The
Dreamers

The Dreamers

SARA FRASER

LITTLE, BROWN AND COMPANY

A *Little, Brown* Book

First published in Great Britain by
Little, Brown and Company in 1995

Copyright © Roy Clews 1995

A CIP catalogue record for this book
is available from the British Library

Photoset in North Wales by
Derek Doyle & Associates, Mold, Clwyd.
Printed and bound in Great Britain by
Mackays of Chatham PLC,
Chatham, Kent.

ISBN 0 316 90904 1

Little, Brown and Company (UK)
Brettenham House
Lancaster Place
London WC2E 7EN

Introduction

All have their dreams. Some remain content only to dream. Others strive to make their dreams a reality. This is the story of Dreamers who fought to make their dreams come true . . .

Chapter One

Redditch, Worcestershire. March, 1909.

The shaft of light dimly illumined the bottom of the pit where the dead woman's fat, naked body lay facing upwards. The light created a grotesque mask of her garishly painted face, and glistened blackly on the viscid coils of entrails bulging from the terrible slashed wound in her fish-white belly. The man felt powerless to move as he stood at the edge of the pit peering fearfully into its depths. Then the dead woman's eyes suddenly opened and locked upon his own. Her rotting features contorted in a lewd smile and she lifted her flabby arms and opened them wide in invitation.

'Noooooo!'

The man screamed in terror as he tumbled helplessly forwards to be locked in the embrace of her cold, mottled-fleshed arms, his mouth greedily clamped by her glutinous rancid lips.

'No Bella! No!'

'Harry! Harry, wake up! Wake up!'

Hands grabbed his shoulders and shook him hard and he came to dazed consciousness, gasping for breath, the clammy sweat of terror beading his face and body.

Emma Vivaldi released her grasp and straightened her body, staring in consternation at her husband as his dark eyes flickered wildly around the room.

'What is it, Harry? What's ailing you? You're acting like you've got the DTs.'

He pushed himself upright to a sitting position and sat shaking his head, his chest heaving as he dragged long shuddering breaths into his lungs.

Then when he had calmed a little he asked her, 'What time is it?'

'It's gone half past nine. I've been up and about for hours,' she told him, and her voice held angry resentment. 'I thought it was about time you roused yourself, seeing as how you've a business needs attending to.'

He made no answer, only thrust aside the tangled bedcovers and got to his feet. He shucked the long night shirt over his black curly hair, disclosing his pale torso, once lithe and muscular, now beginning to carry excess layers of puffy flesh.

'You're putting on too much weight,' she criticised. 'You need to cut down on your drinking. It's making you fat as well as giving you nightmares.'

Harry Vivaldi ignored her disparaging words as he quickly dressed himself in collarless shirt and trousers, pulled socks and boots onto his feet, and taking up a jacket began to go out of the bedroom.

'Where are you going? Aren't you having a wash and shave? What about your collar and tie?' she questioned disbelievingly. Unable to credit the fact that her fastidious dandy of a husband could so neglect his personal toilet.

He made no reply, and she remained standing where he had left her, listening to his footsteps receding along the corridor and down the stairs, and the slamming of the front door signalling his departure from the house.

She shook her head in puzzlement. 'What the hell's got into him this morning?'

A pert-featured young girl poked her mob-capped head around the edge of the open bedroom door.

'Shall I do this room now, Mrs Emma?'

Her mistress nodded absently as with slender fingers she reached to tuck away a long tendril which had escaped from her high-piled mass of glossy chestnut-coloured hair.

The maid-servant, dressed in her cleaning rig of gingham gown and voluminous canvas apron, bustled into the room and began to strip the bed covers, prattling artlessly as she did so.

'Mr Harry 'ull catch his death o' cold, going out without

4

a big coat on on a morning like this 'un is. It's freezin' outside. Theers icicles a foot long hanging off the back drainpipe. Why did Mr Harry have to goo out like that, Mrs Emma?'

Emma shook her head, her black eyes mirroring her own puzzlement. Then frowning she went from the room.

For a moment or two the girl stared after her beautiful young mistress, then grinned slyly and muttered, 'I bet you and him 'ave bin having another row if the truth's to be told. I 'eard him come home last night pissed as a bob-owler.'

Satisfied she had arrived at a correct conclusion she hummed happily to herself and went on stripping the bed.

The bitterly cold wind struck savagely at Harry Vivaldi's exposed head and hands as he hurried through the town's centre streets, his laboured breath pluming whitely from his open mouth. At this hour of the morning he encountered only a spattering of other people, and these paid him no attention as they walked with hunched shoulders and downcast heads in vain effort to minimise the effects of the wind's assault.

After some hundreds of yards he entered the down-at-heel George Street, with its clangorous factories and workshops, mean-fronted Mission hall, sleazy ale houses and grimy terraces of back-to-back tenements. Some distance along the street's shabby length he turned into a covered entryway, which led to a cramped court containing four tenements faced by an odourous communal privy and washhouse. With cold-stiffened fingers he fumbled for a key and unlocked the door of the second tenement, the solitary ground floor window of which was covered by nailed boarding. For a brief instant the memory of the nightmare assailed him and a sensation of dread held him motionless before the unlocked door. Then he summoned all his scant reserves of courage, drew a long harsh breath, and blundered into the room, slamming the warped door shut behind him.

With a pounding heart he peered through the gloom. A pile of empty packing cases filled one corner of the small dirty room, and the rest of the space was a jumble of oddments, broken backed chairs, and a small table. He fumbled his way towards the far wall and taking a box of lucifers from his pocket he lit the single gas jet. The sharp hiss of burning gas softened as he adjusted the flame and a pale light drove back the dark shadows. Breathing hard, he moved the pile of packing cases and crouched to carefully examine the uneven stone paving slabs which constituted the floor beneath them. Despite the chilled dank air he was sweating heavily, and the fingers with which he traced the cement filled cracks between the slabs were trembling uncontrollably.

At last he vented his pent-up breath in a gusty sigh of relief. Nothing had been tampered with. Everything was as he had left it. Easier in his mind, he quickly repiled the packing cases into their original position, and then slumped down upon one of the rickety chairs. With trembling hands he pulled a cheroot from his cigar case and gratefully lit up and inhaled deeply of the fragrant smoke.

A loud knocking shook the panels of the door, and he started violently and the cheroot fell from his suddenly nerveless fingers.

'Is anybody in theer? Is that you in theer, Mr Vivaldi?'

The sensation of relief was so intense that it left Harry feeling weak and spent. The voice belonged to the woman who lived in the next-door tenement. Fighting to steady his voice he called.

'It's alright Mrs Croxall, it's only me.'

With legs that felt spongy he went to the door and opened it.

The shabby woman smiled at him with broken blackened teeth. 'I 'eard noises in 'ere, Mr Vivaldi, and I thought it might be somebody who hadn't got any right to be in 'ere.'

He forced himself to return her smile. 'Many thanks, Mrs Croxall. It's a comfort to know that my property is being so well guarded.'

He recognised the curious gleam in her eyes as she saw his unshaven features and the lack of a collar and tie, and felt driven to try and make an explanation of his uncharacteristic dishevellment, so utterly at odds with his usual immaculate appearance.

'I needed some packing material for an urgent order, Mrs Croxall. And with this place being so dusty I thought it best I came in old clothes.'

"Ud you like me to give the place a clane out, Mr Vivaldi? I could soon have it all spick and span for you,' she offered eagerly. 'I can do it now if you likes. Since I bin laid off from Morralls I'se bin looking about for some other bits o' work. I'd only charge for me time, I'd supply me own soda and cloths.'

'No!' he almost shouted, and cursed himself as he saw the shock engendered in her by this vehement refusal. Quickly he attempted to soften his rejection. He struggled to speak more easily and to smile. 'No, what I mean to say, Mrs Croxall, is that I'd certainly like you to keep this place clean, but just at present it wouldn't be convenient.'

He saw the resentment burgeoning in her expression at this rejection, and his mind raced.

'I'll tell you what you could do for me, though. You know where I keep my van at the back of the Royal, in the yard there?'

She nodded her head, and he went on more easily. 'If you could meet me there in a couple of hours I could show you what needs to be done to the van in the way of cleaning it.' He was able now to smile charmingly at her. 'And you'll not supply your own cloths and soda, Mrs Croxall, I wouldn't dream of allowing you to do that. I shall pay for everything that's necessary.'

Mollified, she nodded in eager acceptance, and he finished in dismissal, 'I'll see you there then, in two hours time. Now I'll have to get on with this sorting out here, so I'll say goodbye for the present, Mrs Croxall.'

'I can give you a hand to sort out what you wants from here, Mr Vivaldi,' she pressed, but he smilingly shook his head.

'No, it'll be quicker doing it myself, thank you all the same, my dear. I'll see you in a couple of hours.'

He closed the door, and stood tensely listening until he heard the woman move back into her own house, then

7

sighed with thankful relief, extracted another cheroot from his case and lit it. Seating himself once more on the rickety chair, he sucked hard on the tube of tobacco, drawing the smoke deep into his body then allowing it to dribble from his mouth in long wreathing tendrils.

Calmer now, he was able to consider his nightmare more rationally, and felt angered at his own frantic reaction to it.

'I acted like a bloody fool!' he told himself disgustedly, 'letting a bloody dream panic me like that.' He pursed his full lips reflectively. 'Wonder why I dreamed what I did though. I've never done so before. I wonder if I am starting to get the DTs, like Emma said?' He rejected this thought with an abrupt shake of his head. 'No! That can't be so. I'm not that much of a drinker.'

'Maybe it's your conscience troubling you?'

It was as if a stranger's voice had whispered in his mind, and angrily he dismissed the accusation. 'Conscience? Why should I have a conscience about what happened to Bella? It was her own fault!'

By now the cheroot was little more than a stub, and taking a final puff, he dropped it to the ground and crushed it to shreds beneath his boot. Then mindful of what he had told Mrs Croxall was his reason for coming here, he took a small packing case from the pile and carried it with him as he left the house once more securely locked.

Emma Vivaldi was sitting at the great scrubbed table in the large kitchen of her home, sharing a pot of tea with her cook, housekeeper, friend and confidant, the fat motherly-featured Mrs Elwood.

The oval face of the younger woman was pensive, and her black eyes mirrored her troubled thoughts, as she sat silent and withdrawn, the untouched cup of tea growing cold before her.

Sitting opposite, Mrs Elwood regarded her mistress shrewdly, and urged, 'Drink your tay, my duck. No man's worth letting a good cup o' tay goo cold for.'

The black eyes sparked irritably. 'What makes you reckon it's him that's worrying me. Perhaps it's your

8

bloody tay that's bitter.' Under stress the young woman's speech patterns tended to revert to her slum origins.

The older woman chuckled comfortably. 'I knows you too well, my duck, doon't I. I can always tell whats the matter wi' you, can't I.'

'Youm too bloody clever by half, you am!' Emma snarled. 'You wants to watch out that it doon't land you in bloody trouble. You know what happens to clever cats, doon't you?'

'Oh ahr, they gets their tails chopped off, doon't they.' The woman slapped her massive rump with one meaty hand. 'Theer's a powerful lot to be chopping at theer through, arn't there. It 'ull take more than a bloody chit like you to do it.'

Despite herself, Emma could not help but grin, and retort, 'Not if I used a bloody big cleaver to do it with.'

Mrs Elwood's fat face shone, and she chortled, 'You'd do better to use it to chop off your bloody husband's drinking arm, my love. That 'ud stop his bloody gallivanting, 'udden't it.'

Half angry, half laughing, Emma nodded agreement. 'I reckon that's what I'll have to do in the end, Mrs E., and that's a fact that is!'

Their conversation was interrupted by the hurried advent of the second of the two young maidservants that Emma employed.

'If you please Mizz Emma, you told me to tell you when Mr Harry was here.'

Emma nodded grimly. 'He's come back, has he. Alright Dolly, I'll be up directly.' She winked at Mrs Elwood. 'I'll find out where he went running off to this morning looking like something the bloody cat had dragged in.'

'You make sure that you does find out, girl,' the cook urged, 'because it all sounds a bit fishy to me.'

Harry Vivaldi was shaving in the bathroom, and Emma stood in the doorway waiting silently until he had finished and was splashing cologne water liberally upon his throat and cheeks before asking him.

'Where did you go off to this morning?'

'Only to George Street.'

9

He turned and smiled at her, and she was forced to concede that despite the incipient thickening of features and dark shadowed eyes induced by heavy drinking he was still an exceptionally handsome man.

'I needed a small packing case,' he explained easily. 'I've got to deliver an order I managed to confirm last night.'

'How could you remember taking any orders last night? You were too drunk to stand when you got home,' she challenged angrily.

He vented a sigh of exasperation, and moving past her went into their bedroom.

She followed, and while he changed into fresh clothes resumed her verbal onslaught. 'I'm getting tired of the way you're going on, Harry! Neglecting the business! Drinking day and night! Throwing money away as if it grew on trees!'

He ignored her diatribe, and instead whistled tunelessly as he carefully studded his stiff white collar and tied his silk cravat.

In the face of his apparent indifference Emma's fiery temper exploded, and she shrieked, "Ull you lissen to what I'm tellin' you, you bastard!'

'Tsk, tsk!' he snicked his tongue sneeringly. 'You're showing your background again, Emmy! Screeching like a slum-rat! What will the servants think?'

He pulled on his waistcoat and jacket, and stood preening in front of the full-length mirror, making the final adjustments to his appearance.

Emma exerted an immense effort and modulated her voice. 'I had a note from Mr Miller yesterday. He wants me to call in and see him when it's convenient.'

A wary gleam invaded her husband's dark lustrous eyes. Miller was the manager of the Capital and Counties Bank, where their joint accounts were held. With a well assumed air of casualness he asked. 'Did he say what he wanted to see you for?'

She shook her head, and challenged suspiciously, 'Do you know something that I don't, Harry? Do you know why he wants to see me?'

He forced a smile of denial. 'Of course not, darling. I

10

expect he just wants you to sign something or other. You know what these bank managers are like.' His smile metamorphosed into a sneer. 'After all, your son-in-law is one of them, isn't he?'

'What do you mean by that?' She reacted aggressively to the sneer.

He assumed an exaggerated air of bewilderment and spread both arms wide as if in supplication. In that physical posture his Mediterranean ancestry overlayed three generations of familial British citizenship.

'I mean Old Hector's son, Franklin. You remember Old Hector, don't you? He was the old man man that you married for his money and fucked to death in short order!'

'You bleedin' wop!' she screeched furiously, and flew at him like a wild-cat, hands raised, fingers hooked, nails seeking to rend and tear.

He side-stepped her wild onrush and deftly tripped her, sending her crashing onto the floor, then before she could recover herself he was out of the room and down the stairs. Snatching up his Homburg hat, gloves and gold-knobbed cane from the hallstand he shouted mockingly, 'Don't bother keeping dinner back for me tonight, darling. I've a business appointment to keep so I'll be late.' Then he disappeared through the front door.

Upstairs in the bedroom Emma still lay upon the floor. Crying tears of mingled rage and chagrin she hammered at the soft, thick carpeting with her fists, and drummed her feet in futile anger.

The biting wind had dropped and now the air was still and beginning to be slightly warmed by the watery sun. Harry Vivaldi paused on the pavement outside the railed courtyard of his porticoed front door and adjusted his hat to a suitably dashing angle, then carefully drew on his fine kid gloves. He turned to look at his opulent home, Cotswold House, and grimaced. Matters had not turned out in the way he had expected them to when he had first moved into this fine house.

Mentally he swiftly reviewed the course of his marriage,

11

now barely more than two years old. In the very beginning of his relationship with his beautiful wife, she had dominated the affair. Then that dominance had swung his way when she fell in love with him. Now, it appeared that her love was swiftly cooling, and once again she was attempting to re-assert her initial dominance.

He frowned unhappily. The shared physical passion which had given them both such ecstatic pleasure was also rapidly waning on her part, and their last few sexual congresses had been joyless satiations of fleshly hungers.

Soured in his mood, he stood staring bleakly across the Recreation Garden with its fountain and bandstand, and the flanking, green swarded churchyard of the tall-spired church of St Stephen with its surrounding sentinels of great elm trees and scattered tombstones. Separated by only a strip of pavement, the two tracts of land formed the central triangle of the town. Around its space were ranged shops, offices, banks, hotels, taverns, the hospital and houses, and the hilly roads and streets, courts and alleys of Redditch radiating outwards in all directions.

The grandiose stuccoed frontage of the Capital and Counties Bank was situated further along the road known as Church Green East, on which Harry was standing. Deep in thought, he strolled slowly in its direction. Although he had denied any knowledge of the bank manager's reasons for asking Emma to call on him, Harry knew only too well what the matter was about.

There was a sudden clamour of bells from the church, and then a single bell tolled mournful peals. Harry automatically counted the strokes. There were nine.

He mentally translated the bell's message. The nine strokes were known as the 'Nine Tailors', denoting that a man had died. If it had been a woman, then six strokes would be tolled, and for a child, three strokes.

There was a long pause, then another peal of bells, after which the single bell's tolling resumed. Once more the man counted. There were forty-two strokes, which denoted the man's age.

'Forty-two. He wasn't all that old then. I wonder if I knew him?'

12

A shaft of black gallows humour suddenly caused Harry to grin and mutter aloud, 'I hope he was one of my creditors.'

By now he had reached the Capital and Counties premises, and for a moment he toyed with the idea of going in to see the manager, and asking him not to speak with Emma. But instantly realised the futility of such a course of action. Then he remembered that he was to meet Mrs Croxall in the Royal yard. He frowned at the thought.

'I'd best go and meet the cow.'

The Royal Hotel stood on the Market Place, facing the bank across the easternmost point of the Church Green triangle, and the broad entryway to the huge yard, and its stabling and sheds, was at the side of the hotel.

'I'll deal with Emma when I have to.'

He resolutely dismissed all thoughts of the coming storm with his wife from his mind, and with a flourish of his gold-knobbed cane went towards the Royal Hotel. Mrs Croxall, bucket and brush in hand, was waiting outside the largest of the collection of sheds and workshops that lay around the broad, empty expanse of bare ash-strewn ground.

Harry greeted her with a smile, and unlocked the big rusty padlock that secured the great double doors. The interior of the shed resembled a warehouse, with its large floorspace and high, wooden trussed roof. Inside was a large pantechnicon van painted dark green with big yellow letterings on both of its tall sides: 'Vivaldi's Moving Pictures and Talking Machines'. The young man stared sourly at the garish logo. His once high hopes of making a fortune with this travelling combined show and retail business had long since been dashed.

Harry's idea had been to circulate the outlying rural villages and hamlets and farmsteads surrounding Redditch with his stocks of gramaphones, vodaphones, zonophones, phonographs, and the latest selections of recordings. He would provide music for parties, dances, wedding celebrations etc, then sell those talking machines and recordings to the revellers. He had also bought a moving picture projector, with the intention of putting on

13

picture shows in village halls and barns.

His rosy visualisation of making lots and lots of easy money had proven to be solely that however. A rosy visualisation! The reality had been seemingly endless wearisome hours spent in travelling over bad roads, through all types of weather, for scant rewards.

If Harry had been a hard worker, prepared to make sacrifices of time and personal comforts, then his idea could well have succeeded, and he might have made a good income. But he hated hard work, and wanted his creature comforts and social pleasures. As he himself readily admitted whenever he was happily drunk, 'I was not born to be a bloody ant slaving all my days away. I was born to be a butterfly and flutter from flower to flower sipping nectar.'

And so inevitably his journeyings around the countryside became increasingly shorter in duration and distance.

Harry's business failure had been compounded by his gambling. He was a reckless gambler, with a sadly misplaced confidence in his own judgement and cunning. As his gambling losses increased so he was forced to part with most of his stock in trade to settle his debts. Unknown to Emma, all of his travelling stock of talking machines and records, his film projector, lamps and reels, and the two horses that drew his pantechnicon had now all been lost. All that he had left were a few talking machines and records in his rented lock-up shop in the Market Place, and the pantechnicon. The lock-up shop and this shed could not be counted as assets, because their owner was threatening Harry with imminent eviction for non-payment of the rent.

Over the last weeks, in a desperate effort to recoup his losses, he had been gambling almost incessantly and losing heavily. To meet the pressing demands of his creditors, some of whom were more than ready to enforce their demands for payment by violent means, he had drawn money from the joint business account he held with his wife. To avoid the necessity of confessing his losses to her, he had forged her signature on the cheques he had presented. Now the account was overdrawn by more than

14

a hundred pounds, and Harry knew that the reason for the bank manager wanting to see his wife was to discuss this overdraft.

'What am I going to do?' The young man again felt a fast increasing weight of foreboding. 'Emma will go bloody mad when she finds out. It could mean the end of our marriage . . . I might even get charged with fraud and forgery for signing her name to the cheques! I could get sent to jail for it!' The afterthoughts were the more disturbing.

'Well, does you want me to start claning, Mr Vivaldi?'

The hoarse question brought Vivaldi from his depressing reverie. 'The van, my dear. I want you to give the van a real spring clean, inside and out.'

The woman nodded. 'Alright, Mr Vivaldi.'

'When you've finished come round to my shop. It's just a few yards up from the Royal. I'll pay you then.'

'Alright, Mr Vivaldi.'

Harry fumbled absently in his waistcoat fob pocket, and to his pleased surprise his fingers encountered some coins. As Mrs Croxall went to fetch water he quickly checked the coins. There were two sovereigns and a florin piece. His low spirits lifted instantly.

'I'll pop into the shop and see what's happening. If it's quiet I might go to Johnny Banks' for a couple of games.'

John Banks was the proprietor of the Billiard Hall, which was also situated in the Market Place, and, very conveniently for Harry, the Billiard Hall occupied the floor above his own lock-up shop.

'But first, I'll pop into the Royal and have a livener.'

Whistling happily, Harry went on his way.

15

Chapter Two

Adrian West's motorcar created a sensation when it appeared in Redditch just before midday. Although the townspeople were mechanically sophisticated, since there were some motorcycles and even a very limited amount of motorcars manufactured in the district, still nothing to match Adrian West's 60 horsepower Mercedes had ever been seen in the town before. Its long bonnet and sleek bodywork was of pristine whiteness, etched with gold decoration. Its twin seats were luxuriously upholstered in hand-tooled, red moroccan leather. Mounted at each side of its radiator were two massive acetylene lamps with burnished brass cases, and there were numerous brass-cased oil lamps providing side and rear lighting. The engine roared as with seemingly effortless ease the motorcar sped up the steep incline of Fish Hill, and at the northernmost point of the Church Green triangle erupted upon the flat plateau of the town's centre.

Adrian West, muffled in a fur-collared, ankle-length driving coat, leather gauntlets, flat cap turned backwards on his head, great goggles masking his eyes, and a silken scarf tied around the lower part of his face, drove his motorcar around and around the roads bordering the Church Green, and the roaring of the powerful engine carried into the streets radiating from the central triangle, causing cart and van horses to start and shiver, and dogs to bark, and bringing curious onlookers to stare at this wonderful machine.

When the sleek white, gold and red monster spluttered to a halt outside the front door of the Royal Hotel, a crowd quickly gathered and hurled eager questions at the driver.

Adrian West loosened his silk scarf so that he could answer. 'It was produced in America for the Daimler Company.'

'I had it imported directly from Long Island City.'

'It's got overhead inlet valves.'

'It's 9-2 litre producing 60 horsepower.'

'Yes it is. I'm not telling tall stories, my friend. It really is a 60 horsepower engine.'

'Top speed is about 75 miles an hour, that's if the lighter racing body is fitted. With this body I could probably reach about 65 miles an hour.'

'Yes, this is the make that won the Gordon Bennet race over in Ireland. But it was the 90 horsepower model.'

'How much did it cost?' West grinned and shook his head. 'That's my own personal business, my friend. Let me just say that it was a hell of a lot. Now, where can I find a safe shelter to leave my car for a few hours?'

Among the crowd clustering around the motorcar was Harry, staring with envious greed at its sleek lines, and glistening paint and brasswork. When he heard the driver's last question he spoke out on impulse.

'I've got a safe place for you, and it's very close.'

West pushed up his dust-smeared goggles, disclosing a pair of unusually piercing light blue eyes.

'That's very kind of you, Mr???' His accent held a slight transatlantic twang.

'I'm Harry Vivaldi – that's my shop over there.' Harry offered his hand, which the driver took in a firm grasp.

'My name is Adrian West. I'm the proprietor of the Royalty Theatre Company.'

He gestured invitingly to the vacant seat at his side. 'Come aboard, Mr Vivaldi. Where is this shelter of yours?'

Harry pointed behind him to the Royal yard. 'It's just up here, Mr West.'

'Would you like a quick spin in her first?' The man questioned, and Harry nodded eagerly.

'Very well then. Just crank the engine for me, will you please?'

Harry took the long starting handle and with a couple of swings fired the engine into roaring life once more.

17

Proudly aware of the envious faces staring at him, he climbed up beside the driver and with one hand holding his Homburg hat down firmly upon his head, surrendered himself to the sheer exhilaration of speed as the car went bucketing along the road.

All too soon for him the ride was over and the car arrived back at the Royal yard. Accompanied by a crowd the Mercedes growled up to the massive shed, and within scant moments was safely parked in its cavernous interior.

West stared with interest at the pantechnicon, and asked, 'That's your business, is it, Mr Vivaldi? Moving Pictures and Talking Machines?'

'Yes, but at present I'm thinking of going in for something else.' Harry tried to give the impression of a successful businessman. 'It's a wee bit cramping of my style being tied down to the shop, as I am. I rather fancy branching out into something a little more exciting.'

'Do you really?' West eyed his companion guardedly. 'Doesn't it pay well enough, the business you're in now?'

Harry shrugged expansively. 'Money's not everything, is it? I'm the sort of chap who needs fresh challenges.'

The other man strolled the length and breadth of the vast shed, staring closely at the wooden roof with its rows of large skylights. Then he asked, 'There is an electric light company in this town, isn't there?'

Harry nodded.

'I suppose it would be possible to have the electric light rigged in this place?'

Again Harry nodded. 'Oh yes. There's a cable running into the Royal Hotel there. So it wouldn't be too much expense to have the supply extended to here.' He frowned curiously. 'But why do you ask me that?'

West shrugged offhandedly. 'Oh, no reason, old chap. No reason. Just curious, that's all.'

He smiled and invited bluffly, 'How about joining me for a drink? I'd like to repay your kindness for letting me use this shelter.'

Harry was happy to accept.

In the Select bar of the Royal Hotel, Harry was able to study his companion more closely. Adrian West looked to be around forty years of age. Tall, broad shouldered and of a flamboyant manner and appearance, he was clean shaven, and florid faced. His hair was light brown, silvered at the temples, and he wore it in long theatrical waves. He was not conventionally handsome, but he was very personable, possessing an easy charm, which he exerted upon the fluttering barmaid until she blushed and simpered and showed every appearance of being utterly captivated.

Harry, accustomed to being the subject of female interest, was at first a trifle piqued at being so overshadowed by his companion, but he also soon found himself succumbing to the other man's charm and within a very short space of time the two men were on first name terms.

During the course of their conversation Harry learned that his companion was the sole owner of a travelling theatre company. He was also the company's leading man. West claimed to have successfully toured in many parts of the world, America, Australia, Canada, South Africa, and even India. For the past year and a half however he had been touring the British Isles.

'I've got my own prefabricated building,' he told the younger man. 'Had it constructed to my own design, of course. Takes only a couple of hours to erect it. Saves all the trouble and bickering that one has to suffer if one hires existing halls.'

'Where is your company now?' Harry questioned.

'Merthyr Tydfil,' West informed him, and shook his head. 'Sad mistake to go there. It's all rain, hymns, and coal dust. The Welsh aren't ready yet for sophisticated modern drama.'

Time passed, and the two men matched each other drink for drink, and as the alcohol enveloped Harry in its mellow glow, he began to look upon his new acquaintance as a man after his own heart. A boon companion. And in all truth Adrian West was easy enough to like. He had a fund of good stories and a ready laugh, and was free and easy with his money.

Eventually Harry wanted to know what had brought

19

such a widely travelled man of the world to Redditch, and West explained that he was exploring the possibility of bringing his travelling theatre to the town, and setting it up for the rest of the winter, until the summer travelling season came around once more.

'You see, Harry, my boy, I know my business. It isn't any good my setting up in a city such as Birmingham or Worcester. There is too much competition from the established theatres and Halls. And there are too many other attractions for people to go to of an evening or weekend. But a town like Redditch is just the place for a company like mine. There's not a deal in the way of entertainment available, apart from the alehouses, and the Public Hall, so there isn't the amount of competition here. Also, you've got the industries here that women are employed in in large numbers, haven't you, such as the Needles and the Fishing Tackle. So a lot of those women will have some money to spare for their own pleasures. Now a respectable woman can't go to a pub for her entertainment, can she? But she can go to a theatre. So I would expect to have her come to my theatre at least once a week, maybe even more. Anyway, I'm going to spend a few days here exploring the possibilities.'

'Well then, if you haven't yet made any arrangements for lodgings, why don't you come and stay at my house while you're doing your exploring?' Harry invited eagerly. Unwilling to lose this glamorous new-found boon companion.

Initially West demurred. 'I wouldn't dream of it, Harry my boy. I wouldn't dream of putting yourself and your lady wife to such inconvenience.'

His demurral only increased Harry's eagerness to have him as a guest, and the young man insisted vehemently, refusing to accept any denial, until at last West graciously surrendered and accepted his offer of hospitality.

Harry beamed with gratification. 'Come on then. We'll go and introduce you to my wife.'

The other man winked at him. 'Hadn't we better have just one quick one for the road first, my boy?'

The young man laughed and willingly agreed.

Emma Vivaldi had heard the roaring of the engine when the Mercedes car had been driven round and round the Church Green, and she had stood at the drawing room window and watched it pass her house. Although she knew nothing about motorcars she had been impressed with its rakish opulence and had wondered who it belonged to.

Now she was in her bedroom dressing to go out. She had decided to call in and see Miller, the bank manager. The roar of a powerful engine penetrated into the room, and she went to the window and peered downwards, then uttered a gasp of surprise. The long-bonneted Mercedes car had come to a halt outside her house, and her husband was sitting in the seat next to the goggled driver.

Hurried footsteps sounded on the stairs and along the corridor, and then her door was knocked and Becca's excited voice called.

'Mizzis Emma? Mizzis Emma? Come and look what the Master's brung home.'

'I've seen it, Becca.' She opened the door and smiled at the rosy cheeked girl. 'You'd best get on downstairs again and take the gentlemen's coats and hats from them.'

The girl scurried downstairs once more, and Emma followed more slowly.

She heard the front door open and the entrance of the two men.

'Where's your mistress, Becca?' Harry Vivaldi's tone was jovial, and the slight slurring of his speech betrayed the fact that he was half-drunk. 'Go and fetch your mistress, my dear, and tell her that we have a guest.'

Emma grimaced wryly. At least Harry was a good-tempered and hospitable drunk. Unlike her own father for example, who turned violently anti-social when in his cups.

She rounded the corner of the broad staircase and came into view of the big hallway, where the men had by now divested themselves of their greatcoats, hats, and gloves.

Adrian West drew breath sharply at the first sight of the young woman advancing down the stairs towards him. She wore a dark green gown, with fitted bodice, long sleeves, and a high, lace trimmed collar. Her complexion was flawless, and her black eyes and mass of glossy chestnut hair highlighted the beauty of her oval features. Her body was slender and shapely, and when she smiled as she did now, her full lips disclosed small, white, even teeth. West thought that she was one of the most gorgeous women he had ever seen.

He advanced to meet her, and as she reached the bottom of the staircase he bowed gracefully. 'My name is Adrian West, Mrs Vivaldi. I'm honoured to meet you.'

She studied him curiously, taking in the long hair, the profusion of heavy gold personal jewellery, the theatrical flamboyance of his expensive clothing, then her black eyes sparked mischievously.

'I'll bet you're an actor, Mr West? And if you're not, then you should be, looking like such a Fancy Dan.'

For a brief instant he was taken aback by her forthright candour. But his acute ear instantly detected the harsh accent of the slums underlying her speech, and his equally acute brain instantly impelled him to react instinctively.

He laughed and answered easily. 'I most certainly am an actor, Mrs Vivaldi. And with your looks, you ought to be an actress.'

Emma was delighted with his reaction, and now she proffered her hand. 'I think that I'm going to like you, Adrian West!'

He gazed admiringly into her eyes while he bent and kissed her hand. Then told her with a grin, 'I already know that I'm going to like you, Mrs Vivaldi.'

Harry Vivaldi observed them uncertainly, unsure of how he felt about this display of apparent instant camaraderie between his wife and his new-found friend. He coughed, and broke in upon their shared absorption as they stood with their hands still clasped, looking at each other.

'I've invited Mr West to stay with us here for a couple of days, my dear.'

'Of course he must,' Emma agreed readily, then could not resist adding spitefully, 'I shall enjoy having someone to talk with.'

Harry blinked hard at her, and challenged peevishly, 'I talk to you, don't I?'

Emma smiled, but her tone was acid. 'You talk at me when you've been drinking, Harry my dear. Which means that I'm talked at all the time, doesn't it? And that's not quite the same as holding a conversation, is it?'

Adrian West kept a neutral expression on his face, but inwardly recognised. So that's the way of it, is it? Discord reigns in the matrimonial home. He felt a sudden tightening of his groin as the thought occurred. Perhaps this gorgeous creature is in the market for another man? His excitement heightened as he dwelt on that thought, and let it expand. And perhaps I might be just what she's looking for?

She smiled again at him, and before she released his hand he thought that she momentarily increased the pressure of her fingers upon his own.

'You are very welcome here, Mr West. I'm sure that we shall become good friends.'

Harry suddenly experienced a sharp sense of unease as his wife and new-found friend smiled at each other, and found himself wondering if he had acted wisely in bringing them together.

Then his own overweening vanity forced him to thrust this disturbing train of thought away. He had yet to meet the man who could take any woman away from him.

Nonsense. I'm thinking nonsense, he told himself, and to avoid dwelling on the matter invited heartily, 'Come on into the drawing room, Adrian, and have a drink.'

Emma, well aware of the effect she had had on Adrian West, decided to forgo her visit to the bank manager, and instead enjoy the company of this exciting newcomer.

'I'll join you, gentlemen.' She winked roguishly at West. 'I fear that you'll find me to be a very fast woman, Mr West. I not only drink spirits, but I smoke as well.'

The man was utterly charmed with her, and he chuckled delightedly.

'I adore fast women, Mrs Vivaldi. They are the very breath of life to me.'

And in that instant he resolved to set up his theatre here

23

in Redditch. Adrian West was an inveterate womaniser and spared no effort or expense in his pursuit of any female who took his fancy. He wanted this gorgeous woman, and he was prepared to stay here in this town until he succeeded in having her.

Later, while the three of them sat far into the night smoking, drinking, talking, laughing, other ideas stirred in West's mind, as he discoverd that Emma Vivaldi had far more to offer than solely physical beauty. She had quick wit, intelligence and humour, a sparkling vivacity, and a grace of movement that no other woman he had met had ever possessed in such abundance.

'She's wasted here,' West told himself over and over again. 'She's wasted on this drunken sot, and wasted on this one-horse town.'

He had for some years cherished certain ambitious dreams. Ambitious dreams which he had been unable to bring to reality because of a variety of reasons. Now, as he watched Emma, and delighted in her company, he began to believe with an ever increasing conviction that through her lay the road to fulfilment of those long cherished dreams: that through Emma Vivaldi he might at long last be enabled to make those dreams a reality.

She laughed at something he had said, and her black eyes were dazzling as they met and held his own.

'Oh yes,' he told himself, as he experienced a curious sense of recognition. 'Oh yes. This is the one. This is the woman that I've been needing. This is she.'

Chapter Three

Next morning the weather was once again dull and overcast, and a cold wind swept the town. Adrian West and Harry Vivaldi breakfasted by themselves. Emma remained in her bed.

West was acutely disappointed that she had not joined them, but inwardly chided himself for experiencing that disappointment. 'You're acting like a love-sick schoolboy, you damn fool! She's just another woman, that's all, and you've had enough of them to know that all cats are grey in the dark.'

But no matter how scathingly he chided himself, the sense of disappointment, and the eager longing to be in Emma's company still continued to gnaw at him. He was honest enough with himself to accept the fact that he was suffering from an instant infatuation with the woman.

Harry was somewhat surly and withdrawn. Mainly this was the result of his massive hangover. But there was also another cause for his surliness. The gaiety of their impromptu gathering of the previous night had made him feel amorously inclined, and when he and Emma had retired to their bedroom he had tried to make love to her. But she had turned on him like some vicious wildcat and had fought him off. So his sexual frustration was adding sourness to his mood. Furthermore, on awaking this morning she had also told him that today she would be going to see the bank manager. So all in all, Harry's lot was definitely not a happy one.

West was grateful for his host's silence, because he had a great deal to exercise his mind. He had gone to his bed and lain sleepless for many hours, continually visualising

25

Emma, and letting his vivid imagination run wild. He had also formulated certain plans, which he intended to put into immediate train.

When they had finished their meal West invited, 'If you've nothing better to do, Harry, how would you like to spend the day with me? There are some arrangements I'd like to make.'

Harry reacted somewhat churlishly to the invitation, and mumbled grumpily, 'Well, I've got my business to attend to, you know.'

The older man smiled secretly. He had garnered sufficient information the previous night from Emma's unguarded gibes at her husband to know that his business was practically moribund.

'These arrangements I want to make could also concern you, if you so wished, old chap,' West informed him.

'Concern me?' Vivaldi frowned suspiciously. 'How concern me?'

'I'm thinking of offering you a proposition, Harry. A business proposition,' West told him, and sitting back in his chair he produced a gold cigarette case from his inside pocket and opening it, proffered its contents towards his companion.

'Try one of these, Harry. They're Turkish, and rather good.'

The younger man's expression betrayed a dawning of sudden hope. Perhaps he was going to be offered a way out of his current, and perennial, financial difficulties. He made an effort to cheer his mood and after he had taken and lighted a cigarette, he forced a smile.

'What sort of proposition, Adrian?'

'A partnership in a new venture I'm thinking of starting. Are you interested?'

'Well, yes. I'm always interested in anything that might make me some money.' Vivaldi leaned forwards across the table towards his friend. 'What is this venture?'

'Moving pictures, Harry. I'm thinking of starting a moving picture company.'

The younger man's swarthy features twisted in disappointment, and he shook his head dismissively. 'I've

26

already tried that game, Adrian. Once the novelty wore off the audiences stopped coming.'

Now Adrian West shook his head dismissively. 'You've not understood me correctly, Harry. I don't mean to show moving pictures. I intend to make them.'

'To make them?' Vivaldi stared in surprise, and the other man slowly nodded his head.

'But how? Where? What about?' the younger man volleyed, and West held up both hands laughingly.

'Steady the buffs!'

Harry Vivaldi subsided into silence.

'Well? Are you interested?' West asked, and after a short pause Vivaldi nodded.

'Good!' West smiled with satisfaction. 'Now then Harry, I'm prepared to put up all the initial investment and stand the expense of starting this venture. What I propose is that you will work on salary for me, until such time as it's up and running. Then, if you so wish, you can buy into the company.'

He paused, as if inviting comment, and Harry, hardly able to believe in this stroke of good fortune, nodded eagerly. 'I'm agreeable.'

'Good.' West smiled expansively. 'Now, I need to ask you a few questions concerning your own current financial position. You must be completely honest with me, because believe me, it will prove to your own advantage to be so.'

Again he paused as if awaiting answer, and after a few moments' frantic inner debate, Harry once again concurred.

'Very well then, now what I need to know is . . .' Adrian West lowered his voice and directed a stream of searching questions at the other man. After some time West nodded as if satisfied, and rose to his feet.

'Come on, Harry, stir yourself. There are a lot of arrangements to make, and time is pressing.'

The offices of Dolton Enterprises were situated in Evesham Street, the thoroughfare which ran southwards from the town's central crossroads in front of St Stephen's church. The premises comprised the two ground floor

27

rooms of the three-storied building.

When Adrian West and Harry Vivaldi entered, Ozzie Clarke, general manager of Dolton Enterprises, was standing deep in conversation with his chief rent and debt collector, Caleb Louch.

Clarke was in his mid-thirties, a strong-bodied, pleasant-featured man, with close-cut curly brown hair and a heavy moustache, and resembled a prosperous farmer in his brown tweed suit and shiny leather gaiters. His companion, Caleb Louch, was burly, brawl-scarred and shabbily clad, with a battered bowler hat perched on his bullet head.

When he saw Vivaldi, Louch grinned ferociously.

'I was just coming to look for you, my bucko!'

Clarke glanced at Adrian West and motioned his rent-collector to silence. Then he smiled and enquired pleasantly, 'Can I be of any assistance to you, gentlemen?'

At a desk on one side of the room a neat young typewritist was sitting busily working at her machine. She paused and stared with interest at the flamboyantly dressed Adrian West.

'You are Mr Clarke, I take it?' West sought confirmation, which Clarke supplied with a nod of his head.

'Is there anywhere we can speak privately?' West asked, and directed an apologetic smile towards the young girl, who preened and fluttered under this attention. 'My business is of a personal nature.'

'Of course, come into my office.' Clarke dismissed Louch with a grin, and led the two newcomers into the rear room.

Once they were all seated facing each other across the broad, leather-topped desk West came immediately to the point.

'My name is Adrian West. I am the proprietor of the Royalty Travelling Theatre Company. I'd like to take over the leases on the present agreed terms and conditions, of the shed in the Royal yard, and also the shop in the market place that my associate Mr Vivaldi presently holds. I will of course immediately settle any outstanding rentals or

28

charges that Mr Vivaldi owes to your company. And, in view of those outstanding rentals, I am prepared in addition to pay six months rentals in advance on both properties in token of my good will. Also I wish to rent a section of ground in the Royal yard on which to erect a temporary wooden structure for a period of three calendar months initially, the temporary structure being a travelling theatre. I can of course supply references as to my suitability as a tenant. I hope that this will be possible.'

Clarke placed his elbows on the desk top, clasping his hands together and steepling his fingers. He smiled pleasantly.

'Yes, Mr West, I'm confident that it will be possible. Subject of course to your references proving satisfactory, and the outstanding and advance rentals being paid in full.'

West nodded. 'Then we have struck a bargain, Mr Clarke. If you will have the contracts drawn up, then I'd like to sign as soon as possible.

Clarke pursed his lips speculatively, and said coolly. 'There is one small matter, concerning your associate here, which needs immediate attention though, Mr West. And, with your permission, I'd like to sort it out while I have the opportunity.'

West gave a theatrical gesture of assent. 'Please do, Mr Clarke.'

'Thank you,' Clarke acknowledged smilingly. Then his manner altered radically, and he frowned at the nervous Harry Vivaldi.

'There's been no mention made of the house in George Street, Vivaldi. You owe us two months rent on that as well. When can we expect to be paid?'

Harry swallowed hard, and his discomfiture was apparent.

West intervened smoothly. 'I'm sorry, Mr Clarke, the error is mine. Mr Vivaldi had told me about the house, but it had slipped my mind. I meant to include it with the other properties in my offer to you.'

Harry Vivaldi relaxed gratefully, and Ozzie Clarke grinned contemptuously at him, then told West, 'Very well, Mr West. We will include the house in George Street, subject to the present terms and conditions of the lease, and the rentals now owed being paid in full.'

With exchanged protestations of pleasure and good will the men took their leave of each other.

Outside in Evesham Street West turned on his colleague.

'Why didn't you tell me about the house in George Street?'

Harry had had time to recover his composure, and he spread his hands and smiled disarmingly. 'It had truly slipped my mind, Adrian. It's just a place I use as extra storage space.'

West doubted this statement, mindful of the immense storage capacity of the shed in the Royal yard, but he wasn't concerned enough at this point to argue. Things were going just as he wanted them to do, and so his spirits were high.

'Come on, Harry, let's go and have a celebratory drink. The treat's on me,' he invited, and Harry happily accepted.

Back in the offices of Dolton Enterprises the neat typewritist finished the letter she was typing and took it into the rear office.

'There you are, Mr Clarke.' She smiled flirtatiously at her manager, and arched her back so that her pert breasts strained against the front of her trim white blouse.

'Thank you, Doris.' He took the letter without looking at her, remaining intent on the papers before him. 'You can go and have your lunch now, if you like.'

She scowled petulantly at his bent head, and flounced out of the room, then hurried out to meet her friend. While they ate sandwiches in the nearby tea rooms, she confided indignantly, 'He must know that I fancy him, Harriet. I've shown him enough encouragement to do something about it. Yet he doesn't show a spark of interest.'

'Well, you know what they say, don't you?' Her friend, secretly gloating at the much prettier girl's chagrin, offered barbed sympathy. 'They say that Ozzie Clarke is in

30

love with your boss lady, don't they. They say he's in love with Cleopatra Dolton.'

'In love with her?' Doris challenged furiously. 'In love with the bloody Queen of Egypt? Youm talking sarft, Harriet. Bloody Cleopatra Dolton's old enough to be his soddin' mother!'

Harriet held her silence, but inwardly hugged herself with gleeful, spiteful satisfaction.

Chapter Four

By early evening the cold wind had risen again, but now it carried flurries of stinging rain upon its whirling gusts. Despite the inclement weather, the meeting at the Temperance Hall in support of The National Service League was well attended, and when Admiral Sir Henry Cumming rose to speak almost all of the hall's five hundred seats were filled.

The vast majority of the audience were male, but here and there dotted among the tophats, Homburgs, bowlers and flat caps was the wide-brimmed, flower or feather decorated hat of an occasional female.

Cleopatra Dolton sat towards the front of the hall, flanked by her three sons, Simon, aged seventeen, James aged fifteen, and the youngest Andrew, eleven-years-old and swelling with pride at being allowed to come to this grown-up gathering. Cleopatra Dolton's physical appearance belied her forty-three years. Her olive skin was still unlined, her lips moist and tempting, her throat smooth and rounded. Beneath the dark clothing her breasts were full and firm, her waist slender, her hips shapely. There were many men in the hall who directed sidelong glances at this widow's sultry charms, and fervently wished that she belonged to them.

The Admiral spoke well and clearly. In the first part of his address he concentrated mainly on the situation regarding the comparative naval strengths of the great powers. He shocked his audience from their inbred complacency concerning the British Empire's maritime supremacy when he told them that the two most powerful battleships in the world were in fact American. The recently completed USS *Wyoming* and her sister ship the USS *Arkansas*, compared to which the new British Dreadnoughts were smaller and mounted a far inferior weight of broadside. Admiral Cumming gave his audience further cause for concern when he revealed that Germany was also engaged upon the construction of a fresh class of Super-Dreadnoughts, to which the new British Dreadnoughts might also prove to be inferior in weight of broadside.

Next Cumming turned to the subject of land power, and again he recited a series of unpalatable facts concerning the relative trained military manpower available to the Great Powers in the event of mobilisation. Even with the addition of her Indian and Colonial troops Great Britain was still lying eighth in order of army strength.

At the back of the hall, sitting in the rear-most row of seats a tall, well dressed man was listening intently, and as the Admiral went on to proclaim the necessity of introducing a system of universal military training into Great Britain to match that of the Continental powers, the tall man's hard-etched features denoted a grudging agreement.

The Admiral finished speaking and there was prolonged and enthusiastic applause. From among the other local dignitaries seated on the platform, the chairman of the meeting, Colonel C.F. Milward, needle manufacturer and Justice of the Peace, rose to call for volunteers to organise petitions in favour of National Military Training to be presented to Parliament, and again there was prolonged and enthusiastic applause.

Simon Dolton, a slender-featured, delicate looking youth, with his mother's dark hair and eyes, turned to her excitedly. 'May I help with the petitions, Mother?'

Cleopatra Dolton regarded him fondly, 'I doubt that you'll have time for it, Simon. You'll be returning to school shortly, won't you?'

On her other side her two younger sons chimed in. 'We can help. We can begin tomorrow to collect signatures.'

She smiled and surrendered. 'Very well then, if you want to.'

33

The audience rose to their feet, and the singing of the National Anthem filled the hall with booming sound.

After the anthem the crowd began to leave the hall and go out into the dark drizzling night and the tall man went with them. As he turned up the collar of his greatcoat and pulled the brim of his bowler hat down to shield his eyes against the chill drizzle, he heard his name called.

'Johnny? Johnny Purvis?'

He halted and looked around, and a fair-haired younger man dressed like a clerk came up to him, limping noticeably.

'How are you, Johnny?' He smiled warmly and held out his hand. 'I trust you remember me. It's Foley, Foley Field.'

John Purvis returned the smile and shook the proffered hand heartily. 'Of course I remember you, Foley. How are you? Do you still work at the bank?'

The younger man grinned wryly. 'Where else could I go?' He tapped his thigh. 'This tends to limit my options of employment. But how about you? Are you back in Redditch to stay, this time?'

The older man nodded.

Cleopatra Dolton and her sons emerged from the Hall's entrance, and as she unfurled her umbrella to open it, Simon told her excitedly, 'Look, Mother, there's Foley Field. I must tell him about my passing the Sandhurst entrance exam.'

She grimaced. 'Must you tell him now, Simon? Only it's late and I want to get home out of this weather.'

'It'll only take me a moment, Mother,' he cajoled. 'I'll not stay longer than it takes me to tell him.'

'Make sure that you don't. We'll walk slowly on,' she instructed, the sternness of her voice offset by the softness in her eyes as she looked at her beloved son.

The youth hurried to where Foley Fields was standing talking with the tall, middle-aged man whose features were shadowed by his pulled-down hat.

'Pardon me for interrupting your conversation, Foley,' he said apologetically as he reached them, 'but I must tell you my news.'

34

Foley Field turned to the interrupter and smiled in welcome. 'Hello Simon. Excuse me for a moment will you, Johnny?'

'I've passed the Sandhurst entrance exam, Foley,' Simon Dolton was glowing with excited pride. 'I'm to enter the Academy next year, with any luck.'

'That's wonderful, Simon! Well done!' Foley Field congratulated the youth with genuine pleasure. 'What arm of the service do you want to make your career in?'

'Why, the cavalry, of course.' The youth grinned, and joked, 'And you're to blame for that choice, Foley, with the stories you've told me about when you served in the Yeomanry in South Africa.'

The man laughed, and retorted. 'This gentleman here could tell you some stories about the cavalry in South Africa, Simon. And about service in India and the Sudan as well. He's seen a deal more action than I ever did.' He turned his head towards John Purvis.

'Let me introduce my friend, Simon Dolton, to you, Johnny . . .'

As he spoke the middle-aged man abruptly jerked out, 'I have to go, Foley.'

And swinging on his heel walked quickly away into the murky gloom.

For a brief instant Foley Field stared after him in shocked amazement, then recollection flooded through his brain, and he experienced acute embarrassment. He stared at the youth, and could only shake his head helplessly.

'I'm truly sorry, Simon,' he uttered, his expression displaying the discomfiture he was feeling. 'I'm truly sorry, I'd completely forgotten.'

The youth's sensitive features showed his own horrified shock, but he managed to blurt out, 'It's not your fault, Foley.'

He also abruptly turned and hurried away.

When he overtook his mother and brothers she stared at his tense face with anxious concern. 'What is it, Simon? What's happened to upset you so?'

He shook his head impatiently. 'Nothing, Mother. Nothing's happened. I'm perfectly alright.'

35

'No you're not,' she stated vehemently, and ordered the younger boys, 'Walk on ahead, you two. We'll catch up with you.' Then faced her eldest son and instructed firmly, 'Now tell me, Simon. What has upset you?'

For a few moments he hesitated, his troubled expression betraying his emotional strain. Then he drew in a sharp hiss of breath, and almost whispered:

'Do you know who it was that Foley was talking to, Mother?'

She shook her head impatiently. 'Of course I don't. I paid them no attention.'

Simon Dolton appeared to be struggling for control, as he informed her in a shaky voice, 'He was talking to John Purvis! He was talking to the man who killed my father!'

It was Cleopatra Dolton's turn to struggle for control, and for some moments she could make no reply. Then she said quietly, 'Look Simon, we can't discuss your father's death while standing here. Let us go home, and then you and I will have a long talk.'

The woman and her sons walked on in a strained silence, the two younger boys aware that something had occurred to cause tension between their elder brother and their mother, but not knowing what it was.

The Dolton family's house was situated on the Red Lane on the western edges of the town, beyond the railway station. It was one of a grouping of several fine Regency buildings, and like its immediate neighbours, was fronted by sweeping lawns shaded by fine old trees.

Mrs Danks, their gaunt-bodied, dour-featured house-keeper, opened the door to greet them, and instantly divined that something untoward had happened.

'What's the matter?' she demanded to know. 'What's upset you?'

Cleopatra shook her head. 'Will you see to the boys' supper, Mrs Danks?' She turned to her eldest son. 'Go into my office, I'll come into you directly.'

As the boys went their separate ways Cleopatra Dolton whispered to her housekeeper, 'John Purvis is back in the town. Simon's just run into him. That's what's caused the upset.'

The other woman scowled accusingly. 'If you'd ha' listened to me, and we'd ha' moved out of this town, then there 'udden't be any of this upset, 'ud there?'

Cleopatra waved her hand in impatient dismissal. 'Don't let's go over that again, Mrs Danks. Just see to the boys' supper, will you?'

Grumbling, the woman took herself off, and with a troubled heart Cleopatra went into her eldest son.

Her office was in fact the one-time study and library of her dead husband. Not that that crude and brutal man had ever made any use of the room for its original purpose. He had preferred noisy public bars to quiet study rooms, and drinking with his cronies to reading alone.

Simon greeted his mother's entrance with an offered apology. 'I'm sorry I reacted as I did, Mother. But meeting that man was a shock to me.'

Cleopatra gestured towards the two leather covered chairs which flanked the fireplace.

'Let's sit down, my dear.'

They seated to face each other, and the woman unpinned her wide-brimmed hat and veil and laid them aside. Then in her low-pitched, husky voice she told her son, 'You must not blame John Purvis for your father's death. He was acting in my defence.'

The youth scowled angrily. 'Acting as your fancy man, so gossip has it.'

'Gossip is a damned liar!' The woman's dark eyes glowed with her instant fury. 'There was nothing between myself and John Purvis. We were not friends, or even close acquaintances for that matter.'

'If that was the case, then why did he kill my father?' the youth challenged aggressively.

Cleopatra Dolton fought back her own anger, realising that nothing could be gained by indulging in heated exchanges. She asked in a quiet voice, 'Can you remember what my life, and your life, was like when your father was alive?'

The youth's dark eyes became troubled, and he waved his hand before him as if to ward off the question.

'No, Simon!' The woman spoke sharply. 'I will not

37

permit you to refuse me the truth! It's seven years since your father's death, and it's time for complete honesty.'

The youth shook his head, unwilling to speak, but his mother pressed.

'Tell me, Simon! Tell me what you remember about our life when your father was still alive!'

As if reluctant to bring back unhappy memories, the youth grudgingly mumbled, 'It was not happy.'

For a few moments the woman stared hard at him, and inwardly battled against her own reluctance to voice her thoughts. Then she resolved to speak out fully.

'I want you to listen very carefully to what I am going to tell you, Simon. It distresses me to recall what I would sooner forget. But unless you know the truth, then your father's death will always come between us. Will you hear me out?'

After a while, he nodded.

'Very well.' The woman hesitated while she marshalled her thoughts, and then went on.

'Your father, Arthur Dolton, was a brutal husband, and a cruel, unfeeling father. For many years he treated me as if I were a dumb beast. His trade of butcher suited him. He enjoyed inflicting pain on those who were weaker than himself. He ill-used me without reason, and without any justification.'

The boy shook his head and gestured as if in denial of her words, but she would not be deflected from her purpose.

'No! You have agreed to listen to me, and now you will do just that. I should have told you all this years since.' She drew long ragged breaths as her own bitterly painful memories returned in force to torment her.

'For many years Arthur Dolton constantly beat me and raped me. There were times when he would have killed me if others had not intervened to prevent it. And to you and your brothers he never showed any physical affection or demonstrated any love.'

Simon knew that his mother was telling the truth, and yet paradoxically, he felt driven to deny that truth. Because he loved his mother so deeply, and felt for her so

38

keenly, he could not stand to hear her talk of the pain and degradations she had endured at the hands of his father. Now he found himself resenting her for forcing him to face what he would preferred to have left buried deep in his memory.

'If my father was so evil, then why did you not leave him? Why did you not run away?'

She regarded her son with pity, knowing the torment he was suffering.

'Where could I have run to? And how would I have supported you three boys? At least by staying with Arthur Dolton I could ensure that your physical needs would always be met, and that you would someday have social standing in the world.'

He frowned and shook his head in rebuttal. 'If he did not love us, surely we were better away from him?'

Arthur Dolton had never shown any love or tenderness towards his children, and Simon had always felt that somehow it must be his own fault that this had been so.

'No, Simon!' Cleopatra told him gently. 'You were not strong, tough children, able to bear want and hardship. When you were smaller you were all three very delicate, and your health was precarious. To take you into poverty would have meant your deaths.'

'How can you know that?' Simon challenged.

Now she showed a flash of temper. 'I can know that, because I was born and bred in poverty! I was birthed in Silver Street, one of the worst slums in this town, as you well know, and my own mother died when I was still little more than a baby. All my brothers and sisters died before they reached the age of eight. I was the only one to survive. And by God there were times without number when I wished I had not done so. When I wished that I were lying beside them in their graves.'

Her face looked suddenly old and haggard, and she shuddered visibly as terrible memories assailed her. Memories of her own father, half-insane with drink, violating her child body. Forcing her to have sex with him night after night after night, until she was pregnant at the age of fifteen, and taken into the workhouse to give birth

39

to a child who mercifully was stillborn. Equally mercifully her father had died very shortly afterwards, and alone in a harsh world the young girl had struggled to make a life for herself.

Arthur Dolton, a rich, successful butcher, had been her escape from hopeless poverty, and despite the fact that her marriage had been a bitter disillusionment, she had survived it, and had come through finally to her present wealth and independence.

'Mother, don't distress yourself so. Please don't!' Her son was staring at her haggard features with concern, and she shivered, and violently shook her head to eject the awful memories from her mind.

She forced a bleak smile to her lips. 'I'm alright, my dear. But I must finish what I have begun.'

He began to protest, then saw the obduracy in his mother's eyes, and subsided in acceptance.

'It was in the summer of 1902 that I first met John Purvis. He had just returned from the Boer War.' Her tone now was one of reminiscence. 'I remember that he was a very kind man. He showed you his pistol at the Coronation Day Sports meeting on the Musketry Ranges. Do you remember that, Simon?'

The youth nodded. 'Yes, I do remember. I thought he was a hero.'

'I think he truly is,' his mother stated with conviction. 'Anyway, gossip had it that John Purvis and I were lovers. That he was my fancy man.' She hissed in disgust.

'It was all lies. Our relationship was that of acquaintances, nothing more. Anyway, to cut a long story short, your father came to hear this gossip, and it made his treatment of me even worse. Then, on one occasion after he had badly injured me, and put me in real fear of my life, I finally decided that I must leave him, and take you boys with me to protect you also. I truly believed that Arthur was capable of committing any outrage. I feared that he might even turn on you boys and kill you in one of his drunken rages.

'Of course, I needed money if I was to run away and take you with me. So I decided that I would sell my jewellery.' She smiled wryly. 'In all fairness to your father, when I first married him he was very generous with his gifts to me. So, I went to John Purvis' lodgings to ask him if he would sell the jewellery for me. I daren't try and dispose of it in person, in case word got back to your father that I was doing so. If he had found out, then I knew that he would most definitely cripple or kill me.'

Her expression became distant, and her voice detached as the memories completely enfolded her.

'Arthur Dolton found out that I was at John's lodgings, and he came after me. He burst into the room, and attacked John. There was a fight, and your father was killed.'

She halted and stared intently at her son. Then she stated vehemently, 'It was an accident, Simon! Your father's death was an accident! John Purvis never intended to kill him. He was only acting in self-defence, and to protect me from harm. I swear that is the truth. I swear it on my mother's grave!'

Simon recognised the truth of what she was saying, and was able to accept it. 'I believe you, Mother,' he told her quietly. 'I truly believe you.'

She gusted a long sigh of relief, and her tense body visibly relaxed. She went on in almost conversational tones.

'John Purvis was sentenced to four years' imprisonment for manslaughter. I wrote to him, saying how sorry I was, and offering any help I could give him.' She shrugged her shoulders. 'He replied to my letter, thanking me for my concern, but refusing any help, and telling me that I should put what had happened firmly behind me, and continue with my life. He stressed that my children's welfare should be my sole concern, and that I should not think of him any more.'

Again she shrugged.

'I've not seen John Purvis to speak to from that day to this. I know that on occasion he has returned to the town for brief periods, and that he still owns his house in Mount Pleasant. And that is all.'

She smiled sadly at her eldest son. 'And now you know

41

all, my dear. I hope that knowing all will help you to come to terms with what happened.'

He fleetingly returned her smile, then became very serious. 'In all truthfulness, Mother, deep in my heart I've known all for a long time now. Ever since I became old enough to think for myself, and to evaluate matters. It was just that there was something inside me which couldn't accept it.'

'And can you accept it now?' She wanted to know.

He nodded, and rose to come to her. Bending he kissed her gently on her cheek.

'Thank you for being so honest with me,' he whispered. 'Yes, I can accept it, and I love you dearly.'

With that he went quietly from the room, leaving Cleopatra sitting staring into the empty fireplace.

A wave of bleak sadness swept over her, and tears stung her eyes. She let her emotions whelm freely, and the tears fell down her cheeks. It was some considerable time before her weeping came to an end, and the house was still and silent. She wiped her eyes, and blew her nose hard, and as on so many many occasions in her past she summoned her inner resources of fortitude to face whatever life might hold for her in the future.

'I won't let anything defeat me,' she resolved with grim determination. 'And whatever must be done to ensure my boys' future, then I'll do it.'

Chapter Five

On Wednesday morning Adrian West attended the Petty Sessions held at the police station and applied for, and was granted, a licence to erect his travelling theatre in the Royal yard, and to give public performances of plays, variety acts, and moving pictures for a period of three calendar months.

After his application had been granted he loitered for a while on a rear bench in the courtroom, watching the cases being brought up before the magistrates. It was the normal bill of fare for the Petty Sessions. An assault. A couple of cases of using indecent language in public. Several drunk and incapables, and drunk and disorderlies. One of driving a horse and cart recklessly. One of drunk in charge of a horse and cart. A battered wife applying for a restraining order against her violent husband. Two bastardy cases. . . .

West listened without any great interest as the succession of sordid insights into other people's sad lives were presented before the court. Then his interest suddenly quickened, as he heard the clerk of the court present the next case to the magistrates.

Dolton Enterprises were applying for an ejectment order against one of their tenants for non-payment of rent. Ozzie Clarke entered the small courtroom to give his evidence, but it was not the man Adrian West was interested in. It was the woman who accompanied Clarke, and came to sit on the end of the rear bench where West himself was sitting.

West covertly studied this newcomer. She was dressed in a long charcoal-grey cape, but its folds could not disguise

43

her proudly jutting breasts, or hide the sultry beauty of her face, set off by the dashing wide-brimmed hat turned up at the side and plumed with white feathers that she wore on her dark hair.

He shrewdly judged her to be around forty years of age, but in her case maturity only served to enhance the sensuality she exuded.

'Are you Clarke's wife?' West wondered. 'If you are, then he's a lucky man.' Then he grinned sardonically to himself. 'Or a worried one. You look a lot of woman for one man to handle.'

An exchange of raised voices from the magistrates' bench deflected West's attention from the woman.

One of the magistrates, a clergyman, was sharply challenging Ozzie Clarke.

'Your tenant has five children under the age of seven years, Mr Clarke. Do you not think you are acting with undue harshness in seeking his ejectment from his dwelling place?'

Clarke's pleasant features flushed, and he appeared uncomfortable.

'The man owes more than a month's rent, sir.'

'That may be. But he has told the court that he has been unable to work for three weeks because of an injury he has sustained at his place of employment.'

The tenant, a weedy-bodied, shabby man, with a broken-peaked flatcap pulled low on his forehead, was sitting on the front bench facing the magistrates, and now he twisted his grimy, grey-stubbled features in an expression of pain, and rubbed the small of his back with both hands. Groaning audibly as he did so.

'You knew that Mr Tomlinson had been unable to go to his work, did you not, Mr Clarke?' the clergyman pressed hectoringly.

Clarke shook his head, and mumbled, 'No sir, I did not.'

'Oh indeed!' The clergyman adjusted his pince-nez to glare witheringly. 'Then you do not concern yourself with your tenants' welfare in any way? Even in this present case, where so many tiny infants are put at risk of losing their home?' he accused scornfully. 'That is hardly a Christian

44

attitude to display, is it, Mr Clarke?'

Clarke shrugged unhappily, and mumbled an inaudible reply.

'What's that you say?' The magistrate cupped his hand to his ear, and leaned towards Clarke, then ordered aggressively, 'Speak up, man!'

West heard the sharp hiss of indrawn breath from the woman, and then she was on her feet.

'Mr Clarke is acting on my instructions in applying for this ejectment order.' Her voice rang out clearly, bringing all eyes swinging towards her.

'Who are you, madam? And how dare you interrupt the proceedings of this court?' the clergyman demanded irascibly.

'I am Mrs Cleopatra Dolton, the owner of Dolton Enterprises,' she informed him coolly. 'And I am interrupting these proceedings because I can see that this man Tomlinson is making a fool of the court with his lying tales of injury.'

The senior magistrate leaned across to his pince-nezed colleague and whispered urgently in his ear, then himself asked Cleopatra Dolton, 'Are you implying that Mr Tomlinson is telling lies about being injured at his work, Mrs Dalton?'

'I am not implying anything, sir,' Cleopatra Dalton's husky voice rang out confidently. 'I am stating it as a fact. Tomlinson has been one of my tenants for a year now. During that time he has on three occasions been in arrears with his rent. Always he has claimed that those arrears have been incurred because he has suffered injuries which keep him from his work. For the sake of his children I have in the past accepted his excuses, and on the first occasion I even wrote off those arrears. This time however I have had enquiries made concerning these alleged injuries that Tomlinson claims to have suffered. And I discovered that on the day he claimed to have been injured, he was not even at his place of work. And far from being injured, he spent most of the day and night in an alehouse and was carried back to his home because he was too drunk to walk.'

The magistrates scowled down at the squirming Tomlinson, and the senior demanded, 'Is this true, Mr Tomlinson?'

The weedy man babbled incoherent sentences and excuses, but the magistrate had heard enough, and he slammed his hand down upon the bench.

'The ejectment order against the defendant is granted. The court orders that he must vacate his present dwelling place within a period of seven days from this date.'

'Thank you, sir.' Cleopatra Dolton inclined her head, then swept from the courtroom, with Ozzie Clarke hurrying to catch her up.

On impulse, Adrian West also jumped to his feet and hurried after the couple. He found them standing a little way along the road outside the doors of the new Post Office. As he neared them he could hear Cleopatra's husky voice taking Clarke to task.

'Why did you not tell the magistrate what a lying hound Tomlinson is? The way you acted it looked as if we were heartless villains.'

Clarke shook his head and looked shamefaced. 'I couldn't help but think of his kids. All those little 'uns to be made homeless. It worries me.'

It was the woman's turn to shake her head. 'You're too soft for your own good, Mr Clarke.' Her tone was mild, and it was more statement than rebuke. 'Of course it's a shame for his kids. But we can't afford to let heart rule head in this business. There are dozens like Tomlinson in this town, who would do us down without any scruples at all, if we were soft enough to let them.'

'It's still a shame for his kids,' Clarke asserted doggedly.

The woman's sultry features hardened. 'The shame for his kids is having a worthless scum like him for a father. And there's nothing you or I can do to change that fact, is there? I can't afford to house men like him for free. I've got my own children to think about. Do you think he would have any pity on me, or on you, if the situation was reversed?' she challenged.

And reluctantly Clarke shook his head. 'No, he most probably wouldn't.'

46

'There's no probably about it, Clarke,' Cleopatra stated flatly, 'it's a certainty.'

They walked on side by side, and West followed closely behind them, enjoying watching her proud, upright carriage and the glimpses of her profile as she turned at times towards the man by her side.

'By Christ! She'd make a wonderful Lady Macbeth,' he decided. 'She's got that quality of ruthlessness that's needed for the part.'

The couple rounded the corner of the Church Road on which the Police Station was situated, and went along the broad promenade of Church Green West with its rows of shops facing the tall, spired St Stephen's. At the central crossroads the couple parted. The man went straight on southwards along Evesham Street, the woman turned westwards down the approach to the junction of the Unicorn and Bates Hills.

West followed the woman. By now he was very keen to meet her, and he toyed with the idea of overtaking and introducing himself to her as one of her new tenants. But some instinct held him back from approaching her, and he trusted his instincts enough to obey their dictates.

As she walked down the Unicorn Hill towards the railway station he maintained the same distance behind her, and when she halted momentarily at the entrance drive to the railway station he slowed his pace. Then she again walked on over the bridge which crossed the railway lines and he quickened his pace once more.

She passed by the grimy enclave of streets and courts clustering around noisy factories which separated the railway lines from the leafy slopes of the Red Lane with its opulent Regency houses, and still West followed discreetly.

When she entered the grounds of one of the fine houses he sauntered past, covertly watching her go into the house, which he assumed was her own. Then he continued on up the slope to the top of the rise where the ancient woodlands stretched before him. He turned there and retraced his steps past Cleopatra Dolton's house, and told himself delightedly, 'What a town of pleasant surprises this is turning out to be. First I meet Emma Vivaldi, and now

I've seen Cleopatra Dolton. Either one of them will do for me. And if I could have both of them, then I'd be in paradise.

He had already decided how he would introduce himself to Cleopatra Dolton. I'll call at her house one evening, he thought, and ask her permission to have the electric cable run into the shed in the Royal yard. But before I do that I'll make a few more enquiries about her.

West was a firm believer in making full and careful reconnaissance before entering into a campaign of seduction. He sauntered back towards the town, and as he began the climb up the steep slope of the Unicorn Hill he spotted yet another attractive woman coming down the hill towards him. She was poorly dressed, in a shabby blue gown with a threadbare shawl wrapped around her upper body and a straw boater perched on her fair hair. But West found her thin pale face piquantly pretty, and noted her fine grey eyes.

As they closed on each other he lifted his curly brimmed bowler hat and smiled broadly at her.

'Good morning.'

Her eyes only flickered across his face, and frowning slightly she ignored his greeting and hurried past.

He shrugged carelessly, and told himself, 'Ah well, Adrian, you cannot expect to charm them all, can you?' And he went light-heartedly on his way, savouring the prospect of sharing an intimate lunch with the delectable Emma Vivaldi.

Samuel Hulland, local Relieving Officer of the Bromsgrove Poor Law Union, stared curiously at the slender young woman standing on the front door step of his home in Oakley Road, Redditch. She wore a shabby blue gown, and straw boater hat, and had a threadbare shawl wrapped around her shoulders and pinned across her strangely protruding chest. After a moment or two he realised that the misshapen configuration was due to the fact that she had her left arm tied up in a sling.

'What can I do for you, Missy?' He was still chewing a piece of his midday sandwich.

48

The young woman's pale face was thin and drawn, and her wide brow furrowed as if she were in pain. But her grey eyes were calm and steady before his dour regard.

'Doctor Protheroe Smith said I was to come to see you, Mr Hulland.'

Her soft cultured voice was strangely at variance with her shabby clothing.

'Oh did he now?' Hulland's dourness became tinged with aggrievement. 'I wonder why he didn't stop to think that I might be having a bite to eat seeing that it's lunchtime, and that I might not want to be pestered.'

'I'm sorry,' she apologised. 'It's my fault that I've disturbed you at this hour, not the doctor's. But my need is urgent.'

From inside the house a woman's aggrieved voice sounded shrilly, 'Will you shut that door, Samuel. Youm letting all the heat out.'

The man scowled and muttered beneath his breath, turning his head to shout, 'In a minute.'

When his eyes swung back to the young woman on the doorstep he caught her in an unguarded wince of pain as she cradled the protuberance of her damaged arm.

More sympathetically, he asked her, 'Is it pauper relief you want to apply for, Missy?'

She nodded, and a flush of embarrassment coloured her drawn cheeks.

'Very well.' His manner became brisk and businesslike. 'Look, to save you having to hang about here in this cold you just give me your name and address, and I'll come round to see you later to make the necessary enquiries.'

'Thank you, very much.' She seemed genuinely grateful for his show of consideration. 'My name is Laura Hughes, Miss Laura Hughes, and my address is Number Three Court, Hill Street.' She hesitated, and then added, 'That's off Unicorn Hill, by the Lamb and Flag public house.'

The man chuckled grimly. 'No need to give me directions, Missy. I knows this town like the palm of me hand.'

Flustered, she apologised. 'I'm sorry, I wasn't thinking.'

'No need to apologise.' His manner was by now

becoming almost genial. 'You get on off home now, and I'll call later today.'

'Thank you, Mr Hulland.' She turned and went down the slope of the hill towards the Railway Station, and for a few moments he stood watching her.

'What's a clean, well-spoken young 'ooman like you doing in bloody Hill Street?' He wondered aloud.

'Samuel! Will you come in and shut that door!' his irate wife screeched, and he scowled and muttered beneath his breath, and obeyed.

At the bottom of the slope Laura turned right and went up the sharp rise of the Unicorn Hill. Halfway up she came to the fetid muddy entrance of the unsavoury Hill Street, with its huddled, decayed tenements, broken doors and rag-stuffed windows.

As always at any hour of the day or night the passage of someone up the narrow, rutted, refuse-strewn roadway brought frowsty heads to doors and windows to challenge the interloper. Recognising Laura, however, the hostile challenges were not issued, and her progress was punctuated with friendly greetings, and questions about her damaged arm.

'I slipped and fell at work.'

'Yes, it's broken, in two places.'

'Doctor Protheroe Smith set it for me.'

'Yes, it was painful, it still is.'

'No, that's alright, thank you, I shall manage very well.'

'Yes, I will call for you if I need any help.'

The rough kindliness and sympathy of her neighbours cheered her, and filled her with a warmth of gratitude, and not for the first time she fervently wished that those self-styled 'respectable' elements of the town's population could witness the depths of compassion and readiness to help that were to be found among the feared and reviled slum dwellers of the town.

She passed through the covered entryway and entered the mean court that was her home, its cramped oblong of tumbledown tenements blocking all access for fresh clean air and sunlight, and its confined centre space dominated by the big stinking refuse heap in the middle of the court.

The heap was bounded by baulks of rotting timber, from between the cracks of which oozed rivulets of putrid liquid which puddled and saturated the earth until it resembled a filthy, foul-stenched bog.

When Laura had first come to live here some two years past the sight and stench of the refuse heap had made her feel physically ill. Now she hardly noticed its reek, and accepted it as an integral part of her surroundings, only on occasion marvelling at how usage had inured her once fastidious senses to such purulent abuse.

She entered her own dwelling, and as always the contrast between the exterior court and this interior with its clean-scrubbed floor and walls, table and stools, the fragrant scents emitted by the bunches of herbs and dried flowers hanging from the uncovered ceiling joists, gave her a sense of pleasure.

The cottage was very small, there was only this room, with a minute back scullery, and upstairs two tiny bedrooms reached by a steep narrow staircase. Going to the bottom of this staircase Laura called softly, 'Hello Tommy. It's only me, Laura. Are you alright?'

There sounded a bumping on the ceiling above her head, and a male voice answered in a series of unintelligible moaning grunts.

She smiled, and called again, 'I'll come up and fetch you in a while, Tommy. But I've a few things to attend to first. Be a good boy now, and lay quiet until I come up for you.'

There was more excited moanings and grunts, coupled with bumping on the ceiling boards and Laura's smile saddened, and she sighed heavily, 'Poor Tommy!'

She unpinned her shawl and with careful fingers lifted the edge of the cloth sling to stare ruefully at her thickly padded and splinted left arm. The initial sickening pain had now lessened to a dull throbbing ache which she knew she could endure. What was worrying her now was how she was to manage to care for the man in the tiny bedroom above her head.

'What's brung you home so early?'

Maria Cull, one of the neighbours, came into the room without knocking. Then, seeing Laura's splinted arm she exclaimed, 'What the bloody hell's you bin doing to yourself?'

Once more Laura explained how she had slipped and fallen at her place of work.

'You just sit yourself down and I'll brew you a cup o' tay, my duck!'

The hard-featured, raw-boned woman took Laura by the hand and guided her down onto one of the trio of three-legged stools which comprised the room's seating.

'You stay theer, while I does the needful. I'll get a bit o' fire gooing as well while I'm about it. I'll fetch in a shovelfull from me grate. And doon't you bloody well stir, or I'll bloody well fetch you a clout across the yed.'

Laura made no protest against the other woman's rough-voiced commands and threats. Caring for others did not come soft-voiced in Hill Street. It came disguised with harsh bluster, but it was a truly genuine caring nevertheless. So she remained quietly seated, grateful for the opportunity to rally her physical strength because she was still suffering the after-effects from the shock of her injury.

In only scant minutes Maria was back with a mug of hot sweet tea, and while Laura sipped pleasurably at the steaming drink, the other woman busied herself in getting a fire going in the small black-leaded grate.

When the flames were leaping high and warming the dank air of the room Maria seated herself on another stool and regarded Laura with concern etched upon her hard, battered features.

'Who was it set your arm?'

'Protheroe Smith.'

'How long did he say you'd be off work?'

Laura shrugged, and flinched as the unthinking movement sent pain stabbing through her arm.

'He couldn't say exactly, but he thinks for several weeks.'

Maria pursed her lips and nodded thoughtfully. 'You'll be needing to apply to the Board then, wun't you? You'll be needing relief.'

'I've already done so. Doctor Smith sent me to see Samuel Hulland, and he said he would call and see me later today to make the necessary enquiries. He seemed to be a kindly man, so I should think that I'll be allowed relief.'

'Ahr, I see.' Again the other woman nodded. 'He aren't a bad sort, Sammy Hulland aren't. But some o' the Board am real mean souled bastards, and no mistake. And it's them who'll have the final say-so, aren't it. All Sammy Hulland can do is to put your case to 'um.'

The Board was the local Board Of Guardians, who dealt with the administration of the Poor Laws in the district and granted the various types of Pauper Relief.

Maria jerked her head meaningfully upwards. 'I reckon Tommy 'ull have to goo into the work'us though.'

'No! He can't!' Acute fear and dismay flooded through Laura, causing her to exclaim fiercely, 'I won't let them put Tommy in the workhouse.'

'It aren't a matter o' what you'll let 'um do, my wench!' Maria told her roughly. 'The Board aren't agooing to pay that loony bugger outdoor relief, am they. Not when it's chaper for 'um to put him into the Work'us.'

'No!' Laura shook her head and repeated stubbornly, 'No, I'll not let them put him away. Rosie would turn in her grave if Tommy was to be put away like that among strangers.'

The other woman appeared to lose patience. 'Doon't talk so sarft! Rosie's dead and gone, and nothing that happens on this earth is gooing to cause her any upset, is it. You'se got to think of yourself, girl. God only knows you'se bin a good 'un looking arter a loony who'se no kin of your own all this time. But how am you gooing to look arter him now, with you crippled like you am. The relief money wun't be enough to keep you hardly, ne'er mind feed Tommy as well. And like I said afore, the Board wun't give you nuthin for him.'

Laura's expression was sullen with determination. 'I'll manage somehow. Neither of us eat that much anyway.'

Maria expelled her breath in noisy disgust. 'Doon't talk sarft, girl. It aren't only the bloody feeding on him that I'm on about. How am you gooing to manage to dress him and see to his needs? And what happens when he throws one of his fits? Gawd strewth! It takes three on us at least to hold the sod when he's playing up. With you in the state youm in he could bloody well kill you afore any on us could get in here to help.'

This last argument struck home, and although Laura still shook her head in determined rebuttal, doubt entered her mind.

Again Maria expelled a noisy breath of disgust, then she shook her head, causing frizzed tendrils of greasy hair to fall about her raddled cheeks.

'Well, I'se had me say, and you must do whatever you reckons is best, my wench. Now doon't you moither your yed about looking arter Tommy today. I'll pop across later to feed him, and see to his needs. And I'll get him settled in for the night. You just sit easy and rest yourself. A broke bone is a bad shock to your system, and you needs a bit o' peace and quiet to settle yourself down agen.'

'Thank you, Maria.' Gratitude for the other woman's unasked for kindness brought tears stinging Laura's eyes, and she was forced to blink hard and draw a deep breath to stop herself from crying.

'No need to thank me, girl,' the woman told her gruffly. 'You'd do the same for me if I was in your place, I knows that.'

Alone in the room once more Laura stared deep into the glowing coals of the small fire and could not prevent a feeling of dread creeping over her.

What am I going to do? she thought helplessly. It's true what Maria says, I'll not be able to care for Tommy while I'm like this. I'll not be able to wash or dress him, and if he should throw one of his fits, I'll be helpless against him.

She bit her lip worriedly. 'What am I going to do? What am I going to do?' Again and again she asked the question, but could find no answer to it.

She went upstairs to find that Tommy Spiers was sleeping, and stood for some while staring down at him. He was a man in his early thirties, but looked far older. He was painfully thin, and his complexion was pallid and unhealthy. He lay now on his back, his jaw gaping and a trickle of saliva falling constantly from the corner of his slack mouth. He snorted and snuffled as he breathed, and at times uttered unintelligible murmurings. She checked the ropes which held his limbs and body secured to the old iron bedstead, with just enough slack to enable him to move a yard or so from its confines. For his own safety she was forced to keep him tied up while she was at work so that he could not wander.

At the side of the bed was a tin mug filled with water, and a piece of bread smeared with pork fat. There was also a bucket which he could use for his personal offices.

Laura took the half-full bucket with its foul smelling contents downstairs with her and went outside to empty it onto the refuse-heap. Then she went out of the court and down the slope to the old hand-worked pump which constituted the only water-supply for the street. As she pumped the long handle and washed out the bucket she wondered once more about how she was going to manage to care for Tommy Spiers, and once more no easy answer presented itself. Heavy hearted, she slowly returned to her own tenement.

Samuel Hulland came to Hill Street late that afternoon. He was well known as a frequent visitor to this mean thoroughfare, and his advent met with a mixed reception. Obsequious greetings from those to whom he had granted, or was currently granting relief, scowls and muttered insults from those whose applications he had spoken against before the Board, or had summarily rejected.

He entered Number Three Court and shouted, 'Laura Hughes? Are you here?'

The shabby door opened, and the young woman beckoned. The man frowned in recognition, and queried as he entered stooping beneath the low door lintel, 'Didn't Rosie Spiers used to live here?'

'That's right,' Laura confirmed. 'Her brother still does.'

'I see.' Hulland nodded his bowler-hatted head, and in sudden remembrance told her, 'I recollect hearing now that somebody was looking after him, after his sister died

55

down in London there while she was in prison. She was stupid to get mixed up with them Suffragettes. It could never do her any good, a working wench like she was.'

'The Suffragettes are the only hope that working women have to better their conditions,' Laura stated positively.

'Am you one of them? A Suffragette, I mean?' he queried.

Laura nodded. 'I am.'

He stared at her with an ambiguous expression, neither hostile or supportive. Then he went on in a conversational tone, 'I knew young Rosie, and her mam and dad well. After the old folks went to the Bromsgrove Union I advised Rosie to let her brother be put in there as well. But she wouldn't hear of it.'

He shook his head slightly as if puzzled.

'When you said you lived here in Hill Street, I never dreamed that it was you who'd taken over looking after the loony.'

'He isn't loony!' Laura snapped in angry defence. 'He's just a little backward, that's all.'

The man's manner visibly hardened in the face of her aggressive rejoinder.

'Well, whatever you wants to say he is, he'll have to be put away now, that's for sure.'

'Why will he?' Laura was made both nervous and indignant by this statement. 'I can care for him here. I've done so for two years now.'

'You warn't applying for relief then though, was you, Missy?'

'What difference does that make?' she challenged spiritedly.

'The difference is that if you was prepared to spend your own money looking after him, then that's nobody's business but your own. But if youm applying to the ratepayers of this town for money to keep him with, then they've got a say in the matter, arn't they.'

The sudden realisation that she would gain nothing, and risk losing a lot by continuing to argue with this man caused Laura to bite back her rising anger. She forced herself to ask reasonably.

'Please, Mr Hulland, I'm in need of your advice in this matter, because I'm very ignorant of how the pauper relief system works.'

Mollified, he was prepared to be gracious, but could not resist gibing, 'After two years in Hill Street you ought to be an expert on pauper relief, missy. The buggers who lives here knows all there is to know about scrounging as much as they can get from the ratepayers.'

Laura would not allow herself to make any retort to this, and taking her silence as a token of her readiness to be suitably humble, he went on.

'I takes all the details from you as to your needs, and present assets. If I decides that youm in need of relief, then I places your case before the Board of Guardians, and makes recommendation as to what type and how much relief youm entitled to. If youm in urgent need, and I considers that it's justified, then I'm also empowered to give you something immediately at my own discretion to tide you over until the Board can hear your application.' He looked smugly satisfied, and remarked, 'It's a very fair and Christian system to my way of thinking, as I'm sure you'll agree.'

It was Laura's turn to regard him ambiguously, and murmur, 'I'm sure it's very Christian indeed, Mr Hulland.'

There was a trace of suspicion in his watery eyes as he stared at her. Then he produced a bulky notebook from his greatcoat pocket and a stub of pencil.

'I'll just take the details then. What's your full name?'

'Laura Victoria Hughes.'

'Place and date of birth?'

'The 7th of March 1883, and I was born in Buxton, Derbyshire.'

The man laboriously wrote it down, breathing adenoidally through his open mouth.

'I take it youm single?'

'Yes, I'm a spinster lady,' she answered, with a hint of self-deprecation in her tone.

'What's your father's name and occupation?'

'George Alfred Hughes. Anglican clergyman.'

Hulland stared in open surprise. 'A clergyman?'

She nodded, and smiled ironically. 'Do you find it strange that I should be a clergyman's daughter?'

'I finds it strange that a clergyman's daughter should be living in Hill Street,' he stated bluntly.

The ironic smile still lurked around her lips as she replied, 'There are many worse places where a clergyman's daughter might be found, Mr Hulland.'

Using one forefinger he tipped his bowler hat slightly back from his brow and rubbed the reddened band of flesh on his forehead. Indicating the printed sheet of paper before him he said, 'I doon't rightly know what to put down here wheer it says "Usual occupation of applicant". I suppose you being a clergyman's daughter I should rightly put you down as a gentlewoman, shouldn't I?'

She chuckled wryly. 'I don't really think that that would be an accurate description at this time, Mr Hulland. I've spent the last two years working at the Steam Laundry in St George's Road. Mainly in the heavy wash shop. I suppose you could put my occupation down as "laundress", though myself I'd be inclined to say washerwoman.'

He frowned at her levity. 'What must your dad think of you working at such a menial job, I wonder? I shouldn't think he's very proud of having a daughter working in a laundry, is he?'

Her grey eyes sparked with a sardonic amusement. 'I don't really think that my father is greatly concerned about what I do to earn my living, Mr Hulland. He's been dead for several years.'

Flustered, the man began to mouth an apology, but Laura Hughes shook her head.

'Please, it makes no matter, Mr Hulland.'

'Have you got any other relatives who could help you financially?'

She shook her head. 'No one, I'm afraid. I am quite alone in the world.'

He expressed a gruff sympathy, but she made light of her situation. 'I'm well used to it, Mr Hulland.'

He went on to ask her a few more questions concerning

her financial assets and outgoings, and when the form was completed laid aside his pencil and stared at her uncertainly.

'Now, youm an unusual case, Missy, because youm a young 'ooman who is caring for a man who is no kin to you. A man that whatever you'd like to call him, is definitely not able to care for himself. A man who most people would agree should be put somewhere safe for his own sake.'

When, despite her previous intentions, Laura opened her mouth to protest, Hulland held up his hand to forestall her.

'No! hear me out first, Missy. Then you can have your say. You see, what you might not know is that Rosie Spiers made an application for relief a few years back when her was taken poorly and couldn't work for a while. Now the Board said that because her Mam and Dad had previously bin took into the workhouse, then there was nobody to look after her brother properly while Rosie was poorly.

'Well, poor Rosie kicked up merry hell about it, and at last the Board took pity on her, because the loony was her one and only brother after all, and agreed to grant outdoor relief to both on 'um.'

'There you are then!' Laura could not help interjecting. 'There has been a precedent set. So how can they rightfully refuse to grant myself and Tommy relief in this instance?'

Exasperation heightened his tone. 'It doon't count as any set precedent, young 'ooman! Because when the Board made the order, they also put it down in writing that it was a one and only. They made it plain that if at any time in the future Rosie Spiers had to apply for relief again, then it 'ud only be granted to her. And that her brother, Tommy Spiers, 'ud have to be taken into the work'us.'

'That's not fair!' Laura burst out.

'Oh yes it is fair, young 'ooman. It's fair to the rate payers. When Rosie Spiers was poorly she was granted medical relief as well, and a nurse was paid to come and see to her. But the nurse had all sorts of bother with that

59

bloody loony brother when he had his violent turns, and she told the Board that she wouldn't never put up with that sort of thing again. So the Board had to ensure that it wouldn't happen again.'

'But I can care for Tommy!' Laura protested heatedly.

Hulland was beginning to have difficulty holding onto his patience with this difficult young woman.

'Look here, I've told you what the situation is, Missy. And you must like it or lump it. You can be granted outdoor relief, but Tommy Spiers can't. And that's that! And what's more, the Board might well decide that you can only be granted that relief if Tommy Spiers is took into the proper place for him. And that's the loony ward of the work'us, in my opinion!'

Laura's own temper surged out of control. 'Bugger your opinion, Mr Hulland! And bugger the Board of Guardians! I'll manage without your relief!'

He stared at her as if stupified at hearing such language coming from her lips.

'I'll thank you to get out of my home, Mr Hulland! Right now, if you please!' Laura pointed towards the door, and even in this moment inwardly cringed with embarrassment as she realised how melodramatically she was behaving.

Hulland shook his head as if nonplussed. 'But what about your application?' he uttered.

'I've withdrawn it!' Laura informed him grandly. 'Now will you please leave my home.'

After a couple of moments he shrugged, and muttering beneath his breath, he went out of the low doorway.

As he disappeared Laura slumped down onto the stool and exclaimed with dismay, 'Why did I do that?'

Remembering her dramatic words and actions she was torn between tears and laughter. 'Why did I do that?'

'How did you get on, my duck?' Maria Cull came through the doorway. 'Has Sammy Hulland give you anything?'

Laura drew a sharp breath and shook her head. 'No, Maria. I told him to get out.'

60

She went on to explain why she had acted as she had, and the other woman regarded her with increasing consternation. Then when Laura had fallen silent once more, she questioned, 'But what 'ull you do now, my duck? How 'ull you live?'

Laura shook her head, then added quickly, 'It's alright though. I've got three days' pay to come from the laundry. I'll go down and fetch it first thing tomorrow morning. I can get some fish and chips on tick for tonight's meal.'

The fried fish shop just around the corner on the Unicorn Hill was accustomed to giving credit to many of its customers after their meagre housekeeping money had run out in mid-week.

'Three days' pay aren't going to keep you long though, is it?' Maria stated bluntly. 'You want's your bloody yed looking at, you does, my wench. Fancy telling Sammy Hulland to bugger off! And just for the sake of that yampy-yedded bugger upstairs. You needs your bloody yed looking at, you does.'

Laura felt unable to argue further about her decision to keep Tommy with her. She could only shake her head wearily. With a final admonition to Laura to have Tommy taken into the workhouse, Maria went away.

The young woman sat for almost an hour as dusk came and darkness fell on the land. Again and again her thoughts traced the same route, and again and again she was reluctantly drawn to the same seemingly inevitable conclusion. If she was to keep Tommy Spiers here with her, then she would have to bury her pride and seek help.

Rising she used a wooden spill to take a light from the glowing coals in the fireplace to the small oil lamp on the table. Taking the oil lamp she went upstairs and opened her old battered travelling trunk. Rummaging through the sparse contents she found an envelope, writing paper and pen and ink.

Downstairs once more she penned a long letter explaining what had befallen her, and asking for financial aid. Then she carefully addressed the envelope to:

61

Miss Miriam Josceleyne,
co/ The Women's Social and Political Union.
    Clement's Inn.
    The Strand.
    London WC2.

Laura placed the envelope on the mantelshelf above the fireplace and sat resentfully regarding it. She knew that her friend Miriam Josceleyne would be more than willing to help her, but she felt a sense of shame and self-scorn that she should have to go begging for charity.

'Here I am at twenty-six years of age a penniless pauper,' she castigated herself scornfully. 'I've had all the advantages of a good upbringing and a liberal education. I preach the cause of Women's Suffrage to poor, downtrodden wretched women, and tell them that they should rise up and fight to better themselves, and they look at me as if I'm strong and fearless, and capable of dealing with any difficulties. Yet at the first instance of difficulty I must go running to my friend seeking help, like a small helpless child runs to its mother.'

Suddenly she jumped up and grabbed the envelope, and threw it onto the fire, then there came the sounds of Tommy Spiers' voice, and a thumping on the ceiling above her head. She remained standing watching the flames lick around the edges of the envelope, the paper scorch and curl and burn to ashes.

The noise from above her head increased in volume, and she shouted wearily, 'Alright, Tommy. Be quiet now. I'm coming.'

With a heavy heart, she turned away from the fireplace and clambered up the narrow stairs.

Chapter Six

The painful throbbing of her arm prevented Laura from sleeping soundly, and through most of the night she lay awake. Her mind was troubled also by the prospect that lay ahead of her of having to survive and support Tommy without any assistance, and unable to work herself.

When daylight came, despite the fact that she felt tired and out of sorts, Laura rose from her bed with a sense of relief that she could now busy herself physically and thus keep her heavy sense of foreboding at bay. She peeped into the tiny rear bedroom where Tommy lay snuffling and grunting and twitching in unquiet sleep, and the sudden thought crossed her mind that it would be a blessing if death took him.

She recoiled in horror and self-disgust. What's happening to me? What sort of an evil bitch am I becoming?

She hurried downstairs, her thoughts and emotions in turmoil, and over and over again the same horrified demand rang through her mind: What's happening to me? How could I ever have thought something like that? What am I becoming?

In the minute scullery she had left a bucket of water, and now she poured some of the water into the tin bowl and awkwardly washed her face and neck with one hand. Afterwards she cleaned her teeth, using the tooth powder sparingly because now she did not know when she might be able to afford to buy another tin of it. Then she returned upstairs and dressed herself, wincing at times as the movements painfully jarred her splinted arm.

For a time she sat down on her bed and considered her

course of action, wondering how she was going to cope with washing and dressing the man in the next room. She knew that she could call on her neighbours for their help, and that they would give it. But she also knew that each and everyone of her neighbours had more than enough to cope with already in caring for their own families, without adding this fresh burden to their heavy loads.

'No,' she decided finally. 'It's my decision to keep Tommy with me. So it's up to me to care for him, broken arm or no broken arm.'

The resolve lifted her spirits, and helped to drive the dark forebodings of the night from her mind. She smiled almost gaily.

'If he won't let me wash and dress him, then he'll just have to stay dirty and undressed.'

Briskly she returned downstairs, and taking the bucket went out to fetch fresh water. Several women were queuing at the pump, and they greeted Laura cheerily, asking how her arm was, and how she was coping with Tommy.

She answered with confident assertions that all was going very well, hiding her own doubts and fears so successfully that she actually started to feel an inner confidence that everything would indeed go well.

But when she had returned to the house, and stood looking down at Tommy's haggard, dark-stubbled face, and smelled his foul breath, and saw the saliva trickling from the corners of his slack-lipped mouth, her heart momentarily sank once more, and she was strongly tempted to leave him sleeping, and do nothing until she was actually forced to do so.

Her greatest fear was that he would erupt in one of his violent fits, and cause her injury, even death. This fear burgeoned uncontrollably as the memories clamoured in her brain of all those other times when he had become violent and it had taken all her strength, and the strength of whoever had come to aid her, to hold him down and secure him safely.

She actually turned and stepped away, then forced herself to halt and go back to him again.

64

'I can't give in to it.' She forced herself to fight the fear. 'And it's not that often that Tommy becomes violent, after all. It's only occasionally.'

But even as she tried to reassure herself, a voice warned in her mind: But it only takes that one occasion for him to cripple or kill you, doesn't it?

She suddenly remembered an occurrence many years past when as a small child she had been nipped and badly frightened by a boisterous puppy. Her father had dried her tears and told her firmly, 'It was your own fault that the puppy turned on you. He saw that you were afraid of him. You must never ever show any animal that you fear it. That only serves to give them the courage to attack you. If you appear unafraid, then they will not dare to turn on you.'

'God forgive me!' Laura chided herself disgustedly. 'I'm beginning to think about Tommy as if he were an animal, and not a poor afflicted human being.'

Her self-disgust helped her to overcome her fear, and she shook his boney shoulder, and told him firmly, 'Come on, Tommy. It's time for you to get up!'

She fumbled at the ropes that secured him and using her one hand and teeth managed to loosen the knots so that he could get free of his bonds.

To her relief she found it far easier than she had thought it would be to lead him into the scullery and wash him, then to direct his dressing. He kept on grunting, and patting her face, and grinning at her to show his pleasure at her being there. Laura experienced waves of tenderness for him, and remorse that she had feared him.

'The poor soul really needs me', she told herself repeatedly. 'I'm all he has in this world.' She felt fiercely protective of him, and hugged him when he was dressed, telling him, 'I'll look after you, Tommy. Don't you fear. I'll not let them put you away!'

He snuffled and grunted and stared at her without any real understanding of what she had told him.

She found the most difficult part of dressing him to be tying the laces of his boots with her single hand, and again was forced to use teeth and fingers combined to fashion

65

the looped knots and draw them tight. While she had her head bent over his boots, Tommy gurgled as if with laughter, and kept on tugging at her hair until she was forced to speak sharply to him to make him stop.

She put on her straw boater, and shawl, and taking him by the hand led him from the house, telling him, 'We're going for a nice walk, Tommy, and after I've completed my errands perhaps we shall go and see Rosie. That's if you're a good boy.'

'Rosie, Rosie,' he slurred gutturally, evincing signs of pleasure. 'Rosie. Rosie.'

Tommy Spiers loved being taken to the grave of his sister, Rosie, in the cemetery situated against the wooded western edges of the town beyond the railway station. He would spend hours at a time patting the raised mound of earth and stroking the small stone plaque that Laura had had placed upon the grave, a plaque that she had only been able to afford to have inscribed with Rosie's name and dates of birth and death.

Laura led the shambling man by the hand up through the town centre and eastwards across the flat central plateau to her destination.

The Redditch Steam Laundry distantly advertised its presence in the quiet terraces of St George's Road by the plume of smoke rising from the tall chimney that towered above its flat roof. Close to the premises it was possible to see the clouds of steam issuing from various points, and to hear the splashing of water and the voices of the washerwomen raised in song or laughter or acrimonious dispute.

Horace Rea, the foreman, was standing outside the double doors where the vans delivered the dirty laundry and collected the finished products. When he saw Laura he hurried to meet her.

'How am you, my duck?'

'I'm alright, thank you.' Laura was a trifle puzzled by the man's apparent concern. Although he was not an unduly harsh taskmaster, he had always appeared indifferent to the welfare of the women who worked at the laundry.

'What's you come for?' he wanted to know.

66

Laura stared at him in surprise. 'I've come for my money, Mr Rea.'

He seemed uneasy, and rubbed his chin with his fingers. His eyes did not seem able to meet her own questioning regard squarely, but kept shifting uneasily.

'How much have you got to come, do you reckon?' he questioned, and now Laura was really amazed. Horace Rea always knew to the very halfpenny how much wages each and every employee was entitled to.

'Three days and a half shift, Mr Rea,' she informed him, and could not help but challenge, 'But you already know that surely?'

He blew out his breath noisily, and his expression denoted his unease.

'No, my duck. You arn't got that much to come, I'm afraid,' he told her, without meeting her eyes.

'But I've worked three days and a half shift,' Laura protested.

'Oh yes, I aren't disputing that, my duck,' he agreed readily. 'But Mr Pinfield knows about them sheets you dropped in the dirt, when you fell and hurt your arm.' Pinfield was the laundry manager.

Laura shook her head bemusedly. 'What about the sheets?'

Again the man's fingers rubbed hard at his chin, and his eyes darted rapidly in all directions to avoid her searching gaze.

'Well, in all the excitement o' getting you up, the sheets was trod on real badly. They got real dirty and they all had to be washed and ironed again. They was best Irish linen them sheets was, you know.'

'Of course I know,' Laura told him acidly. 'It was me who washed and ironed them in the first place.'

'Yes, then you knows very well that they was a special job, doon't you? A special job done for one of Mr Pinfield's particular friends.'

'So I was told,' Laura assented grimly. By now she was beginning to nurture a strong suspicion about what was to come.

'Well then, you knows the rules, doon't you?' Rea's own

sense of guilt caused him to suddenly feel unreasoning anger against this young woman. He saw it as her fault that he was being placed in this uncomfortable position.

'The rules am that any mess-up of articles is paid for out of wages due. That's Mr Pinfield's ruling in this case. And it's nothing to do wi' me, young 'ooman, so it's no use you a blaggardin' me about it.' The words gushed from his mouth in a breathless torrent of mingled resentment, anger and apology.

'Mr Pinfield has instructed that youm to have a day's wages stopped to pay for the sheets having to be washed and ironed again. That's what Mr Pinfield has told me to do, and it warn't my place to contradict him. He's the master here, not me. I'se had to stop you a day's wages, because that's what Mr Pinfield has told me to do. And he's the boss, not me. So there's nothing I can do about it. And you must just like it or lump it, my wench. Because Mr Pinfield has said that's what's to happen. And that' an end to it!'

'Where is Mr Pinfield now?' Laura demanded indignantly. 'I want to see him about this. The money he's stopping me is more than it could cost to wash and iron those sheets again.'

'Mr Pinfield's not here. He's had to goo away on business. But even if he was here he 'udden't agree to see to you. It's against his rules to see anybody who'se bin give the sack.'

'Given the sack? Why has he sacked me? I'll be able to work again in a few weeks.' Laura was flabbergasted. To be given the sack was to be discharged from employment. 'Why has he given me the sack?'

'Well, youm not able to work now wi' your arm broke, am you, my wench. So we'se got to get somebody in your place, aren't we. That's obvious, that is.' The foreman appeared to be affronted at Laura having the gall to want to know why she had been fired from her job.

He turned on his heel and stamped into the building, shouting back at her as he went. 'You must wait theer. You can't bring that sarft-yedded bugger inside. He might cause damage. I'll bring your money out directly.'

68

Laura stood holding Tommy's hand, and didn't know if she felt more like laughing or crying. The bitter irony of the situation made her want to laugh savagely. The sheer injustice made her angry, but she knew the futility of allowing that justified anger to goad her into further confrontation. She was absolutely powerless against her late employer's decisions.

She spoke to Tommy, even though she knew he would not understand, but the need to vent her feelings was all-powerful.

'Do you know, Tommy, if I had walked into that place as a clergyman's daughter and gentlewoman coming to collect a handkerchief, and I'd slipped and fallen because someone else had spilled grease on the floor and made it dangerous to walk on, then all the world would have been on my side, and ensured that I received due recompense for my injury.

'But because I was in that place as a washerwoman and a pauper, then I have no voice. It doesn't matter that the floor was in a dangerous condition, and it doesn't matter that my fall was no fault of my own. And it doesn't matter that the cost of re-washing and re-ironing those sheets was less than half of the money that I'm being stopped. It doesn't matter a damn! Justice is only for the rich in this country, Tommy. For the rest of us it is only an impossible dream.'

For a while black despair whelmed over her, and when the man tugged against her hand, wanting to go from this place, she scowled at him and shouted, 'Will you stand quiet! Behave yourself, will you!'

This unaccustomed display of fury penetrated his dulled mind, and he looked fearful and shuffled his feet, not understanding why she should behave towards him like this.

Laura sighed and pitied him, and forced herself to smile and speak gently. 'Just be good, Tommy. Then we'll go and see Rosie. You'll like that won't you? Going to see Rosie.'

'Rosie, Rosie, Rosie,' he snuffled and grinned happily, displaying his knarled, decayed teeth. 'Rosie, Rosie, Rosie.'

Rea brought Laura her money wrapped up in a screw of newspaper, and she took it from him without a word.

Uncomfortable, he rubbed his chin, and muttered, 'I'm sorry about this, me duck. It warn't any doing of mine.'

Laura felt unwilling to ease his feelings by telling him that she knew it was not his fault. Fully aware that she was behaving spitefully, she ignored him completely and walked swiftly away, tugging Tommy with her. By the time she had covered a hundred yards, she could not help but smile ruefully at her own behaviour.

I'm acting like a child, aren't I. Then she told herself forcefully, And why shouldn't I act how I please? I'm sick and tired of behaving like a gentle-lady, and in return getting treated like a piece of dirt.

She wanted to do some shoppng for food and necessities while in the town centre, but realised that while she had Tommy with her she would not be able to do so. Even though he was behaving docilely she dared not risk letting go of his hand, and there was no way in which she could carry the purchases with her broken arm.

She decided that she would take him down to Rosie's grave, and after that return to Hill Street and secure him to his bed, while she went to do the shopping.

There was only a smattering of small clouds in the sky, and the breeze was gentle. As Laura led Tommy into the cemetery grounds she found herself enjoying the fine day.

This is better than being smothered in steam and fumes, and mauling filthy laundry about, she told herself as she drew appreciative breaths of fresh sweet air.

The cemetery was as always quiet and very peaceful. It stretched across gently rising slopes and giant fir trees and ancient yews sheltered the graves and the small, steeply gabled burial chapel that stood in the centre of the oldest part of the cemetery.

She pulled Tommy with her past the expensive monuments and tombs of the town's wealthier deceased until they reached the area where the poor of the town were buried. There were no massive, elaborately scrolled stones here. No tall columns. No carven angels, or cherubs, or crosses. Only rows of anonymous mounds, some overgrown with weeds, their occupiers long neglected and forgotten. Some remembered with tin cans or jam jars placed upon the cropped grass, holding pathetic offerings of wild flowers and grasses picked from the surrounding woods and hedgerows.

Laura compared the differing sections and smiled ironically. 'Even in death, we are still divided. Hill Street and the Red Lane will never come together as equals. Not even in front of the Judgement Seat.' Her smile widened as she fancifully imagined the Day of Judgement, with the rich being respectfully ushered in first to be presented to their Maker, and the poor being held back by angel sentinels so that their rude, crude presence should not impede or offend their betters.

At Rosie's graveside she sat on the adjoining grave mound while Tommy grunted and snuffled and stroked the small square stone plaque with every appearance of pleasure, repeating over and over again, 'Rosie, Rosie, Rosie, Rosie, Rosie . . .'

Knowing that he would stay here, completely absorbed in what he was doing, Laura rose to her feet and sauntered among the graves. Stopping at intervals to read the fulsome tributes scrolled upon the tombstones, and smiling wickedly to herself as she imagined what might have been inscribed should the complete truth have been told of those who lay here, apparently uniform in their saintly goodness while alive.

Because of the folds in the ground she was not aware of another person being near her until she came to a small hollow where the tombstones were thickly clustered, and heard a man's voice. She felt in something of a quandary, not wishing to intrude, yet at the same time drawn by curiosity to see who it was that was speaking. She moved forwards cautiously until she was able to peep around a tall monumental column and saw the speaker immediately in front of her, and very close.

He was crouching with his back to her, and was completely alone. Puzzled, she glanced about her, searching for his companion, but quickly realised that there was no one there. She stood listening, and could overhear enough to understand that the man was actually talking to whoever rested beneath the new-looking marble tombstone that he crouched at. He seemed to be relating a story, and expressing regrets and offering explanations.

Embarrassed at intruding upon such a private scene she turned to go, and trod upon a scatter of gravel which crunched beneath her foot. Instantly the crouching man rose and whirled around, his body tensed and ready to spring.

Laura gasped in shock at his rapid movement, and flustered, began to apologise, 'I'm so sorry. I did not mean to intrude. Only I heard your voice and wondered who you might be.'

She stared at him, uncertain of her own reaction to what she saw.

He appeared to be in his early middle age, just over six feet in height, and strongly built. He was well dressed, in a dark green, tweed suit and broad-brimmed slouch hat. His close cut hair and moustache were dark brown, shot with streaks of grey, and his hard features with their clear blue eyes were attractive, if a trifle grim and fierce looking.

He nodded brusquely. 'Please, there's no need for apologies. I should apologise to you for alarming you by my talking aloud.' He smiled bleakly and disclosed a flash of strong white teeth. 'It's one of the more bizarre habits that I've acquired over the years, I'm afraid.'

He raised his hand to the brim of his hat in a military style salute. 'I'll bid you good-day, ma'am.'

With that he was gone, marching erectly away down the rows of graves, and was quickly lost to her view.

Laura stood for a moment or two trying to evaluate how she felt about this brief, but disturbing encounter. Then she moved closer to the tombstone to read the names inscribed upon its white face. 'Ezra Purvis'.

She uttered a faint exclamation of shock as remembrance struck her. 'Maria Purvis.' Again she repeated both names aloud, 'Ezra Purvis – Maria Purvis.'

She stared wildly in the direction that the man had taken. 'Then you must be Johnny Purvis! You must be! No one else would come to this grave and talk to it in the way

72

that you were doing. You must be Johnny Purvis.'

A flood of recollection assailed her, recollection of the multitude of colourful stories she had been told concerning this notorious man. That he had spent many years in the Army. That he had killed the husband of Cleopatra Dolton. That he had been the lover of her own close friend, Miriam. How he had returned to Redditch after the Boer War, a rich man. How he had been sent to prison for the death of Arthur Dolton.

Her thoughts in a whirl, Laura slowly made her way back to Rosie's graveside and when she reached it conjured up in her mind the visual image of her dear friend, Rosie.

'Oh Rosie, you'll never believe who I've just met. I've just met Johnny Purvis.'

Still immersed in her vivid recollections, she gently took Tommy Spiers by the hand and led him away.

Chapter Seven

In the select bar of the Royal Hotel Harry Vivaldi sat nursing a small whisky, taking only occasional sips of the golden liquid, trying to make it last as long as possible because he had no money with which to buy another drink when this one should be finished. Hugh Rountree, the landlord, had refused him any more credit until his existing slate had been wiped clean. The young man was alone in the small room, and could hear the talk and laughter of drinkers in the adjoining saloon and public bars. But he felt no urge to join their company – his mood was too depressed. It was a week now since he had brought Adrian West into Cotswold House, and he was beginning to consider his guest's continuing presence as very much a mixed blessing.

He scowled glumly. Never mind blessing, I'm beginning to wonder if it might not prove to be a bloody curse. Emma's not let me so much as kiss her since that flash bugger came to stay, he thought.

At first Harry had not been over-resentful of the apparent fascination that West seemed to exercise upon his wife. At least it had appeared to put all thoughts of going to see the bank manager out of her head. And it had diverted her from badgering him about his failure in business, and his excessive drinking.

But now the young man was feeling increasing uncertain about the relationship between West and his wife. They seemed altogether too fond of each other's company, and at times made him feel as if he were the interloper, as they sat engrossed in conversations which excluded him.

Another fast deepening cause of irritation was the fact that although West had talked airily of employing Harry in his new venture, up to this point in time he had not offered to pay Harry any wages on account.

The young man swore beneath his breath. 'The flash bastard! Here I am neglecting my own business for his sake, and he's not yet paid me a penny piece. He's willing enough to treat me to drinks, I'll give him that, but it's not the same as having money of my own in my pockets, is it?'

The more he dwelt on this, the more resentful and indignant Harry became, until he ended by feeling that he had been treated very cavalierly, if not actually cheated, by the other man.

'I'm going to have it out with the flash bugger,' Harry decided now. 'He either puts up some cash, or shuts up shop in my house.'

He lifted his glass and found to his disgust that there was barely a taste of the golden liquid left in it.

The portly-bellied landlord came through the bar's connecting door, and Harry smiled obsequiously, and lifted his glass questioningly. The landlord frowned, and silently shook his head. Harry grimaced in dismay and equally silently left the premises.

Outside in the Market Place he stood for a few seconds undecided as to where he might go. The notion of opening his shop for business he dismissed instantly. The prospect of sitting in the half-empty showroom waiting for non-existent customers held no appeal whatsoever for him. He toyed with the idea of going to the billiard hall, but remembered that he had exhausted his credit there also, and was forced to dismiss that idea. For the same reason he also had to dismiss any idea of going to another public house.

'I wonder if it might be worth trying to cash a cheque at the Capital and Counties?' he considered briefly. Then a visual image of the stern, saturnine features of the bank manager entered his mind, and he realised the hopelessness of that proceeding.

Finally, he reluctantly decided that he might as well go home. At least he could get a drink there, even if the prospect of Emma's temper if she saw him drinking when he should be at his shop was something of a deterrent.

He shrugged resignedly. 'Well, where else can I go at this hour? I've got no money, have I. And I've run out of slates.'

He grinned in sardonic humour. 'And I'm certanly not a chap who enjoys a country walk. So there's nothing else for it but to go back home, is there. Damn and blast it!'

During the week that Adrian West had been a guest at Cotswold House Emma Vivaldi had found herself being increasingly drawn to him. She enjoyed his company, and admired his sophisticated manners, his confident flamboyance, and his wide knowledge and experience of the world. She would listen enthralled as he talked of the countries he had travelled and the people he had known. She thought him the most glamorous being she had ever met, and found herself frequently making comparison between him and her husband – much to the latter's disadvantage.

The young woman had some time previously accepted the unpalatable fact that her marriage to Harry Vivaldi had been a mistake on her part. But she was realistic about life, and so did not waste time in pointless self-recrimination. In her world women were conditioned to accept a low expectation with regard to marital happiness. They were also conditioned to believe that for a woman to have no husband was extremely unfortunate. A woman who had not been able to gain a husband was in many quarters regarded as a figure of fun, to be mocked at as an old maid, whom no man had ever wanted. Even widows were regarded as objects of pity, and were expected to be eager to remarry if they could only find a man willing to give them his name. It was considered unnatural for any woman to live without a man to protect her. The cruel fact that in all too many cases the wife needed to be protected from the brutality of her own husband was completely disregarded by society.

And so, like countless other women, Emma had been prepared to continue in this unsatisfactory relationship rather than run the risk of being a subject of derisory regard.

She knew that as husbands went, there were very many worse ones than Harry. He did not ill treat her, or physically abuse her in any way. In fact, it was she who physically attacked him when her temper was roused. And Emma could readily admit to herself that it was her own fault that she was married to him. That it was she who had manoeuvred him into marrying her. After the experience of her first marriage to a physically and sexually repulsive old man, her overwhelming lust for the young and handsome Harry Vivaldi had irresistibly impelled her to ensnare him.

It was mid-afternoon and she was sitting in her drawing room, reflecting on her present situation.

'I'm twenty-five years old. I've already buried one husband, and I'm lumbered with another one that I no longer want. Everybody warned me not to wed Harry, but I wouldn't listen, would I. I had to scratch the itch between my legs, didn't I. Bloody fool that I was.'

She sighed despondently, and then chided herself irritably. 'Will you stop feeling so bloody sorry for yourself! There's hundreds and thousands of poor wenches who'd give their eyeteeth to be sitting where you're sitting right now. You've got a fine house, and plenty of money. Alright, you don't want your husband anymore, but at least he doesn't knock you about, and if you tell him no when he's trying to have a bit, then he doesn't force himself on you, does he?

'He's turned into a bloody drunkard, and that's a fact, but there's drunks and drunks isn't there? At least he's good tempered with it. Not like bloody Feyther. Just remember what sort of life your Mam has of it, then you'll appreciate how well off you are.'

The thought of her mother brought a troubled frown to the young woman's smooth features. Her parents still lived in one of the worst slums in the town, Silver Street, where Emma herself had been born. Winston Farr, Emma's father, was a chimney sweep – that was when he bothered to work at all. He was a drunken, violent brute, who treated his wife and children very badly. Emma was constantly urging her mother to leave her father. To take her numerous brood of children and run away from his violence. She had offered to buy her mother a house wherever she wanted to live, and to support her and the children financially. But Amy Farr stubbornly refused to leave the man.

'You must be bloody mad!' Emma scolded her mother in her mind. 'To put up with how that bad bugger serves you.'

Emma regularly gave sums of money to her mother, but knew that Winston Farr took most of it and drank it away in the alehouses of the town.

She rose and went to stand looking out of the tall window. At this time of the day the road outside was fairly quiet, and during the long minutes she stood at her vantage point she saw only a horseman go clipping past, a couple of delivery carts, and a few pedestrians passing along the pavements, or strolling in the recreation garden. Then she was distracted from her reverie by the sound of a motor engine, and smiled expectantly. Adrian West was coming along the Church Green East in his Mercedes.

The splendid machine spluttered to a standstill outside Cotswold House, and the actor-manager bustled through the front door, discarding his driving coat and accoutrements in the hallway, before entering the drawing room.

'There you are, Emma.' He smiled and took her hand to kiss it, then still retaining his light hold on her fingers he led her to sit beside him on the chaise longue.

'I've cabled my people to come up to Redditch next week,' he told her, 'and made arrangements for their accommodation.'

'Where will they stay?' she enquired.

'I've rented a furnished house from Dolton Enterprises. It's one of those large ones in Worcester Road. It will do very well, because it's handy for the station, and for the town centre.'

He chuckled amusedly. 'And for a couple of my chaps it's ideally situated. There's a doctor's surgery next door

78

where they can get treatment if they fall down and injure themselves on the way back from the pubs.'

He became serious. 'In a way I could wish that the troupe wasn't coming.'

'But why?' She could not understand why he should be saying this. 'You said only this morning how eager you were to begin putting on shows here.'

'Yes, I did.' He smiled ruefully. 'But it means that I shall be deprived of your company, doesn't it, my dear?'

She frowned slightly. 'Why does it?'

'Well, now that the company's accommodation has been arranged I shall have to leave here, won't I?'

'Only if you choose to leave,' she told him sharply, disturbed at the prospect of his leaving her house.

'But I can hardly continue to take advantage of your kindness now that the alternative accommodation is available,' he protested. 'I don't think that Harry, good generous fellow though he is, would be happy to keep on providing me with board and lodging for the next three months. And I should not be happy to do so either. I should regard it as an abuse of hospitality.'

Her full lips firmed determinedly. 'Harry has nothing to do with it, Adrian. This is my house, and you are my guest. I won't hear of you leaving. You must stay for as long as you are happy here.'

He opened his mouth as if to make further protest, but she smiled radiantly at him, and coaxed, 'Please Adrian, say that you'll stay on here. I should sorely miss you, if you were to go and live elsewhere.'

After a moment he accepted graciously. 'If it is really what you want, Emma, then I'll be more than happy to stay. But, and I do insist most firmly on this point, I shall only stay if you will agree to let me become a paying guest.'

She demurred, but he was forcefully adamant on this point, and at last she gave way and accepted.

'Do you want some tea?' she wanted to know, and when he said that he did, she told him gaily, 'Sit here and relax, I'll only be a moment.'

Smiling happily, she went to the big kitchen at the rear of the house, to speak to Mrs Elwood.

79

'Mr West wants some tea, Mrs E. Will you make some sandwiches as well please? I'm sure he must be hungry. Use the smoked salmon – he likes that.'

The fat woman stared speculatively at her mistress's smiling face, and told her bluntly, 'You'se took a real fancy to that bloke, aren't you?'

Emma's fair skin coloured, and she challenged defensively, 'What if I have?'

The cook shrugged her massive shoulders. 'I only hopes that you knows what youm adoing, my girl. That's all.'

'It's none o' your business,' Emma snapped petulantly.

The other woman was unabashed. 'That's as maybe. But I'm telling you, all the same. Youm playing wi' bloody fire agen, girl, and you might get your fingers burned.'

'You don't know what you're talking about,' Emma scoffed dismissively. 'Just because I like talking to the bloke, it doesn't mean anything.'

Mrs Elwood's big mob-capped head nodded ponderously. 'Oh yes it does. You seems to be forgetting that I'se known you for more nor seven years, my wench. Ever since you fust stepped foot in this house as a bloody parlour maid. I knows what youm thinking. I'se seen you like this afore, aren't I?'

The younger woman coloured even more hotly, and snapped, 'Just get on and make the tea, will you. And stop talking sarft.'

Then she flounced out of the kitchen before the cook could make any reply.

When she returned to the drawing room Emma was piqued to see that her husband had come home.

'What brings you back so early, Harry?' she questioned, and her chagrin at having this pleasant interlude with Adrian disturbed by her husband betrayed itself in the sharp tone of her voice.

Harry detected her mood, and reacted equally sharply. 'Can't a chap come home any more? Good God above, Emma, if I don't come home you accuse me of all sorts, and when I do come home you snap at me as if I were an unwelcome intruder.'

Not wishing to precipitate a clash in front of their guest,

Emma tried to modulate her tone. 'No, I'm not having a go at you, Harry. It's only that I was surprised to see you here so early. I thought that you'd still be in the shop.'

His swarthy, drink-puffy features were sulky, and he muttered, 'You don't seem to mind my not being in the shop when I'm doing favours for other people, do you?'

West smiled secretly, knowing at whom this barb was aimed. Then he decided to take advantage of the opening it presented for him. He knew that Harry had nothing, and that it was Emma who possessed and controlled the money. It was she that he needed to win over to his plan. But, wise in the ways of women, he knew also that he must approach his objective from an oblique angle. Frontal assault might prove fatal to his plans. Emma had already given him sufficient proofs that she possessed all the perversities of her sex. So he directed his words towards the man.

'Well now, I for one am very pleased that you've come back early. Because it gives me the opportunity of discussing with both of you together the proposition I talked to you about previously, Harry.'

The couple stared expectantly at him, Emma in surprise, because neither of the men had mentioned anything about any proposition to her, Harry with burgeoning hope that at last something might be going to come to fruition.

West smiled warmly at Emma. 'I had not mentioned anything to you before, my dear, because I wanted to make all the necessary arrangements before doing so. But now those arrangements have been completed, and I'm ready to go ahead.'

He directed the warm smile towards Harry. 'Are you ready to begin working for me, Harry, on a full-time basis?'

Harry breathed a sigh of relief, and nodded eagerly.

Emma frowned doubtfully. 'But what about your business, Harry?'

It was West who answered her. 'Harry is wasting his time and talents in that business, Emma,' he declared with an absolute certitude. 'He is worthy of much better things.

He's not cut out to be a shopkeeper. What I'm offering him could lead to success beyond your wildest dreams.'

'Doing what?' Emma's previous experience of life had imbued her with a healthy scepticism. Wild claims and promises were too easily uttered. She wanted hard proof before she would display any enthusiasm.

'I'm going to make my own moving pictures, Emma,' West informed her. 'They are the entertainment of the future, and there are fortunes waiting to be made by those who get into the business now.'

Emma's expressive features mirrored her doubt, and West smiled and invited, 'Come on, tell me why you don't believe what I'm telling you. Because I can see by your expression that you doubt me.'

Emma pondered for a few moments, then pointed out with some degree of diffidence, 'When the moving pictures started, everybody wanted to see them. But once the novelty had worn off, then they became just another end-of-bill variety turn, didn't they?'

West nodded smilingly, and said, 'Please, go on.'

The young woman spoke more confidently and firmly now. 'Look at the public hall, here in Redditch. A few years ago, when they had a moving picture on the bill, it was standing room only. But now people go to see the stage acts and variety turns, and nobody really bothers about the pictures so much.'

The man laughed, then radiating confidence he said, 'You're making the mistake of passing a judgement based on too narrow a basis, my dear. The public hall is not primarily a picture theatre, is it? It's used for a whole variety of functions. In the context I'm speaking of, the public hall cannot be used as the yardstick by which to measure the impact of moving pictures.

'Now let me tell you what is actually happening out there in the big world. The moving picture business is beginning to boom. In America there are now more than nine thousand picture theatres open. Some of the most famous traditional theatres in New York, like the Harlem Opera House, the 23rd Street Theatre, the Union Square Theatre, have changed from putting on mainly vaudeville, to showing mainly moving pictures, and other theatres all across the States are following that lead.

'In Brooklyn there is currently being built a picture house which will seat one thousand eight hundred people.' He repeated the numbers to give due emphasis to them. 'One thousand and eight hundred people!

'The same sort of thing is happening here in Britain. At Bradford they've changed the skating rink into a picture palace. Down in Broadstairs the grand pavilion has been converted.

'I know a man named Wallace Davidson; he used to be in the same business that I am, travelling shows and stock companies. Now he's got control of picture palaces all over this country – Rochdale, Edinburgh, Glasgow, Huddersfield, Bedminster, Bristol, everywhere. And he tells me that they're having to turn money away at every performance because of full houses.

'Albany Ward, another old chum of mine, has got a chain of picture theatres in the West Country, and the same thing is happening there, standing room only notices going up before eight o'clock in the evening, picture theatres packed throughout Devon, Somerset, Cornwall.

'In London, in Birmingham, Manchester, Liverpool, it is everywhere the same. I tell you, my dear, it's the entertainment of the future, and there are fortunes to be made in it.'

Although impressed by what she had heard, Emma still needed convincing. 'If this picture theatre business is doing so well, and coining so much money, why aren't you in that line yourself, Adrian, instead of travelling theatre?'

The question did not disconcert him. 'Because quite frankly, Emma, I haven't got the necessary capital to build new theatres, or to buy and convert existing buildings. But even if I had got that amount of capital, I would still prefer to be making pictures rather than merely showing them.'

His eyes took on a fanatical gleam, and yearning throbbed in his voice.

'I'm an actor, and a good one. I'm a stage director, and a good one. But always I am limited in what I can do by the sheer physical limitations of space that the stage imposes.

83

But just imagine what spectacles might be staged if one had the entire outdoors to work in. If one can set scenes against actual physical backgrounds. Take, for example, a play like *Henry the Fifth*. On the stage we have to represent the siege of Harfleur with a handful of players and a painted backdrop of walls and flaming buildings. Just imagine, however, if that scene were to be staged with real castle walls, and real flaming buildings, and instead of a handful of players, having hundreds, even thousands of men storming real walls. What a spectacle it would be. It would be true life itself. True life brought onto the screen . . .'

His voice trailed away, and for a few moments he sat with a distant look in his eyes as though he was staring at something which lay beyond the confines of the room they sat in. Then, abruptly, he gave a slight shake of his head, and appeared to take cognisance of his immediate surroundings once again.

He smiled wryly, and half-apologetically told Emma, 'I tend to get carried away by my own enthusiasm.'

But now he had fired Emma's vivid imagination also, and she questioned eagerly, 'Could it be done? Could you really make a moving picture with all those people and real walls and flames and all that?'

'Yes, certainly,' he asserted positively. 'Naturally the equipment that is used now is still somewhat crude, in comparison to what it will become eventually. But even with the present-day cameras, I'm sure it could be done.'

It was Harry who injected a note of pragmatism into the conversation. 'But can you make money at it?'

West grinned, 'Of course.' He held up his hand and ticked off on his fingers the facts he was stating.

'Let me give you an example. We can make a comedy picture such as *The Wedding that Didn't Come Off*, with a length of just under four hundred feet, a one reeler, for just the price of the celluloid film and the electric light, and the players' wages. In total it might cost, say, three pounds to make. We can sell a copy of that picture for at least six pounds and ten shillings. And we can produce hundreds of copies of it at a cost of only shillings for each copy.

'Initially I shall use my own actors and actresses from my

troupe to make the pictures. But I've all sorts of ideas and plans for the future. I can see the time when I'll be utilising the finest acting and performing talents in the world to make my pictures.

'My idea is to set up our own distribution network to either sell or rent out our pictures both here and abroad. I've already got some contacts in the picture theatre business, as I've told you. So we have a head start in marketing and selling our products.'

'Would there be a place for me in this business?' Emma wanted to know, her enthusiasm beginning to take fire.

West laughed in satisfaction as he realised that he had won her over. 'A place for you, Emma? But of course there would be a place for you!'

'What as?' She smiled in excitement.

'That depends on you, my dear,' he told her. 'You could either become an employee of the new company I'm forming, and earn a salary. Or you can become a full partner, and share the risks and the profits.'

Emma's black eyes were shining. 'What do I have to do to become a full partner?'

'That's easily answered,' West chuckled. 'You just scrape together every penny that you can lay your hands on, and you match the amount of capital that I intend to invest in the new company, and take the chance of gaining a fortune. Remember what Bonny Dundee said, Emma.'

Half serious, half laughing, West struck a dramatic pose, and declaimed sonorously, ' "He either fears his fate too much, or his deserts are small. Who will not put it to the test, to win or lose it all!" '

Emma sobered suddenly, and then determination glinted in her eyes and she lifted her chin and declared ringingly, 'I've never been feared to risk anything. I'll match you penny for penny in this new company, Adrian. And I'll be your full partner in it.'

The man held out his hand towards her, and she spat on her own palm and slapped it resoundingly against his outstretched palm in the ancient symbolic token of a sealed and binding bargain.

'It's settled then, is it, Emma?' West questioned

seriously. 'You and I are to be full business partners?'

She nodded, and equally seriously confirmed, 'Yes Adrian, it's settled. You and I are to be full business partners.'

Harry Vivaldi witnessed what had happened with a sickening realisation of his own impotence. Although, as her husband, he was considered by the law to be the master of his wife, he knew that in his case it was a nominal mastery only. Because of the Married Woman's Property Act passed in the latter decades of the previous century, Emma still retained the control of the money and property that her first husband had bequeathed to her. And because of her own courage, intelligence and independent spirit, Harry knew that he could never assert dominance over her by fear or by force.

Harry's highly developed sense of self-preservation told him now that the best course for him to take was to accept what had happened and voice no protest. He knew that his relationship with his wife was very tenuous at this moment in time, and that if he tried to prevent her doing whatsoever she wished, then he stood in real danger of that relationship being severed completely.

So outwardly he smiled and offered the new business partners his heartiest congratulations. Inwardly, he resolved to watch and wait and bide his time until he could take full revenge upon both of them for not having bidden him to join the feast.

Chapter Eight

'Does you want me to take summat down to Uncle's for you, my duck?' Maria Cull called outside Laura's open front door.

Laura was washing Tommy in the scullery, and she had not heard clearly what the other woman had said.

'I'm in the back here, Maria. What was it you wanted?' she shouted back.

Tommy grunted loudly, and tried to pull away the wet rag that was scrubbing his neck and shoulders.

'Keep still, Tommy,' Laura told him sharply. 'You must be washed, so it's no use you playing up.'

'Gawd Strewth! He looks like summat the bloody cat's dragged in, doon't he?' Maria had come to the scullery doorway, and was regarding the man's scrawny, pallid torso with a jaundiced glare.

Laura, fond of him though she was, had to admit to herself that Tommy presented an unappetizing spectacle. Dressed only in a pair of flannel long johns which were too baggy for his stick thin legs, his pallid, skinny upper body was naked, a heavy stubble covering his throat and chin, and his hair a shaggy uncombed mop.

She smiled ruefully. 'He'll look better when I've finished washing and brushing him.'

It had been three weeks since her accident, and she was now able to make a limited use of her fast-healing broken arm. But this was the first occasion since she had broken it that she had dared to attempt to give the man a thorough wash.

'What was it you wanted, Maria?' she asked again.

The other woman nodded towards the sheet-wrapped

bundle she had put on the small table in the front room. 'I'm taking some stuff to Uncle's. I wondered if you wanted me to take anything in for you?'

Laura's thin, pale face betrayed anxiety. 'I've nothing left to pawn, Maria. I've only got the clothes I'm wearing left, and Tommy's clothes. I daren't take any more coverings off the beds in case the weather turns cold again.'

Although it was the second week in April, and the weather had been exceptionally mild, she knew only too well the treachery of the month.

The older woman nodded understandingly. 'Yes, youm right theer, my duck. It's no use not been able to slape because of the bloody cold, is it?'

She noisily sucked on her long snags of decayed front teeth and peered speculatively at Tommy.

'What clothes has he got, Laura?'

'He's got his jacket and trousers, and a shirt. And a couple of vests and drawers. And his boots.' Laura informed, while she went on scrubbing the wriggling, grunting man, wielding the wet rag on his throat and face now. Then she added in remembrance, 'Oh yes, and he's got that old smockcoat of his father's as well, but I need that to put on his bed. His blanket's too thin to keep him warm until the summer comes.'

'Well then, youm alright to send his jacket and trousers, and his boots, aren't you?' Maria declared.

Laura shook her head. 'I can't do that. What will he wear to go out in?'

'He wun't have to goo out, 'ull he?' the other woman stated matter of factly. 'He'll have to stay inside.'

'But he can't do that. He must have some exercise and fresh air!' Laura protested.

'If bloody fresh air is needful then he can goo out in your back theer, carn't he?'

Maria was referring to the narrow strip of yard at the back of the tenements. Enclosed by high blank walls so that the sunlight never penetrated, and the greasy bricks saturated with slimy mould, it resembled nothing more than a cold damp cavern.

'I wouldn't put a dog out there, never mind this poor creature,' Laura told her indignantly.

'Well then, put the bugger out in the court. He'll be decent enough if you puts his drawers and vest on, and ties a bit of blanket round him,' Maria advised airily.

Laura thought of the foul-stenched midden heap in the centre of the court, and chuckled mirthlessly.

'That would be a worse place for him than the backyard, wouldn't it? If I took my eyes off him for a second he'd go swimming in the midden heap.'

'That 'ud be the best thing for the sarft bugger, I reckon.' The other woman joked, but there was a cruelty underlying her humour. 'For him to goo swimming in the midden heap, and bloody well drown hisself. You'd be free of the useless sod then, 'udden't you.'

Laura reacted to this harshness with a flash of temper, and snapped heatedly, 'Don't start on about that again, Maria, please! I've told you until I'm sick of repeating myself, Tommy stays with me.'

'Well, if you wants to be a fool to yourself, then so be it.' Maria took no offence at Laura's show of temper, and once more asked equably, 'Am you sure that you doon't want me to take his clothes and boots down to Uncle's? They aren't gooing to stay theer for ever, am they. You might be able to start work again shortly, and then you can fetch 'um out, carn't you. I'm only talking sense, my wench. A few days without his clothes aren't agoing to kill the sarft bugger, are they?'

Unwillingly, Laura was forced to reconsider the suggestion. Her plight was truly desperate. She had not eaten for two days now, and knew that if she did not soon have food, then her own health would begin to deteriorate. As it was she felt sick and weak with hunger.

Engrossed in her thoughts she did not realise that she was continuing to scrub Tommy's face with the wet rag, making the skin red and sore, until he suddenly emitted a howl of outrage and struck out savagely against her arm.

The blow was very painful, and she cried out in shock, and as though her cry had triggered a reaction in his damaged brain, Tommy's features suddenly contorted, and his white face suffused darkly with an unearthly greenish purplish hue. His mouth gaped, and a terrible long-drawnout scream erupted from its glistening, reddened depths.

'Gerrout 'ere!' Maria bellowed as she grabbed Laura's shoulders and jerked her backwards into the other room.

Before Laura could recover her wits the woman had slammed the scullery door shut and had rammed her body against the cracked panels to hold it shut against the onslaught of Tommy. As the man rained blows upon the thin wood, it shook and shivered beneath the impacts, and all the time he kept on howling and screeching like a maddened beast.

'Run down to the corner and fetch the men!' Maria shouted. 'Goo onn! I wun't be able to keep the bugger in for much longer. He'll have the bloody door down in a minute!'

Laura ran from the tenement and down the rutted slope of Hill Street to the corner where a group of men and youths were lounging against the big plate glassed windows of the Lamb and Flag public house.

'Alfie, can you come? Tommy's having a fit!' she gasped out to a man she recognised.

Immediately he shouted to the others to follow him, and set off at a run back up the slope. Laura ran after them, but her long skirt hindered her progress, slowing her pace so that she was not able to keep up with them.

By the time she re-entered the small courtyard the cursing, shouting men had already wrestled Tommy outside and were clamping his heaving twisted body to the filthy ground. His eyes were bulging from his head, and Laura shivered with horror as she saw their reddened, maniacal glare. From his mouth animal-like shrieks volleyed, and in her torment it seemed to Laura that the awful tumult went on and on and on without end.

Then, at long last, it abruptly ceased, as the heaving body suddenly slumped and became limp. And Laura breathed a prayer of thanks for the mercy of the silenced shrieking.

Alfie Fisher looked closely at the senseless man, and told

90

his companions gruffly, 'Right lads, let's get the mad bugger tied up.' He stared at Laura's white strained face, and advised her with gruff sympathy, 'You'd best let us take him to the doctor's and get him certified, my duck. He needs to be put away. Protheroe Smith 'ull soon have the van brought for him.'

Twisting her hands together in distress, Laura shook her head. 'No Alfie. He must stay here. Can you take him upstairs to his bed for me please?'

The unshaven, tough looking faces ranged before her showed doubt and puzzlement, and two or three voices were raised to support Alfie Fisher's advice, urging her roughly.

'Doon't be so sarft, girl, have the bugger certified!'

'Let us take him now.'

'He needs to be put away.'

'He'll end by bloody killing you, you silly cow!'

She shook her head wildly. 'No! No, I won't have Tommy put away.'

Despite their renewed urgings, she remained adamant in her refusal, and at length they were forced to accept and to accede to her pleas to carry Tommy up to his bed.

With Maria Cull's help she secured him with the ropes once again, and then the men left as she thanked them profusely.

When she and Maria were alone with the stertorously breathing man, the older woman smiled archly, and enquired, 'How long 'ull it take him to get over this fit, Laura? It was a real bad 'un this time, warn't it?'

Laura noded, and with one finger touched the senseless man's features, scratched and bruised and bloodied in the violent struggle.

'Yes, it was a very bad one, this time,' she murmured, almost absently. 'I'll need to bathe his face, won't I? I hope he's not been hurt too badly.'

'So then, what do you reckon? 'Ull it take a while for him to recover this time?'

Again Laura nodded. 'Yes, I should think so. I'll have to keep him in his bed for a few days that's for sure.'

Maria Cull cackled with laughter and declared

triumphantly, 'Well then, the sarft bugger wun't be needing his clothes and boots, 'ull he? So I'll take 'um down to Uncle's wi' my stuff, and get a few pence on 'um for you.'

Laura could not help but smile ironically herself. And after a moment's reflection, she nodded agreement.

More than two hours had passed before Maria returned from the pawnbrokers, which was only a little distance up the Unicorn Hill from Hill Street. And Laura expressed surprise at how long the business had taken.

'It's real busy theer today, my duck. What with so many folks being laid off from their work, there aren't bin many paypackets coming into the houses lately. Old Charlie Vincent must be making a bloody fortune out on us poor craturs!'

Laura nodded, then remarked. 'Still, he's not so bad as some of the other pawnbrokers in the town, is he? He usually gives a couple of pennies over the odds for the pledges doesn't he?'

'Does he bollocks!' Maria spat out scathingly. 'Charlie Vincent is just like all the other soddin' pop shops. He'd screw you down to the last ha'penny, and then scream that you was robbing him.'

She laid some coins and pawn tickets down on the table.

'Here, I got a tanner on the boots, and fourpence for the jacket, and threepence for the trousers. Now does you see what I means about the greedy old bastard screwing you down to the last ha'penny. He could have give at least tuppence more on each on 'um, and still made a profit if he had to sell 'um. Them boots am near brand new.'

She saw Laura's worried eyes, and urged with a rough kindliness, 'Look, my duck, doon't goo biting me yed off. But youm gooing to have to have Tommy put away. He's dragging you down into an early grave. You arn't got more meat on your bones than a bloody stick.'

She paused, and studied Laura's thin body and pale drawn features with a genuine concern, then urged hoarsely, 'Let me goo and fetch the doctor to him. He needs to be certified for his own sake, as well as for yourn, Laura. Just look at the state on you. Youm ready to drop, arn't you?'

Laura closed her eyes and for a brief instant the temptation to accept what the other woman was offering was almost irresistible.

'How much rent does you owe now, my wench?' Maria pressed. 'It's got to be three weeks, at least. You knows what's gooing to happen doon't you. The bloody Queen of Egypt 'ull have you out on the bloody streets afore you can say Jack Robinson. Then what 'ull you do, my duck? You'll both on you have to goo into the bloody work'us then, wun't you?

'Think on yourself now, Laura. You'se done more than enough for Tommy. He's no blood kin to you, is he? And you'se looked arter him ever since poor Rosie died. You'se done more nor enough for him. You must think about your own needs now. Let me goo and fetch the doctor to him.'

Laura was forced to summon up all her remaining reserves of strength and resolve, to tell the other woman, 'Please, just leave me alone will you, Maria! I know that you mean well. But I'd sooner be in my grave than let them put Tommy away in the lunatic ward. Will you please go now, and just leave me alone.'

Maria shook her greasy frizzed mop of hair in disgust. 'Alright then, my wench. I can see that theers no use talking to you, is there. Give us a shout if you needs me.'

'I will, and thank you, Maria.' Laura felt near to tears, and remorseful that she should have spoken so sharply to this kindly woman who was only trying to help her. 'I'm sorry if I've offended you in any way.'

The other woman turned at the door and smiled bleakly. 'Theer's no need to tell me sorry, my wench. You'd oughter be a bit more sorry for yourself. Then you might stand a chance of living out your rightful span.'

Laura stared at the coins lying on the table, and her empty stomach twisted in painful reminder of its condition. A wave of sick giddiness caused her to sway, forcing her to hold onto the edge of the tabletop to steady herself.

'I must have some food, or I'm likely to faint.'

Despite the devouring need, she still hesitated. 'But

93

what about the rent I owe? Caleb Louch will want something on account this week, won't he? Otherwise there'll be an ejectment order served against Tommy and me.'

Again her stomach twisted painfully, and she knew that unless she ate something soon, then she would be unable even to think clearly, never mind maintain any ability to do physical work. The long, long months of privation and worry, of scant rations and hard toil, had eroded her reserves of strength, and she feared that she was very near to collapse.

Suddenly she snatched up a coin and hurried out of the house. The succulent, appetising odours of the fish and chip shop enveloped her as if in a warm blanket, and the juices of hunger moistened her dry throat. As she watched the greasy handed proprietor shovel golden potato chips into a big cone fashioned from old newspaper, she could hardly restrain herself from snatching them from him, and cramming them into her ravenous mouth. But even in this extremity the engrained mores of her childhood would not permit her to act in such an unladylike manner. All the same she was still forced to exert every atom of self-discipline that she possessed to carry the cone with its steaming contents back into the privacy of her own house, before greedily cramming the golden chips into her ravenous mouth.

In mindless delight she crammed and chewed and gulped and crammed and chewed and gulped, until her stomach was full and the fierce clamourings of her hunger were satisfied.

Then, she stared at her greasy hands, and felt the thick smearing of saliva and juices on her lips and chin, and was filled with a sudden shame that she could have behaved so much like a starving dog. Slavering at food and bolting it down in such a bestial manner.

'What am I becoming?' she muttered in burgeoning self-disgust. 'What in heaven's name is happening to me. What am I turning into?'

Quickly she ran into the scullery and washed her hands and face in the bucket of water. Scrubbing furiously with

94

the wet rag until her skin burned, and every trace of the grease was cleansed away.

Then she went upstairs to check that Tommy was alright. He lay on his back, his jaw gapped wide, snoring and snorting, and Laura felt intense relief that she did not have to do anything for him at this time.

Downstairs once more she sat on one of the stools and rested her elbows on the tabletop. Despite herself, she could not help but dwell on what Maria Cull had said to her concerning the owed rent.

This tenement, like the others in the court, was owned by Dolton Enterprises, by Cleopatra Dolton. Cleopatra Dolton, nick-named the Queen of Egypt by the local wags, bore the reputation of being a ruthless businesswoman, who would eject tenants who fell behind with their rents without mercy.

But Laura knew her differently. Some two years previously, soon after she had begun to take care of Tommy, Laura had fallen behind with her rent, and had experienced serious financial difficulties because she needed money to pay for Rosie's funeral. She had gone to see Cleopatra Dolton and had explained what the problems were, and had asked for time to settle her debts. The woman had not only agreed to give Laura time, but had also paid for Rosie's burial, written off the arrears of rent, and instructed her rent collector, Caleb Louch, to continue to let the tenement to Laura at the existing level of rent, even after many of her other tenants had had their rents increased. And she had done all this without seeking thanks or plaudits. In fact she had told Laura to keep it a secret, and not to speak of it to anyone. However, she also had strongly advised Laura to have Tommy taken into the workhouse lunatic ward.

Paradoxically, it was because of Cleopatra Dolton's previous kindness and generosity to her, that Laura now felt unable again to ask the woman for help.

'How can I go cap in hand to Mrs Dolton now, after I disregarded her advice to have Tommy put away? After all, she could quite rightly say that it's my own fault I'm not receiving any Relief from the Guardians. That if I'd taken her advice in the first place, I'd not be in this predicament now.'

Laura's spirits fell plummeting down and down, as she envisaged the louring features of Caleb Louch, the debt and rent collector of Dolton Enterprises.

'He'll have no mercy on me this time, will he?'

She toyed with the coins remaining on the table. Her rent was half a crown a week. Two shillings and sixpence. She had spent three pence on her meal of potato chips. The coins on the table totalled ten pence.

'I wonder if Caleb Louch might take that on account?'

Even as the hope crossed her mind, she erased it. 'No, he warned me last week, didn't he, that I'd have to start paying off the arrears by at least sixpence added to the week's rent.'

She felt perilously near to weeping with despair, then rallied and fought back the tears.

'No, I'll not give in yet. After all today is Saturday, isn't it? Who knows what bargains I might find tonight?'

Saturday was market day in Redditch, and stall holders came from miles around to sell their wares in the market place. Many of the townspeople were in the habit of doing their weekend shopping after the pubs had closed, and so the stalls stayed open for business late into the night.

As was customary after one of his fits, Tommy remained in a comatose state for many hours. Laura was happy to leave him so, and made no attempt to rouse him. To save the oil that remained in the lamp she did not light it, but sat in darkness when night fell. She kindled no fire in the small grate either. The woodbox at the fireside was empty. Fortunately the night was mild, so that the shawl wrapped tightly around her shoulders served to keep her reasonably warm.

She welcomed the night, and patiently waited for the hours to pass until even the most hardened Saturday night revellers should have tired and gone to their beds.

Then, in the darkest early hours of the morning she took an old cloth bag and went out into the sleeping town. Cautiously she made her way towards the market place, and hid in the shadows of the churchyard while the last remaining stall holder packed his covered cart with his stock, extinguished his flaring naphtha lamp and trundled away. A ragged old man was wielding a large-headed broom and a broad-bladed shovel, sweeping up the litter of rubbish left behind by the market shoppers and sellers and piling it into heaps, to be collected by the horse drawn dust-cart on the following day.

It was almost an hour before his task was done, and he too shuffled away into the darkness. Then, moving as silently as she was able, and always keeping a wary eye open for the appearance of a patrolling policeman, or belated passerby, Laura came from her place of concealment and crossed to the heaps of rubbish. Swiftly she rummaged through the odourous, sticky wet contents, examining the discarded vegetables and fruits, the scraps of bread and meatstuffs, the spoiled sausages and crushed pies and pastries. And whatever she judged to be usuable, she put into her bag.

Once she was forced to crouch low and hide, as a policeman slowly strolled along the roadway. And she breathed a silent prayer of thanks that she had heard him whistling a tune as he came around the corner from the Evesham Street. Otherwise he would inevitably have seen her.

Laura knew that to scavenge in this manner was not strictly against the law, and that if he had seen her the policeman would probably have merely ascertained her identity. But the shame of being discovered at this task would have been beyond bearing for her. As it was she suffered agonies of self-disgust and shame because she was acting the scavenger. But the stark alternative was actual starvation for both herself and Tommy. Laura had accepted that this was the bitter price she must pay, if she was to keep Tommy from being committed to the Lunatic Ward.

But now, as she kept grimly to her task, she was forced to keep on reminding herself, 'This is only until my arm mends, and I can find work again. It won't have to last forever, but only until my arm mends and I can find work again. It will not last for ever.'

At last she was done, the last heap of rubbish sifted, the last half-rotten potato consigned to her cloth bag. And Laura was able to scurry back through the darkened town centre to the haven of Hill Street.

But her work was not finished yet. She placed the bag on the table, and sorted out a length of rope. Then once more left the house.

This time, however, she did not turn towards the centre of the town, but instead went westwards down the Unicorn Hill in the direction of the railway station. Just before she reached the railway bridge she struck off the main road and down a short entrance driveway into the big railway goods yard, with its huge store sheds and platforms and serried ranks of sidings. She searched throughout the length and breadth of the yard for pieces of scrap wood, which she could use as fuel for warmth and cooking. By now her injured arm was throbbing with a dull, painful ache, but she would not allow herself to rest.

When she had found all the wood she could, she tied it into a bundle and slung it across her shoulder, then climbed back up the steep hill, panting with the effort.

In her dark house, she at last lighted the oil lamp, and by its pale glow carefully sorted through the foodstuffs. Cutting the rotted and bruised parts of the vegetables and fruits away, trying to salvage what she could from the crushed pies and pastries, the scraps of bread, the staling meatstuffs. All that was unusable she took out to the midden heap, and hid it deep within the fetid mass.

When that task was done, she felt desperately tired, but forced her aching body to make the effort of fetching a bucket of fresh water from the pump. She washed her arms, and face and neck thoroughly, and while drying herself with the rough towel, she closely regarded her spoils. With frugal rationing, there should be enough food here to sustain herself and Tommy for three or perhaps even four days. The wood she had collected filled the box at the fireside.

Laura experienced a sense of sardonic satisfaction. 'I'm really becoming rather good at scavenging, aren't I?'

She finished drying herself, feeling almost giddy with

tiredness. Then, utterly spent in mind and body, Laura turned out the lamp and went thankfully to her hard, narrow bed.

Chapter Nine

Ozzie Clarke had spent the morning in his office, poring over the account books of Dolton Enterprises, and just before the noon hour he sat back, stretched his powerful arms and yawned widely. Standing, he took his curly-brimmed bowler hat from its peg and put it on as he moved into the outer office.

'Going out, Mr Clarke?' The neat typewritist smiled at him.

He returned her smile, and his eyes dwelt appreciatively on her trim, shapely body and pretty face. Ozzie had always been an admirer of female beauty, and it pleasured him in both a sexual and aesthetical sense to have this pretty young girl to look at during the long, sometimes tedious working hours.

'Yes, Doris, I'm just going to have a word with Old Walter.'

'Did you know that there's a travelling theatre come to the Royal yard?' the girl asked him.

'I heard something about it,' he told her.

'They say it's going to stay here for three months.' The pretty face betrayed a hint of yearning. 'Do you know, I always wanted to be an actress.'

Clarke chuckled, and complimented her, 'Well, you're certainly pretty enough to be one, Doris.'

She blushed with pleasure at the compliment, and preened her trim body. With artless vanity she informed him, 'All my friends tell me that I'm the best looking girl in this town, Mr Clarke.' She lowered her eyes in demure flirtatiousness. 'Do you think I am, Mr Clarke?'

To tease her, he feigned a frown of puzzlement. 'Do I

think you're what, Doris?'

She giggled, delighted by his playful reaction. 'Do you think I'm the best looking girl in town?'

He laughed and nodded. 'Certainly I do, Doris. You are without doubt the best looking girl in the town.' He had put an emphasis on the word, girl, which she noted.

'But I'm not really a girl, any longer, am I? I'm a woman now.' She had become serious.

'I'll be eighteen years old next month, won't I, Mr Clarke? There's a good many girls married and with children at that age, aren't there.' He nodded agreement.

To try and provoke some sign of jealousy from him, she went on, 'Do you know, there's already been a young man has asked me to marry him.'

'Has there?' He smiled. 'Well, I hope that you don't go breaking his heart for him, Doris.'

'It doesn't matter if I do. He's only a rodmaker down at Allcocks,' she stated, with the heedless cruelty of youth. 'Besides, he's far too young for me.' She stared straight into the man's eyes. 'I prefer older men, who are successful in life. Like you are, Mr Clarke.'

Ozzie knew that this young girl found him attractive, and although he was naturally flattered by this, he had no desire to take advantage of her youthful inexperience. Or to hurt her feelings by a blunt rebuff. So now, he merely smiled and let her veiled invitation pass without comment.

'I must get on and see Old Walter. If Mrs Dolton comes in, would you ask her to wait for me please. I'll not be more than a few minutes.'

The girl's small mouth pouted petulantly. It seemed to her that every time she had any sort of brief conversation with this man, he always somehow or other brought Cleopatra Dolton's name into the exchange.

She tossed her head and told herself, 'Bugger him! And bugger the bloody Queen of Egypt, as well.' Then she craned her neck to watch Ozzie Clarke stroll away along Evesham Street.

'He is lovely, though, isn't he? I'll get him in the end.'

The Redditch Meat Company comprised five butchers

shops situated in Redditch and its satellite villages. The original company had been founded by Arthur Dolton, the late husband of Cleopatra Dolton, with a single shop, the premises near the southern end of Evesham Street, to where Ozzie Clarke was now making his way. When Arthur Dolton had died, his company had grown to three shops, and Ozzie had been the head butcher and manager. It was from these beginnings that the present Dolton Enterprises had expanded and diversified into real estate, property and farming, helped in its rapid expansion by a legacy of money and property bequeathed by an old lady to the dead Arthur Dolton's estate.

Between Ozzie Clarke, bachelor, and Cleopatra Dolton, wife and widow, there had always existed a sexual tension. In his youth and young manhood he had been something of a ladies' man, and had had many affairs. At first he had regarded this sensual older woman as just another sexual trophy to be gained. The fact that she was the wife of his employer, a man he disliked and despised, only added a piquant savour to the prospect. But in her he had met more than his match.

Cleopatra Dolton had tantalised and tormented him, sometimes appearing to be within reach, to be ready to welcome his advances. Then, when he accepted those apparent invitations and made those advances, always rejecting him coldly. Only to again invite with her eyes, her gestures, her nuances of speech, and to again elude him, and retreat into the fortress of rejection. Throughout the years his feelings towards her had alternated wildly between desire, dislike, infatuation, resentment, anger, obsession. But never had he ever ceased wanting her.

Now they had reached a plateau in their relationship. As Dolton Enterprises had expanded, she had been forced to admit openly to him that she needed his strength and shrewdness to help her achieve her objective of financial success. And in proof of that she had promoted him to becoming her right hand man and closest confidant in the business, and had rewarded him commensurately. Cleopatra increased his salary with each expansion of Dolton Enterprises, so that now he was a man of considerable substance in material possessions and wealth.

In return he gave her his absolute loyalty, and devoted practically the whole of his waking hours to the furtherance of her business interests.

He still wanted her above any other woman he had ever known. But with the passage of years, as he had mellowed and the fires of youth had begun to cool, he had slowly been able to come to terms with their ambiguous relationship. He accepted now that what he felt for her was a deep and abiding love. And he set himself to wait patiently in the hope that the day might come when she would reciprocate his feelings, and love him in return.

Walter Spiers, the shop manager, greeted Ozzie Clarke with an immediate complaint, rubbing his hands against the front of his blue-striped apron as he whined in his cracked, wavering voice, 'That new bloke I took on aren't any bloody good, Ozzie! Calls hisself an improver? He arn't got nothin' that could be improved. He's bloody useless. A lazy idling bastard! He's knows nuthin' and doon't want to know anything.'

'Sack him, then,' Ozzie retorted.

The heavily lined features of the old man contorted doubtfully. 'Well now, that aren't so easy to do, is it. Arter all, the bugger lives next door to me, doon't he. And he's kin to my missis, arn't he. And his missis is very thick wi' my missis. Her 'ull goo scrawking to my missis iffen I was to hand the bugger his sack, and then my missis 'ud give me a bloody earache, 'udden't her. And apart from that, he's a big, narsty tempered bugger, arn't he. He could do me a real mischief, couldn't he. And I 'udden't be the first bloke or 'ooman to get a kicking from him, 'ud I.'

Clarke hissed impatiently, 'You want me to do your dirty work, do you, Walter?'

The old man's toothless gums bared in a broad grin, and Clarke could not help but give a wry grin in return. He nodded slowly.

'Alright then, you old bastard. I'll hand him his sack. Where is he now?'

The old man snorted indignantly. 'He's doing what he does best. He's bloody skiving off out the back theer.'

'I told you what he was like, didn't I, Walter,' Ozzie taxed the manager. 'But you would insist on giving him a job, wouldn't you.'

The man looked sheepish, and excused himself. 'Well, it was my missis, warn't it. Her kept on and on werritin me, until I had to give in to her to get a bit o' peace.'

A female customer came into the shop, and Ozzie instructed quietly, 'Serve her Walter, I'll go and see to the other business.'

He passed through to the rear of the shop, where the cold store rooms, chopping blocks, salting and wash troughs were situated, and laid his bowler hat on one of the scrubbed work surfaces. Then he went out into the yard.

A burly, rough looking young man was lounging back on a pile of empty sacks, smoking a cigarette. When he saw Ozzie he went to snuff out the cigarette and get to his feet.

Ozzie stopped him with a wave of his hand. 'No, that's alright Reg, you might as well finish your fag.'

The heavy features stared at him doubtfully, and Ozzie repeated pleasantly, 'Yes, go ahead and finish your fag, Reg. Because it's going to be the last one that you'll ever smoke on my bloody time.'

Reg Duggins stared puzzedly, as his slow moving mind examined the implications of that statement. 'What's you mean, Mr Clarke? Aren't I entitled to me rightful work breaks?' he challenged aggressively. 'Carn't a bloke even have a bloody fag now, or what? What's this place, a bloody slave camp, is it?'

'What I mean, my buck, is that I'm giving you the sack. You're finished here, so take off that apron and get out of this shop, and don't come back.'

'The sack?' Duggins acted as if he could not believe what he had heard. 'I'm being given me sack? What the bleedin' hell for? I aren't done nothing!'

'That's right, Duggins. You aren't done nothing.' Ozzie's normally pleasant expression had metamorphosed into a glower. 'You're a useless, lazy bastard.'

The other man slowly clambered to his feet and moved to stand facing Ozzie, his head thrust forwards threateningly, his big fists clenched.

'You wants to watch your fuckin' big trap, Clarke,' he growled menacingly, 'or else I mi . . .'

Before he could complete the word Ozzie Clarke's fist smashed against his mouth, crushing and splitting the lips, breaking teeth, bringing blood spurting.

Duggins reeled back, and Clarke went after him, pumping blows into the man's overhanging beer gut, pinning him against the wall, ramming his forearm into the fat throat, smashing his forehead against Duggins' face again and again and again.

'Stop it, Ozzie! Leave off him! You'll kill the bugger else! Leave off him!'

Walter Spires, unable to contain his curiosity, had left the customer waiting while he came to see what was happening in the back yard. He wrapped his scrawny arms around Clarke's upper body and tried to pull him away from the helpless Duggins.

'Leave him, Ozzie! Youm bloody killing him! He aren't worth getting topped for, is he! Leave him, for Gawd's sake! Leave him!'

Panting heavily, Clarke stepped back from his opponent, and freed his grasp.

Half senseless, the moaning, bleeding man slumped to the ground.

'Can you hear me, Duggins?' Clarke demanded, and when the groaning man made no reply, he kicked savagely against the prone body, drawing a squeal of pain in return.

'I said, can you hear me?' he demanded once more, and this time Duggins grunted assent.

'Then listen very careful. I've sacked you. Understand? And I want you gone from here. And if you ever step foot in any shop belonging to us again, I'll finish what I've started here today. Understand?'

Again his boot thudded into the prone body, only with less venom this time, and Duggins squealed his assent.

Clarke turned to face the anxious Walter Spiers. 'How many days are owing to this bastard, Walter?'

The old man shook his head and grimaced guiltily as he muttered, 'Well, none really, Ozzie. He aren't got no wages to come.'

Ozzie scowled. 'I see. That's the way on it, is it? You've been subbing the bastard his wages, haven't you? Even though it's against the company rules.' The old man hung his head and shuffled his feet.

Clarke regarded him grimly. 'You know my ruling on that, and yet you still did it, you stupid old bleeder. By rights I should be handing you your sack as well for disobeying my orders.'

'Oh no, Ozzie, doon't do that!' the old man pleaded in real alarm. 'I didn't want to give him any subs, but he kept on to me, and he was turning narsty when I 'udden't give him any subs. So what else could I do?'

'You could have come to me, you old fool! That's what I'm here for.' Ozzie shook his head disgustedly. 'I don't know. You'll never bloody well learn, will you, Walter.'

The old man detected the softening note in the younger man's voice, and his anxiety lessened as he realised that he was going to escape punishment for what he had done.

Ozzie Clarke pulled his expensive gold watch from his waistcoat fob and checked the time. 'I'll have to be getting back to the office. I'm expecting Mrs Dolton. Get this piece of offal cleaned up a bit, and then get him out of here. Remember to take the apron off him, won't you.'

'I will, Ozzie. I'll do that.' Relief made the old man profuse in his protestations. 'I'll do that. I'll do that straight away. Theer's no call for you to worry about that. I'll have the apron off him.'

'Alright Walter, alright.' Ozzie grinned, his normal good temper reasserting itself. 'Just remember that next time you take anyone on, make sure that they're some use, will you.'

'I will, Ozzie. You can be sure on that. I will, I will. I will . . .'

Ozzie Clarke left the shop with the fervent protestations ringing in his ears.

As he walked back along Evesham Street towards his offices he sucked at his bleeding knuckles, cut by Duggins' teeth, and painfully flexed his fingers, which were swelling and bruised from the force of his blows. He grimaced and told himself, 'You're getting too old and soft-bodied for

106

fighting, you bloody fool. A little scuffle like that, and your hands are giving you gyp. Thank Christ that bastard wasn't a real hardcase or you could have ended up with two broken hands for your trouble.'

Cleopatra Dolton was waiting alone in the office. Elegant in a forest-green gown and black shoulder cape, a Parisian toque bonnet on her glossy, piled hair, its dark veil thrown back to disclose her olive-skinned features and lustrous dark eyes.

She saw him glance briefly at the typewritist's empty chair, and explained, 'I told her to go for her lunch, Mr Clarke. I hope you don't mind, but I wanted to see you in private.'

He nodded acceptance. 'That's alright, Mrs Dolton.'

Despite their years of close acquaintance they always addressed each other with formality. Deep down, both of them privately admitted that this formal manner was in fact a defence mechanism. It guarded Ozzie from making any further advances towards the woman, and it guarded Cleopatra, in her lonelier, more vulnerable moments, from the temptation to surrender to those advances.

She noticed his damaged knuckles, and the reddened bruising on his forehead, and commented, 'You've had trouble with someone, I see.'

Her long years of slum life had left Cleopatra Dolton very familiar with the tokens of physical violence.

'Yes, with Duggins, the new improver old Walter took on. I had to give him the sack, and he objected to it.'

A grim smile lurked at the corners of her full lips. 'I take it that you've dealt satisfactorily with his objections, Mr Clarke?'

He nodded. 'I have, Mrs Dolton. There'll be no more nonsense from him.'

Then he changed the subject abruptly. 'I'm glad you're here. I wanted to talk to you about the properties in George Street.'

He led the way into his own office and spread some sheets of paper before her.

'Here are the tenders for the jobs. Newbold's is the lowest, but they can't begin before the end of May.

Huxley's and Avery's tenders are about equal, and they both promise to start within two weeks. Huins is the highest tender, and they reckon they could begin immediately.'

Cleopatra closely studied the various tenders, comparing the estimates, the labour costs, the types of materials proposed.

She owned a considerable number of properties throughout the district, many of which could be justifiably classed as slums. It was a cherished ambition of hers to modernise and renovate these slum properties, and to fund that project she had long since increased the rents on most of the properties, much to the outrage and bitter resentment of the tenants. But until this point she had not had sufficient floating capital available to begin that process of modernisation and renovation. Now enough capital had been accumulated, and she was ready to make a start.

After long discussions with Ozzie, they had decided that the properties in George Street would be the first to be dealt with. Mains water supplies were to be laid on, and a proper sewerage system, with individual water closets replacing the communal earth privies. Each house was to be piped for gas lighting in all rooms, and the fabric and roofs of the buildings to be repaired and renovated.

After she had finished her perusal of the tenders the woman remarked, 'There's not a deal of difference in any of the quotes, is there, except for Newbold's. Their quote does seem a bit too low to me. They can't be showing any profit on it at this price, can they?'

Ozzie shrugged his broad shoulders.

'Which of the other three does the best quality work?' she queried.

'They're all pretty good, so long as we keep a close eye on them.'

'So, who do we choose?' Cleopatra stared expectantly at the man. 'It's up to you, Mr Clarke?'

Since she had already throughout the years given him ample proof that she relied on, and trusted in his judgements, Ozzie had no compunction about making the decision.

'We give it to Newbold's. They're up and coming, and

108

eager to make their mark. I'm not worried about their tender being so low, because I'm sure that they won't try skimping on anything to make up the difference. I think that they see this job as a chance for them to challenge the bigger firms and make a name for themselves.'

He grinned, and for a moment resembled a mischievous schoolboy. 'Besides, I've already dropped a few hints about all the other work that we'll be asking tenders for in the very near future.' He winked broadly. 'Mind you, I don't expect their future tenders will be so low as this one. Not once they've made their name.'

She concurred without further discussion. 'Alright then, Mr Clarke. Newbold's it shall be.'

After further brief discussion about the other businesses, she made as if to leave. Then she paused and told him, 'Oh yes, there was something else I wanted to see you about, wasn't there. A private matter.'

Her manner became warmer, more confiding, and Ozzie Clarke was forced to remind himself of all those other occasions when her manner had been warm and confiding, and he had dared to hope for something other than a business relationship.

Just watch it, boy, he warned himself silently. Don't go jumping the gun again.

Her hand rested on his arm, and she moved closer to him, so that he could smell the sensuous fragrance of her scent, and feel the warmth of her sweet breath upon his face.

'There is a man named Adrian West come recently to the town, Mr Clarke. The proprietor of a travelling theatre, I believe. Do you know him?'

He nodded, and felt a sinking in his heart. Dreading that perhaps she was romantically interested in the dashing newcomer.

'He's taken over the leases of the properties we rented to Harry Vivaldi,' he told her, then went on to question, 'What about him, Mrs Dolton?'

She smiled, and dropped her voice so that she spoke in an intimate whisper.

'Well, on two evenings recently he has called at my house wanting to speak with me.'

Ozzie could not control the demon of jealousy that instantly sprang to torment him. 'Oh, has he!' His tone was a growl, and in the depths of her lustrous dark eyes pleasure briefly gleamed.

Cleopatra might not yet be ready to take this man into her bed or her heart, but she acknowledged to herself that she found him sexually attractive, and that she needed his strength and protection. She most definitely did not want anyone else to lay claim on him. The knowledge that Ozzie loved and wanted her was a constant source of deep satisfaction to Cleopatra. And it pleased her to treat him with kindness or cruelty according to her mood. The fact that someday he might grow tired of being held at arm's length, and seek for love elsewhere, she would not allow herself to dwell upon.

Now she delicately twisted the dagger of spiteful torment. 'I admit that I did take a peep at him. He's certainly a most interesting man in appearance.'

She gloried in the darkening glower this compliment induced upon Ozzie Clarke's features. Then she relented. 'Of course, I refused to receive him, and he had to leave his card on both occasions.'

'I see.' Ozzie experienced a sudden relief, and his glowering features lightened a little.

She increased the pressure of her fingers. 'What could he want to see me about, Mr Clarke, I wonder?'

He shrugged and shook his head. 'I've no idea, Mrs Dolton. He hasn't mentioned your name to me at all, while we've been doing business.'

She smiled, and requested huskily, 'Could I ask a great favour of you, Mr Clarke?'

'Of course.' He nodded brusquely, wary and uncertain at what might be coming. Made unhappy again by the instantly renewed fear that she could be interested romantically in the newcomer.

'I'd like you to see the man on my behalf, Mr Clarke, and ask him what his business is with me.' She spoke as if indignant that West should be so presumptuous as to call on her without invitation. 'You may make it perfectly plain to him that you deal with all matters concerning Dolton

110

Enterprises, and that any business he might think he has with me, is to be taken up with you first.'

Relief coursed through Ozzie, and now he was able himself to smile broadly and to assure her that he would be very happy to carry out that task.

The telephone started to ring, and she smilingly told him, 'You'd best answer that hadn't you, Mr Clarke.'

He turned away from her to lift the receiver, and when he glanced back she had gone.

111

Chapter Ten

'Give me a bit more! Give me a bit more!' the woman urged feverishly, and lifted her thighs so that she could wrap her legs around the man's plunging hips.

'Don't stop! Don't stop!'

Her fingers dug into his buttocks in frantic attempt to pull his maleness even deeper into her body.

'Give it me, Addy! Give it me! Don't stop! Don't stop!'

He shuddered, and groaned, and his plunging hips suddenly stilled as he slumped down upon her, noisily sucking air into his straining lungs.

Moaning in desperate need she went on kneading at his buttocks, digging painfully with long nailed fingers, her hips thrusting jerkily against his weight as she sought frantically for satiation of her fierce hungers.

With almost brutal force the man freed himself from her imprisoning arms and legs to push up and away from her, and she wailed in protest as he rolled off her to lie panting on his back.

'No, Addy, no.' She turned and mounted him, her hands grasping his now limp manhood and forcing it against the pulsing wetness between her thighs, her mouth greedily sucking at his lips.

'Get off me, damm you!' he shouted in sudden anger, and thrust her brutally from him.

For a few moments she lay on her side, her sweat-sheened face mirroring shock. Then the anger of frustration swept through her. 'You're fucking somebody else, aren't you, you bastard?' she screeched in accusation.

'Who is it? Is it that dirty cow Hetty? Are you fucking her?'

'No!' Adrian West denied.

'Then who is it?' The woman was now squatting back on her heels, her fine breasts heaving up and down as she agitatedly drew in great gulps of air to fuel her strident shouting. 'I can always tell when you're fucking somebody, you bastard! Because you can't perform then, can you! You can't keep it up! A couple of minutes and it's all over, like now! Who is it? Come on, tell me! Who is it?'

He scowled at her reddened face, contorted and ugly with jealous fury.

'I've told you already. There isn't anybody,' he spluttered indignantly. 'God above, woman! I can't keep at it for hours every time! I'm not bloody steam powered, am I!'

From below them there sounded the slamming of a door, and he hissed at her, 'Just be quiet now, will you. There's somebody come in.'

'I don't give a damn who's come in. Let them all hear, for all I care!' she retorted defiantly, but her voice was noticeably quieter.

He rose from the rumpled bed and quickly began to dress.

'I have to go, I've got things to attend to.'

She glared at him sullenly, her luxuriant mane of fiery ginger hair tumbled about her dimpled white shoulders, and her blue eyes shimmering with tears of anger.

West felt a sudden pang. She was undoubtedly a very attractive woman, and he was unwilling to create a complete rift between them.

He smiled and coaxed. 'Come now Beatie, don't be cross with me. There is no one else, I swear it. It's just that I've been working very hard lately, and I'm not feeling too well. I'm badly run down, Beatie. That's why I haven't been able to make love to you as I'd like to. As soon as I've got this new venture of mine up and running, why then, it will be just like it was before between us. I promise you.'

He leaned over the bed towards her and kissed her tenderly on her red painted mouth.

'I love only you, Beatie. You know that!' he whispered. 'Now, don't be cross with me.'

He continued to kiss and caress her, whispering endearments into her ears, and slowly she allowed herself to be coaxed back into good humour. By the time he had finished dressing and was leaving, all was apparently well between them once again.

West left the house and walked briskly up the Worcester Road in the direction of Evesham Street. He considered the woman he had left behind him. In the world of the theatre she was Beatrice de la Fournay, of the Château de Petit Barscon, French aristocrat's daughter, heiress to great estates. In real life she was Bridget Dooley of Scotland Road, Liverpool, Irish docker's daughter, heiress to nothing.

She was the leading lady of his troupe, a good actress, and his longtime mistress, and he would be very reluctant to part with her. But increasingly of late she had become ever more demanding of him, both in bed and out of it, continually nagging him to marry her, continually upbraiding and accusing him if he failed to satisfy her sexual needs. Continually prying ever more aggressively into his personal affairs.

'Ah well, there's nothing to be gained by worrying about Beatie now.' He dismissed all concern about her from his mind. 'I've other fish to fry, haven't I?'

He smiled happily as he thought of Emma Vivaldi. 'If I'm forced to choose between the two of them, then it's got to be Emma.'

Then, ever the optimist, he added, 'But if I play my cards right, there's no reason at all why I should ever have to make the choice, is there?'

He reached Evesham Street, and hesitated a moment before the doors of the public house on the corner. Although it was mid-afternoon when most people were still at their workplaces, he could hear the hubbub of voices and laughter coming from inside the Vine Inn, and was tempted to join that congenial sounding company.

Then he shook his head, and moved on. 'No, I'll leave it until later.'

At the central crossroads he turned eastwards down the Market Place. In front of Vivaldi's shop he halted once

114

more, and stood scowling at the locked door.

The window of the shop was plastered with posters advertising the Royalty Theatre and its forthcoming programmes of productions, and Harry was supposed to keep open for the sale of tickets for the theatre. His own talking machine business was practically moribund, but West had some ideas for utilising it, and so had insisted that Vivaldi still continued to trade, although he was now a full-time employee of West's and Emma Vivaldi's new company.

'I expect the bastard's getting drunk somewhere.' West's ever intensifying contempt for the other man was mingled with jealousy. After all, Harry was still Emma's lawful husband, and although West was doing his best to seduce her, she was still remaining faithful to her wedding vows.

He swept on down towards the entrance of the Royal yard. The streets were quite busy with people, and there were many women who felt a frisson of romantic yearnings as they stared at the flamboyantly attired actor-manager, with his caped cloak flying, his wide-brimmed hat rakishly angled, his well-cut suit, fine linen and the dashing manner with which he saluted those who greeted him in passing.

Although he had only been in the town for scant weeks, West had become known to many people, and was fast becoming a popular character among the more fashionable and 'faster' elements of the population.

The prefabricated wooden building that was the Royalty Theatre was an impressive structure, its high frontal façade painted to resemble an oriental palace with minarets and domes. The cavernous interior could seat five hundred bodies on sloping ranks of wooden benches, and there were half a dozen side boxes for the richer, more select patrons.

For front, auditorium and stage lighting it had three separately wired electrical circuits, the power generated by petrol driven engines driving dynamos. For heating there were the more traditional cast iron stoves, ranged strategically around the structure.

West was a hard taskmaster. The programme of

entertainment comprised a different play every night, plus a children's matinee on Saturday afternoon. His troupe of players were expected to help with scene-shifting, cleaning the theatre, drumming up trade when audiences were sparse, erecting and taking down the structure, striking and re-setting during performances, painting the flats, attending to the props, caring for the costumes, and all the other myriad of tasks which needed to be done.

The doors were open, and West entered the gloomy interior, his footfalls thumping hollowly against the wooden flooring.

'Henry? Are you here?' he called loudly, and after a few seconds a small, grimy featured, scruffy looking man, sucking a clay pipe which emitted acrid smelling clouds of tobacco smoke, and wearing a battered top hat on his bald head, emerged from the gloom at the rear of the stage platform.

Henry Snipe regarded his employer sourly. 'What's you want?'

'Did you grease those pulley blocks? They made enough noise to wake the dead last night,' West wanted to know.

'Course I 'ave. And I've stripped down that bloody engine, as well. There was nothing really wrong with it, like I told you. You was getting your arse in a twist for nothing, as per bloody usual.' The man's tone was as sour as his expression.

Snipe was the only person in the troupe whom West allowed to speak to him in such a surly, insolent manner. If any other of his employees had dared to address him so, West would have dismissed him or her on the spot. But Snipe had full licence to speak and behave as he pleased, because despite his insolence, surliness and apparently contemptuous opinion of his employer, he was in actual fact totally and completely West's creature. They had been together ever since West had taken over the company that had once been his father's, and Snipe's loyalty to the younger man was an absolute, as he had proven on many occasions during their long years together. He was prepared to do literally anything in West's service. And quite apart from all this, he was a multi-talented

116

handyman, who could seemingly turn his hand to any sort of practical task.

'When will you have the ramp ready?' West asked next.

The other man took the pipe from his toothless mouth and hawked and spat. Then growled, 'When does you want it ready for?'

'You know bloody well when!' West snapped impatiently. 'I'm trying the horse out this afternoon.'

A sly grin twisted Snipe's almost lipless mouth. 'No need for you to get so bloody aerated. I can have it up in ten minutes. Everything's laid out the back.'

'Get on with it then, while I go and see about the horse,' West ordered, and stamped away.

At the far side of the big yard was a row of stabling, where Walter Read and his son Frank based their horse dealing concern. Both father and son had served in the army as Cavalry Roughriders, and a major part of their business was the breaking and training of horses for other people.

As West neared the stables he could see the elder Read and another man standing ouside the open doors watching Frank Read leading a big glossy coated black horse out from its stall.

'Good afternoon, gentlemen,' West saluted the two men, and waved a hand in Frank Read's direction. 'And good afternoon to you also, Frank.'

Walter Read, a lean tough whip of a man, dressed like his two companions in riding breeches, cord jacket and high boots, acknowledged West with a grin.

'Come to have that look at my horseflesh, have you Mr West?' He turned and explained to his companion. 'Mr West here is the manager of the playhouse theer. He want's to use a horse in one of his plays.'

John Purvis nodded, and his startlingly blue eyes briefly studied the flamboyant newcomer. His lips twitched in a smile and he quipped, 'I didn't know that there had been a play written about the Charge of the Light Brigade.'

West laughed easily. 'Not yet, to my knowledge, sir. But if there was a large enough stage in existence, then I don't doubt but that somebody would very quickly write such a piece.'

While the newcomer briefly talked to Walter, Purvis took a longer look at him, searching for what else might be there beyond the exaggerated theatricality of appearance and mannerisms. He sensed that the outward foppishness disguised a tough and ruthless inner core.

'Ahr, I dare say I can find you a beast that'll suit,' Walter nodded. 'But you'll have to wait a while, because me and Mr Purvis here are busy right now.'

'That's quite alright, Mr Read. I've plenty of time.' West smiled, and stared at the horse that the younger Read was now leading in a tight circle.

'Trot him up and down a bit, Frank,' Walter Read instructed, and as the young man started to run told the two men with him, 'That's one o' the finest young 'uns I've had in my stables for many a long year, gentlemen. Make a crackin' hunter, he 'ull.'

Curious to test the actor's knowledge, Purvis asked him, 'What do you think, Mr West?'

The actor smiled. 'I'd need to make a closer examination before I'd dare to venture any opinion, Mr Purvis.'

Walter Read was also curious to see if this foppish man was any judge of horseflesh.

'Have a good look at him, Mr West,' he invited. 'Then tell us what you think.'

Realising that this invitation was in the nature of a test, the actor hesitated briefly, before accepting.

'Very well, gentlemen.' He stepped forwards a couple of paces, and requested the younger Read, 'Frank, can you let me have him please.'

The young horse shied nervously, and tossed its head, eyes rolling whitely, as the actor took the leading rein from the hands of the young man.

Then West started to talk to the horse in a soft soothing voice, and as the beast quietened to gently stroke and pat its neck and shoulders. He ran his hands down the top of the neck and the legs, his fingers lingering and gently kneading the joints. After a thorough examination of the entire body, he then checked the teeth. The entire process took several minutes, before he beckoned Frank to him and handed him the leading rein once more.

118

'Will you just keep him standing for a couple of seconds, please.'

West moved back a few paces and intently scrutinised the animal. Then he moved further back and requested, 'Run him up and down again, will you please.'

After half a dozen passes in both directions, West signified that he had seen enough, and he returned to John Purvis and Walter Read.

'Well now, what does you reckon to him. Aren't he a prime bit of flesh?'

The actor nodded. 'Yes, it's a fine beast. He's got good shoulders. They slope perfectly, and are nicely lean and muscular. The fronts look a bit chesty to me, but then that's only a personal prejudice of mine. I've never liked any suggestion of heaviness there at all in a hunter. But he should make a good fencer.

'The only fault I have to find is that he's perhaps a trifle long in the back for a really top-class hunter. Having said that, his loins are exceptionally muscular, so that shouldn't prove to be a problem. The other thing that would cause me a little concern is the near foreleg. I thought I felt a bit of fillings in the fetlock where the suspensory ligaments come round the joint. Has there been trouble there?'

Walter Read frowned, then grinned and nodded. 'Just a bit. But nothing to worry about.'

West turned to Purvis and arched his eyebrows in silent question. Purvis nodded and congratulated, 'You know your horseflesh, Mr West. Your findings and opinions coincide almost exactly with mine.' He grinned at Walter Read.

'So Walter? I think my original bid should stand, don't you?'

Grimacing doubtfully, the horse dealer shook his head. 'I dunno, Johnny. I was counting on getting my price. It's an exceptional fine beast.'

'I'll tell you what, let's split the difference,' Purvis offered, and when Read still grimaced doubtfully, added, 'That's as high as I'm prepared to go, Walter.'

After more doubtful grimacing and head shaking, the man grudgingly agreed, and the bargain was sealed with a

119

resounding slap of their hands.

'Will you keep him here for the rest of the week, Walter?' Purvis requested, and the horse dealer puffed out his cheeks in mock indignation.

'Gawd strewth, Johnny! Aren't it enough that you's robbed me on the price, without me having to give you free feed and stabling for a week?'

Purvis laughed easily. 'Add it to the bill, Walter. Add it to the bill.'

West had already noted that Purvis' clothing was made from top quality cloth, and well tailored, and that the high riding boots were of the very finest leather. He could guess also that the price of this fine animal before them would be a high one. Always eager to enlarge the circle of his acquaintances, particularly if they gave indications of being wealthy, he sought in his mind for some way of prolonging his meeting with John Purvis.

'Are you a local man, Mr Purvis?'

Purvis nodded. 'Yes I am, Redditch born and bred. But I've spent long periods away from the town.'

'Johnny's an old army man,' Walter Read informed, and baited good humouredly, 'Mind you, he was only a foot slogger for most of his service. Not a cavalryman like me, and my boy over theer. But you did end up in the cavalry, didn't you, Johnny.'

'Irregular Cavalry, in South Africa,' Purvis confirmed.

'Irregular Cavalry?' West was genuinely interested. 'You were in South Africa during the war, then?'

'Yes,' the other man nodded. 'I served as an infantryman for the first year or so, and then transferred to the Irregular Cavalry. The North Cape Horse.'

'Johnny was an officer,' Walter Read put in, and winked broadly. 'They'm the ones who swanked about all day, while the sergeants like me did all the work.'

Purvis took the ribbing in good part and merely chuckled amusedly.

'Right then, Mr West, now what can I do for you?' Read asked.

'I need a very docile animal, Mr Read,' West explained. 'I want to ride it onto the stage. It needs to be used to heat

120

and noise, and not take fright at sudden commotions, or people rushing about around it.'

The horse dealer rubbed his sharp pointed nose and pondered briefly.

'I've got an old mare that would suit. But she's down in my paddock at present. I can have her fetched up here in a couple of hours if you doon't mind coming back then?'

'No, that will be fine, thank you,' West agreed readily, and turned to the other man, 'Listen Mr Purvis, how about joining me for a drink?' he invited. 'I'd very much like to hear more about the Irregular Cavalry, and the war.'

The hard-etched features showed a trace of doubt, then cleared, as Purvis accepted. 'Yes, why not, Mr West. I've nothing pressing to be done.'

The two men passed a congenial couple of hours in the Royal Hotel, talking about the Boer War, and exchanging reminiscences about places where at differing times during their lives they had both been. Each found the other man interesting, and enjoyed listening to the varying tales of soldiering and play-acting in different parts of the world, and they were quickly on first name terms.

West found that he greatly liked this ex-soldier, whose hard, dour exterior disguised a ready humour and pleasant personality.

Nearly two hours had passed, and Purvis reminded him, 'I should think that old Walter has fetched that mare up for you now, Adrian.'

The actor was unwilling to part company so soon. This man was such a refreshing change from the normal run of his drinking companions.

'Oh, I'm in no great hurry. The mare can wait for a while. There's something I'd greatly like you to see, Johnny. I'm sure you'll find it interesting. We only need to walk a little way up the yard here.'

Purvis had also enjoyed the past couple of hours with this new acquaintance, and he was quite willing to spend some more time with him.

'Fine, let's go then.'

The two men walked side by side to the large shed, and West unlocked the big padlock securing the great double

121

doors and led the way inside.

'Here it is, Johnny,' there was a note of pride in the actor's voice. 'Here's my new moving picture studio.'

The pantechnicon van had been pushed into one corner of the long shed. In the centre of the floor, directly beneath one of the big skylights a broad square platform had been erected, around which were ranged a variety of shapes shrouded in dustsheets.

'Come and have a closer look, Johnny.' West began to strip the dust sheets from the objects they covered, and he talked constantly, his enthusiasm so infectious that Purvis found himself being caught up by it himself.

'These are Westminster incandescent arc lamps to supplement the natural light. And these are Cooper-Hewitt lamps. I've had the electric light company run a cable into here. At first I thought about generating my own power, like I use in my theatre, but the size of engine I'd need to power these lamps would be too big and noisy.'

His voice throbbed with pride and excitement as he pulled the shroud from a big rectangular box mounted on a heavy-looking metal tripod.

'And this is the finest camera in the world. It's a Biograph. I had to send to America for it.'

Purvis examined the camera curiously. The rectangular box was constructed of highly polished wood, with a rounded, brass-cased lens protruding from one end, and a brass hand crank set into one side.

'The lens is a f/3.5 Zeiss Tessar from Germany; it's got a better image-resolving power than any other lens yet produced. The film is fed into this wooden magazine on top here and is carried over these rollers by friction. This beater-movement roller places the sections behind the aperture, and it utilises the Latham Loop to keep the action smooth.'

Purvis was finding the technical explanations a little difficult to absorb fully, but he concentrated hard on what West was excitely telling him.

'At the moment of exposure two registration holes are punched into the exposed film section, so that we can have a precise matching when release positive prints are made from the camera negative. The punchings are sucked out of the camera body by these little spinning blades here. These here look, just behind the camera shutter. They create a momentary vacuum and they blow the punchings out of this hole here, in the bottom righthand side of the box.

'This is the reflex viewer. Using that I can focus the lens with absolute precision. That takes up quite a lot of time, though, because I have to swing the wooden magazine on top here, out of the way, and then I have to slide this metal frame with the ground glass into its place. I focus the lens on the glass, then remove the frame and put the magazine back in position.'

West took hold of the crank handle and rotated it a few times.

'It's this that takes real skill. The cameraman must turn this crank at a uniformly steady rate. Two turns per second precisely. A fraction of deviance makes the film jerky. There is a governing device fitted here, of course, but it doesn't really help very much. It all has to depend on the cameraman's skill.'

The actor moved to strip off another shrouded object.

'Now this is something that I've always thought should have been persevered with.'

Purvis smiled as he saw an ordinary looking wooden cabinet with a gramophone on top of it.

'But it has been persevered with, Adrian,' he stated. 'I've bought a new one myself only a few weeks past.'

The actor shook his head. 'No, you misunderstand me, Johnny. I'm not referring to talking machines, as such. I'm referring to the fact that a few years ago a company named Walturdaw were making talking and singing moving pictures using this special cabinet and sound box to record the voices and synchronise them with the picture.

'I knew one of the partners, a chap named Eddie Dawson, and he took me to their studios at Wembley Park, just outside London.'

Purvis interrupted him. 'But talking and singing films are still being produced. I was in Sheffield a few weeks past, and at the Empire Theatre they were showing

George Robey and Victoria Monks. I went to see the show myself, and the sound was really very good.'

'Yes, yes, Johnny, I know the sound can be very good, but it hasn't been sufficiently persevered with to make real talking pictures, has it?' West impatiently waved aside the interruption.

Again his excitement took wing, and his eyes shone with his enthusiasm. 'The moving pictures are the entertainment of the future, Johnny. They are going to sweep everything else away. They aren't just a passing fad, like roller-skating proved to be. They are going to get bigger and bigger and bigger, and spread out all over the world. There is nothing that can stop it, Johnny. It really is the coming thing! Did you know that Charles Urban and his partner gave an exhibition of natural coloured films only last month in London at the Palace Theatre? Just think of it! Natural colour!'

He began to walk up and down in front of his companion, gesticulating with his hands as he talked excitedly. 'Do you know, Johnny, I'm going to sink everything I have into this business. Every single penny that I possess. Every single penny that I can beg, borrow or steal. There are fortunes to be made, and I intend to make mine. We're so lucky to be in at the beginning of this. I know that today a film lasts only ten minutes at the most. The vast majority are much shorter. It's farcical what is happening now – condensing *Romeo and Juliet* into a ten minute pantomime, shooting the *Destruction of Pompeii* in a tiny studio with a painted backdrop as Vesuvius, and half a dozen players as the population. It's farcical! But I can see a time coming when a moving picture will be able to last for an hour, or two hours, or three or four or five hours. I can see a time coming when there will be hundreds and thousands of players acting their roles out against eruptions of real volcanos. A time when a play by Shakespeare or Sheridan will run its full length. A time when we shall recreate a battle like Waterloo on the actual ground it took place upon, with entire armies fighting each other.'

He came to a standstill and stared at the other man

intently, nodding his head and repeating with utter conviction, 'That time is coming, Johnny. And it's coming faster than anyone realises. That time is coming!'

Then he shrugged, and laughed softly. 'I'm sorry for ranting and raving like this, Johnny. I'm afraid I get quite carried away at times.'

Purvis had recognised the sincerity in West's words. 'Please, don't apologise. I've enjoyed listening to you.'

He checked his pocket watch. 'And now I really do have to go, Adrian. It's been a pleasure meeting you.'

'And for me as well, Johnny. A real pleasure.' The actor meant what he said. 'But surely this needn't be our only meeting? I'd like you to come to the performance on Saturday, as my guest. We'll have a meal and a few drinks afterwards? What do you say?'

Purvis accepted. 'Yes, I'd like that.'

'Good!' The actor grinned with satisfaction. 'The curtain goes up at half past seven. I'll have the best box in the house reserved for you. Bring a guest if you wish.'

'Well,' Purvis' features were doubtful. 'I'm not sure, about the guest I mean. But I'll definitely come myself.'

He proffered his hand, which West shook heartily.

'Until Saturday then, Johnny.'

'Until Saturday,' Purvis replied.

Chapter Eleven

The nightmares about the dead woman were becoming a nightly occurrence, and familiarity was not creating contempt. On the contrary, Harry Vivaldi's nerves were becoming increasingly strained as a result of them. That strain was beginning to tell on his temper, and the charm he had always exerted effortlessly, was becoming ever more difficult to sustain. He had begun to snarl at the two maidservants, and at times even spoke sharply to the formidable Mrs Elwood, and between himself and his wife there was now almost continual bickering.

'Why should this be happening?' he asked himself over and over again. 'Why should I keep on dreaming about Bella dragging me down into the grave with her? What happened wasn't my fault. I've nothing to feel guilty about! It's never troubled me in my conscience! So why am I now having these nightmares about the bloody cow?'

A disquieting notion occurred to him. 'Are they being sent as a warning to me? Am I in danger myself?'

The anxiety this thought provoked made it necessary for him to gulp down his whisky and call for another large measure, which he instantly gulped down as well, in an effort to calm his fears.

Seated by himself in the tiny snug bar of the Royal George public house in Evesham Street, he fervently wished that he could recover some measure of his old lighthearted persona.

'It's just not fair,' he grumbled self-pityingly. 'Everything's just starting to go well for me, and now I can't enjoy myself because of these bloody awful nightmares.'

He shouted for another large measure of whisky, and

fought against the powerful urge that had assailed him all day – the urge to go to the house in George Street, and examine the stone-flagged floor.

'No, I won't give in to it. The bloody floor is alright, I know it is. Christ Almighty! I was there only yesterday, wasn't I? I checked it then, didn't I, and everything was fine.'

He sighed gustingly, remembering the curious eyes of Mrs Croxall, as she had told him, 'Why Mr. Vivaldi, what ever does you find to do in theer? Youm coming near on every day now, aren't you?'

He had fumbled some reply, fighting to stop himself shrieking at her to mind her own business, and to stop spying on him. But he was well aware that that reply had not satisfied her, and that she was entertaining all sorts of wild surmises as to why he spent so many hours locked in that fetid little room in George Street.

A sharp visual memory of the previous night's dream suddenly invaded his mind, and he shuddered uncontrollably. The actual content of the nightmare was slowly getting worse – becoming more terrifying. Now Bella was succeeding in holding him longer and longer in her icy cold, mottled arms, and her rotting rancid lips were seeming to suck the very life from his body. In every succeeding dream he was becoming weaker, more powerless to fight free of her foul embrace.

He drained the glass without actually tasting the spirit it contained. Then abruptly slammed it down on the table, and scurried from the public house. He hurried through the streets and several people spoke to him, but he was unaware of their greetings. All his thought was centred on his destination.

Despite the warmth of the day the tenement in George Street was dank and chill, and Harry Vivaldi shivered slightly as he entered the darkened room. Locking the door behind him he rapidly hurled aside the heaped packing cases until the stone slabs beneath were uncovered. Then he dropped on to his hands and knees and, with eyes only inches from the ground, he used fingers and sight to minutely examine each slab and its

127

surrounding mortared jointing. Over and over again he covered every square inch of the floor searching for some sign, however minute, of cracking or disturbance, but as on all the other occasions he found nothing untoward.

He had been so engrossed in his task that he had lost all track of time, and was painfully surprised by the stiffness of his joints and muscles when he rose from his constricted, awkward posture.

Slowly he replaced the pile of packing cases in their original position, and was beginning to turn the key to unlock the outer door, when a sudden sound from the room directly above his head caused him to cry out in shock and fear.

The sound came again, a scratching followed by a soft thump on the floorboards, and Vivaldi experienced sheer terror, as sweat started from his pores and he was trapped in petrified motionless rigidity.

He could not tell how long he remained like that. But his pounding heart caused the blood to thud in his ears as he strained to detect further sounds from above.

'It's only rats!' he kept telling himself, 'it's only rats!'

He used the sentence as a religious man might use a prayer, hoping that the repetition of the words would somehow bring about a factual truth. 'It's only rats! It's only rats! It's only rats!'

Slowly his terror lessened, and he was able to force his rigid body into motion. He unlocked the door and went out into the light of day, with the sensation of escaping from a tomb.

'Well I never, it's you down here agen, is it, Mr Vivaldi. I shall soon start to think that you'se got a fancy 'oomon hid away in theer, the times you bin spending in theer lately.' Mrs Croxall bared her decayed, jagged teeth in a grotesquely arch smile. But her eyes were avid with curiosity.

She moved as if to try and peep through the open door into the room, and Harry Vivaldi slammed it shut and re-locked it.

He forced a smile, uneasily aware that his face must be pallid and sweaty, and in the next instant the woman confirmed that awareness.

128

'You doon't look well at all, Mr Vivaldi. Youm all grey and sweaty. Am you feeling poorly?'

He nodded jerkily. 'Yes, that's right, Mrs Croxall. I'm not well, I'm not well at all.'

She grunted sympathetically. 'You gerron home and have a lie down, Mr Vivaldi. That's the best thing you can do.'

Again he nodded jerkily. 'Yes, I will, Mrs Croxall, I'll go and have a lie down at home. That would be best, wouldn't it?'

As he moved away she called after him. 'Oh by the way, Mr Vivaldi, there was a stranger bloke here earlier. He was asking after your lady friend!'

Harry's earlier terror returned in full force, and it was all he could do to stop himself from completely surrendering to panic.

'My lady friend?' he jerked out.

'Yes, that 'ooman you was living here with, Mr Vivaldi. Bella! That was her name, warn't it?'

He nodded, and drew a long ragged breath, steeling himself to turn back and face the woman.

'Who was he?' he managed to grunt out. 'This stranger who called? Who was he?'

She shook her head. 'He didn't give any name. He was an old bloke. A bit shabby looking. I shouldn't think he was come to give her a fortune by the looks on him.'

Mrs Croxall's mouth gaped and she cackled with raucous laughter. 'He didn't look as if he'd got enough money for his own wants, never mind hers! He warn't Lord Derby, that's for sure.'

Vivaldi felt a burning desire to grab this woman by her flabby throat and to squeeze the life from her. But by now his own highly developed sense of self-preservation was coming to his aid, impelling him to mobilise his wits and cunning, and enabling him to impose some control over his rampaging fears.

'What did you tell him? About Bella, I mean? Did you mention me at all?' He managed to keep his tone neutral. Knowing that if she detected any hint of abrasiveness she would react hostilely.

'I just said that her 'ad upped and gone years ago, and I hadn't a clue wheer her was now.'

He nodded. 'I see. And me? Did he ask anything about me?'

Once more she gave him the grotesquely arch smile. 'He aren't her jealous husband come to give you a good hiding, by any chance, is he?'

Harry Vivaldi shook his head, and returned her smile, but his effort resembled more of a sickly grimace.

'I shouldn't think so, Mrs Croxall. At least, if Bella ever did have a husband, she never mentioned him to me.'

Before Mrs Croxall could reply the sound of heavy, iron-shod boots clattered up the covered entryway, and her coal heaver husband appeared in the yard. Black faced from his day's work, and surly looking, still wearing the leather hood and back covering of his trade. Harry had always feared this big, muscled man who bore a justly deserved reputation for violence.

He scowled at Harry as he passed him, and then shouted at his wife, 'Has you got my grub ready? You'll 'ave my fist around your bloody earhole if you aren't. Standing 'ere yapping to this flash bleeder instead o' seeing to your job.'

'It's ready!' she hastened to assure him. 'I'll put it out for you now.'

She scurried after his burly figure, calling over her shoulder to the young man.

'That old bloke arsked me if Bella 'ad bin living wi' anybody, and I told him yes. And I told him wheer you was living now.'

She disappeared into her house with a slam of the door.

Harry moved into the dark entryway, and stood with his forehead pressed hard against the greasy damp wall.

'Oh my God!' He felt sick with dread. 'Oh my God! What's going to happen now? What's going to happen now?'

Chapter Twelve

The jangling of the door bell reached the ears of Mrs Elwood in the kitchen. She was busy making bread dough, red-faced and sweating from the heat of the oven, sleeves rolled up, massive forearms white with flour.

'Bugger it!' the woman grunted, as the bell continued its jangling.

The two maids were tubbing blankets in the wash house across the large back yard.

Grumbling pettishly, the fat woman left off from kneading the dough and wiping her hands on her apron, and waddled through the house to open the front door. She scowled when she saw the shabby elderly man who stood there. Her eyes made instant evaluation of his social standing, and that evaluation placed him very low in the social scale.

'The tradesmen's entrance is around the back,' she told him sharply. 'But you needn't bother gooing round theer, because we aren't buying anything today.'

She shut the door in his face, and was waddling back towards the kitchen, muttering indignantly to herself about the lower classes forgetting their place in life, when the bell again commenced a loud jangling.

'The cheeky bugger!' she exclaimed in affront. 'I'll bloody soon put him to the right about. Cheeky bugger!'

'What's your game?' she demanded angrily as she swung the door back. 'I'se already told you that we doon't want nothing. Now get off about your business.'

The stoop-shouldered, meagre-bodied little man politely lifted his battered bowler hat from his balding pate, disclosing long greasy strands of hair brushed across

131

the pallid skin.

'I needs to see the marster of the house, missis. I'se got an urgent matter to discuss with him.'

His accent was the nasal sing-song of the nearby city of Birmingham.

The woman's eyes squinted suspiciously in their puffballs of fat. 'Who does you mean? The master of the house?'

'Mr Vivaldi, missis. Mr Harry Vivaldi.' His pinched features, although not aggressive, were stubbornly determined. 'And I aren't agoing to shift from here until I'se seen him, missis.'

'What's your business with him?' she demanded.

'It's personal.'

'You can tell me what it is,' she pressed.

He rubbed the hairy nostrils of his long nose with his black nailed fingers, and shook his head. 'No offence to you, missis, but it's personal.'

She scowled and tossed her mob-capped head. 'Well you carn't see him. He aren't here.'

'Where can I find him?'

'How the bloody hell should I know,' she puffed indignantly. 'I'm only a servant. Mr Vivaldi doon't have to tell me wheer he's going, does he.'

The pinched grimy features again denoted stubborn determination. 'Alright then, missis. I'll just wait here until he comes back.'

'What's you mean, you'll wait here?' Mrs Elwood questioned.

'Just what I said, missis. I'll wait here until he gets back.'

The woman could not believe what she was hearing, and her temper exploded at what she saw to be this stranger's effrontery. 'You bloody well wun't wait here, you cheeky bugger! You'll gerrof out on it right now, or I'll bloody well shift you out on it.'

He bared a set of stained, ill-fitting false teeth in a weasel-like snarl. 'I'm waiting right here for him to come back.'

'We'll soon see about that!' she bellowed, and moving with a surprising agility for her bulk, she grabbed his puny

132

shoulders, spun him around, and physically propelled him across the forecourt and through the ornamental ironwork gate onto the pavement.

'Now gerroff with you!' she ordered, and slammed the gate shut.

He turned to face her, and declared defiantly, 'This is a public highway, missis. And I'm going to stand here for as long as I wants.'

Again her temper exploded. 'Oh am you now? We'll soon see about that, you cheeky bugger!'

She surged through the gateway and grabbed his puny shoulders and propelled him forcefully along the pavement. He made no attempt to struggle against her superior strength. And when she released him and began to make her way back to the gate, he followed her. She swung on him, and advanced threateningly. He retreated. She retraced her footsteps. He followed. She launched an attack. He retreated. She stood glaring. He stood stubbornly. She advanced. He retreated. She went back towards the gate. He followed.

By now, interested passersby were stopping to watch the bizarre antics of the ill-matched couple, a carter halted his horse, a workman called to his mates to come and see, three housewives abandoned their gossiping to stand gleefully nudging each other.

Mrs Elwood made one final despairing rush at the little man, but was unable to match the speed of his retreat. Then in disgust at her own impotence, and made uncomfortably conscious of the grinning faces peering at her, she walked with what dignity she could muster back to Cotswold House, angrily aware of the fact that the little man was inevitably following behind her.

As she reached the front door, he came to a standstill on the pavement outside the gate, and shouted.

'You tell Mr Vivaldi that Albert Thomas wants to see him, missis. Has you got that? Tell him Albert Thomas wants to see him.'

Uncertain of what to do, Mrs Elwood tried to immerse herself in her work. But the thought of the little man kept on tormenting her, and she went to peep through the drawing room window. Albert Thomas was standing outside the gate, staring at the house. Muttering angrily the woman returned to the kitchen, but still at intervals was driven to go and peep through the front windows. And always she saw him standing on the pavement.

When the maidservants, Becca and Dolly, had finished their washing and were with her in the house again, she sent them at intervals to check if the little man was still outside, and each time they came back to tell her that he was.

They pestered her with questions until she weakened and told them what had happened, and they found it highly amusing, and then kept on going to peer out of the front windows, giggling with each other, and egging each other on to wave cheekily to the watching man, until Mrs Elwood came to scold them away.

Three hours passed, and Albert Thomas still continued his vigil. The cook herself was beginning to see some humour in the situation. Her onetime liking for Harry had long since metamorphosed into a contemptuous dislike, and she welcomed anything that might cause him embarrassment. But her genuinely deep affection for her mistress gave her cause for concern in case the little man should intend any harm towards Emma.

'You never knows these days, does you,' Mrs Elwood told herself. 'With all these bloody nutcases being allowed to roam the streets. It might be really Emma that the bugger's after, and not that bastard husband of her'n. I wonder if I ought to fetch a copper to shift the bugger?'

Yet again she left the kitchen and went to the front of the house to peep out of the window.

The pavement outside the gate was empty. She drew the curtains back from the glass pane to see more clearly, and her gaze swept from side to side. There was no sign of the little man's shabby figure anywhere along the roadway. The fat woman gusted a sigh of relief, then her heart sank, and she cursed sibilantly. Albert Thomas had moved into the recreation gardens, and was sitting in the band kiosk, from where he could still maintain a clear view of the front of Cotswold House.

The cook remained at the window, wondering what to do. Emma was visiting her mother. Adrian West was at his theatre. And Harry would undoubtedly be ensconced in one or other of the many public houses. She did not expect any of them to return to the house before early evening.

She glanced at the clock on the tower beneath the spire of St Stephen's church. It was twenty minutes past two o'clock. Again her gaze moved to the little man's motionless figure, and then her attention was caught by a ponderously pacing uniformed man crossing the road at the top of the Fish Hill. She peered hard. It was Police Sergeant Haines, who had recently been transferred to the Redditch station from another area.

Mrs Elwood went quickly from the house and hurried down the road to intercept him. His heavy bovine features were impassive as he listened to her gabbled account of Albert Thomas' calling at Cotswold House, and their subsequent altercation.

'And where is this man now, madam?'

She flung out her arm. 'He's over theer, sitting in the kiosk.'

'Where?' he questioned, and when she swung to look, she saw that the kiosk was empty.

She squinted her eyes and swung her head from side to side, staring wildly in all directions. There were a few pedestrians in sight, but none of them resembled Albert Thomas.

'He was theer just a minute ago. He was theer when I come out from the house to spake to you.'

'Come on.' The sergeant paced ponderously onwards and entered the northern gate of the recreation garden. She followed a pace behind him, breathing heavily. There was no one in the gardens or at the kiosk.

'Did this man assault you in any way, madam?' the policeman wanted to know.

She shook her head. 'No, he didn't try to lay hands on me. But he 'udden't goo off about his business.'

'Did he utter any threats towards you or anyone else?'

Mrs Elwood was a naturally honest woman, and could not bring herself to lie without a very pressing need to do so.

135

'No. He never made any threats.'

'Did he attempt to force his way onto the property, once you'd ejected him, madam?' Once more she answered in the negative.

The bovine features frowned grimly. 'Well then, madam, I have to say that it doesn't appear that this man committed any offence that he could be charged with. He's got the right to sit in a public place, and to make use of the public highway.

'In fact, you've admitted to me, that it was you who laid hands on him. If I was you, madam, I'd be careful about laying hands on people. You could end up by getting into trouble yourself.'

He nodded, and paced ponderously away in the direction of the police station.

Mrs Elwood angrily stuck her tongue out at the policeman's back, and began to walk back towards Cotswold House.

In the churchyard, sheltered behind a thick tree trunk, Albert Thomas stood watching her waddle back into the house. He glanced up at the church clock, and his pinched features frowned with disappointment. 'I can't wait any longer to catch Vivaldi, else I'll miss my train.' Then he consoled himself with the promise, 'But I'll be back. Don't you worry about that, Vivaldi. I'll be back to see you.'

When Emma Vivaldi returned home later that afternoon, Mrs Elwood told her about the caller.

The young woman shrugged dismissively. 'I expect that it's somebody else the bastard owes money too, Mrs E. I'll tell him about it when he comes home. That's if he's sober enough to be able to hear me.'

'How was your mam?' the cook asked.

Emma's beautiful face became clouded. 'Not well, Mrs E, not well at all. And me Dad is playing her up as usual. And she won't hear of leaving him, as usual. I'm getting sick and tired of it all.'

She paused, and then blurted in sudden anger, 'I feel like packing my traps and going as far away from all of them as I can. The way I feel at this minute, I wouldn't

136

give a bugger if I never saw any of them ever again. Not me husband nor me bloody family neither.'

She shook her head and hissed vindictively, 'Bloody men! There's not one of them any bloody good! There's me Dad giving me Mam a life of misery. There's that sodding husband of mine forging my signature to cash cheques. I should have had the bugger charged with forgery, when I found out what he'd been doing, shouldn't I? I'm too soft for me own good, letting him talk me out of it, with all his pleadings and promises to be better. The bastard's as bad now as he's ever been. Worse, in fact! He's never bloody sober now! I don't think Adrian will put up with him for much longer, and that's a fact.'

'Well, you 'udden't listen to me, 'ud you?' Mrs Elwood chided resentfully. 'I told you not to wed Vivaldi, didn't I?'

'Oh yes, you've told me lots and lots of things haven't you,' Emma sneered viciously. 'It was you who told me to wed Old Hector, warn't it? And I had to spend four years getting into bed with the filthy old bastard, didn't I?'

'You knew well what sort o' bloke you was getting into bed with when you wed him,' the fat woman retorted spiritedly. 'And you'm a rich 'ooman now because you got wed to him. I did you a favour there, you ungrateful little bitch!'

'Doon't you becall me, you fat cow!' The younger woman had by now reverted to pure slumcat. 'And doon't make out that you was doing me any favour! You didn't have to fuck the dirty old bastard, did you?'

'Doon't come the lily white wi' me!' the older woman sneered. 'You knew well what you was going to have to put up with. And you was quick enough to chase arter Johnny Purvis, warn't you? And quick enough to jump into bed wi' Vivaldi. And youm getting ready to jump into bed with Adrian West, aren't you? That's if you arn't done it already.'

Emma's highly developed sense of comedy, and her wicked humour, always made it very difficult for her to sustain any anger with those whom she knew to be her genuine friends, such as the woman before her. And now the basic ridiculousness of this dispute caused her to giggle suddenly.

'No, I aren't been in bed with Adrian West. But I intend

to be in bed with him in the very near future. So put that in your pipe and smoke it, you jealous old cow!'

'You wicked, loose-living little bleeder!' The older woman tried to look shocked and appalled at this display of utter shamelessness. But then her fat cheeks quivered, her huge belly shook, and she cackled with laughter. 'Youm a bloody caution, you am, Emmy Farr. A bloody caution!'

The young woman grinned, and agreed with an air of tremendous satisfaction, 'I am, aren't I. I really am!'

The two women hugged, and laughed, and laughed, and laughed.

Chapter Thirteen

Ozzie Clarke and Cleopatra Dolton were sitting side by side at the rolltop desk in the library of her house. The man was making an administration report to his employer.

' . . . so the electric light company have run their cable into the shed, and West has paid me the increased fire insurance premium, and settled for the installation bill.'

He glanced sideways at her handsome face, and added, 'West told me that that was all he called here to see you about, but I reckon that's a bit of guff. He could have come to the office about it, couldn't he?'

Clarke could not help but go further, it was as if his jealousy for her was an ache which he was driven to continually probe, like a child probes an aching tooth.

'If you want my opinion, Mrs Dolton, I think he's taken a fancy for you. He seemed most put out when I told him that I would be dealing with him in the future about all matters, and that he wasn't to come here pestering you.'

Cleopatra was in a disturbed state of mind, which at this particular moment she was finding increasingly difficulty in concealing. Although her sexual experiences with her father and her husband had not brought her anything more than a rarely occurring and fleeting physical pleasure, and for the most part only repulsion and disgust, still she was a woman who had powerful sensual hungers. In the loneliness of her bed her vivid imagination created fantasies which drove her to try and satisfy her own sexual needs. But her hands and fingers could never replace a man's hands and fingers, could never become the hard rod of maleness.

There were many many times during the dark hours of

the night when she craved for the weight of a man, craved for the urgent greedy thrusting of a man, craved for the smell and the feel and the taste of a man, and in her frustration would writhe and toss and cry out in wanting.

Her celibacy was enforced upon her by her own fierce pride, and her deep rooted determination that she would never allow any man ever again the opportunity to inflict upon her the humiliations and sufferings that men had inflicted upon her in the past. But now, at this moment, sitting in such close proximity to an attractive, virile man, whom she knew loved and wanted her, Cleopatra's repressed sexual desires were clamouring and beginning to torment her unbearably. She feared that if this man were to make any physical advance towards her, she would not be able to restrain herself, but would uncontrollably seek for satiation.

'Now here's the rent arrears.' Ozzie, unaware of the effect his proximity was having on the woman, so rigid was the control she imposed upon her outward demeanour, opened another ledger. 'We've got two tenants who are a month in arrears, and one who is three weeks, one who is two weeks, and three who are one week.'

Cleopatra's dark lustrous eyes were fixed upon Clarke's strong hands, tanned by the sun, the nails so clean and well manicured, just a spattering of fine brown hairs on the skin, and she could not help but press her thighs hard together in a vain attempt to assuage the fierce lust that possessed her as she visualised those strong hands caressing her intimate body.

'You'd better take yourself out from here right now, girl,' she warned herself. 'You're randy enough to tear his bloody clothes off his back.'

'We've got ejectment orders against one of the month arrears, and the three week arrears. They're both bad lots who are just trying it on. But the other one of the month's arrears is a difficult case to decide upon.'

Cleopatra was not really listening. Her sexual hunger was now an unbearable torment, and she could only think of escape from this dangerous position she was in. She knew that if at this moment he was to pull her close, she

140

would give in to her own lusts.

Without thinking she blurted out, 'Get an ejectment order against the other month's arrears as well, Mr Clarke. These people are just trying to make fools of us. Then tell Louch to give all three of the ejectment orders a final chance to pay, and if they don't settle immediately, have them out.'

She rose to her feet, her manner now betraying agitation, which caused Ozzie to stare at her curiously, and to ask her, 'Are you feeling alright, Mrs Dolton?'

She reacted irritably, snapping at him curtly, 'Of course I'm alright. Why should I not be?' Then she took a grip of herself, and went on more evenly.

'I'll see you tomorrow, Mr Clarke. Will you find your own way out?'

As she hurried from the room he shook his head at his employer's strange vagaries. Then he checked the names of the tenants he was to evict.

'Billy Shrimpton, Arthur McGuire, and Laura Hughes.' He shrugged resignedly. 'So be it then. If they don't pay up, out they go.'

Chapter Fourteen

Caleb Louch walked into the bar of the Lamb and Flag public house, and his entrance caused a sudden hush to fall upon the room. He grinned challengingly as his hard eyes swung from drinker to drinker. Some of them met his challenging stare with a defiant or equally challenging regard. Some looked guilty and their eyes slid uneasily from his. Still others tried to smile and greeted him fawningly, like dogs giving due deference to the leader of the pack.

James Jakeman, the publican, moved along the rear of the counter to take Louch's order. He pulled the beerpump handle, filling the pint pot with rich dark porter topped by a creamy froth, and placed it in front of Louch, waving aside the other man's proffered coins.

'That's alright, Caleb, have that 'un on me. You did me a good turn letting me have that bit of info' the other day.'

'Youm welcome to it, James. I doon't like to see any decent man being cheated by bloody toe-rags.'

Louch lifted the foaming pot and drank deeply from it, then smacked his lips with relish and placed it half emptied on the counter.

Louch had established a very good understanding with the publicans of the town. It was the custom for publicans to allow trusted customers to drink on credit, and settle the debt the following payday. This was called having it on the slate. But like all credit systems there were those who tried to abuse it. Some topers would run up a slate at one public house, but instead of settling the debt promptly, would then transfer their custom to another public house and run up a slate there also. Others would plead poverty to avoid settling the debt when it was due. They would claim to have been laid off work, or to have been ill. Yet others would spend their money in one public house, and simultaneously obtain drinks on the slate at another.

Louch, as a debt and rent collector, regularly visited the many public houses in the district to check if those in his account books who owed money were in fact drinking it away. With his encyclopedic memory for names, faces, dates, debts and rent arrears, and the myriad snippets of information contained within the dog-eared pages of his thick notebooks, he was regarded as an infallible source of information by the local publicans who needed to keep a check on their own slate runners.

No one was waiting to be served, so the publican leaned on the counter and began to chat to the debt-collector.

'You looking for anybody in particular, Caleb?'

The burly man shook his bulletlike head. 'Nobody special, James. I got to go to Hill Street on a bit of business, so I just called in case I might see Tommy Blunt in here.'

It was the publican's turn to shake his head. 'He aren't bin in for a while now. They do say as he's off the drink these days.'

Louch's strong yellow teeth bared in a momentary rictus that was more ferocious snarl than smile. 'And he'd better stay off it as well, until he's settled up wi' me, if he knows what's good for him.'

Jakeman stroked his heavy moustache reflectively. 'I always thought Tommy was a straight enough bloke, Caleb. He's always cleared his slate wi' me nice and prompt.'

'It's since his missis took to her bed to have the last babby that he's gone off the rails, James,' Louch whispered hoarsely, and tapped the side of his nose to signal that this was confidential information that he was about to impart, causing the publican to look suitably gratified and hunch closer.

'Blunt's bin chasing after a young wench for months now, unbeknownst to his missis, o' course. Well, with his missis being took so badly arter birthing the kid, and having to stay in her bed, Blunt is acting like a young pup that's bin let off his chain. He's throwing all his money

143

away treating the young wench, and he's forgetting about paying his bloody rent, and his tallies for his furniture.'

Louch lifted his pint pot and drained it, and the publican instantly took it from him and refilled it. Once again waving aside payment, he hunched close to listen.

Louch tasted his fresh drink, and congratulated Jakeman, 'This is a lovely pint, James. You keeps the best cellar in the town, no doubt about it.'

The publican showed his pleasure at the compliment by inviting expansively, 'Well, theer's another in the barrel for you when youm ready, Caleb.'

Louch was too shrewd in operator to risk killing the goose that lays the golden eggs. 'No thank you all the same, James.'

And he insisted forcefully on the man accepting the money for the second drink. 'You'll take it, James, and no argument!'

After the publican had taken the coins from him, Louch went on with his story.

'Tommy's bin lifting this wench out to Hopwood and filling her wi' shorts and grub, and he's bin buying her presents. Oh the stupid barstard's really in love, no doubt about it. Anyway, that's wheer his rent and tally has bin gooing. So I had a little word in his ear larst week.'

Jakeman grinned sycophantically. 'I'll bet that put the fear o' Christ up him, didn't it, Caleb?'

'Ahr, he looked a bit green about the gills. I mean to say, James, I'se got some pity for his poor missis, but it won't stop me having him and her and the kids out on the bloody street, if he comes the cunt.'

Then he dropped his voice to a whisper. 'If you'll take my tip, you'll not let Blunt run up any slate with you until I gives you the whistle.'

'The bugger wunt get so much as a bloody smell on it, never mind a taste, Caleb. And thanks very much for the tip. It's appreciated.'

'And Elias Snow over theer.' Louch jerked his head slightly to indicate a man sat playing dominoes with some cronies at a table by the door. 'Has he got much on the slate this week?'

144

'A couple o' bob,' the publican informed him. 'Why? Am you after him, Caleb?'

Again the strong yellow teeth bared in the rictus grimace. 'Not this week. But young Canadine at the White Swan is. Snowey arn't cleared his slate since three weeks back.'

Louch winked meaningly. 'So I shouldn't let the bugger run up too much on his slate here, my friend.'

He gulped down the rest of his porter and nodded farewell.

As he passed the table where the men were playing dominoes he halted briefly and said loudly, 'You wants to get rid o' that double three, Snowey, or you could get stuck with it.'

'You bastard, Louch! Just keep your bloody nose out on it, 'ull you!' The man reacted furiously to having his key domino revealed to his opponents, who chortled and jeered delightedly at his discomfiture. Louch laughed uproariously at the man's impotent rage, and went on his way.

The queue of haggard shabby women at the water pump watched the rent collector walking up Hill Street, and for the most part their regard was hostile. Those who knew the man as their own rent collector knew the reason for him being here on a mid-week day. He always came in mid-week to deliver the final ultimatum: pay all arrears of rent instantly, or be thrown out onto the street. The necessary ejectment order issued by the Magistrate's Court would be in his back pocket, and all the women present had witnessed Louch carry out ejectments before.

'Here he comes, the blood sucker himself.'

'He's got his chucking out face on him!'

'Bloody heartless bastard!'

'I wonder which poor cratur is for the chop!'

The last speaker was a robust, dark-haired woman who looked like a Romany gypsy, with her dangling brass earrings and brightly coloured scarf tied about her hair.

'Well, it wun't be you for the chop, 'ull it Rosie?' another woman sneered nastily at her. 'You always manages to come to some accommodation with him, doon't you?'

'What does you mean by that, Aggie Winkworth?' the gypsy-like woman demanded aggressively.

Aggie Winkworth was unimpressed by the display of aggression. 'I means just what I says, Rosie. Just so long as you lets him have a bit of what he fancies when you aren't got the rent money to give him, then youm never going to be up for the chop, am you?'

'That's a wicked lie!' Rosie's swarthy features flushed dully. 'God should strike you down dead for saying such, you evil-tongued bitch!'

Her opponent only laughed in harsh scorn, and swaggered away with her bucket of water.

The group fell silent as Caleb Louch came abreast and passed them. He ignored them completely, not even glancing in their direction. A couple of the women sighed with heartfelt relief as he continued on up the slope, and inwardly breathed a prayer of gratitude that for today at least they were not the primary quarry of this feared man.

The women watched to see into which tenement he would enter, with the same sense of nervous, tense anticipation that spectators at an execution might experience. Their emotions were a dichotomy: pity for the victim, and at the same time a perverse pleasurable excitement at the prospect of witnessing someone else's traumatic ordeal.

They hissed in unison when he disappeared into an entryway.

'It's the Culls he's come for.'

'No, it carn't be. Eddie settled all he owed last week. He told me so hisself.'

'That's right, Maria told me the same.'

'Is it Ethel Ryder then?'

'I shouldn't have thought so. Ethel's always very careful to keep herself straight, aren't her?'

'Is it the Watson's?'

'No, they'm on the relief.'

'I'll bet it's Laura. Her aren't bin able to do a tap since her broke her arm, has her?'

'It carn't be her. I saw Sammy Hulland go theer to see her. Her 'ull be getting relief, wun't her?'

146

'No, her wunt. Maria Cull told me that the silly little cow told Sammy Hulland to bugger off.'

'Never! Her never did!'

'She bloody well did. I'm telling you! Her told him to sod off, because he wanted her to have Tommy Spiers put away.'

'Rosie's right. Maria told me the same thing. Laura warn't give any relief because her 'udden't have Tommy put away.'

'Stupid silly cow! Her want's her bloody yed looking at!'

'I'm buggered if I'd let meself get kicked out onto the bloody streets for the sake of a yampy-yedded bugger like Tommy Spiers.'

'Youm right theer, Mary. By rights he should have bin put away years ago.'

'It's Laura's own fault, aren't it, having this come on her.'

This last statement drew a general consensus of agreement.

'Ahr, it is.'

'Her's brought it on herself.'

'Silly cow!'

In the small, immaculately clean room, Caleb Louch laid the sheet of paper on the table and told Laura Hughes bluntly, but not unkindly, 'That's the ejectment order granted by the Bench at last week's petty sessions.'

Sitting on a stool at the table, dressed in his vest and long johns, a blanket wrapped around him, Tommy reached out and patted the sheet of paper, grunting and chuckling to himself, and bobbing his head erratically.

Laura Hughes stared at the ejectment order, and tears of despair blurred her vision.

Louch stood looking down at the young woman's bowed head, noting the cleanliness of her bunned hair, and the neatly darned shawl around her painfully thin shoulders, and hardened though he was, could not repress his pity for her.

He knew a good deal more about Laura Hughes than she realised. He knew something of her family background, and her involvement with the Suffragette movement. He knew how she had come to be here in this slum, caring for a

147

mentally disturbed man who was no kin to her. He knew why she was not receiving Poor Relief. He also shrewdly surmised how she had managed to obtain food and fuel enough to keep herself and Tommy from starving or freezing to death.

'Now my wench, it's my job to ask you if you can pay the arrears of rent you owes.' Louch spoke with uncharacteristic gentleness. 'And of course I already knows the answer. But I have to ask to make it all legal.'

Laura had managed to force back her tears, and was able to meet the man's sympathetic eyes. 'No, Mr Louch. I can't pay the arrears. If I could, then I would, believe me.'

He nodded. 'I do believe you, my wench. Well, by rights I have to tell you to get out of this house. And to use whatever force is necessary to get you out if you refuses to shift.'

He frowned at Tommy, who, seemingly oblivious to his surroundings, was now examining his thumb with intense curiosity, the string of saliva trickling from the corner of his slack mouth and dripping from the point of his chin.

'Wheer's his clothes?'

'I had to pawn them. And his boots,' the young woman answered quietly, and she again bowed her head to hide the tears that now she could no longer force back.

'You knows that I'se got little choice in this matter now, doon't you?' Louch explained, and there was almost a note of apology in his voice. 'The thing is, you'se got to get out from here today. Though I suppose you could always try and see Mrs Dolton, and tell her why you'se got into this state. I mean, it's no fault of your own that you broke your arm.'

'No, Mr Louch, but it's considered my own fault that I'm not getting pauper relief to pay my rent with, isn't it?' Laura wiped the tears from her eyes, and spoke bitterly. 'If I was to agree to have poor Tommy put away, then I'd get relief, wouldn't I, and I wouldn't find myself in this position. I can't go and ask Mrs Dolton for more help. She's already been very kind to me. But she told me that I should have Tommy put away, so she'll not be ready to help me again, will she? And I wouldn't expect her to.'

'Then why doon't you have him put away?' the man questioned, somewhat impatiently. 'If you was to do that now, why then I'd be able to let you stay on here. Because the Board o' Guardians 'ud help you then, and Dolton Enterprises 'ud be guaranteed their rent. Christ above, girl, does you enjoy playing the martyr?'

He asked this final question sharply, and she reacted equally sharply. 'Of course I don't enjoy playing the martyr, Mr Louch!' she retorted vehemently. 'And it was never my intention to appear as if I was acting like a martyr. But I gave my solemn promise to Rosie Spiers, that I wouldn't let Tommy be taken into the workhouse. And I shall keep that promise no matter what it might cost me!'

His tough features grimaced in dismissive disgust. 'No you won't, girl. Not now. And it wun't be the work'us this loony bugger 'ull be gooing into neither. It'll be the mad'ouse he'll be put in, the very minute that he's steps foot outside this door. Does you think that the police 'ull let him goo running around the bloody town dressed in his underclothes with a bloody blanket wrapped round him? See some sense, 'ull you, girl. Let him be put away by the Guardians, and look after yourself.'

Her features became a stubborn mask of rejection, but he continued his urgings.

'Listen to me now! If you'll let 'um take him away, then I'll hold back from evicting you. You can goo and see Sammy Hulland straight now, and he's certain sure to allow relief.'

She made no sign, only stayed with her head turned from him, her faced still stubbornly set in rejection. Louch was beginning to lose patience, and he cursed beneath his breath, but decided to make one final attempt at persuasion. Normally he would not have bothered to try and save someone from eviction. But he respected this young woman, and admired the courage and determination she had displayed during her years of hardship.

'Let me put summat else to you, my wench. The way it stands now, is that youm both going to be put out onto the street. If nobody takes you in and gives you shelter, then

149

you'll both be classed as homeless vagrants. I know that
you arn't got any money, so you'll have no defence against
that charge. And that means that you'll be sent to prison as
a wilful vagrant, and Tommy here 'ull be committed to the
lunatic asylum.'

Laura knew this was a fact, but she persisted in clinging
to the wild hope that she and Tommy would find help of
some sort.

Louch, as if recognising what she was hoping for,
brutally pointed out the truth. 'Does you think that
somebody 'ull take pity on you, and give you shelter, girl?'
He shook his head, and scathingly answered his own
question.

'Youm living in bloody cloud cuckoo land, if you thinks
that that 'ull happen. If youm on your own, there'll be
them as 'ull be willing to give you shelter, my wench. But
you arn't agoing to find anybody who'll be willing to give
the loony any place under their roof. For Christ's sake, see
some sense, 'ull you girl!'

He fell silent and stood staring at her, trying to judge
what effect, if any, his words had had on her resolve.

Her expression remained unchanged, but deep within
the recesses of her mind, she knew that what the man had
said was only the truth. If she persisted in her stubborn
refusal to give Tommy up, then both of them would
inevitably end up in even worse straits than they already
were. She heard Louch begin to speak again, and could no
longer wilfully shut out what he was saying from her mind.

'If you has Tommy put away today, then that'll give you
a chance to get back on your own feet, wun't it? You'll still
have a roof over your head. And later, when your arm's
better, and you can start work again and settle your debts,
why then there's nothing to prevent you from fetching
Tommy back out to live with you, is there? If he's in the
mad ward at the Bromsgrove work'us, it aren't the same as
him being committed to the lunatic asylum at Barnsley, is
it? Because he wun't have committed any criminal offence,
will he? Because if you has him taken in now by the Board
of Guardians, he'll only be classed as a pauper loony, not
as a criminal vagrant loony.'

His arguments mercilessly eroded Laura's resistance. She knew that what he was saying was only the truth. And despite her bitter reluctance, she must either do as he advised, or risk losing Tommy for ever.

Finally, she nodded, and told him sadly, 'Yes, Mr Louch, I do accept that what you tell me is right. I shall do as you advise. Would you be very kind and watch over Tommy for me, while I go and see Mr Hulland? I'll be as quick as I can.'

Sensing how bitterly she felt this defeat, he forbore from applauding her decision. Instead he only told her quietly, 'Yes, my wench. You goo and see Sammy Hulland. I'll watch Tommy for you.'

Chapter Fifteen

It was early evening when they came to fetch Tommy Spiers. There were four men, with a small, enclosed and windowless black van drawn by a bedraggled looking horse.

Two of the men were Samuel Hulland, the vaccination and relieving officer of the Bromsgrove Union, and Doctor Protheroe Smith, medical officer and public vaccinator of the Bromsgrove Union. The other two men were peaked-capped, dark uniformed male orderlies from the lunatic asylum at Barnsley Hall.

As the doctor had earlier explained to Laura, Tommy was to be taken initially to Barnsley Hall to be assessed by the medical staff there, as to his suitability for transfer to the workhouse in Bromsgrove.

The appearance of the black van lurching up the rutted slope of Hill Street created a sensation. It was by no means the first time that this van had come to the street to take away one of its inhabitants, but it was not such a frequent occurrence as to make the street blasé and uninterested. Even the bar of the Lamb and Flag emptied as the customers poured out to follow the black van, and James Jakeman cursed long and hard, before locking the bar doors and joining the exodus.

The wildly excited urchins capered about chanting and screeching at the tops of their strident voices:

Black, black, big black van,
Come to get a mad mad man.
Eeny meeny miney mo,
Catch that loony by his toe.

Tie him up in a great big ball,
And cart him off to Barnsley Hall!

The more soft-hearted onlookers scolded the urchins and tried to make them stop their chanting, but others protected the children, and several heated altercations erupted, during which the strident shrieking continued undiminished.

Black, black, big black van
Come to get a mad mad man.
Eeny meeny miney mo,
Catch that loony by his toe.
Tie him up a great big ball,
And cart him off to Barnsley Hall!

Laura's immediate neighbours had gathered in a protective phalanx around the entrance to the court, and they refused to allow anybody but the two officials and one of the orderlies to enter the fetid confines. The second orderly remained to hold the horse and guard against mischievous children clambering all over the van.

Maria Cull had sorted out an ancient pair of trousers and a ragged jacket belonging to her husband to clothe Tommy Spiers. And now she waited with Laura inside the tenement, Tommy sitting on stool between them.

When the three men entered the cramped room Tommy welcomed them with high-pitch gruntings and snufflings and immediately began to stroke and pat the Doctor's full-length beard. The medical man smiled and talked pleasantly to the idiot, and removed the ragged jacket from his scrawny upper body.

'You won't be needing this, my friend. I've brought a nice new coat for you to put on. You'll be a real dandy when you're wearing this coat.'

He nodded to the orderly, who produced a rolled, white-canvas strait-jacket from behind his back.

'Oh no!' Laura protested in dismay. 'You can't put that dreadful thing on him.'

The doctor spoke to her soothingly. 'My dear young

lady, it is for his sake that we use this. It prevents him from doing injury to himself or to anyone else.'

'But it's not needed!' Laura continued to protest. 'He won't harm anyone.'

'He may well become disturbed when he is taken out from here and put into the van, young woman. We must ensure that all precautions are taken to ensure his own safety, and the safety of others.'

Laura's distress caused her to begin to cry, but still she stood arguing, until Maria intervened and pulled her away from the doctor and Tommy.

'Come on, my duck. The doctor knows what's best. Come on now. Doon't upset yourself so. Come on away now.'

Laura could not bear to watch as with smiling encouragement the doctor and orderly deftly slipped the straitjacket onto the grunting, grinning Tommy Spiers. And then, in concert with each other, quickly tightened and secured the straps.

Tommy stared wildly down at his canvas prison, and his eyes dilated in terror. The men started to lead him out from the room, and he jerked and struggled against them, grunting and snuffling in distress. The doctor nodded, and together with the orderly exerted his full strength to drag Tommy out. The idiot howled in terror and anguish and Laura rammed her palms against her ears in a futile effort to shut out the sound of the terrible shrieking howl. But nothing served to diminish the power of its penetrating ululations, as the men dragged Tommy through the narrow entryway and out into the street.

There was an outburst of jeering and catcalls from the onlookers, and their mood threatened to turn against the officials as they saw how roughly the struggling, screaming idiot was bundled into the back of the enclosed van and its rear-opening doors slammed shut and locked behind him, imprisoning him in darkness.

The van trundled down the slope, lurching and bucking over the deep ruts, and the terrible, terrified shrieking from its black interior seemed to bounce off the walls of the tenements and reverberate through every rancid nook and cranny of the mean street.

154

Back in the room, Laura Hughes was sobbing as if her heart was broken, shoulders heaving, her breath a jerky gulping, all control gone.

Maria patted the thin shoulders of her friend and told her over and over again, 'It aren't your fault that he's gone, Laura. It aren't your fault. It aren't your fault.'

But no words of comfort could ease the despairing grief that Laura Hughes was suffering.

It was many hours before Laura could begin to think about what had happened, and to consider what she should now do. She felt that she had betrayed Rosie and Tommy, and her guilt was all-enveloping.

In her mind she promised her dead friend, 'Tommy won't stay there for a minute longer than I can help, Rosie. I'll bring him back to live with me, I promise you. I promise you that from the bottom of my heart.'

For further long hours she sat motionless in the darkness, immersed in her sombre thoughts. Then she rose and lit the lamp. From her battered trunk upstairs she fetched paper, pen and ink.

'It's my selfish, stupid pride that's caused Tommy to be taken away like this,' she castigated herself without mercy. 'Well I'll not let my own selfishness stop me now. I can swallow my pride, and swallow it with ease. Because it's proved itself to be a wicked thing which brings only grief and torment to that poor soul who I promised to care for.'

She wrote a short letter, then sealed it in an envelope and addressed the packet to:

Miss Miriam Josceleyne
co/ The Women's Social and Political Union
Clement's Inn
The Strand
London WC2.

She stuck a stamp on the letter, then wrapped her shawl around her shoulders and went immediately to post it.

155

Chapter Sixteen

London

In the minutes before seven o'clock in the morning, a small group of men, women and children gathered on the roadway outside the massive castellated, turreted gatehouse of Holloway Female Prison. Separated from the building by a short entrance drive, the crowd stood for the most part in silence. Some smoked, one or two paced restlessly up and down the pavement, others peered through the spiked iron railings which cordoned off the prison grounds from the public thoroughfare.

Some uniformed policemen appeared and stood overlooking the crowd. Then, as the clocks whirred and chimed the hour of seven o'clock, a small door in the recess at the side of the great iron-studded main door of the prison opened and one by one the released prisoners emerged.

Most of the women were poorly dressed, and their ravaged faces bore the marks of years of physical and mental abuse. They trudged dispiritedly down the stone-setted driveway and through the tall gateposts topped by ornate gas lamps, and appeared curiously subdued and apprehensive to embrace their freedom once again. Because for them that freedom was only the passport to more suffering, want and hardship and the prison that they were leaving had at least sheltered, fed, cleansed and protected them.

Some of the women were met by relatives and friends, by husbands, sons or daughters, and went tearfully away in the company of their loved ones. A few of the younger

156

women wore the tawdry finery of the prostitute, and were greeted raucously by their bullyboys and ponces.

Two women walked down the driveway side by side carrying the babies that they had given birth to while in prison. One of them was hugged and kissed fondly by a man dressed like a workman, in flat cap, muffler and clay-stained clothing, and he took the baby and cuddled it tenderly, before the pair went off side by side. The other baby-carrying woman had no one to greet her, and she trudged away sad-faced and head bent.

A large fat woman, garishly coated, her hat a mass of gaudy feathers, was intercepted by two hard-featured, bowler-hatted plainclothes detectives, and was re-arrested to face other charges. She howled in furious outrage and poured a stream of verbal filth from her mouth. The bullyboys and ponces egged her on to make a fight of it, and jeered the detectives until they themselves were confronted and warned by a uniformed constable and sergeant, and they swaggered away, their newly released women on their arms.

A little distance apart from the remainder of the small crowd two well dressed women stood staring anxiously through the iron railings towards the prison doors. Then they turned to each other with smiles of relief, as from the small recessed door a petite, slender figure emerged.

As the small woman walked down the driveway curious stares were directed at her. Unlike her fellow released prisoners this woman was extremely neat and clean in appearance, and her clothing, subdued in colour, was of good quality. Her pale, delicate features bore none of the ravaged scars inflicted by drink or ill usage, and her green eyes, though shadowed and weary, were clear and tranquil. Although she was in her mid-thirties she gave the impression of youth with her slender figure and almost translucent skin.

The two well dressed women moved forwards to intercept her as she came through the gates.

'Welcome back, Miriam,' the taller of the pair greeted her, and the small woman smiled.

'Amelia! Thank you for coming to meet me!'

157

'Let me introduce a new sister to you, Miriam.' The tall woman made the introductions.

'Alice Paul, of New York City. Miriam Josceleyne, one of the foremost fighters in our cause.'

'I've heard a great deal about you, Miss Josceleyne.' The good-looking, dark-haired American woman stared admiringly at Miriam. 'But you are different to my visualisation of you.'

Miriam chuckled. 'I have been told such before, Miss Paul. Most people seem to expect me to look like a female version of Attilla the Hun.'

Then she suddenly coughed heavily, and taking a large handkerchief from her pocket pressed it against her mouth with both hands, as the bout of coughing racked her slender body.

Amelia Hunt's expression showed alarm, and she muttered to the American woman, 'Miriam is not at all strong. And every time she goes into prison her health deteriorates. Yet she'll not listen to any advice we give her. She refuses to rest, or to take proper care of her health.'

Miriam's bout of coughing slowly stilled, and after a while she was able to straighten her slender body and to smile reassuringly at her companions' concerned faces.

'I've only got a cold. Nothing more. I'm perfectly well.'

'You really must rest yourself, Miriam, and obey Doctor Charles' instructions this time,' Amelia Hunt scolded. 'Now come along, we'll go and find a cab and take you back to Clement's Inn. More of the sisters are waiting to welcome you there.'

Left more shaken and spent by her fit of coughing than she cared to admit, Miriam allowed herself to be taken arm in arm between the other two women and led away from the gates of the prison.

A burly inspector of police spoke to the trio as they passed him. 'Good morning, ladies. Free again, I see, Miss Josceleyne.'

His manner was friendly, and Miriam Josceleyne acknowledged pleasantly, 'Yes, Inspector Bedford, I'm free again to torment the politicians.'

He chuckled grimly, and his shrewd eyes briefly rested

on her features, left unhealthily flushed and damp-sheened by the terrible bout of coughing.

'If I were you, Miss Josceleyne, I'd give up tormenting the politicians. All these visits to Holloway don't seem to be doing you very much good.'

'I shall stop tormenting them, Inspector, at the very moment that they give me what I want,' Miriam retorted defiantly.

His manner hardened perceptibly. 'I think that you've got a long time to wait for that, Miss Josceleyne. Only about thirty per cent of men in this country have the right to a vote. So I can't really see the government giving you women the vote before the rest of the male population gets it.'

'We shall see, Inspector. We shall see.' Her lips set in a stubborn line. 'Goodbye, Inspector.'

She walked on, then could not help turning her head and calling back over her shoulder, 'Or perhaps I should say au revoir, Inspector, because you and I are certain to meet again, aren't we?'

He smiled grimly, and saluted by touching his gloved fingers to the peak of his cap.

His sergeant came to stand by his side and watch the three women walking away arm in arm. He puffed out his breath, causing the ends of his bushy moustache to lift and fall.

'I expect we'll be taking some o' that lot in agen before very long, won't we sir?'

'I expect we shall, Sergeant Thompson,' the Inspector agreed, and his eyes dwelt on the retreating figure of Miriam Josceleyne with a grudging admiration. 'That little woman has got guts though. I'll give her that.'

Then he jerked out in exasperation. 'Bloody suffragettes! They're a pain in the arse!'

As the closed carriage made its way through the bustling streets, Miriam tried to pay attention to what her new acquaintance, Alice Paul, was telling her about the growth of an American Women's Suffrage movement. But Miriam was finding it increasingly difficult to follow the other woman's words. She felt giddily light-headed, and

159

uncomfortably hot, and her chest was sore and painful. At intervals bouts of coughing racked her body, and brought tears streaming from her eyes. Clammy sweat beaded her broad forehead, and fits of acute nausea assailed her.

'So you see . . . then I said . . . of course not . . . if . . . well most of our women . . . it's worse in the mid-west . . . the nigger women will . . . the president says . . . we say . . . they say . . .'

Alice Paul's voice came and went in disjointed waves of blurred sound, and a curious darkness impinged on Miriam's vision. Pain throbbed through her skull, and she felt as if a hammer were pounding against the inner surfaces of her temples. Then the carriage jolted across a big pothole in the road and Miriam's eyes rolled upwards and she fell forwards in a dead faint.

'Oh my God!' Alice Paul was shocked into panic. 'Oh my God, what's wrong with her? What's happening? Oh my God!'

Amelia Hunt was made of sterner stuff. She coolly propped the limp body back onto the narrow seat, and shouted to the cab driver, 'Never mind going to Clement's Inn, take us to Cleveland Square, Bayswater, and hurry, I've a very sick woman here.'

As the cab jolted and swung in its sudden change of direction Amelia Hunt rapidly explained, 'I'm taking her to Doctor Charles' house. He's our regular doctor.'

Doctor Cyril Charles bore a distinct physical resemblance to His Imperial Majesty, King Edward the Seventh, and like that monarch indulged his gross appetites to excess. He was, however, an experienced and competent medical man, and although the sudden arrival of the three women interrupted his breakfast hour, and spoiled his leisurely consumption of a huge bowl of kedgeree, he accepted that disappointment philosophically enough.

His servants carried Miriam Josceleyne into his surgery and laid her on the broad leather couch which he used for examinations.

She had regained a dazed consciousness by now, and at first struggled against the restraining hands, but as full

160

consciousness returned she obeyed his instructions passively and answered his questions, as he made a careful examination.

He repeatedly percussed her chest and back, and afterwards sent her into the toilet to provide him with samples of her sputum and urine.

When he had finished his examination Miriam straightened her clothing and asked him bluntly, 'What is the matter with me, Doctor?'

He frowned. 'I cannot answer that at this moment, Miss Josceleyne. I have to make tests of the sputum and urine samples, and study you for a further space of time before I can justify any firm diagnosis of your disorder.'

'Please, Doctor Charles, don't treat me as if I were stupid.' She spoke very firmly and calmly. 'I have the right to know what it is that is wrong with me. You must have drawn some conclusions already after your examination. After all, this isn't the first time that I've come to you with similar symptoms, is it?'

'No, it is not the first time you have come to me with similar symptoms, Miss Josceleyne. And I shall once again give you advice, and I expect that you will once again ignore that advice,' he spat out in sudden annoyance.

She paid no heed to his petulant outburst, and demanded, 'I want you to tell me the truth, Doctor Charles. I have the right to know.'

When he still demurred she spoke more sharply, and her stubborn determination radiated from her.

'If you will not tell me what I wish to know, Doctor Charles, then I shall merely go elsewhere to obtain the answer to my question. There are a great many medical men in London, are there not? And I'm quite sure that I shall easily find one who will do as I ask.'

He smiled bleakly and surrendered to her pressure. 'Very well, Miss Josceleyne. I will make an exception to my usual practice and give you a blunt answer. I have a strong suspicion that you may be developing pulmonary phthisis.'

'You mean consumption?' she sought clarification.

He nodded. 'Yes, Miss Josceleyne, I mean consumption.'

'I see.' Her delicate features momentarily clouded, but

161

then she visibly rallied against the shock of this information.

'Tell me, Doctor Charles, if I have indeed developed consumption, is there any treatment which is effective against it?'

He smiled confidently. 'Yes indeed there is, Miss Josceleyne. If after further tests and examination I conclude that you have contracted the disorder then I am confident that I will be able to effect a cure.'

'How long will these further tests and examinations take?' Miriam wanted to know.

'Not long,' he informed her gravely. 'In the meantime, I must insist that you rest completely, spend as much time as possible in your bed.'

He seated himself at his desk and began to scribble on a sheet of notepaper.

'I want you to follow this dietary regime I'm noting down for you until such time as my tests are completed. Also to follow the other instructions I shall note down, concerning hygiene and disinfection. All these must be implemented immediately.'

She nodded.

He finished writing and rose to hand the paper to her, then he patted her thin shoulder encouragingly.

'Now do not worry yourself unduly, Miss Josceleyne. I'm confident that all will be well. Come and see me in three days from now. At about eleven o'clock in the morning if that is convenient.'

'Very well, Doctor, and thank you.'

The two women were in the waiting room of the surgery, and they greeted Miriam with anxious questions.

'Are you feeling better?'

'What did he say?'

'Did he know what is ailing you?'

'He hopes to know shortly,' Miriam answered.

She felt an overwhelming need to be alone with her own thoughts, and she told Amelia.

'I think it best that I go straight back to my rooms, Amelia. I don't really feel well enough to come on with you to Clement's Inn. Can you make my apologies to the ladies there for my absence?'

162

'I'll come to your rooms with you,' Amelia offered immediately. 'You may need some help.'

'No, thank you very much, but I really would prefer to be alone just now. I just need to rest and be quiet for a time.'

Reluctantly Amelia accepted this, and the three of them parted outside the doctor's house.

Miriam's rooms were in a quiet side street in Kensington, and her walking route to there from Bayswater crossed Hyde Park and Kensington Gardens. She walked slowly through the streets and made her way into the parkland through the Marlborough Gate.

Directly before her stretched the long curve of the Serpentine, with the sunlight sparkling on its dark green waters, and Miriam smiled and drew deep breaths of the tree and grass-scented air. She strolled along the path at the water's edge and her eyes, jaded by the confines of high walls and cells and drab convict garb, took pleasure from the myriad colours and sights surrounding her.

Hordes of white-robed nursemaids paraded with their charges – tiny boys in sailor suits, little girls with be-ribboned hair and dainty parasols, chubby, lace-bonneted babies in bassinets.

Squads of soldiers, some uniformed in the glory of scarlet, blue and gold, others in the more prosaic khaki, were practising semaphore, waving flags that snapped and fluttered in the air, and preening themselves as they caught the bright eyes of the passing nursemaids glancing towards them.

Old ladies in black velvet and satins sat sedately on chairs, watching people feeding the flocks of ducks and waterfowl. Beefy, moustached men and skinny, pimple-faced boys and youths, jackets cast aside, sleeves rolled up, launched their model sailing craft out across the waters. Further out, the rowing skiffs manned by oarsmen of many differing shades of expertise splashed and wallowed from bank to bank, and swimmers shouted angrily at the oarsmen to take care where they wielded their long-bladed poles.

Fashionable young women and elegant matrons

163

sauntered under the leafy trees, their sleek menfolk strolling proudly beside them, and on the grass dirty, ragged tramps and derelicts lay snoring peacefully, oblivious to the children playing noisily around them.

Phaetons, brakes, dogcarts, victorias, broughams and landaus crewed by resplendent coachmen and footmen decorously bore their pampered owners along the carriage roads. In Rotten Row dashing horsemen and horsewomen cantered and trotted and walked their splendid mounts for the onlookers to envy and admire.

Miriam immersed herself in the pleasure of freedom, of being able to walk where she pleased, to stare at what she pleased, to stand or go on as she pleased. Then, as time passed and she wandered from one extremity of the parkland to the other, she became increasingly aware of a gnawing sense of inner loneliness. She had no one with whom she could fully share this simple pleasure of freedom. Of course she knew that friendship and company awaited her in Clement's Inn where her fellow suffragettes gathered together. But Miriam Josceleyne knew that the friendship of women was not enough to assuage this loneliness. She hungered for the loving company of a man. She needed the spiritual union of hearts and the physical union of bodies. She needed to love and be loved by a man.

Once in her life she had briefly known such a loving union. But it had been cruelly snatched from her, and now in this green parkland, in this warm sunlight, she yearned sadly for the man she had loved and lost.

A feeling of desolation struck through her, and she turned and walked out from the park and made her solitary way to her empty rooms.

Chapter Seventeen

Three days after her release from Holloway Miriam was readying herself to keep her appointment with Doctor Charles. During those three days she had been forced to acknowledge that she was afflicted with something more serious than the simple feverish cold she had chosen to believe her symptoms indicated. She had suffered from heavy night-sweats, high temperatures and pain in her chest, plus the repeated bouts of racking coughs, and a general feeling of bodily weakness. And at this moment in time she was feeling distinctly unwell, and enduring a throbbing headache.

Various suffragette friends had come to visit her since her release, and she had hidden her state of health from them. Although she had been pleased to see them, after a brief while in their company she had longed for them to go away and leave her in peace. All she wanted to do was to sit and be quiet.

She was leaving the house when she met Amelia Hunt coming up the pathway towards the front door, and her heart sank. The way she was feeling at this moment with her headache worsening and a sense of nausea periodically souring her stomach, the last thing she needed was Amelia's hearty good fellowship.

'Where are you going?' the woman demanded.

'To keep my appointment with Doctor Charles.'

'Then I shall come with you.'

'No Amelia, I really would not dream of putting you to the trouble.'

'It's no trouble,' Amelia declared. 'Company will do you good, my dear. You're looking rather peaky and out of sorts. You shouldn't keep yourself to yourself so much. It's not healthy.'

Inwardly Miriam grimaced in rueful surrender.

As they walked up the road Amelia Hunt produced a letter which she handed to Miriam. 'This came yesterday, my dear.'

Miriam needed glasses to read with and she fumbled in her reticule for her spectacle case. Then clucked her tongue in annoyance.

'I've forgotten to bring my glasses.'

'Can I read it for you?' her companion offered, committing a breach of social etiquette.

Miriam could not help but resent the other woman's attempt to intrude upon her privacy, and she answered more sharply than she intended, 'No, that won't be necessary.'

The other woman visibly bridled at this sharpness. 'I was only trying to help, Miriam.'

Miriam experienced an instant sense of remorse. She knew that the other woman possessed a good heart, and was only trying to be helpful, yet even as Miriam acknowledged these facts, still all her senses screamed out to be merely left alone.

She drew a long ragged breath, and stated quietly, 'I know that you were trying to be helpful, Amelia, and I do truly appreciate your kindness. But I really would prefer at this time to be alone.'

Amelia's homely features twisted resentfully, and she blurted out aggrievedly, 'Very well, Miriam. If that is what you prefer. I know where I am not wanted!'

She turned on her heels and stalked away, every inch of her body radiating her resentment of this rebuff. Miriam's heart sank with dismay. The last thing she wanted to do was to hurt the other woman. For a brief instant she opened her mouth to call Amelia back, then shook her head.

'No, it's no use. I really cannot stand to have her with me at this moment, good soul though she might be.'

Made troubled and unhappy by what she had done, Miriam slowly walked on.

166

Doctor Charles finished yet another long and searching examination, and then while Miriam waited nervously, stood toying uneasily with his pince-nez.

At last he shook his head and told her gravely, 'I'm very sorry, Miss Josceleyne, but my tests of your sputa, and my examinations, have led me to conclude that you have contracted pulmonary phthisis.'

Even though in the bottom of her heart Miriam had been expecting this result, yet she could not help but clutch at any straw.

'Is that beyond doubt, Doctor? Could it not be just a bronchial infection, or a type of fever?'

Again he regretfully shook his head. 'I'm sorry, Miss Josceleyne. But there is no doubt. I have detected quantities of tubercle bacilli in your specimens of sputa, and of course your other symptoms and the results of my examinations all serve to confirm my diagnosis.'

He paused, then offered, 'Of course, if you so wish, you may obtain another opinion. I can recommend several very sound fellows in this field.'

Miriam shook her head. 'No, Doctor, that will not be necessary. I have every confidence in your professional judgement.'

He remained silent, giving her time to come to terms with what he had told her. Miriam felt confused and uncertain, yet strangely felt no fear. She was a well read and intelligent woman, and knew that this was not necessarily a death sentence.

'How serious is my condition?' she asked quietly, and added, 'and please, Doctor Charles, do not tell me anything less than the truth. I am not an hysterical woman, and am quite able to bear unpleasant news.'

He pondered briefly, then nodded. 'Very well, Miss Josceleyne, I shall comply with your wish. You have contracted the less serious form of phthisis, namely the chronic. I say less serious because the acute phthisis, otherwise known as galloping consumption, can lead to death very quickly. However, the chronic condition can be arrested, and even improved and virtually cured in many cases. Of course this necessitates a long and intensive regime of treatment.'

'Where would this treatment take place?' Miriam wanted to know.

'There are a wide variety of sanatoriums and hospitals specialising in the treatment of phthisis, both here and abroad, mostly at the seaside or in mountain regions where the air is pure and healthful. Naturally, I do not consider the London air to be at all beneficial, Miss Josceleyne – quite the opposite in fact. I consider London air, or indeed any city air to be deleterious in the extreme.'

'I would have to leave London then?' Miriam sought confirmation, and he nodded.

'Yes, that would be my advice to you.'

'Is it absolutely essential that I enter a hospital or sanatorium?' she questioned.

He paused before replying judiciously, 'There are several schools of thought regarding this matter within the medical profession, Miss Josceleyne. I am personally inclined to the belief that home treatment is better in the majority of cases, where the patient has the loving care and attention of their dear ones, and also has skilled medical help on call. That is with the proviso that the climate is temperate and healthy, and the physical surroundings comfortable and hygienic.'

He smiled kindly at her pale face, and suggested, 'Look, Miss Josceleyne. Why don't you spend a couple of days considering what you would prefer to do in the matter of treatment and care? Then come and see me again, and we will fully discuss all the options, and make the necessary arrangements to follow the course you finally decide upon.'

With relief she readily agreed, but asked one final question, 'How infectious is this disease, Doctor? Am I a danger to my acquaintances?'

'Not if certain precautions are taken on your part, Miss Josceleyne. You should always sleep alone if practicable; if not practicable then particular attention should be paid to having a good-sized and well ventilated bedroom. This must be kept very clean and well aired.

168

'It's generally accepted now that the tubercle bacilli can not be transmitted to others on the breath, so you may converse quite freely. Do not however kiss anyone on the mouth, and when you are forced to expectorate it is advisable to catch the sputa in a paper handkerchief and burn it immediately. Or alternatively there are pocket-flasks especially designed for this purpose which can be purchased from the chemist. You should put disinfectant into the flask before using it.'

He saw the fleeting expression of distaste upon her face, and told her sympathetically, 'I realise that for a gentle-lady such as yourself the crudity of such a proceeding can be very distressing. But you must not on any account swallow any expectorations. This can only spread the baccilli throughout the digestive organs of the body, and is a most dangerous proceeding. Therefore, Miss Josceleyne, you must overcome your feelings of delicacy in this matter for your own sake.

'I would also advise that your living apartments be frequently disinfected, and it is desirable that as little furnishings as possible be contained within them. Always use wet dusters when dusting, to prevent any dust-borne bacilli being inhaled.'

'What disinfectant should I use?' Miriam had become totally absorbed by what she was being told, so much so that it was almost as if she were discussing a stranger.

'A solution of carbolic acid, strength about one part in twenty should be perfectly adequate.'

After a brief exchange of other conversation Miriam took her leave and left, after making arrangements to call on the doctor within a couple of days.

Again she took her way homewards through the parkland, but this time she paid little heed to the people and surroundings she passed by. Instead she walked absorbed in her own thoughts, curiously examining her emotions.

She found that even though she had been given such grave news, paradoxically her mind was now much easier. The enemy had been identified, and now she could make plans for the battle against it. She would not allow herself

169

to countenance any possibility of defeat in this coming struggle. On the contrary, she felt a burgeoning confidence that she would gain the victory.

It was with almost a light heart that she arrived back at her rooms, and once there suddenly remembered the letter that Amelia Hunt had passed on to her. Finding her reading glasses she scanned the envelope, noting the Redditch postmark, and tore it open. It took only seconds to read the few lines contained on the sheet of notepaper, and as she absorbed the neatly penned words she felt a flash of anger at herself.

I've been so selfish these last years, she thought. So involved with what I was doing within the movement that I've paid little or no heed to what was happening back in Redditch. Poor Laura!

She stood staring at the sheet of notepaper for some seconds, visualising what grim reality and depth of torment lay hidden behind the restrained message contained in the brief sentences, and remorse assailed her.

I've been so selfish, so unforgivably selfish.

She went to look out of the window, peering across at the terrace of tall houses facing her. But she was not seeing those tall houses, instead she saw in her imagination the steep hilled, windswept streets of her native town. She smiled bleakly.

They're high enough.

Then she spoke aloud, conjuring up an image of the disease that was festering within her body. 'I don't need to go to any seaside shore or mountain top to fight you. I can do that equally well back at home. Back in Redditch.'

Chapter Eighteen

The House Full notice had been up since five minutes past seven o'clock; every bench in the auditorium was crammed, every side box filled to capacity except one. Seated in the shadows of that box John Purvis could not help but feel a pang of loneliness as he saw and heard the jovial family groups filling the other boxes, and the noisy camaraderie of the benches. He was a man who was comfortable with his own company, yet there were times such as the present, when he wished that he had a wife and loved ones to share pleasures with.

The curtain at the back of his box was suddenly thrust aside and Adrian West, bewigged and painted, wearing the costume of a Civil War Cavalier beckoned with his hand.

Purvis rose and went to him, and the other man apologised.

'I'm sorry to call you out here, John, but I don't want the audience to see me in costume before I make my entrance.'

In the badly lit passage way John Purvis could see the shadowed figures of a man and woman standing behind the actor, who went on speaking rapidly.

'My friends have only just now decided to come to the performance, Johnny, and there's not a vacant seat in the house. Would you mind if they shared your box?'

'Not at all, I shall enjoy having their company,' Purvis asserted.

'Thank you, Johnny. You're a pal!' The actor turned to the couple. 'Emma, Harry, let me introduce you to a newly-met friend of mine, Mr John Purvis.

'Johnny, allow me to present Mr Harry Vivaldi and Mrs Emma Vivaldi.'

As the woman moved forward, Johnny Purvis recognised her beautiful face instantly. It invoked a rush of painful memories, but his self-discipline enabled him to smile pleasantly, and tell her, 'It's been a long time since we last met, Mrs Vivaldi.'

'Oh, do you know each other?' the actor queried with surprise, and Emma, who was herself disconcerted with the shock of this unexpected encounter, nodded.

'Yes Adrian, Mr Purvis and I have met before.' Then, as she quickly recovered her poise, she chuckled with her customary gamine humour, 'But I was only a parlourmaid then, wasn't I, Mr Purvis. I bet that it's a surprise to have me sharing the best box in the house with you, isn't it?'

Purvis responded to her light-hearted question with an easy grin. He had always liked the pretty, pert young parlourmaid who had evolved now into this elegantly dressed, self-assured beauty.

'No, Mrs Vivaldi, I'm not really surprised. It was always obvious that you were destined to rise in the world.'

He shook hands with Harry Vivaldi, who smelled strongly of drink, and mumbled a few words which he slurred so badly that Purvis could not really understand what he had said.

The three of them seated themselves in the box, Emma in the centre with the two men flanking her, and West left them.

As soon as he was seated Harry produced a silver spirit flask and invited Purvis to take a drink from it. Purvis smiled and politely refused, and the other man shrugged and grimaced, then took a long pull from the flask himself. He belched loudly, then his head drooped slowly down until his chin was resting on his chest, and he began to snore.

Emma regarded her sleeping husband with undisguised contempt, and told Johnny Purvis, 'I've got a gift for choosing rotten husbands.'

The man made no immediate reply, only smiled noncommittally, and then told her quietly, 'I'd heard that

172

you married Hector Josceleyne, but I didn't know that you had married again.'

The young woman's expressive features were wryly resigned. 'Two years ago. He didn't drink so much then.'

Beneath the front of the stage was a small orchestra pit, occupied by a trio of musicians, a pianist, a drummer and a guitarist, who were playing a medley of popular airs, to which the rowdier elements of the audience were humming and whistling a discordant accompaniment.

The medley ended, the lights were lowered, and an expectant hush fell upon the auditorium. Then the stage curtains swung open to disclose a set representing the interior of a squalid miserable hut. A real woodfire was burning in a hearth, and there was a moaning of wind and a pattering of rain which sounded so realistic that a wag in the audience shouted:

'Better get your umbrellas opened, chaps!'

'Shhhh!'

'Be quiet!'

'Hush!'

'Shhh!'

The people around him angrily hissed for him to be quiet. Johnny Purvis could not help but smile, and beside him he heard Emma's throaty chuckle.

A voice came from offstage; 'Hullo! Daniel, art within?' There was a loud knocking. 'Daniel, I say, open will you . . .'

'Theer's nobody in, you silly bugger!' the wag in the audience shouted, provoking a mixed reaction of laughter and angry reproaches from the people around him.

The actor kicked the set-door open and entered on stage, making an exaggerated gesture of shock.

'Why, the hut's empty. Where's the old devil gone, I wonder?'

'I thought I saw him in the bar at the Sportsmans Arms!' the wag offered, and advised, 'I should pop down theer, if I was you, and see if he's still theer.'

Again there was an eruption of laughter and angry remonstrations from the audience, but the actor on stage manfully continued.

173

'. . . come in, master, out of the storm.'

And a second player entered.

'. . . Don't be afeared, he'll be a bit rusty to be sure, at our coming in without leave, but that will blow off sooner than the gale outside.'

The howling of the wind suddenly became extremely loud, and the sounds of rain intensified, forcing the newly entered player to shout his opening lines.

'Is the man away?'

'Nay, he's hauling up his boat on the bench, or taking in his nets, and making all snug and taut for the night . . .'

Emma moved her head close to Purvis' ear to whisper, 'What play is this?'

'*Daniel Druce, Blacksmith*.' He whispered back, and she smiled and nodded.

While Johnny Purvis was engrossed in watching the play, the young woman covertly studied his face, and her thoughts were troubled with pangs of regret and guilt as she mentally travelled back over the years.

She had been parlourmaid to Miss Miriam Josceleyne and her elderly father, Hector, at the Cotswold House when she had first met Johnny Purvis. Recently returned from the Boer War, he had come to Cotswold House seeking to purchase another property owned by the Josceleyne family.

Emma had become infatuated with the soldier, despite the difference in their ages, and had made plain to him her readiness to enter upon a romantic relationship. But he had not made any attempt to form any such relationship with her. Instead, to her chagrin, he had fallen in love with Miriam, a timid, frail-bodied, faded spinster, a twenty-eight-year-old virgin, whose self confidence and joy in her life had been ruthlessly crushed by her bullying tyrannical father and married elder brother, Franklin. Both men had treated Miriam as an unpaid handmaiden whose only role in life was to serve them, and obey their dictates without question.

Miriam had returned Johnny Purvis' feelings, and they had become lovers. The faded spinster had blossomed with her new-found love, and had regained self-confidence and joy in her life.

Although she had been a very kindly mistress to Emma, the young parlourmaid had bitterly resented the fact that Miriam had got the man that she, Emma, had panted for herself. And despite her undoubted fondness for her mistress, Emma had not been able to resist poisoning and destroying the relationship between the lovers when the opportunity arose to do so.

Ever since then Emma had been periodically tormented by remorse for what she had done. Particularly when she had seen how the destruction of her love affair had shattered all her mistress's newfound confidence and joy. After she had married Miriam's father, she had retained a close and loving relationship with her ex-mistress, and there had been times when she had been on the verge of confessing what she had done, and doing what she could to make amends. But somehow, when those moments had come, she had never been able to bring herself to make that confession, and still both Miriam and John remained in ignorance of the harm she had done to them.

The very close relationship with Miriam had finally been ruptured when Emma had insisted on marrying Harry Vivaldi, whom Miriam had loathed from the very first meeting with him. The elder woman truly desired Emma's happiness, but she had instinctively known that marriage to Harry would bring her young friend only disillusion and unhappiness. Emma had reacted viciously against the other woman's strictures, and they had quarrelled bitterly.

Miriam had met Laura Hughes, and through her had become increasingly more involved with the Women's Suffragette Movement, spending longer and longer periods away from Redditch. Then, when despite all advice and entreaty to the contrary Emma had married Harry, Miriam had left Cotswold House. From that time on the relationship between the two women had been strained and distant.

The action onstage continued and no further interruptions came from the wag. But Emma paid little or no attention to the proceedings. Instead she became totally absorbed in her covert regard of John Purvis. On her other

175

side her husband continued to snore in a drunken coma, and Emma could not help but wonder how her life would have been if instead of marrying Harry, she had instead married Johnny. The ex-soldier's hard face was now lined, and his close-cropped hair streaked with grey, but maturity suited him, and beneath his well-tailored clothing she sensed that his body was still lean and muscular. She found herself envisaging how it would feel to lie naked with him, close-locked in each others arms, and the heat of sexual wanting moistened her, and the nipples hardened on her firm breasts.

The attraction that Adrian West held for her was still there, but the knowledge that this quiet man beside her possessed a capacity for ruthless violence excited her. And the comparison between Purvis' past life and that of West diminished the latter in Emma's estimation.

The actor manager was now on stage, in the role of a colonel in the Royalist Army, playing the part of a battle-hardened, veteran soldier.

But that's all he's ever done, isn't it? Emma experienced a tinge of contempt. Spent his life dressing up in fancy clothes pretending to be what he's not, nor ever has been.

Again her eyes rested caressingly on Purvis' features. But Johnny here has really done exciting things, hasn't he. He's been a real soldier, and he's fought in real battles, and he's killed men who were trying to kill him ... including Arthur Dolton. He killed him with his bare hands.

The last thought intruded unbidden, but it did not repulse the young woman. Rather, it excited an ancient atavistic lust buried deep within her being.

The musicians suddenly struck up a hymn-like melody, and onstage the character Daniel Druce sank to his knees, cradling a prop baby in his arms, and declaimed, 'A miracle, a miracle! Down on your knees, down I say, for Heaven has worked a miracle to save me. I prayed that this might be, but scoffers mocked me when I prayed, and said that the days of miracles were passed.'

He lifted the prop baby high towards the ceiling.

176

'My Heaven-sent bairn, thou hast brought me back to reason, to manhood, to life!'

There were several others onstage now dressed as Royalist soldiers, and they clustered around the kneeling figure, one of them making as if to touch the baby.

Daniel Druce scowled, and shouted, 'Hands off, hands off! Touch not the Lord's gift! Touch not the Lord's gift!'

All the players struck dramatic poses and remained perfectly still in a living tableau as the music swelled and the drum thundered. Then as the audience burst into applause, Daniel Druce rose to his feet, smiling and bowing as the curtains closed.

'Did you see that? Did you see what that puffed-up fool did?'

The furious whisper came from the rear of the box, and Emma and Purvis turned in shock, to find West's angry face peering through the gap in the box curtain.

Emma assumed an expression of puzzlement, and enquired sweetly, 'What did who do, Adrian? What's upset you so?'

The actor scowled. 'Archibald Mannering. He's upset me. That puffed-up old cretin playing Druce!'

Emma shook her head, and baited with wide eyes, 'But he played the part very well, I thought. The audience loved him, that's why they applauded so.'

'Well he'll get no applause from me!' West declared fiercely. 'He ruined the tableau. How dare he take a bow at the end of the first act? The gall of the cretin! Standing there bowing and simpering like a damned old woman. That's all the old fool is anyway, a damned simpering old queen! He has no business trying to be an actor!

'Well he won't be bowing and simpering in a couple of seconds from now, I promise you. He'll be bloody well weeping!'

His irate face disappeared and they heard him stamping along the passageway. Emma and Johnny looked at each other and burst into laughter.

The lights went up, and during the interval people called to friends, left their seats to chat, or adjourned to the bar which had been set up at the rear of the auditorium by staff from the nearby Royal Hotel.

'Would you like something to drink?' Purvis invited, but Emma shook her head. Indicating her husband she said jokingly, 'He's already had sufficient for all the Vivaldi family.'

For the remainder of the interval they chatted easily about mutual acquaintances, but the one name that they both wanted above all others to introduce into the conversation remained unspoken. For Emma, it was guilt that prevented her from mentioning Miriam. For Johnny Purvis, it was a reluctance to risk reopening emotional wounds that were still not completely healed.

The second act began, and a sensation of close companionship rapidly developed btween the couple, as at intervals their eyes would meet and they would share a mutual reaction towards some incident in the play. Harry still snored and twitched, but for both of them it was as if they were alone in the box.

There was a spectacular finale to this act, when West rode the horse onstage, but the old mare was no actress, and quite ruined the dramatic effect by defecating loudly and odorously in the middle of West's impassioned speech. The audience roared and rocked with laughter, and deafening applause greeted the closing of the curtains with the old mare whinnying and tossing its head as if delighted by the plaudits.

'I'll bet you that Adrian will be here in a second or two to threaten he'll murder the horse for stealing the scene from him,' Johnny quipped, and Emma's laughter pealed high. Then her head rolled and she held her stomach as, as if on cue, the actor's furious face appeared from the gap in the curtain behind them.

'Did you see that? Did you see that damned old nag?'

He glared ferociously at the couple as they both roared helplessly, unable to speak to him, and then he stormed off along the passageway once more.

Slowly their laughter stilled, and Emma experienced a sudden intense sad regret, and she whispered, 'Why couldn't it have been you and I who got married, Johnny? We would have made each other happy, you know.'

178

Her words sobered him, and he looked at her intently. Then answered quietly, 'It wasn't mean't to be, was it, Emma?'

It was as if a barrier suddenly dissolved in the young woman's mind, and compelled by an irresistible compulsion, she told him, 'It was my fault that you and Miss Miriam parted, Johnny. And I'm truly sorry for it.'

He stared at her in puzzlement. 'How was it your fault? You had nothing to do with what happened between me and Arthur Dolton.'

'No, I had nothing to do with that.' Her voice was low-pitched and husky, and she nervously entwined and twisted her fingers. But she kept her black eyes fixed on his, and continued on to tell him.

'That letter, the one that your friend brought to Miriam from you, when you were in the police cells. After you'd killed Dolton.'

'What about it?' he interrupted.

Emma drew a long shuddering breath, and for the first time her eyes slid away from his. She could not look at him and her terrible stress made her revert to the speech patterns of her childhood as she blurted out, 'Miss Miriam never read it. I never showed it to her. I read it and tore it up, then made up the message to send back to you. I told your friend to tell you that Miss Miriam never wanted to see or to hear from you ever again. I took a chance on that, because knowing the sort of chap you was, I thought that your own pride 'ud stop you pestering any 'ooman who'd said she didn't want you.'

Now she did force herself to look directly at him once more, and the nervous twining and twisting of her fingers stilled to a savage gripping which whitened her knuckles with strain.

'Knowing her like I did, I knew that she'd be too broken up by what had happened to do anything but sit and cry. I knew that she'd never be able to pluck up the courage to face you or Cleopatra Dolton herself. All her pride had been took from her, you see, and what bit of self-confidence she'd managed to build up had been knocked down again. And when you was sent to prison

179

and she wrote letters to you, I took 'um and burned 'um, then told her I'd posted 'um to you. So that when she never got no reply she'd think that you didn't want her. And I told her all that folks was saying, about you and Cleopatra Dolton being lovers. That all the time that you was telling Miss Miriam that you loved her, you was going with the Dolton 'ooman.'

The expression on his features was metamorphosing from puzzlement to dawning anger to murderous fury, as he thought through what she had said. For a moment or two a rush of fear made it impossible for her to continue. But then she fought back that fear, and forced herself to go on.

'And because of all that, Miss Miriam believed that you and Cleopatra Dolton were lovers. And that you killed Arthur Dolton because you wanted his wife. And God forgive me, I let her go on believing that. Then she went to live in the Clee Hills for a time to get away from the sneering and talking about you and Cleopatra Dolton. And I still never said anything of the truth to her. I know it was wicked and evil of me, but I couldn't help meself, Johnny.

'I'd never knew a chap like you. And I wanted you for meself. I was so bloody jealous, I was like a mad 'ooman. But I'm sorry for it now, Johnny. I'm sorry I hurt you both like I did. I'm truly sorry!'

The auditorium lights dimmed, and the curtains parted for the next act. Daniel Druce began to speak.

'Eventide, and he's not yet come to claim her. It's hard to have to creep away like a thief in the night, but that it should have come . . .'

John closed his eyes, and his hands clenched into fists.

Emma went on babbling her protestations of apology and regret and remorse, and her words mingled with the words of Daniel Druce and filled John's head with a meaningless, tormenting cacophany.

'. . . through him . . . I'm sorry . . . whom I loved like a . . . I'se cursed meself ever since . . . like a son . . . I wished I'd never done . . . it's doubly hard . . . Miss Miriam was broken-'earted . . . Well, it's better so . . . I'd do anything,

anything . . . it's better so . . . Forgive me . . . Forgive . . . Forgive me . . .'

He could not stand to remain in this box for a moment longer. He shook his head wildly, and jumping to his feet, left the young woman still desperately pleading.

Outside the theatre building the wide yard was seemingly deserted, but the voice of Daniel Druce still carried faintly to his ears.

'. . . would lift that sorrow from her gentle heart.'

Purvis grinned savagely at the irony of that sentence.

'Lift that sorrow from her gentle heart,' he repeated. 'Lift that sorrow from her gentle heart.'

He walked away from the brightly illuminated façade.

'Lift that sorrow from her gentle heart.'

From behind him came the pattering of hurrying feet and his name was called.

'Johnny! Johnny wait! Please wait!'

It was Emma, and he sighed heavily, and a curious stillness overlaid the tumultuous swirlings of his emotions. For all his adult life Purvis had been a fatalist, believing implicitly in a predestined pattern of life. And now that implicit belief enabled him to come to a standstill, and turn towards the oncoming woman. She reached him, and in the reflected lights of the theatre's façade he saw the tears glistening on her cheeks.

'Do you hate me, Johnny?' she demanded chokingly. 'Do you hate me for what I'se done to you and Miss Miriam?'

'Do I hate you?' he repeated aloud, and then almost musingly said it again. 'Do I hate you?'

He pondered silently for some moments, examining his own thoughts and emotions. And was finally able to shake his head and tell her truthfully, 'No Emma. No, I don't hate you.'

She broke into harsh sobs, covering her face with her hands, her body bent and shuddering. For a few seconds he remained still, watching her outburst of grief. Then pity filled him, and he drew her close, gently cradling her head against his chest.

'There now, don't cry,' he soothed gently, stroking her hair with one hand, holding her close with the other.

181

'Don't cry, Emmy. It's all long over and done with now so don't cry. Don't cry . . .'

Chapter Nineteen

Sunday morning dawned fresh and fine, and Johnny Purvis rose from his bed as the chorusing of the birds saluted the coming of day. He flung open the window and stared out across the wooded hillside that stretched downwards into the rich green fertile valley of the River Arrow. Along the far horizon the sun was already rising, and the man drew in deep draughts of the pure sweet air. His mood matched the morning. He felt fresh and alert and eager to meet the promise of the day.

He shucked off his nightshirt and padded on bare feet into the bathroom. While the bath filled with hot water from the gas-geyser he stropped his razor, lathered his chin and throat, and shaved carefully, enjoying the rasping hiss of the honed steel reaping the tough bristles from his skin.

While soaking in the bath he thought back on the happenings of the previous night. He felt no lingering vestiges of anger or resentment against Emma. What she had done could not be altered now, and fatalist that he was, he was able to accept that nothing could have prevented it. And he recognised that her grief and remorse were genuine and deeply felt. Forgiving her had been easier than he had ever imagined forgiveness for a bitter injury could be. They had parted as friends. But before they had parted outside the theatre she had told him all that she could concerning Miriam.

He smiled in wry amazement as he remembered what he had been told. The Miriam he had first known, quiet, nervous, drab little churchmouse, who would not have dared say boo to a goose, had become a militant

183

suffragette, defying the government, the police, and the whole of the male sex. To the forefront in demonstration and conflict, and a familiar with the insides of police and prison cells.

At first he had hardly been able to believe what he was hearing. But later, when he had had time to reflect, he remembered the times during their love affair when she had acted contrary to people's perception of her character, when she had displayed flashes of stubborn courage and determination, and unexpected confidence.

His smile broadened now as he thought about those times. Then he suddenly questioned this present happiness he was experiencing; and realised that it was engendered by the fact that what he had believed to be her rejection of him those seven long years past, had in fact been no rejection at all. That she had loved him despite what had happened between himself and Dolton. That it was someone else's lies and treachery that had thrust them apart, and not a cessation of either's love for the other.

Now he felt a brimming of hope. He had never stopped loving Miriam, not through the years in prison, not since his release, when he had travelled the world in the vain endeavour to find another life for himself, not now, today, back here in the town of his birth.

Emma had promised him that she would now confess to Miriam what she, Emma, had done.

'After Emma's done that, then I'm going to go to Miriam myself, and find out if she still has any love left for me. And if she has . . . ' He smiled happily, ' . . . if she has, then we've still got the rest of our lives to spend together.'

After he had finished bathing, John dressed himself in riding clothes, then went down to the kitchen to brew himself a pot of coffee.

Although he was a very wealthy man Johnny Purvis kept no living-in servants. For most of his life he had lived in intimate proximity with others, as a boy in his parents' cramped terraced cottage, as a youth and man in barrackrooms, camps and bivouacs, ships' cabins and prison cells. Now he was enjoying the peace and tranquillity of his large house, preferring solitude to

184

enforced company – although he readily admitted that he would be more than happy to share that peace and tranquillity with the woman he loved.

He employed a married couple who lived nearby to do the various domestic chores. The husband cared for the grounds, stables and horses; the woman cleaned and cooked occasionally when needed. He paid them well, and treated them kindly, but they knew that should they try to take advantage of his easy-going nature, then he would discharge them from his employment without hesitation. He expected an honest return for his money, and up to this point in time, they had given him that honest return.

'Mr Purvis, are you there?'

It was Terry Perkins, the youngest son of the married couple, who was shouting outside the kitchen door.

Purvis unlocked the door and invited the boy inside.

'Come and have some coffee, Terry.'

The lad, rosy cheeked and sturdy, came smiling into the large room.

'Am you gooing to ride the new 'un this morning, Mr Purvis?' he questioned eagerly. 'He looks a real beauty, doon't he? Has you got a name for him yet?'

'Not yet.' The man poured out a mug of coffee and pushed it towards the boy. 'Here you are, help yourself to cream and sugar. Do you want anything to eat?'

'No thanks, Mr Purvis, me Mam fried me some bread for me breakfast.'

Purvis chuckled, 'Well, another breakfast isn't going to make you overfat, Terry, and I'm having some myself anyway.'

He placed a large iron skillet on the gas stove and sliced several thick rashers of bacon from one of the joints hanging from the roof beams. Then, as the appetising scents of the frying meat filled the air, he sliced tomatoes and cracked open eggs and put them to cook in the sizzling bacon fat.

'There's a loaf and butter in that cupboard, Terry – fetch them out, will you.'

As soon as the food was cooked he divided it equally between two large platters, and grinned amusedly as he

185

watched the rosy-cheeked boy set to eating with tremendous gusto. He chewed steadily himself, relishing the crisp, salt-cured bacon, the rich taste of the big-yolked eggs, the faintly acidic tang of the tomatoes, the yeasty crusty bread and creamy butter.

Appetites satisfied, they leaned back in their chairs, and John lit a cigarette, and for perhaps the eighth thousandth time in his life revelled in that most pleasurable satisfaction of his addiction, the day's first fragrant taste of tobacco smoke.

Between taking gulps from his third mug of coffee, Terry Perkins questioned, 'How much did the new 'un cost, Mr Purvis?' His eyes were shining with excitement. 'Me Dad reckons it must have cost more nor a hundred sovereigns.'

He looked awed at the immensity of such a sum.

'That's an awful lot o' money, arn't it, Mr Purvis. Me Dad reckons its more nor he earns in five years.'

Johnny Purvis chuckled wryly. 'If that's the case, Terry, then your dad must be working for somebody else, and I've got a chap here pretending to be your dad. Because the chap who comes here costs me a sight more than that for five years' work.'

The boy disregarded that answer – he was still intent upon his question. 'How much did the new 'un cost, Mr Purvis?'

'Now Terry, you know that a gentleman never discloses the price he pays for a horse, don't you?' the man teased gently.

The boy's face fell with disappointment and, relenting, Purvis told him.

'Well, if you must know, Terry, I paid Walter Read eighty-five pounds for him. If he'd been in perfect condition I would have gladly paid a hundred and twenty pounds, but he's got a slight fault in the near fore fetlock. There's a bit of filling there. Come on, I'll show you what I mean.'

The man and boy went out to the stable block, and Purvis led the newly purchased horse out into the stable yard. For almost an hour he instructed the eager-to-learn youngster in the finer points of judging the condition and value of horses.

'I'm finishing school this year, you know, Mr Purvis,' the boy informed him, when the lesson was over and Purvis was saddling the horse.

'Are you looking forward to that, Terry?'

'Oh yes, I hates school. I wants to come and work for you, Mr Purvis. I could look after your horses.'

'I've only got three, Terry, the man pointed out, 'and two of those are going to be put out to grass very shortly.'

'Well, couldn't I be your servant then, Mr Purvis? You know, like the Earl as got a servant just for hisself.'

He was referring to the Earl of Plymouth, whose family seat was Hewell Grange, some three miles from the town.

The man smiled kindly, 'Perhaps your dad has other plans for your future, Terry?'

The boy pulled a face. 'Me Dad wants me to goo and work in a factory, like our kid, but I'd hate that. Our kid hates it as well, but me Dad wun't let him leave theer. I wants to come and work for you.'

Purvis shrugged, and reflected for a moment, then told him, 'I'll tell you what, Terry. If when you leave school you've still got a mind to work for me, then you ask your father to come and have a chat with me at that time, and we'll see if something can be sorted out.'

'Oohhh thanks, Mr Purvis. I'll tell me Dad today to come and see you, shall I?' the boy crowed with delight.

'Alright Terry, you do that,' the man surrendered ruefully. He mounted the horse, and with a wave to the boy, trotted away.

Purvis' home, Grange House, was an ancient, tall-chimneyed building constructed from grey stone. It had small arrow-slitted turrets, mossy-tiled, steep-gabled roofs, and its latticed windows were set deep into its weathered sides. Its history stretched back to the Cistercian Abbey of Bordesley, the ruins of which lay in the Abbey Meadows at the base of the Fish Hill, north of the town. Its name was derived from the fact that it had originally been one of the monks' grange farms.

The house was surrounded by a wide square of

greensward, which in its turn was surrounded by thick woodlands. A winding driveway connected the green-sward with Mount Pleasant, the long southward rising ridgeway that connected Redditch to its satellite villages. The driveway itself was like a tunnel, overhung by masses of branches and sided by thick underbrush and shrubbery. Its entrance was between a row of terraced houses and a factory, and sentinelled by two huge chestnut trees.

Each time Purvis entered between those mighty chestnut trees and travelled along that winding green tunnel cut off from sound and sight of Mount Pleasant, his senses filled with the soughing of wind, the rustling of leaves, the scents of trees and grasses; it was as if he were travelling back through the ages. And each time he came to the open greensward and saw the ancient greystone building untouched and unchanged by the passage of the centuries he experienced a never diminishing thrill of pleasure.

But he was a man of this new century also, and appreciated the advances in science that made life more pleasant and easy. He had had water, gas and electricity supplies connected to Grange House, and a modern sewerage system constructed. But the supply lines and pipes were hidden deep underground, and he had spent a great deal of money to employ expert craftsmen to install the indoor-fittings so that the very minimum of alteration was created to the interior fabric of the house.

He guided his horse through the green tunnel at a walk, letting the animal become accustomed to its new rider's voice and body as he talked to it and patted its neck. Once out on Mount Pleasant he turned northwards down the long slope towards the town's centre.

At this early hour the streets were quiet and almost deserted, with only the occasional passerby. But Johnny Purvis knew that before too long the godly would begin to come forth and congregate for the Sabbath Day, and the numerous chapels would resound with massed voices offering their thanks and praises to the Lord.

Purvis grimaced with faint distaste. His own father had been a fire and brimstone lay preacher, and although he had always loved that dour, grim man, it was not until a couple of years before the old man's death that he had ever managed to achieve any closeness with him. The love Ezra Purvis bore for his God had seemed to take precedence over the love he had for his wife and family; and this early experience of religious fervour had prejudiced John against those who too loudly professed to adore the Lord.

He moved slowly through the grimy red-brick terraces, with their numerous alehouses and even more numerous workshops and small factories, noting how many of these latter buildings still possessed the multi-serried windows of the needlemakers.

Redditch and its satellite villages and hamlets were collectively known as the Needle District, a title gained by being the world centre for the production of all types of that article. This nomenclature was now becoming a source of resentment to certain sections of its population, because the district was also the world centre for the manufacturing of fishing tackle, and the people engaged in that trade thought that the district should take its fame from their work. In turn this was disputed by the steel spring workers, and by the cycle and motorcycle manufacturers, who thought that their newer industries should now take the precedence in naming the district.

Purvis grinned as he thought of this feuding.

'No matter what they call the place, it'll still be the same dirty, rough old town . . . And I'll still love it!'

He had travelled in a meandering circle and was now approaching the forked junction of Alcester and Red Lion Streets, east of Church Green. He halted the horse at that junction and sat for a few seconds deciding which direction he would now go in. Turn down Alcester Street which would bring him to other roads leading eventually down to the flat meadows of the Arrow Valley, or continue on towards the central crossroads? Then his attention was caught by the figure of a man dressed only in collarless shirt, trousers and boots running towards him from Church Green East.

As the man neared him Purvis recognised Harry Vivaldi's features, and he raised a hand and went to call out to him. Then instantly he lowered that hand and peered curiously. Vivaldi's face was pallid and sweating, his mouth wide as he panted desperately for breath. Eyes wildly staring, he lurched past near to where Purvis waited, but did not appear to be aware of either the horse or its rider.

'What in hell's name is up with the man?'

Purvis watched Vivaldi stumbling along Red Lion Street, and spurred his mount into a trot to follow. He was fast gaining on Vivaldi when the running man suddenly disappeared around the corner of George Street. Johnny Purvis reached that corner just in time to see Vivaldi disappear into an entryway about halfway up the street's length.

'Walk on.' Purvis moved slowly up the street, by now made intensely curious by Vivaldi's strange actions and demeanour. 'Could anything have happened to Emma?' he wondered. 'By the look of Vivaldi something is obviously wrong.'

Opposite the dark, covered entry he brought his horse to a halt, peering curiously at the shabby tenements facing him. Their curtains were drawn, and the entire street seemed to be still asleep.

Then he remembered. 'These houses are back to backs, aren't they? So Vivaldi has gone to the rear row. He'll not be inside one of these front ones.'

Impelled by an overwhelming curiosity Purvis dismounted and tethered the horse to a convenient bollard. Then he cautiously entered the dark entryway, and moved stealthily along it to emerge into the narrow, foul-smelling courtyard at its far end.

The inhabitants of the row of four houses appeared, like their neighbours in the street, to be asleep. Every curtain was drawn, no smoke rose from the chimneys, no sound of voices or smells of cooking issued from the shrouded interiors.

For some time Johnny Purvis remained standing in the centre of the row, listening hard. Then shrugged and mentally chided himself, 'You're behaving like a bloody peeping Tom! You'd better just go on along and mind your own business.'

With that he turned on his heel and walked away, his boot heels striking the ground and spurs jingling metallically as he abandoned stealth.

Inside the darkened room, Harry Vivaldi crouched in body-torturing rigidity, sweat pouring from him, breath drawn in strangled wheezes, eyes wild and bloodshot, his terrified thoughts racing frantically as he listened to the impacting boot heels and jingling spurs.

It was long long minutes before he could be satisfied that the spurred interloper had definitely gone, and he could recommence his feverish inspection of the mortared joints between the stone slabs of the floor.

Chapter Twenty

The rhythmic swaying of the carriage, combined with the metallic clicking of wheels on rail ties, created a hypnotic effect which had lulled Miriam into sleep, and she awoke with a start as the train juddered to a hissing, clanking halt.

'Redditch, Redditch. Next stops Studley, Alcester, Evesham, Ashford . . . Redditch. Redditch.'

The raucously shouting porter passed the carriage, and heavy doors opened and slammed shut along the length of the train as passengers got on and off.

'Porter?' Miriam beckoned another man to her. 'I need my trunk from the guard's van.'

She waited until she had seen the trunk safely deposited in the left luggage office, and putting the receipt into her reticule, she walked out of the station approaches and up the Unicorn Hill.

It was midday and noisy, horseplaying groups of young girls and youths released from the noisy stuffy factories and workshops for a brief hour of freedom thronged the roadway and pavements.

The sun was high and very hot and the air seemed stale and turgid as Miriam breathed it into her damaged lungs. Her feelings were somewhat ambiguous – pleasure at being back home, mingled with apprehension at what she might find here.

Outside the Lamb and Flag public house men and youths, uniform in their down-at-heel shabbiness, lounged against the peeling paintwork of the front windows. In front of the tumbledown tenements of Hill Street haggard women sat on doorsteps, stools and old wooden chairs, some suckling rag-swaddled babies at their flaccid breasts,

192

others engaged in desultory conversation as they watched the older infants playing listlessly in the dirt.

Voices stilled as the neatly dressed woman passed; and hostile eyes studied her. But no one challenged her passage. A frail-looking creature such as she could present no threat. A couple of the women recognised her and told their friends, 'That's Miss Josceleyne, that is. Her's a friend o' Laura's. Her's one o' them suffragettes.'

This information was received with widely differing reactions.

'If them bleedin' suffragettes had 'usbands and kids to look arter, they 'udden't have bleedin' time to goo gallivanting about like they does.'

'They'm all rich that lot am! Lucky sods!'

'What they says is right. If us women did have a vote then things 'ud be better for us.'

Miriam kept her eyes firmly fixed ahead of her. She was not afraid of these rough-looking women, but she did not want to be detained from her primary purpose. So she avoided catching anyone's eye and being engaged in conversation.

In the rancid smelling court Laura's front door was open, and when Miriam looked through it she saw her friend seated at the small table, body slumped forwards, her head cradled upon her arms.

'Laura?' Miriam called softly.

The young woman lifted her head, and her grey eyes were filled with tears. Smiling through her tears and without speaking she rose and came to Miriam, and they fell into each other's arms.

Later, when the first emotion of their reunion had spent itself they moved to sit facing each other across the table and in turn related what had happened to each of them since their parting so many long months ago. They shared both joy and laughter, tears and sadness, and found an assuagement of their own bleak personal loneliness in each other's company.

Miriam made no mention of her illness. In her turn Laura forbore from relating just how bitter her privations had been since she had broken her arm. But both women's eyes noted the newly formed patternings of lines around eyes and mouths, and the painful wastage of flesh. At last, they fell silent, and sat for a time in companionable silence, the realisation of just how much their friendship meant to each other burgeoning anew within their hearts and minds.

It was Miriam who broke the silence.

'I want to ask a favour of you, my dear.'

Laura Hughes smiled ruefully. 'Well of course I'll do anything that you ask of me, Miriam. But at present my usefulness is somewhat limited. It will be a few more weeks before my arm is fully healed.'

'That makes no matter,' the older woman assured her. 'I'm going to take a house here in town and I want you to do me the favour of living there with me.'

Laura's thin features became troubled, and she appeared to be seeking for words. Then she replied hesitantly, 'I'm very grateful that you should offer me such a kindness, Miriam, but I can't bring myself to live off your charity. I'm finding the fact that I'm on Poor Relief a bitter enough pill to swallow. I couldn't bear to sponge off a dear friend.'

'Nonsense!' Miriam waved the statement aside. 'I'm not offering charity, my dear.' She decided to be completely honest about her illness. 'In all truth, Laura, I need someone to keep house for me. You see, I've become consumptive!'

'Oh no!' the younger woman exclaimed softly in dismay.

Miriam was quick to reassure her friend. 'It's not life-threatening, Laura. If I take care, and follow the necessary regimen, then the doctor has assured me that I'll make old bones. But I have to rest as much as possible until my condition is stabilised. So you see, I am in desperate need of someone to keep house for me.

'It's not charity I'm offering to you, Laura, but a proper job. If you won't accept it, then I'll have to employ someone else. A stranger perhaps. And I'd hate that. So please, Laura, please say that you'll come and live with me.'

She paused, and then added another inducement, 'Tommy can come and live with us as well. And we can

194

employ someone to help us with him if need be . . . Please say that you'll come, Laura. Please, I really need you.'

The younger woman pondered briefly, then nodded and smiled. 'Of course I'll come, Miriam, and gladly.'

Chapter Twenty-One

'Right then, stand by Beatie, make ready Archibald . . . Lights, Henry!'

The huge arc lamps crackled and hissed, and bright white light shone onto the raised platform on which a scene had been set of an opulent room interior.

'Action!' West shouted, and began to crank the handle of the camera.

Beatrice de la Fournay, dressed in a ball gown and glittering with paste jewellery, came onstage followed by Archibald Mannering, resplendent in the scarlet, blue and gold of a general's dress uniform. They began to act out a scene in which the general was to inform the heroine that his son Harry, her fiancé, who was fighting the Boers in South Africa, had been reported missing.

While they played the scene Adrian West kept up a constant shouted barrage of instructions.

'Full face to the camera, Beatie . . . Show more manly grief Mannering, you old fool. More bloody manly sadness. No, not like you're crying over spilt milk, man. You're supposed to be a general, not a bloody old queen! Begin to swoon, Beatie! I said begin to, not bloody well do it! You cretin! Cut! Cut! Cut! Damn and blast it! Can't either of you two follow a simple instruction? Damm and blast you both! You're bloody useless, the pair of you! Bloody moronic!'

As he ranted and raved the elderly Archibald Mannering stood stoically enduring. But the fiery tempered Beatie tore off her tiara and hurled it at him, as she shrieked:

'Don't bawl at me! I'm not one of the bloody walk – ons! I

don't want to do this anyway, it's all extra. And we're not getting paid for it, are we?'

'I pay you too much already,' West bawled back at her, and for a couple of minutes they swopped insults, then the woman tore off the rest of her jewellery and threw it down.

'That's it! I'm off! You can find somebody else to do it!' She stormed from the platform and out of the shed.

Sitting to the side of the camera Emma smothered a fit of laughter at the bemused expression on Adrian's face.

After a few seconds he recovered his customary aplomb, and shouted, 'Kill the lights, Henry.'

He turned towards Emma and shrugged, then chuckled as he saw her fruitless attempt to hide her amusement.

'I'm a martyr to Beatie's artistic temperament.'

'Do you still need me here, Mr West?' Archibald Mannering asked timidly.

West shook his head, then almost instantly changed his mind.

'Wait a while, will you Archie.'

He eyed Emma speculatively. She sensed what was in his mind, and shook her head.

'No, Adrian! I'm no actress!'

'You could become one, Emma.'

'I couldn't!'

'How do you know that, until you've tried?'

'I'll only make a fool of myself. People will laugh at me.'

'No, nobody will laugh at you. There isn't any audience, is there? You'll be acting only for me, and for the camera. Don't you want to see yourself in a moving picture? It will be great fun, I promise you! Great fun.'

Emma was becoming less vehement in her refusal. The novel prospect of seeing herself in a real moving picture was very tempting, and as the man continued to coax and cajole she weakened rapidly.

'But I don't know the words of the part.' Her protest lacked any real force.

'That doesn't matter for now.' West had been nurturing the idea of putting Emma into his pictures ever since he had first met her, and now he was eager to bring that idea

197

to fruition. 'I'll explain what I want you to do, and I'll talk you through it. This will be just an experiment to see how the camera likes you, Emma. Please do this for me. I promise that if you don't enjoy it, then I'll never ask you to do it again.'

At last Emma surrendered. Her lively sense of adventure was by now sparking at this novel experience.

'But I'm not made-up or costumed for it,' she stated.

'That doesn't matter.' West reached out his hand to help her to rise. 'All that needs to be done is for you to take off your hat. Otherwise the lights will cast your face into shadow.'

As soon as she had removed her wide-brimmed hat he guided her up onto the platform.

'Lights, Henry.'

Again the great arc lamps crackled and hissed, and bright white light shone onto the platform.

'Just stand facing the camera, Emma, while I check the lens focus again.'

He quickly swung aside the wooden film magazine and inserted the framed ground glass. The focusing was soon done, and he returned to Emma onstage.

'Now listen carefully, my dear. You are going to be told that your fiancé, the man you love above all others in the world, is missing in action. I want you to forget everything around you, and concentrate only on that dreadful news. I want you to react as if it were reality, and not make believe.

'When I shout "action" this time, Archibald will come to stand here on this spot and he'll tell you the awful news. All you have to do, is to react to that. You needn't speak if you don't want to. And remember to remain facing the camera.'

He left her, and Emma felt apprehensive, tense and excited all at the same time. Anticipation swelling within her made her throat feel constricted, and her breath hard to draw. The heat of the great arc lamps bathed her face, and her heart started to beat ever more rapidly. In her mind she could still hear Adrian's words repeating over and over again, 'Awful news. Awful news. Awful news.'

'Action!'

Archibald Mannering's thickly painted features appeared before her and she heard his voice.

'Charles is reported missing in action, it is believed that he is dead.'

Emma abruptly lost all sense of her own identity. It seemed that her mind was no longer the mind of the woman named Emma Vivaldi. Her being, her persona, her very soul, was no longer Emma Vivaldi. Instead she was a young woman who had just been informed that her beloved fiancé, a man whom she worshipped mentally and physically, had been cruelly torn from her. The shock was at first numbing, and she could only stare blankly at the bringer of this terrible news, and shake her head in denial.

'No, No. That's not true. It can't be true!'

Savage grief tore at her, her fists clenched and lifted and she threw back her head and screamed in denial.

'NOOOOOO!'

Blackness swam before her eyes, blotting out all light, and she swayed and crumpled to the ground.

'Cut! Cut! Cut!' West shouted and came on-stage, his face glowing with enthusiasm.

'Wonderful, Emma. You were wonderful! Wasn't she, Archie; wasn't she, Henry? You were wonderful! Absolutely wonderful!'

Emma opened her eyes, and found that she was once again herself. She grinned up into the man's excited face.

'You're only saying that so that you can have your wicked way with me, aren't you, Adrian,' she teased, but inside she was exulting.

'Listen Emma, let's try something else, shall we? This time I want Archibald to tell you that your fiancé, who had been reported missing, has now been found, safe and well.

'Do you understand, my dear? You're a young woman who has been grieving for her dead fiancé, but now you are going to be told that he isn't dead after all, he's alive and well.'

Elated by this totally new experience, this discovery within herself of a talent which she had been totally unaware of possessing, Emma eagerly agreed.

199

This time, as she waited for Adrian to call 'action' there was no trace left of her previous sense of apprehension. Instead, as she thought of her dead fiancé, she felt an all pervading depression weighing heavily upon her. Her existence was bleak, pointless, and she had no real desire to continue living. Death would come as a loving friend to take her in its arms and bear her away into dark oblivion.

She saw Archibald's face grinning happily at her, and felt anger that he should be happy, when her own beloved Charles was lying rotting in his grave.

The fool's got no right to be happy. No right, no right.

'Charles is alive! Alive! Charles is alive and well!'

She heard the words, and jerkily mouthed them back at the man as if she could not comprehend their meaning.

'Alive? Charles is alive? Alive?'

A spark of hope flared deep within her being, and she was suddenly filled with a terrible fear that those words had been only figments of her imagination.

'Alive? You are telling me that my Charles is alive?' she challenged fiercely, demanding that he convince her that those words were true.

'Yes, Charles is alive!' the man repeated forcefully, and an almost unbearable sense of relief and happiness erupted in her mind. Tears of joy cascaded down her cheeks, and she could only smile and let those tears fall freely.

'Cut! Cut! Cut!'

West shouted, and again came to her in excited, smiling congratulation.

This time Archibald Mannering added his own plaudits without any prompting from West, telling Emma in all sincerity, 'That was marvellous, Mrs Vivaldi. A truly marvellous bit of business.'

Now it was Emma who was begging West, 'Let's try something else, Adrian. Can I try something else? Tell me what to do next! Tell me!'

For more than an hour West tested Emma with widely differing scenarios. He called for her to portray ever varying degrees of happiness, sadness, excitement, slyness, wickedness, cruelty, joy, grief, kindness, piety, despair, doubt; and over and over again Emma found that, chameleon-like, she could assume whatever colouring of emotion was needed, and that more than assume that emotion, she actually experienced it.

At length West called a halt, and told Emma in a voice husky with feeling, 'I knew it from the first time I ever talked with you, Emma. You were born to act in the moving pictures. I'm going straight away now to get this film processed. If the camera likes you even a tenth as much as I think it will, you'll be a sensation!'

Until such time as he should set up his own film processing and drying rooms West had come to an arrangement with a local photographer, Walter Terry, whose premises were situated towards the southern end of Evesham Street, next door to the offices of Dolton Enterprises.

Ozzie Clark was standing in the doorway of Dolton Enterprises when the flamboyant figure of the actor/manager swept towards him, cloak flying, wide-brimmed hat set at a rakish angle.

'You're in a hurry, Mr West; is there a fire?' he asked jokingly.

The other man laughed, and tapped the can of film he was carrying with his well-manicured fingernails.

'I believe I've something in here to set the world in flames, Mr Clarke.'

Clarke was already interested in the other man's plans to make moving pictures, and now his curiosity was instantly aroused.

'Have you made a picture then?'

'Not a picture as such, Mr Clarke. But I've just filmed a young lady whom I believe well may prove to be the finest moving picture actress in the country.' He bowed gallantly. 'Now please excuse me, I must hurry.'

He swept on and disappeared into Walter Terry's shop. Almost an hour elapsed, and Ozzie was sitting at his desk when the actor reappeared in the office.

'Mr Clarke, the house in George Street that I've taken over the lease of?'

'What about it?'

201

'I'd like to use it as my film processing laboratory. Walter Terry is doing the work for me at the moment, but it's not really satisfactory. I need my own premises.'

Clarke opened one of the desk drawers and drew out a sheaf of papers.

'Let's see now, that's in Number Seven Court, isn't it?' He quickly glanced through the papers. Then informed West, 'It's one of the tenements that we intend to refurbish and modernise this year.'

He pursed his lips and thought for a few seconds.

'This processing laboratory. Does it mean that you'd have to alter the fabric of the building?'

'No, not at all. I just need to install some washing and developing tanks, and fit up a drying room where I can hang the film.'

'But how about when the workmen need to pipe the gas and bring in the watermain connection? Would they be able to do so without you needing to move out?'

'I would think that we could arrive at some satisfactory working arrangement, Mr Clarke.'

Again Clarke pursed his lips thoughtfully. Then he offered, 'Look, how about you and I going there now, and you can show me what you would actually need to be doing there.'

West readily agreed, and Clarke selected a bunch of keys from the board where dozens of other key-bunches were hanging, put on his curly-brimmed bowler, and led the other man from the offices.

As they walked to George Street Clarke bombarded the other man with questions about the moving picture business. West replied with obvious enthusiasm, telling his companion of his dreams of creating great pictures. He also had another motive for convincing Clarke that there were fortunes to be made in this new and exciting medium. His own finances were by now being stretched to the limit, and he knew that to bring his dreams to reality he was going to need more ready money than he and his partner, Emma, could command. His dreams of recreating great events would entail the employment of thousands of extras and lavish sets and costumes, and this

202

in turn would necessitate spending very large sums of money. West was now actively seeking investors. And although he was uncertain as to how rich the man with him might be, he had made enough enquiries to know that Clarke's employer, Cleopatra Dolton, was very wealthy indeed, and he hoped to get to her money through this man who was her trusted business manager.

As they went through the gloomy entryway and into the court they heard the sounds of voices, and found a man and woman standing outside the door of the house they had come to look at.

'Hello Mr Clarke.' Ada Croxall stared curiously at the newcomers. 'We doon't see you round here very often.' She bared her broken teeth in a grotesquely arch grin and simpered, 'I 'opes you aren't come to tell me the rent's bin put up again.'

'No, Mrs Croxall. We've just come to have a look inside here.'

Clarke moved to the door and tried to insert the key into the lock, but it wouldn't penetrate the keyhole.

'It's no use you trying to open it, mate.' The stoop-shouldered, meagre-bodied little man standing by Ada Croxall politely lifted his battered bowler hat, disclosing the few strands of greasy hair plastered across his dandruffed scalp. 'The bugger's locked it, and he wun't open up.'

'Who won't open up?' Clarke demanded in puzzlement.

'Mr Vivaldi,' Ada Croxall put in eagerly. 'He come running in from the road not five minutes since, and he went in theer and locked the door, and now he wun't give answer. We bin shouting through the door for ages, aren't we, Mr Thomas?'

The little man nodded. 'I spotted him leaving his house, just when I was agoing to call on him theer, and he run off from me, so I followed.'

West stepped up to the door and called through the warped, cracked panels, 'Harry? Harry, are you alright? It's Adrian. Adrian West.' He rapped the door smartly with his fist. 'Harry? Can you hear me? Are you unwell?'

He took off his wide-brimmed hat so that he could press

his ear against the door panel and listened hard, then frowned and shook his head. 'I can't hear anyone moving inside.' He swung round to the man and woman. 'Are you sure that you saw Mr Vivaldi go in here?'

The woman scowled indignantly. 'O' course I'm bloody well sure. What does you take me for, Mister? A bloody mawkin or summat?'

She turned to Clarke. 'Mr Vivaldi's always gooing in theer. And he stays in theer for ages. Gawd omly knows what he finds to do, because the bloody place must be perishin' cold and damp now nobody lives in it.' A baleful gleam entered her eyes and she cast a resentful barb at Clarke. 'Like all these bloody houses down this yard am cold and damp, for all that your boss has put our bloody rents up.'

'What was it you wanted to see Mr Vivaldi about?' West asked the little man. 'Perhaps I might be able to help you. I'm a paying guest in his house.'

Albert Thomas' ill-fitting, badly stained false teeth bared in a snarl, and for a moment West fancied he saw a distinct resemblance to a rabid weasel in the other man's pinched features.

'I wants to know what he's done wi' my missis, mate. I wants to know wheer my Bella's gone.'

West stared in astonishment, and Ada Croxall told him, 'Bella was living here wi' Mr Vivaldi, afore Mr Vivaldi got wed to Emma Josceleyne, Emma Farr as her used to be when I fust knowed her.'

Hostile envy gleamed in the woman's eyes, and she sniffed in loud disparagement. 'I knew Emma Farr when her was a raggedy arsed morsel in Silver Street, and hadn't got a shoe to her foot. Never mind her uppity ways now, her's never bin any better than her ought to be, and that's a fact. I knows her too well to be fooled by her fancy clothes and fine airs and graces. Leopards can't never change their spots, and Silver Street always sticks. You can't wash it away, or hide it under fancy clothes. It always sticks!'

West was fascinated by these revelations concerning his hostess and devoutly hoped for future mistress. If it had not been for the pressing mystery of what Harry was doing inside the house, he would have pumped the woman for more information. But regretfully he decided he must pursue the primary objective – which was to get an answer from Harry Vivaldi.

Now he pounded the door until it shook beneath the thundering blows, and bellowed, 'Harry? Open this damned door, will you? What in hell's name are you doing in here?'

Again he hammered long and hard, 'We're not leaving here until you do open the door, Harry. So you might as well open it right now, and save us all a deal of waiting.'

There was the sound of a key being turned in the rusty lock and the door opened to disclose Harry's grey, clammy-sweated face.

'Good God!' West exclaimed in shock. 'What's the matter with you, man?'

'I feel ill,' Vivaldi jerked out in a tremulous voice. 'I need to lie down.'

'Wheer's my missus?' Thomas demanded. 'What's you done wi' my Bella?'

'I don't know where she is. She left this town years ago,' Harry told him.

'I doon't believe that you doon't know wheer she is, mate!' the little man stated stubbornly. 'So you just tell me straight.'

As Vivaldi shook his head, West intervened angrily.

'Look here, sir, can't you see that Mr Vivaldi is ill? Stop badgering him.'

'I'll badger the bugger until he tells me what I wants to know, mate,' the little man snarled, baring his stained false teeth. 'And neither you, nor another ten like you 'ull stop me.'

Vivaldi groaned loudly, and swayed and sagged down onto his knees, his hands still clutching the edge of the door.

'Help me, Adrian. I'm ill,' he pleaded faintly.

'There's nothing wrong wi' you, mate, youm just bloody shamming!' Thomas jeered. 'Now wheer's my missus?'

West lost his patience. 'If you don't leave here right now,

205

then I'll make you leave,' he threatened the little man.

Thomas was unafraid. 'You and whose army, mate?'

The actor's temper exploded. Grabbing Thomas by the collar of his shabby threadbare overcoat he forced him backwards towards the entryway.

The little man made no attempt to struggle. His aggressor released his collar and pushed him hard into the entryway, telling him:

'Get down that entry.'

Albert Thomas stood his ground.

'You cheeky bastard!' West shouted furiously, and roughly taking hold of the little man he frogmarched him down the length of the entryway and out into the street.

Once again Thomas made no attempt to resist.

In the street the actor shoved the little man away, causing him to stumble, and breathing heavily from his exertions warned:

'Get away from here, or I'll do you an injury.'

They remained staring at each other for some seconds, then West shouted, 'Get away, damm you!'

Thomas shook his head. 'Not 'til I finds out what I wants to know, mate.'

West started to raise his fists and move against the other man, but Clarke came from behind him and grabbed his shoulder.

'Leave it, Mr West. I'll help you get Vivaldi back to his home.'

The actor was loth to turn away from Thomas, but then Clarke nodded towards the curious eyes staring from the doorways and windows.

'You're only giving these people a free peepshow, Mr West. That's not a very professional thing to do, is it?' He grinned. 'Or do you want me to go round with the hat?'

West reluctantly allowed himself to be steered back into the entryway.

Thomas straightened his disarranged coat collar, pulled his bowler hat firmly down on his narrow head, and waited.

Clarke and West reappeared in the street supporting the apparently dazed Harry, stumbling between them. As they made their way through the town in the direction of Cotswold House, Thomas followed close behind, shouting at frequent intervals, 'Wheer's my missus, Vivaldi? What's you done wi' my Bella?'

Excited urchins and curious loungers trailed behind the bizarre procession, and Thomas continued his heckling until Cotswold House was reached. Then, as the front door closed behind Harry and his helpers, the little man shouted, 'You'll have to tell me in the end, Vivaldi. I'll keep on coming back 'til you does.'

Ignoring the questions and catcalls of the onlookers, he walked away.

Inside Cotswold House the two men half-carried Harry upstairs and laid him on the bed, while Emma, Mrs Elwood and the two maidservants fluttered anxiously around them, bombarding them with questions. Neither man was eager to answer.

West only said brusquely, 'Harry's been taken ill.'

Clarke said nothing, and as soon as he was able, made his goodbyes and left.

Later, after Harry had been seen by the doctor and pronounced in no danger of losing his life, then sedated and left to sleep, West sat alone with Emma in the drawing room. He explained what had happened, and told Emma about Albert Thomas' demands.

Her black eyes glinted with anger, and she hissed, 'My husband's making a bloody laughing stock of me, isn't he?'

West diplomatically forbore from making any comment on this statement.

Emma's anger fuelled itself. 'I'm not going to stand for it. I'll throw the bugger out of this house. I'm not going to be jeered at in this town because he couldn't keep his bloody hands off somebody else's wife.'

Inwardly exulting at what he was hearing, West kept a grave expression on his face, and decided to delicately exacerbate the situation.

'Surely Harry is not still seeing this woman, is he? He said that Bella Thomas had left the town some time ago.'

'How can I know who he's seeing when he's not at home. The bugger is out all hours, and I've got no idea where he goes, or what he gets up to.'

West nodded judiciously. 'Yes, you have a point there, my dear.'

Emma jumped up from her chair and began to pace up and down the room, gesturing wildly in her agitation.

'It's not that I give a damn what he's doing. I've been regretting my marriage for a long time now, and I'd sooner have his space than his company. But I'm not going to have him making me a bloody laughing stock in this town. I'm not going to stand for that.'

The actor sat quietly watching her. Savouring the heaving of her high firm breasts, the heightened colour of her cheeks, the flashing of her black eyes. She was very good to look upon, and West felt his manhood engorging with lust, and was forced to cross his legs to disguise his sudden tumescence.

She came to a standstill, and told West, 'Do you know something, Adrian; I'm bloody sure that Harry hasn't told me the full story of what went on between himself and that fat cow he was with when I first met him. He's always stuck to it that she was an old friend of his family who he was giving shelter to as a favour. But that's a load of old codswallop. I've a good mind to talk to this Albert Thomas myself, and get his side of the story from him.'

'But do you know where to find the man?' West queried.

She shook her head, causing the long escaped tendrils of chestnut hair to toss and shimmer against her flushed cheeks.

'No, I don't, but I'll bet you any amount that that bugger upstairs knows where Thomas lives. I'll make him tell me, and then I'll go and see the man myself.'

West recognised his opportunity, and moved with speed.

'No, my dear. That wouldn't be a wise move on your part. If Harry has been hiding the truth from you, then he'll merely continue to do so if you tackle him about it. Particularly in your present mood.'

He rose from his chair and went to face her, standing very close and speaking in such a low tone that she had to lean towards him to hear clearly what he said.

208

'Let me do this for you, my dear. Let me find out from Harry where this Thomas lives, and let me go to see him. I can guarantee that I'll find out everything. And at the same time I'll have some enquiries made as to the present whereabouts of Bella Thomas. I know a private detective agency who are very good at tracing people, and very very discreet. Only you and I will ever come to know what they might discover.'

He placed his hands soothingly on her slender shoulders, manfully resisting the urge to pull her shapely body hard against his own, and to crush his mouth to her temptingly moist lips.

'Well, Emma, what do you say? Will you let me do this for you? It would mean more to me than I could ever say, if you would allow me to help you.'

She stared at him, and in her eyes there lurked a knowing cynicism. With an inviting smile, she asked him, 'And why would it mean more than you could ever say if I were to let you help me, Adrian?'

Instinctively he realised that audacity would prove his best ally.

Returning her smile, he told her, 'Because I think that I'm in love with you.'

Then he swiftly leaned forwards and pressed his lips to hers. His desire exploded as he tasted the sweet moist warmth, and he would have taken her in his arms, but she deftly slipped back. When he stepped towards her she held him off, shaking her head.

He made no attempt to brush aside her hands, only told her smilingly, 'I believe that you and I are truly destined for each other, Emma. There'll come a day when you'll welcome my kisses, and welcome much more besides.'

She grinned like a gamine urchin, and retorted, laughing, 'That's as maybe. But you'll have to wait until that day dawns, won't you? And it could be a long time off.'

'I will wait. You can count on it. For just as long as I have to.' He smiled and bowed with a flourish, then went on breezily, 'And now I'll have to go to the theatre. Will you be coming there tonight?'

She nodded.

'Then I shall have the finest box made ready for you, my dear, complete with champagne in a bucket of ice.'

When he left the house Emma moved to the window and watched him walk away. She thought about what had just taken place between them, and her lips parted in a smile of satisfaction.

You never know, Adrian, she spoke to him in her mind. The day you're waiting for might come a whole lot quicker than you hope it will.

Chapter Twenty-Two

Harry Vivaldi awoke in the early hours of the morning. His head was throbbing painfully and he felt nauseous and sluggish from the after-effects of the sedatives. Fumbling in the darkness he felt for the bedside cabinet and his searching fingers encountered the chill of a glass waterjug. Sitting up in the bed he lifted the jug to his lips and drank greedily, sighing gratefully as the cold liquid lubricated and soothed his parched mouth and throat.

He remained sitting for some time, and as the throbbing in his head eased, and the nausea dulled, he was able to consider the events of the previous day. He shivered with apprehension as full recall came to him. Harry was sadly lacking in both physical and moral courage, and for a while his fears once more overcame him, and he sagged back against the pillows, body trembling, hands shaking, breathing in short harsh pants. For once he was grateful for the fact that he and Emma were no longer sharing a bed or room. If she had seen him like this he knew that she would have badgered him unmercifully to find the reason he was behaving so.

But Harry possessed one attribute that had always stood him in good stead – the instinct of self-preservation. And that instinct was so strong in him that it enabled him when desperate to overcome his cowardice and act decisively. Now, from the depths of his fear, that instinct burgeoned anew, forcing him to begin to think rationally about what he needed to do to save himself from the disaster his panicky actions were almost inevitably going to bring upon his head.

'I've got to box clever,' he told himself over and over

211

again. 'I've got to box clever.'

The craving for alcohol began to gnaw at him, and he got out of the bed to go in search of a drink. Then, with his hand on the doorknob he halted, and shook his head.

'No! It's the drink that's making me act so foolishly. I can't afford to risk any more drinking until I get myself clear from the mess.'

He went back to the bed and got under the covers once again, shivering slightly from the chill of the night air. As his body warmed he began to rack his brains in a desperate search for a solution to his problems. He was so engrossed that he failed to hear the soft padding of bare feet passing his door.

Emma paused and listened hard, straining her ears to detect any sounds, but the darkened corridor was still and silent. She turned the knob and slipped into the room beyond. The curtains had been left open, and the moon's rays lanced through the tall windows and bathed the bed in a silvery light.

As she moved towards the bed the man turned, and gasped in surprise, then levered himself upright.

'Shhhh!' She held her fingers to her lips.

She went to stand at the foot of the bed, and West held out his arms in invitation.

Smiling, she slowly lifted her nightdress and drew it over her head. Then stood erect and naked. The moonlight shimmered upon her silken skin, and the man's breathing quickened as he let his gaze travel slowly up and down her body. Her long hair was a soft cloud about her shapely shoulders, and her breasts were high and proud, her waist slender, her hips lushly rounded, her thighs perfectly sculptured.

He threw the covers aside, revealing his own nakedness and the already hardened rod of his manhood. Emma moved to the side of the bed, and when his hands would have grasped her, she turned them away.

'Wait,' she whispered huskily.

Then she pushed against his shoulder, making him lie back upon the pillows. She got onto the bed and knelt astride his thick calves, and the man's desire became almost unbearable as he felt the smooth heat of her thighs and buttocks against his skin. Once more he reached for her, and once more she turned his eager hands away.

'Wait.'

Her fingers moved teasingly, lingeringly up his muscular thighs, and cupped his genitals. Then she bent and took his throbbing maleness deep into her warm wet mouth. He groaned in delight as her tongue caressed him, and she moved her head up and down, up and down in slow lazy rhythm. His excitement increased to the verge of climax, and his hips jerked uncontrollably.

She lifted her head, and smiled wickedly, as he begged hoarsely, 'No, don't stop. Please don't stop.'

Deliberately she waited until the threat of his climax receded, and all the time her own desire was shuddering through her with ever more urgency. Then she moved further up his body, raised herself above him and taking his maleness plunged it deep into the aching void between her legs. With head thrown back, body arched, breasts swelling, moaning and panting with pleasure she moved her hips in hard, almost brutal motion, and the man's hands moved demandingly across her thighs and breasts and belly, clutching, cupping, stroking, and his eyes were fixed upon her face, and his passion was intensified by the glory of her beauty.

Emma's breathing became a series of moaning gasps as the waves of delight began to crescendo through her body, and the movement of her hips became a violent thrusting. Her lips drew back from her clenched teeth, and she cried out as the shocks of fleshly ecstasy exploded through her, and beneath her the man's cry echoed her own. Then slowly she stilled, and remained astride him in motionless pose.

As his own senses returned West tried to draw her down to him, but she shook her head.

When he started to protest, she frowned and deftly lifted herself free of him and slipped away out of the room, leaving him peering bemusedly at the door closing behind her.

Harry, lying staring into the darkness, still racking his

brain for solutions to his problems, thought he heard faint sounds in the corridor outside his door. He got out of the bed and went across to the door and opened it to look outside. But the corridor was empty and silent.

'I'm even beginning to imagine noises now,' he told himself disgruntledly, and returned to his lonely bed.

Chapter Twenty-Three

Miriam rented a detached house about a mile from the town centre. It stood in its own grounds at the very top of Mount Pleasant, where that road joined the flat plateau on which the village of Headless Cross was built. The house was situated on the eastern side of the roadway and directly behind its back garden the wooded hillsides fell downwards to the broad agricultural plain through which the River Arrow meandered. Elevated as it was, the air was fresh and pure, uncontaminated by the grime and smoke of the district's industries.

She furnished it plainly and sparsely, and her preference for this simplicity was shared by Laura, who had now come to live with her.

To Laura's own surprise she had found that the leaving of Hill Street came as something of a wrench. In the midst of its abysmal poverty she had found true friends, and had known happiness there, as well as heartbreak. So that when the day came when she actually left, she suffered pangs of the heart, and wept as some of the rough inhabitants of the street came out to wish her goodbye and good luck.

The peace and calm of her new home, and the clean fresh surroundings soon cheered her, however, and very quickly she adjusted to her good fortune and began to feel happy and contented.

There was only one blemish on that happiness, and that was Tommy Spiers. Together with Miriam she had travelled to Bromsgrove and applied to the Board of Guardians for custody of him. Her application had been refused. During his stay in Barnsley Hall Tommy's mental condition had deteriorated alarmingly. His violent fits had become much more frequent, and the medical advisors to the asylum had recommended that he be kept in close confinement there. They did not consider him safe to be released into anyone's custody.

Although the doctors had assured Laura that this worsening of Tommy's condition had been inevitable, no matter where he had been living, or whoever had cared for him, still she could not help but feel a nagging sense of guilt. And despite all the evidence to the contrary she could not help but blame herself for having parted with him, feeling that if she had not done so then he would not have deteriorated so quickly, or so badly. But she kept all these guilts to herself, not wishing to burden her friend Miriam with her own troubles, and apart from this, she found her present life good and satisfying.

Miriam had also found a quiet contentment, and an increasing realisation of happiness during the weeks she had been back in her home town. She kept mostly to the house and garden, resting and recuperating her strength. She followed the medical regimen prescribed by Doctor Charles in London, and her consumption did not seem to be worsening. Indeed, she was beginning to hope that her health was improving, and that she might well eventually become completely cured.

The afternoon was hot and somnolent, and the two women sat together in the back garden beneath the gnarled branches of an apple tree, heavily laden with clusters of small fruits. From the open windows of the house there came the sounds of a clock chiming and Laura put aside the book she was reading.

'Three o'clock. Time for your medicine.'

Miriam, small round spectacles perched on the end of her nose, made a pout. 'It's horrible stuff.'

Laura laughed and went into the house, to reappear some moments later carrying a tray on which was set several bottles of differing colours, and a row of highly polished tablespoons. Brooking no arguments she began to measure out spoonfuls from the various bottles and administer the doses to her friend.

'Here's your iron mixture first . . . good. Now you must try this calumba and gentian tincture. It's very good for your appetite. Well done . . . Now your favourite, cod liver oil mixed with syrup of phosphate.'

'Oh no, must I take that horrible creation?' Miriam protested weakly.

'Of course you must. I intend to get you better if I have to pump the stuff into you by force,' Laura told her with mock-severity.

When the last dose had been swallowed, Laura poured out a glass of orange juice. 'Here, this will take away any lingering tastes.'

Miriam gratefully sipped the juice, while her friend returned the tray of medicines inside the house.

Suddenly she started with shock, and almost spilled the glass of juice. Emma Vivaldi had appeared from around the corner of the house.

'Hello Miss Miriam. I did knock at the front door, but no one answered so I guessed that you might be sitting sunning yourselves out back here.'

The young woman was dressed all in white, and carried a white parasol. She wore a straw boater with streaming pastel ribbons perched saucily on her piled chestnut hair, and the toes of dainty satin bootees peeped from under the froth of laced petticoats which rustled silkily as she came to the seated woman.

Despite the rift between them created by the young woman's marriage to Harry, Miriam was still very fond of her former maidservant. And now she rose and embraced the younger woman.

'It's lovely to see you again, Emma. Come, sit down and tell me all your news.'

Despite the warmth of this welcome Emma seemed ill at ease, and did not smile.

'What's the matter, Emma?' the older woman asked with concern. 'Has something happened to trouble you?'

Emma Vivaldi shook her head. 'No, I'm very well, Miss Miriam.' She hesitated, seeming to search for words, then blurted out, 'But when you hear what I have to say, I don't think that you will be pleased that I've come here.'

217

Miriam's thin face became grave, and she told the younger woman quietly, 'Come, sit down. You and I are old enough friends for there to be honesty between us. Whether I shall be pleased or not to hear what you have to say will not do any real damage to our friendship.'

Emma shook her head, and she looked near to tears. 'This will damage it, Miss Miriam. It will end it for good.'

'I think you'd best tell me, and let me be the judge of that,' the older woman instructed with a hint of tartness. 'Now sit down, and let me hear what you have to say.'

The young woman furled her parasol and perched herself on the edge of the garden seat, her body tense as if she was prepared to flee. Fidgeting nervously with the furled parasol upon her lap, she reluctantly met Miriam's questioning gaze, and said hesitantly, 'It's about Johnny Purvis. You and Johnny Purvis.'

The mention of that name caused Miriam Josceleyne to draw breath sharply, but she kept her face impassive, and nodded. 'Go on, Emma.'

Still fidgeting with the parasol, and speaking in nervous, hesitant bursts Emma related the same story to Miriam that she had told Johnny outside the Royalty Theatre.

The older woman's eyes brimmed with tears, and her hands clenched tightly, but she remained silent and showed no other reaction to the unfolding story.

Emma came to the end of her tale, and anxiously pleaded, 'Can you ever forgive me, Miss Miriam? I'm truly sorry for what I did. Truly I am, and I've bitterly regretted it. Can you ever forgive me?'

Miriam bent her head, and clasped her hands together on her lap, gripping so tightly that her thin fingers whitened as the blood was forced from them.

Emma was crying now, and she jerked out chokingly, 'I understand, Miss Miriam. I don't blame you for not being able to forgive me. What I did to you was evil. I can't forgive myself, so how can I expect you to forgive me?'

She rose to her feet, staring tearfully down at the older woman's bent head.

'I'll go now, Miss Miriam. I know that what's been done can't ever be undone. But please believe me when I tell you that I'll regret what I did to my dying day. I'm truly sorry for it, Miss Miriam, truly sorry.'

Miriam shook her head, tears streaming down her cheeks, her hands twisting and turning in writhing embrace upon her lap.

Emma turned abruptly and hurried away.

Laura had stood just inside the house door watching and listening to the interchange between the two women, feeling guilty for eavesdropping, but too concerned for Miriam's welfare to go out of earshot. Now she came out into the garden and, kneeling by the side of the seated woman, took her in her arms.

Miriam wept softly against Laura's shoulder, and the younger woman stroked her friend's hair, and murmured words of comfort. She felt a fast-rising anger against Emma Vivaldi for having upset Miriam Josceleyne so.

Laura had not told Miriam of her own meeting with Johnny Purvis in the cemetery, not wishing to risk causing her friend any distress, and now her blood boiled at Emma for the terrible wrong she had inflicted upon two people who had only ever treated that young woman with kindness.

'I could kill her!' Laura realised. 'At this moment I could take her throat in my hands and squeeze the life from her.'

She stroked Miriam's hair, and cradled her shaking body close, and her own heart felt like breaking as she listened to her friend's heart-rending weeping.

Chapter Twenty-Four

Adrian West was whistling happily as he strode along the green-tunnelled driveway, his mood still elated by what had happened in the dark early hours of that morning. He savoured with intense pleasure the memory of the passionate interlude he had shared with Emma Vivaldi, and with an equally intense pleasure savoured the prospects of all the other passionate interludes that surely would now follow.

Although he had been confident that eventually he would succeed in making the beautiful young woman his mistress, he had not dared to hope that it would happen as quickly, and in the manner that it had.

'She came to me!' He mentally hugged himself with delight. 'She came to my bed, and she made love to me.'

The thought of her mysterious avoidance of him all that day caused him a momentary disquietude. She had eventually left the house earlier that afternoon, and he had only known that because he had asked Mrs Elwood where her mistress was. But then he shrugged it aside.

'I expect she was feeling a trifle shy after what happened. Women in love act that way. It upsets them to think that they've betrayed their feelings so. After all, it's we men who are supposed to be the hunters, and to initiate the lovemaking, isn't it?'

He grinned with smug satisfaction. 'I've got her now, haven't I? She's mine now.'

He emerged onto the flat stretch of greensward, and stared with admiration at the ancient greystone house some scores of yards before him.

'Why it's really quite magnificent, isn't it! You're a lucky devil, Purvis, to be living here.'

As he walked towards the house he once again pondered on the sources of John Purvis' purported wealth. West had of course made enquiries about the man's financial standing, and had listened avidly to the stories told him about the rumoured immense riches that Purvis possessed.

'He joined the army as a youth, and was away for about ten years. Then after the peace was signed at Vereeniging he came back here as a rich man. But where the hell could his money have come from? From what I've heard he was only a ranker in the infantry until the South African War. And then he only gained promotion to lieutenant of Irregular Cavalry during the later campaigns. In the earlier fighting he was still an infantry sergeant-major.'

One obvious explanation naturally had instantly occurred to West.

'Loot! Could it have been loot?'

But that explanation was hard to believe. The Boers were not oriental nabobs with hoards of gold and jewels and precious stones, living in fabulous palaces. They were farmers, living in crude homesteads, counting their wealth in land and livestock.

'I can't imagine that Johnny Purvis could have rustled sufficient Boer cattle to account for what he's supposed to be worth.'

West grinned at the notion of Purvis driving vast herds of cattle across the South African veldt and selling them in the market places of Cape Town and Durban.

'I'm afraid that it's a mystery that only the man himself can solve for me.'

He put the matter from his thoughts, and as he neared the house, saw a young boy come to its front to stand and watch his approach.

'Is Mr Purvis here?' he called.

Terry Perkins made no reply, only continued to stare suspiciously at the man's flamboyant cloak and wide-brimmed hat.

West frowned and came to a halt a couple of yards distant from the tow-headed, rosy cheeked boy.

'Is Mr Purvis here?' he repeated.

221

The boy shook his head, and West felt a surge of irritation at this surly impoliteness, and snapped curtly, 'Well where is he?'

The boy pointed over the questioner's shoulder, and West swung round to see Purvis mounted on a black horse coming at a fast gallop towards them.

The horseman came rapidly closer, and for brief moments West experienced flashes of fear as the distance shortened to scant yards and the thudding of hooves became a thunder, and the bellows of the beast's lungs sounded in his ears, and he saw the wild bulging eyes, the frothing mouth, the bared teeth, the heaving, sweating flanks. Then the onrush swerved and the horse slithered to a halt and reared high, iron-shod hooves flailing, neighing and snorting. The rider soothed and calmed it with voice and hands, and the beast quietened and shook its head and the long mane flicked wildly and stilled.

Purvis grinned down at the actor. Then he dismounted and handed the reins to the boy.

'Give him a good rub down, then after he's cooled, feed and water him, will you please, Terry?'

The boy's pug features radiated hero-worship as he hurried to obey the man.

'How was he, Mr Purvis? Was he as fast as you reckoned?'

'Faster, Terry.' The man grinned with satisfaction. 'And he took a couple of good fences as well. Go on now, rub him down before he catches cold.'

The boy happily led the sweating, frothing beast away around the side of the house, and Purvis invited the actor, 'Come in and have a drink, Adrian. What brings you here?'

As the actor had watched the consummate display of horsemanship ideas had sprung into his mind, and momentarily overlaid his main reason for coming here. So now, when he answered, these new ideas influenced his words.

'Well, there were a couple of things I wanted to talk to you about, Johnny.'

The other man opened the iron-studded front door, protected from the elements by its arched porchway.

222

'We'll talk more comfortably over a glass of whisky, Adrian.'

He beckoned the actor to follow him into the house.

Purvis had converted one of the stone-flagged, high-arched downstairs rooms into a study and library, and it was here that he led his guest. Deep leather armchairs flanked the inglenook fireplace and they seated themselves in these, with a bottle of malt whisky and glasses set on a low oaken table between them.

After both men had sipped their drinks and lit up cheroots, West glanced at the hundreds of books filling the rows of wall shelves and questioned jokingly, 'Have you read all these, Johnny?'

Purvis grinned wryly and shook his head. 'No, not yet, but I'm doing my best to get through them.' His expression grew serious. 'I'm woefully uneducated, Adrian. My parents were too poor to keep any of their kids at school for very long, even though we were all fairly bright. And after I began work, and then in the army, I never had a deal of opportunity to read very much. But I always promised myself that if I ever had time and money enough, then I would buy all the books I wanted, and read to my heart's content.

'I love books, Adrian. I think that all the knowledge and wisdom and humour of the ages can be found somewhere between their covers. For me it's one of life's great pleasures to sit in here of an evening and read.'

His expression became defensive.

'Though I've met a good many people in my life who think that readers like me are very dull, unadventurous bookworms.'

The actor nodded understandingly. 'Well, I'm no bookworm myself, Johnny, but then, I'm no man of action like you've been either. I think that you've earned the right to spend your time reading. I wonder how many of those who would call you a dull bookworm, have ever done or seen what you have, or been where you have? Precious few I should think.'

He skilfully used the trend of the conversation to broach the subject which was his reason for being here.

'But for a man like yourself, Johnny, surely reading cannot be sufficient to satisfy you completely? I don't know what your business is, of course, but I would think that a man with your background would still crave some excitement. Some goal to aim at.'

Purvis considered for a couple of moments, then conceded, 'Well yes, there are times when I feel that in some ways my life is without any real direction. I've no business interests as such to occupy my time.'

'You should do as I've done, and find a new venture, Johnny.' West went on to talk about his dreams of making epic moving pictures, and his enthusiasm and excitement kindled a glow of interest in his listener.

When after long minutes the actor fell momentarily silent, Purvis asked, 'Are you making a picture at present, Adrian?'

'I haven't actually begun shooting it yet, but I've one in mind. I've been very impressed by your horsemanship, Johnny. And there would be a part for you in the picture I'm thinking of making. I'm going to set the story in the South African War. Emma Vivaldi is to be my leading lady.'

'Is she really?' Purvis was very interested by now. 'And will you be the leading man?'

'For this first picture I shall have to be, I think. There's no one suitable for the part in my troupe.'

'What part would I play?'

Adrian West was forced to hide a smile of satisfaction when he heard that question. It was the confirmation that he had ensnared the other man.

'There are two or three parts which you would be admirable for,' he answered, and although his primary object in coming here had been to persuade Purvis to invest money in this first picture, he now decided that he would delay that objective for the time being. With Emma's money there would be sufficient funds to produce and distribute the first picture, and he now judged that it would be better to keep any mention of an investment of money from Purvis for a little later.

I'll do better in the long run, if I get him really interested and involved first, before I ask him for money.

Aloud, he invited, 'I'll tell you what, Johnny. If you're interested in what I'm doing, and you feel that you might enjoy appearing in a moving picture, then come down with me now to the Royal Yard, and let me shoot a few feet of film of you.'

Purvis was both tempted and uncertain. 'But I'll probably make a fool of myself, Adrian. I'm no actor.'

'No, you won't make a fool of yourself, Johnny. I won't let you,' the actor assured him heartily. Then he sobered abruptly, and went on with intense sincerity.

'I've a theory about moving pictures, Johnny. The people in them are for the most part actors and actresses from the stock repertory companies. That goes for the French and Americans, as well as we British. And what happens is that the players act on the film as they would act on the stage. But because the films are silent, and we have to use printed cards instead of dialogue, then the players overact to get the message across to the audience.'

He paused, and lifted his hands slightly upwards, fingers hooked as if he were seeking to catch something in the air, completely absorbed in voicing his own thoughts, not looking at his listener, but instead staring as if he were watching a film screen.

'The players presently appearing in the drama pictures are not the top of the bill people. To put it bluntly, they're second rate hams. And they are trapped in their mediocrity. But even if the player was one of the very finest then he or she would still be playing to a theatre audience. And would still be acting as if they were on a stage, forced to throw their voices, and to overemphasise their gestures to reach that chap up in the gods.'

Now West looked directly at his rapt companion and demanded, 'Are you following me, Johnny? Do you see what I'm getting at?'

Purvis nodded. 'I think so.'

West appeared satisfied, and went on with absolute certitude ringing in his voice. 'You see, Johnny, what the other people who're making moving pictures haven't yet grasped, but I have, is that the actor on film must not play to an audience. He must play only to the camera. He doesn't need to overemphasise his gestures, or project his voice, or exaggerate his facial expressions, because he doesn't need to ensure that the chap sitting way up in the gods, or the woman far back in the stalls, can hear and see what he's doing. All the actor on film needs to do, is to play to that small glass lens, only a few yards distant. The lens is very intimate because it's close, and it can see everything very clearly and easily. And it's impartial, because it has no opinion of its own. All it does is to observe, and record what it observes on film. And it's judgemental only in the sense that it sees clearly, without any distractions, what is before it.'

By now Purvis was beginning to fully grasp what the other man was telling him.

'So you think, then, that to be a stage actor is really a disadvantage when it comes to acting in a moving picture?' he sought confirmation.

'Exactly!' West slapped his hand on his knee to give added emphasis. 'Exactly so! Now I am not saying that a stage actor cannot become a good moving picture actor. But I am saying that to be a good moving picture actor is a totally different discipline from that required to be a good stage actor.'

He rose to his feet and invited pressingly, 'Come with me now, Johnny. I've got to collect some processed film from Walter Terry. I'll show you what I have, and then you'll be able to see very clearly what I've been talking about.'

The only sound in the darkened shed was the whirring of the projector, and the only light the beam from its lens which cast the picture on the hanging screen.

Johnny Purvis sat smoking a cheroot and watched the flickering images on the screen. Although he had seen moving pictures on many occasions, this viewing was different from those other times. He was not seeking for diversion and entertainment, but instead he was studying the images before him with critical eyes. For perhaps the first time he was now conscious of the elongated gestures, the exaggerated facial expressions, the at times almost farcical pantomiming of the players.

The short scenes followed in quick succession, reel

following reel. Then for the first time since the screening began, Adrian West spoke.

'Now I want you to pay particular attention to this next reel, Johnny. I think that it will surprise you, as much as it did me.'

Purvis lit a fresh cheroot, and again gave his full attention to the screen. He hissed in surprise when he saw the young woman's face appear. Unlike the previous players, her face had not been heavily plastered with stage make-up, and so did not appear so harshly grey and black, but more muted and softer in shades. Purvis watched the brief flickering shots of her features displaying a kaleidoscope of varying emotions, and found himself marvelling at the realism of her acting.

When the short reel had run its course, Adrian switched the main lights on and asked eagerly, 'What did you think of her, Johnny? What did you think of Emma?'

Purvis drew deep on his cheroot and allowed the smoke to dribble slowly from his mouth. Then he replied quietly, 'I thought she was wonderful. Everything she did appeared so natural. So realistic. I could really believe that she was feeling those different emotions.'

'And the others? What about them?'

'It was as you said, Adrian. They appeared to overact all the time. They didn't seem realistic. Although to be honest with you, until you'd explained it all to me, I'd never noticed before just how stagey the acting is in these films.'

'Good, I'm glad that you've understood me.' The actor appeared well satisfied.

Johnny was curious about another aspect of what he had seen.

'Why did Emma's face look different from the others, Adrian? The shading didn't seem as strong somehow, not as harshly grey and black.'

This time the other man did not give an immediate answer. Instead he pondered for a while. 'Do you know, Johnny, I particularly noticed that myself this time. Although it's something that I haven't given a deal of thought to before. It's got to be the make-up, obviously.

'You see the make-up we use in the theatre depends

227

heavily on pinkish tones, because we have to overcome the concentrations of the yellow stage lighting. Now Emma wore no make-up for these shots. But there were times when she moved that her features became a little blurred and obscure. So she'll need to be made-up in future.'

He grinned. 'This make-up business is one of the things I'll have to experiment with, to try and create as natural a look as possible. I've still got a lot to learn about this moving picture lark, my friend.'

West moved to switch the arc lamps on, and bright white light bathed the raised platform in the middle of the shed.

'Come on, Johnny, let's take a test shot.'

Purvis at first demurred, feeling unaccountably shy at appearing before a camera, and fearful of making a fool of himself.

But the other man laughed away his objections, and Purvis eventually surrendered to his persuasions and agreed. But he felt stiff and awkward, and was unable to lose consciousness of himself and portray emotions he did not feel. And at last Adrian accepted that Johnny was not a natural actor.

But he would not admit complete defeat. 'Listen Johnny. You might not be leading man material at this point, but there are still a great many parts you could play in my films. I could use you for the outdoor shots, and for the action sequences. Would you be interested in trying for those?'

'Yes, I would.' Purvis was now experiencing a dichotomy of reactions, relief at release from the ordeal of trying to act, but disappointment that he had not succeeded. 'Yes, I think that I'd enjoy doing the action sequences.'

'That's settled then,' West declared. 'You shall be my action man, and my military advisor.'

As they left the big shed and walked side by side down the yard, the actor explained.

'I want to shoot a battle, Johnny: the British attacking a hillside where the Boers are entrenched. Can you help me with it? I'll need your advice about how to stage it so that it looks realistic. And I could use your help in finding the soldiers and Boers. The chaps who play the British will need to look as if they're real soldiers. It doesn't matter so much about the ones who play the Boers. Any roughs and scruffs will do.'

Johnny agreed after only a moment's hesitation. To his own surprise he found that this new and novel proposal was already firing his enthusiasm and imagination.

'We'll have to discuss terms, Johnny,' West said casually.

'Terms?' Purvis queried.

'Why yes. This is a serious commercial business, Johnny, not a hobby.'

'But I don't require payment for helping you out, Adrian. I've no need of the money.'

The actor inwardly debated before answering. Then he came to his decision, and invited casually, 'Why don't you come into partnership with Emma and myself, Johnny? We're going to form a moving picture company. It's the entertainment of the future, you know. There are fortunes to be made.'

He stole a covert glance at the other man's profile, and what he saw there propelled him onwards, and he began to tell Purvis of his dreams of creating epic moving pictures. John Purvis was interested. Very interested. But his finely honed instincts held him back from making any immediate commitment. He listened carefully, without comment until the other man had done.

Then he told him. 'I'll have to think about it, Adrian. The idea does intrigue me, I freely admit. But I'll have to consider all the implications before I commit myself. If I do decide to come in with you, then I'll come in one hundred percent.'

West was wise enough not to persist with any further attempt at persuasion.

Purvis went on to tell him, 'Look, I'll tell you what I'll do. I'll work on this picture about the South African War for nothing. And after it's finished, I'll know then whether I'll be prepared to join your company as a partner.

'So if you're willing to wait until then for my answer, I'll guarantee to give you a firm yes or no at that time.'

'That's fair enough, Johnny.' The actor smiled. 'Now let's go for a drink, shall we? My throat's as dry as the desert.'

Chapter Twenty-Five

In London during the month of June 1909 the politicians David Lloyd George and Joseph Chamberlain clashed fiercely over the former's People's Budget. In order to finance the new old-age pensions and rearmament simultaneously, the Welsh Wizard had levied a super tax of an extra sixpence in the pound on the rich, and had taxed unearned income, alcohol, tobacco and petrol, as well as doubling death duties and motor car duties.

In Seattle, USA, the World Fair opened. In Paris the Ballet Russe gave the first performance of the ballet, *Les Sylphides*. The Antartic explorer, Lieutenant Ernest Shackleton, arrived back in Dover to a hero's welcome. Sixty people died in an earthquake in Provence, France.

In Pitpikas, Finald, Kaiser Wilhelm of Germany met the Czar of all the Russias. The Darwin Museum opened in Cambridge. The Sultan of Morocco forbade the Jews of Fez from seeing his new palace, on penalty of being shot to death. King Edward the Seventh opened the Victoria and Albert Museum in Kensington. And on the 29th day of June, 1909, one hundred and twenty militant suffragettes were arrested after violent clashes with the police outside the Houses of Parliament and Number 10 Downing Street.

In the afternoon postal delivery of Friday the 2nd of July, Miriam received a letter from a suffragette friend in London detailing all the exciting events of the 29th of June. She sat beneath the apple tree in the garden and read the flimsy pages over and over again, repeating excerpts from them to Laura.

Emmeline Pankhurst summoned the Parliament of

Women in the early evening of the twenty-ninth, and the petition to the Prime Minister was read and adopted. Then the deputation set out for the Houses of Parliament ... Elsie Howey galloped ahead on horseback to let the crowds know that the deputation was coming. Apparently the crowds were simply enormous ... The fighting began outside St Stephen's Hall ... The authorities used mounted police.

The crowds sympathised with us ... By nine o'clock the authorities though they had won because Parliament Square had been cleared and the crowds pushed back across Westminster Bridge, and back into Victoria Street ... But then our girls began to come out of hiding places in small groups and dash for the Houses of Parliament ...

'She says the police had no idea where they were coming from. Oh look, they'd rented about thirty different office premises close to the square, that's where they were hiding. No wonder the police were puzzled. While they were doing that other sisters went and smashed windows at the Home Office, the Treasury, the Privy Council Offices ... Oh, and at the official residence of the First Lord of the Admiralty as well. How exciting it must have been, Laura. Oh, I wish I could have been there.'

Miriam's green eyes glowed with excitement as she looked at Laura over the rims of her small, round, reading glasses. Then she sobered and said regretfully, 'I feel so useless, Laura. The sisters are carrying the fight on and I'm doing nothing to help them. I feel as if I've abandoned them, as if I've failed to do my duty.'

'Nonsense!' Laura chided sharply. 'You've done as much for the cause as anyone else, Miriam. And you've suffered as much as anyone else as well, if not more. Your duty now is to yourself, Miriam. You must concentrate on regaining your full health and strength.'

The older woman recognised the truth of that statement, and sighed sadly, 'Yes, you're right, Laura, but ...'

231

'But nothing!' Laura would not listen to any further self-directed recriminations. 'Besides, you're still active in the movement, aren't you? Don't forget we've a rally tomorrow. Shouldn't you be preparing your speech for it?'

'I've already done so,' the older woman became snappish. 'I spent more than two hours on it last night, if you'll take the trouble to remember.'

'Then you'd best rest for a while now, so that you'll be fresh for the rally.'

Miriam's lips set stubbornly. 'I feel perfectly rested now, Laura. I don't feel the need to lie down.'

'You'll take your medicine and you'll go and lie down for at least an hour,' the young woman commanded firmly.

'But there's no need for me to rest. I'm rested enough,' Miriam argued.

Grim faced and silent, Laura fetched out the tray of medicines and measured out the doses, which the older woman swallowed dutifully. When she had taken the final dose Miriam apologised quietly.

'I'm sorry, Laura. I'm acting like a spoilt child, aren't I?'

Laura nodded. 'You are.'

'It's just that I'm feeling so much better and stronger these days,' Miriam Josceleyne explained. 'And I'm afraid to go the way of my mother. She became a professional invalid, you know. Stayed in her bed for years, when she was perfectly capable of being up and about.'

Laura studied her friend closely. Noting the clear pale colouring of her complexion, the clarity of the green eyes, and the slight but noticeable increase of flesh.

'Yes, you are becoming stronger, Miriam, and you appear to be much improved in health. But you still have to take care. Doctor Peirce is pleased with your progress, I know. But he told me only last week that I must see to it that you don't overtax yourself. There is always the danger of a relapse if you try to do too much, too soon.'

Miriam smiled in surrender. 'Very well, Laura. I'll do as you say and I'll have a lie down. But let's have a cup of tea first, shall we?'

Her friend willingly agreed to this small compromise, and while she went indoors to brew the drink, Miriam leaned back in her chair and closed her eyes, enjoying the warmth, and the sweet garden scents, the birdsong, and the bumblings and chirrings of bees and insects.

As always lately her thoughts turned to Johnny Purvis. Emma's story had caused Miriam long hours of grief and regret. But during the weeks that had elapsed since the young woman's confession, Miriam had slowly come to terms with her new knowledge. Johnny had been the only man she had ever loved, or made love with, and despite all that had happened, and the years that had passed since she had last seen him, she knew that deep in her heart she still loved him. Now she hungered to see him once more, and she constantly wondered if he for his part still thought of her, still had any love left for her? Did he hunger to see and talk with her, as she hungered to see and talk with him? Did he hunger to hold her close, to kiss and caress and possess her, as she hungered for those kisses and caresses, that possession?

Tears stung beneath her closed eyelids. It was too late now for them. No matter if he did share her feelings. Her illness meant that unless by some miracle she achieved a complete recovery, they could never be joined in intimate physical loving. The risk of her infecting him with her disease was too great. She drew a long shuddering breath, and the yearning for him was an aching, empty void within her.

The rattling of crockery against metal signalled Laura's return with the tea things on a brass tray, and Miriam fought to control her rampaging emotions, and managed to smile and appear untroubled when Laura set down the tray and enquired, 'Would you like some biscuits, or cake, Miriam?'

'No thank you. I'm becoming disgustingly fat as it is.'

They sat sipping tea, and after briefly discussing the forthcoming rally, fell silent, each with her own thoughts.

In the Redditch district the movement for women's suffrage had polarised into two distinct entities. On the one side there was the Women's Suffrage Society, Branch President the Lady Isobel Margesson of Foxlydiate House. On the other side was the Redditch Branch of the

Women's Social and Political Union, organised by Laura Hughes and Miriam Josceleyne.

The two movements had similar yet divergent aims. The Women's Suffrage Society wanted only the women of the middle and upper classes to be given the right to vote. The Women's Social and Political Union wanted all women of every class to have the right to vote.

The Women's Suffrage Society believed in pacifistic method. The bringing to bear of moral pressure upon the government. The Women's Social and Political Union had become militant, and believed that their cause must be fought with force and physical demonstration.

The Women's Suffrage Society were composed of gentlewomen, the wives, daughters, mothers of professional and landed men. In their ranks were to be found titled, and wealthy women, and all the sycophantic hangers on of the socially superior classes.

The branches of the Women's Social and Political Union also contained many women of title and wealth. But side by side with these marched seamstresses and factory workers, typewritists and barmaids, servant girls and washerwomen, women from farming villages and women from city slums. The two separate movements regarded each other with a degree of hostile contempt, and refused to work together.

The rally had been called for by Miriam immediately after the newspapers had carried the reports of the clashes in London. It was intended to demonstrate solidarity and support for the suffragettes arrested on the 29th June, and had been publicised by the distribution of handbills around the district. Miriam hoped for a good turnout, but at the same time was realistic enough not to expect too much from it. Although many women in the district professed their support for the aims of the Women's Social and Political Union, the actual activists were few in number.

Laura had great misgivings about the rally. Previous rallies that she and her friends had attempted to hold in the town had ended in their receiving rough treatment from the hands of those locals who were anti-suffragette.

Laura was not afraid for herself, she had youth and strength, and her zeal for the cause was not diminished by the prospect of physical violence being directed towards her. Her misgivings were for her friend. Although Miriam's general health had undoubtedly improved, still Laura worried that the older woman's frailty would not be able to withstand any physical assault. She knew that the local police would be keeping surveillance on the rally, but also knew from past experience that certain officers tended to be slow to intervene and protect suffragettes from attack. She felt that certain police officers regarded a few lumps and bruises to be well deserved by those women who dared to challenge the existing state of affairs. Male chauvinism was the way of the world, and many men bitterly resented women forcefully demanding what large segments of the male population still lacked themselves, namely the right to vote.

Laura's lips twisted scornfully. 'It's idiots like them who make it possible for the ruling classes to exploit us all with such callous contempt!'

'What did you say?' Miriam questioned, and Laura realised that she had voiced her thoughts aloud.

'Nothing really, my dear. I was just thinking out loud,' Laura explained, and then said briskly, 'Come now, it's time that you went and lay down.'

While Laura had been engrossed in her own thoughts and misgivings, the older woman had also been thinking deeply. And now she said, 'Do you know, Laura, ever since young Emma told me what she had done with John Purvis' letter, and my own letters, there's been something troubling me.'

'What's that?' Laura asked apprehensively. The subject of Emma's confession had been deliberately avoided by both women ever since the day it had happened. Laura had feared to exacerbate her friend's grief by mentioning it, and for her part, Miriam had wanted to fully come to terms with what she had been told, before bringing the matter up.

'It's Cleopatra Dolton,' Miriam told her quietly. 'I've greatly wronged that woman, by blaming her for what happened, and by thinking the worst of her and Johnny. Do you remember how rude I was to her after she helped to save us from that mob in Holyoaksfield that time?'

Laura nodded slowly. On that occasion she and Miriam and Rosie Spiers had attempted to address a crowd of women about the Suffrage Movement, and they had been attacked by local roughs. Cleopatra Dolton and Ozzie Clarke had been driving past when this happened, and they had intervened and rescued the three women. Miriam had refused to thank Cleopatra Dolton, or even to acknowledge her, and had stormed away.

'I'm going to write and apologise to her for my rudeness on that day, and for so cruelly blaming and misjudging her as I've done. I was considering calling on her in person to do so, but then there's always the possibility that she might refuse to accept my card, isn't there? So I think it best if I write instead, don't you?'

Laura nodded thoughtfully, as she considered the other woman's words. 'Yes, it's best that you write in the first instance. Perhaps you might meet and talk in person afterwards.'

Then she smiled, and went on, 'I'm so glad that you're doing this, Miriam. Cleopatra was very kind to me when I was in sore need of kindness. I've always thought her to be a good person. From what I've heard of her husband and his death, I can't help but believe that she's been sorely wronged by public opinion.'

The young woman hesitated, and then added diffidently, 'I met John Purvis myself, you know. Not very long since.'

'Did you?' Miriam was taken aback. 'But you've never mentioned it to me.'

The young woman shrugged, and excused herself, 'I didn't like to mention it, Miriam. I knew how much grief you'd suffered because of what happened between you all, and I was afraid to stir up unwelcome memories.'

She continued on to explain the circumstances of her meeting with Johnny, and the other woman listened intently. After Laura's tale was finished, Miriam remained silent, appearing to be deep in thought.

236

Laura studied the thin face, and the distant expression in the tired green eyes for some time, then ventured, 'Perhaps now that you know the truth of what happened, perhaps you might even meet and talk with John Purvis again?'

The green eyes met hers, and for long moments they remained locked in silent regard. Then a suggestion of a smile came to hover on Miriam's lips, and she murmured ambiguously, 'Perhaps, Laura . . . perhaps.'

Chapter Twenty-Six

At half past two o'clock on Saturday afternoon the approach driveway to the Royal yard was seething with men, women and children, and as the two women walked side by side through the jostling crowd Miriam smiled at Laura.

'I never dared to hope for such an attendance as this.'

They reached the wide expanse of the yard itself, and Laura indicated the rows of horsedrawn brakes and charabancs festooned with lettered banners.

'I don't think that it's our rally they've come to, Miriam.'

The older woman's elation visibly ebbed as she read the letterings. 'Royal Oak Bowling Club. Odd Fellows Arms Bowls Club. Crown Bowls Club. The Fleece Bowling Club.'

She shook her head and questioned plaintively, 'What are they all doing here?'

Laura asked the same question of a man walking alongside her, and was told, 'It's the big match, my duck. The Redditch and District Bowling League am playing the Warwickshire and Worcestershire Bowling Association.'

Resplendent in scarlet and blue, white crossbelts gleaming, peaked caps jaunty, the Redditch Town Band was counter-marching up and down in front of the ornate façade of the Royalty Theatre playing 'Hearts of Oak', and a score of street urchins marched in ragged formation at the sides of the bandsmen. Across the open space of the yard some travelling showmen had erected their stalls and roundabouts, and the strident chords of a steam organ competed with the martial music of the band.

Sweating, white aproned waiters were running to and from the Royal Hotel carrying aloft trays of drinks to the various groups of bowls supporters clustering around the vehicles among whom the festive atmosphere was already apparent.

At the front ticket office of the Royalty Theatre Adrian West was glowering at the crowds. Standing at his side Harry Vivaldi, spruce and sober, stared enviously at the drinkers, and mentally struggled against the almost overwhelming urge to join them.

'We shan't do any business for this afternoon's matinée,' West grumbled. 'We'll be lucky to get half a dozen in.'

His eyes roamed across the thronging masses and his mood became increasingly sour as he watched money being handed over at the hoopla stalls, the mechanical figures arcade and the coconut shies. The carousel went round and round, the painted horses bobbing up and down, glassy-eyed and grinning inanely, as were the men, women and children who were their riders.

'Bloody morons!' West grunted disgruntledly. 'Sooner spend their money to sit on bloody wooden horses, or to throw balls at bloody wooden coconuts rather than to come inside here and see great drama performed.'

Two neatly dressed women wearing plain, unadorned hats passed directly in front of the theatre and caught West's attention. The taller of the pair, a slender young woman with a thin pretty face and fine grey eyes seemed somehow familiar to him, and he frowned as he tried to recollect where he had encountered her before. Then remembrance flooded him, and he felt a faint shock of surprise. The last time he had seen her had been on the Unicorn Hill, and then she had been very shabbily dressed. Interestedly he examined her clothing, and his knowledgeable eyes recognised the expensive cut and quality of the jacket and skirt, and the white blouse with its frothy laced jabot.

You look as if your fortunes have taken a turn for the better, he observed mentally. Did you come into money, or something?

He kept his gaze on the two women as they threaded through the crowds and moved to join a group of shabby, beshawled working class women and girls, some of them

239

wearing men's flat caps, who were standing in the space between the rows of vehicles and the showmen's stalls and carousels. Curious as to what the connection might be between such disparate classes of women, he acted on impulse.

'Keep an eye on this for me, will you Harry? I'll not be long.'

He went to leave the ticket office.

'Where are you going? What shall I do if any customers come?' Harry questioned him.

West chuckled, 'Just take their money quickly, and don't give them any chance to change their minds, my boy.'

He descended the short flight of wooden planksteps that fronted the entrance of the theatre and began to thread his way through the crowds towards the group of women.

Miriam and Laura stood surrounded by their fellow suffragettes, discussing what was to be done. At this moment the combined noises of the band and the steam organ precluded any speechmaking here in the yard.

'We can hold the rally in the Market Place,' Miriam suggested. 'There are plenty of people there doing their shopping.'

'No, that's no good,' Laura Hughes vetoed the idea. 'The police would only arrest us for obstruction.'

'Let them,' the older woman declared defiantly, and Laura frowned worriedly.

'Miriam, you're not yet well enough to be put back into prison.'

'I won't be put in prison for causing an obstruction,' Miriam argued.

'You can't know that for certain, can you?' Laura's anxiety was increasing. Knowing her friend as she did, she sensed that Miriam was lusting for confrontation with the authorities. The news and letter from London had unsettled the older woman, and left her feeling guilty that she was standing idle while her fellow suffragettes fought the good fight.

The other women had been silently listening to the argument, and now one of the younger ones spoke out.

'I reckon Miss Miriam's right. Let's hold the rally in the Market Place. Never mind what the police might do.'

Other hot-heads voiced their support, and when Laura attempted to argue against it further, Miriam turned on her angrily, 'If you've no wish to attend this rally, then just go away and leave us to get on with it.'

Laura stared at her friend with dismay. She saw and recognised the fanatic gleam in the green eyes, and her heart sank. When Miriam was in this mood, then nothing or nobody would prevent her from doing what she wanted.

'Right ladies, let's unfurl our banners, shall we? We'll march around the yard here, and then make our way into the Market Place.'

Miriam's orders were greeted with a cheer by her supporters, and although some of the group shared Laura's reluctance to risk confrontation with the police, they made no protest. Crudely fashioned streamers and banners were produced, chest sashes were donned, all proclaiming in large black letters the demand 'Votes for Women'.

'Well?' Miriam eyed her friend challengingly. 'Are you marching with us?'

Laura sighed, and nodded, and donned her own chest sash.

With Miriam at the head, followed directly by two women holding a banner on high, the suffragettes stepped off in formation, shouting in unison, 'Votes for Women! Votes for Women!'

West grinned in amused admiration for their spirit, and went back to the theatre.

The town band had come to a halt and ceased playing, and there was a sudden discordant hissing from the steam organ and its music ceased as a valve jammed, so the women's shouts could be heard across the yard. The demonstration instantly attracted the attention of the thronging crowds. The response was initially good natured, and mock cheers and catcalls sounded out, and some shouted gibes.

'Here, Bert, come and see. It's the bloody Prussian Guard!'

241

'Left, right, left, right, left, right, open them legs wider girls, you wun't drop nothing!'

The big drummer of the town band mockingly began to beat out the step and the deep thumping of his instrument counterpointed the chorused shouts.

'Votes for women! Votes for women! Votes for women!'

The suffragettes circled the big open space between the bowling clubs' transport and the showmen's stalls and roundabouts, and the street urchins rushed to march behind them in gleeful parody.

Sensing the mood of the crowd the bandmaster grinned and winked at his men. 'Come on, Lads, let's give 'um the "British Grenadiers".' The band struck up the rousing march, and the contrasting images of a crack regiment, and the clumsy, uncoordinated marching of the suffragettes brought roars of amusement from the onlookers.

Some of the suffragettes paid no heed to the jeering laughter, but others blushed hotly with embarrassment, and bitterly regretted that they had come to this rally. One even left the small procession and scurried away to hide her shame.

Then, as the suffragettes completed their third circling of the open space and Miriam, head held proud and high, began to lead them past the rows of brakes and charabancs, a man seated on one of the brakes hurled the contents of his pint pot over the head of one of the banner carriers.

A roar of jeering acclamation greeted his action, and as the woman shrieked in shock and fear and dropped her end of the banner, other men on the brakes and charabancs likewise hurled the contents of their glasses and jugs over the hapless suffragettes. In only seconds the women were drenched, beer and cider running down their faces, dripping from their hair, saturating their clothing. Some of the onlookers voiced their protests at what was happening, but the vast majority clapped and cheered the assailants on, and as the supply of liquid diminished other missiles were lifted and flung at the suffragettes.

Police Inspector Wagstaff had been standing in

company with West and Vivaldi on the wooden steps of the Royalty Theatre watching what was happening. While only liquids were being hurled at the procession of women he made no move to intervene. He was an opponent of universal suffrage generally, and women's suffrage in particular. But then he saw stones and rotting fruits and vegetables and lumps of wood beginning to hurtle through the air and he lifted his whistle to his lips and blew a series of short sharp shrills. From various points around the yard and approach-drive his sergeant and several constables came running to him. He placed himself at their head, and forming a wedge, they buffeted their way towards the women through the swarming, shouting mass of bodies.

The appearance of dark blue uniforms halted the barrage of missiles, and the shouting of the crowd quietened as ears strained to listen to what the policeman was going to say to the drenched, bruised and shaken suffragettes.

'I order you to disperse and go about your business,' he told Miriam brusquely.

The small frail woman presented a woeful spectacle. She was dripping wet, and blood was trickling from a small cut on her forehead which had been inflicted by a hurled stone. Her broad-brimmed hat was wildly askew, and now she attempted to straighten and repin it. Breathing hard she told him defiantly, 'We've committed no crime, Inspector. We have the right to pass along this yard. It's a public place.'

His florid features scowled, and the long spikes of his waxed moustache lifted and quivered. 'You're acting in a manner likely to cause a serious breach of the peace. If you don't do as I say, then I'll have you arrested.' He directed his scowl towards the other suffragettes, who had all nervously moved up closer to their leader to hear what he had to say.

'And that goes for all of you as well. You're behaving in a manner likely to cause a serious breach of the peace, and if you don't put away those flags and sashes and disperse, then I'll have the lot of you arrested.'

'It's these men who are creating a breach of the peace, Inspector,' Miriam's pale complexion was now flushed with anger. 'We have been assaulted, and you are making no attempt to arrest those who carried out that assault.'

The policeman did not answer her accusation. Instead he merely repeated, 'If you do not instantly disperse, then I'll have you all arrested.'

'We have the right to hold our rally,' Miriam stated.

'Not in this town you don't,' the Inspector growled.

'By whose authority do you say that?' the woman challenged, and the Inspector tapped the silver badge on the front of his peaked cap.

'That's my authority.'

'I'm not afraid of badges, Inspector,' Miriam told him spiritedly. 'I shall not hesitate to employ lawyers to challenge that authority you claim to have to prevent our holding a perfectly legal rally. Naturally I shall not resist arrest. Quite the opposite in fact – I shall go willingly. But then we shall see what the judgement of the courts will be on this matter. We shall see what the courts make of your failure to protect us from assault, and of your failure to take any measures to apprehend the offenders.'

'What's your name, madam?' the policeman growled, his caution alerted by her well-bred accent and confident manner.

From experience Miriam had learned how to fight with officialdom, and she now brought into action the weapon of her social position.

'Josceleyne. My name is Miriam Josceleyne. My brother is Franklin Josceleyne, a senior officer of the Metropolitan Bank, and I am related to the Gray Cheapes of Bentley Manor.'

Wagstaff became instantly wary in the realisation that this bedraggled little creature standing so defiantly before him was in fact a gentlewoman, who if she was speaking the truth possessed locally powerful and influential connections. But he could not afford to let the avid spectators see him give way.

While he thought rapidly, Laura, saturated and dirt-stained, tugged on Miriam's arm and spoke urgently.

244

'Listen to me, Miriam. It makes no matter if you and I are arrested, but our sisters have got families and children to think about. They can't afford to risk being fined, or perhaps worse. We must do as he says for their sakes.'

Her argument caused the older woman to hesitate uncertainly, and at that point the flamboyantly elegant figure of Adrian West suddenly appeared at the inspector's elbow.

'Yes, Mr West, what can I do for you?' Wagstaff's manner became noticeably friendlier.

'Please do not think that I'm attempting to interfere in any way, Inspector, but I could not help but hear what's been said here, and I have a suggestion which might help in this unfortunate situation.'

'Oh yes,' Wagstaff stared suspiciously at the other man.

'If you'll allow me, Inspector,' the actor smiled charmingly and turned to Miriam and Laura. 'Now ladies, I wonder if you would do me the honour of being my guests.'

They both stared at him blankly, and his smile broadened.

'My theatre is empty, ladies. I've cancelled this afternoon's matinée performance. Would you do me the honour of holding your rally there? I can guarantee that you'll not be disturbed or interfered with by any unwelcome intruders, and there is ample seating for as many people as might wish to attend and hear what you have to say. There will of course be no charge for entry or the use of the premises.'

He turned to the police officer.

'Would this suggestion be acceptable to you, Inspector? The ladies will not cause any obstruction, or risk provoking any breach of the peace if they are inside my theatre, will they?'

The Inspector was happy to agree. This solution would give him a way out of what was developing into an uncomfortable situation.

'Ladies?' West raised his eyebrows in question.

Laura gave Miriam no chance to voice any opinion.

'Thank you very much, sir. We'll be most happy to accept your kind offer.'

245

Led by West, the suffragettes trooped into the theatre. Harry Vivaldi stared bemusedly as the soaked women went past him, and asked the actor/manager, 'But what about the matinée?'

'I've just cancelled it,' West smiled.

Leaving the women in the darkened auditorium, West went to the rear of the structure where the dressing rooms were located. The troupe were already dressed in costume and were applying their make-up. West called them all together, and ordered Henry Snipe, 'I want the full lights put on, Henry. Front of house as well.'

To the curious troupe West explained what had happened, and informed them that he had cancelled the matinée. They greeted the news with whoops of pleasure at this unexpected holiday. But he frowned and told them, 'Oh no, you're not going gallivanting, my friends. You're going to drum up business for this rally. I want it to be a great success.'

The fiery-haired Beatrice de la Fournay stared at him suspiciously.

'Why are you helping these suffragettes? Have you taken a fancy to one of them?'

He returned her suspicious stare with a broad smile, and shook his head.

'No, Beatrice, my love. I've not taken any fancy to any of them. Am I not entitled to make a quixotic gesture occasionally? To do someone a favour out of the goodness of my heart?'

Her suspicion was not allayed, and she retorted sharply, 'Quixotic gestures aren't your style, Addy. Not unless there's something in it for you.'

His smile hardened a trifle, but he only answered lightly, 'Let me assure you all, ladies and gentlemen, that there is nothing in this for me. Now, get out front and drum up some business.

'Beattie, I'll leave it to you to organise the town centre coverage. Remember to make it plain that it's free entrance. I want to see that House Full notice up in very short order.

'Rodney, Archie, you two take the door, and don't let any drunks or rowdies in.

'Winnie, take the kettle drum, and Sid, you take the trumpet.'

They dispersed grumbling, but he knew that they would all do as he had told them, and he was confident that the house would soon be full.

He went back into the now brightly lit auditorium, and told Miriam and Laura that they were to use the stage as they saw fit, and that his troupe would be spreading the news of the rally throughout the town centre.

'Regretfully I must leave you now for a short time, ladies, but I hope to be back before the rally is over.'

Both women thanked him with a grateful sincerity, but he waved their protestations away, and with a final elegant bow left them happily preparing for the rally.

Harry Vivaldi was still standing at the front of the house, and the actor told him, 'I want you to keep a close eye on what happens, Harry. If any hecklers or drunks manage to sneak past the door chaps, then turf them out straight away. I'll be back presently, I've some business to attend to.'

With a casual insouciance West strolled out of the Royal Yard and up the busy Market Place, thronged with the afternoon shoppers and loud with the shouts of stall traders carrying their wares. He crossed over the central crossroads and went into White's Restaurant at the junction of the Unicorn and Bates Hills. The main dining room was packed with families having tea and sandwiches and cakes. West frowned as he sought among the close-set tables for the man he had arranged to meet here.

Reginald White, the big-paunched proprietor came hurrying to him, soft hands spread wide in apology.

'I couldn't keep your table, Mr West. What with all these bowling clubs coming into town, I've been packed out since well before lunchtime. The gentleman you're wanting is upstairs.' The restaurateur winked knowingly. 'I thought you might prefer to talk business in private, Mr West.'

The actor nodded in gracious appreciation. 'You thought correctly, Mr White. But then, that's what makes you such a successful man, is it not?'

Gratified by the compliment, the fat man himself led the actor upstairs to the small room above the main dining area.

A large-bodied, red-faced man wearing a bowler hat, stiff high collar, and heavy blue serge suit, was sitting bolt upright by the window. A quick glance satisfied West that the room contained only this single occupant, and he slipped a gold coin into Reginald White's eager hand.

'Many thanks, Mr White. I'd like a pot of tea sent up, if you please. And then no further disturbance.'

'Certainly, Mr West, sir. Certainly.'

After greeting each other the two men stayed silent until the harassed-looking waitress had brought the tea, and departed.

As he had promised Emma, West had himself found out from Harry where Albert Thomas lived, and had gone to see him. But the little man had given him short shrift, and had refused to tell him anything. So now it was with eager anticipation that he asked, 'What have you got for me, Mr Tillotson?'

Ex-Detective Sergeant Tillotson frowned.

'Well, Mr West, the first thing I'd like to say, is that I wish you hadn't gone to see Thomas like you did. It made things very difficult in that direction for my enquiries to proceed.'

Although he smarted at this rebuke, West ate humble pie. 'Yes, I'm sorry for that, Mr Tillotson.'

'Well, never mind that now. We managed to get over it alright.' The big man stroked his handlebar moustache and looked smug.

'I've had three of my best men on this case, Mr West. They managed to trace Bella Thomas right back to when she was a babby. I knows as much about that woman as I knows about me own missus.'

West controlled his impatience, and smiled encouragingly.

'Do you know her present whereabouts, Mr Tillotson? Have you discovered where she is living?'

The man slowly shook his large head, and West frowned in disappointment. Tillotson noted that reaction, and informed portentously, 'It's my belief that the woman aren't living nowhere, Mr West.'

West narrowed his eyes, but forbore from speaking, only motioned the other man to continue.

'My men are human bloodhounds, Mr West, veritable human bloodhounds,' the big man declared in hushed, awed tones. 'Once they're put to the scent, then they never fails to run down their quarry.'

'I appreciate that they possess unhuman characteristics, Mr Tillotson,' West's impatience caused him to gibe acidly, 'but I'm not really interested in their kinship with the animal kingdom. If you have something to tell me, then let me hear it.'

The other man's red face showed a sulky resentment at this reproof. But recollecting the large sums that West was paying him for the services of his detective agency, he smothered that sulky reaction, and stated evenly, 'My meaning is, that I suspect the woman, Bella Thomas, to be dead.'

'Dead?' West could not hide his shock.

'Dead!' Tillotson stated firmly.

'But on what grounds do you base that belief?'

'On the grounds that my men have failed to find any trace of her.'

'But just because they've failed to trace her is not proof that she is dead, Mr Tillotson,' West objected reasonably. 'She could have changed her name, or gone abroad. After all, it's two years or longer since she left Vivaldi. She's had time enough to hide herself away, if that's what she wanted to do. Time to wipe out all her tracks.'

The private detective regarded his companion as if he pitied the ignorance which had given voice to that statement. Puffing out his cheeks, he expelled a noisy gust of breath.

'Mr West, I don't think that you fully appreciate the quality of my men. And I don't think that you appreciate the effort that I've personally put into tracing this woman, Bella Thomas. And as I've already reported to you, we've found no trace of her.'

'But if she was dead, then surely there would be a record

249

of her death?' the actor argued. 'There would be a death certificate.'

The big man laid one meaty forefinger along the side of his large, drink-purpled nose. 'That would depend on the circumstances of her death, wouldn't it, Mr West?'

The actor instantly divined the detective's allusion, and exclaimed in protest, 'Surely you're not suggesting that Bella Thomas has been the victim of foul play, or has done away with herself, Mr Tillotson, and that her body is lying hidden somewhere?'

The broad red face was impassive. 'At this point in time I'm suggesting nothing, Mr West. But at the same time, I'm not rejecting anything either. What I am telling you, is that she can't be traced, and my personal opinion is that there is a strong possibility that she's dead.'

He fumbled inside his tightly buttoned jacket and produced a large thick envelope.

'There's my men's reports, Mr West, and a full accounting of the fees and expenses. I'd be very grateful if you could settle the account at your earliest convenience.'

The actor stared in puzzlement at the other man. 'But I haven't yet dispensed with your services, Mr Tillotson.'

Tillotson shook his head. 'There's nothing else I can do for you, Mr West. If I was to continue searching for this woman, then I'd be taking your money under false pretences. Because in my opinion, she's no longer in the world of the living. I'm an honest man, Mr West.' A grim smile curved his lips. 'There are a few of us left in this wicked world, you know.'

He rose ponderously. 'I'll be bidding you good day, Mr West. I'm sorry that we've not managed to achieve complete success in this case.'

West looked up at him, and demanded, 'You are certain then that she is dead?'

'It's my belief that she is,' the man confirmed stolidly.

'And you also believe that there is a possibility that she met her death at the hands of someone else? Or that she has killed herself?'

West was beginning to look very thoughtful.

Tillotson shrugged his big shoulders. 'Anything is possible, Mr West. But finding proof is another matter altogether.'

West hesitated for a moment or two, then asked, 'Would you be prepared to continue to investigate what may have happened to her?'

'No, Mr West, I would not,' the man answered, with apparent regret. 'Since I left the police service, I've managed to maintain a very amicable relationship with my former comrades. I wouldn't want to put that in jeopardy by meddling in matters that are strictly their affair.'

'But you've been implying to me that Bella Thomas could have been murdered, Mr Tillotson. Or could have killed herself,' West challenged. 'Surely if that is your belief, then it's your duty to investigate further?'

Once more the other man shook his head. 'No, Mr West. I'm a private detective now. I'm no longer a policeman. You employed me to trace Bella Thomas' whereabouts. She can't be traced. That's the start and end of it as far as I'm concerned. If you think that there's been foul play in this matter, then you must go to the police with your suspicions, Mr West. Good day to you.'

He lifted his bowler hat in formal farewell, and walked ponderously through the door.

West sat staring at the envelope on the table in front of him for a very long time. Examining in his mind all the possible implications of his now rampant suspicions. Then he opened it and taking out the sheaf of papers it contained, began to study them closely.

Chapter Twenty-Seven

Harry Vivaldi stayed at the ticket office in company with the two designated doorkeepers, while a surprisingly large number of women, many with children and babes in arms, and a few men entered the theatre. The troupe straggled back from their peregrinations around the town, and the women among them went into the auditorium to join the rally, while the men sneaked away and into the public houses. The two doorkeepers also disappeared, and Harry found himself alone.

He stood on the front steps glumly watching the passing scene. By now the bowls match had got under way on the Royal Hotel bowling green, and periodically he could hear the plaudits of the supporters. Away over the yard the showmen were doing good business with the children and young people, and outside the side entrance of the Royal Hotel the Redditch town bandsmen were guzzling beer.

Harry began to feel sorry for himself. It seemed that everyone was having an enjoyable time except for him. He stared enviously at the scarlet-coated bandsmen, and licked his lips longingly. He craved a drink. It had been almost a month now since he had last tasted alcohol, and the abstinence was becoming harder to bear with each passing day. On the plus side however, it appeared that with that abstinence had come relief from his nightmares. He had not dreamed of Bella for over two weeks, and had kept away from the house in George Street.

Neither had he seen Albert Thomas, since the day that Adrian West and Ozzie Clarke had rescued him from the man.

'Perhaps the bugger's died,' Harry hoped now. 'But that

252

would be too much to hope for, wouldn't it?'

As if to confirm that pessimism, at that very moment Harry sighted the short, bowler-hatted figure of Thomas coming towards the theatre entrance.

'Jesus Christ!' the young man exclaimed aloud, as panic overwhelmed him, and he looked wildly about him for an escape route.

But the other man had already seen him, and was shouting, 'Vivaldi, I wants a word wi' you.'

The young man's senses clamoured to take wild flight, but then his instinct for self-preservation came to his aid. Almost miraculously he was able to bring his panic under control, and to face the oncoming Thomas with an outward show of coolness.

'Box clever now,' he told himself. 'Box clever.'

When the small man reached the bottom of the theatre steps Harry moved to the edge of the top step.

Thomas' pinched features were filled with loathing as he stared at the handsome, dapper figure standing above him.

'What does you think youm playing at, Vivaldi. Sending your bullyboy to me shop to nosey into my personal business?'

Vivaldi stared with shocked amazement. 'My bullyboy? Your shop?'

'Doon't try coming the bloody innocent wi' me, mate. It was the bugger who was wi' you the last time I came over here,' the little man snarled. 'Well it didn't work did it, whatever it was you'd got in mind for doing it. Because I soon told him to bugger off, didn't I?'

Vivaldi shook his head in bafflement. 'I don't know what you're talking about, Mr Thomas.'

'Doon't give me that old codswallop! You sent that bastard alright!'

'Who do you mean? Who was it came to your shop?'

'That bugger who laid hands on me the last time I was over here. That bloody Fancy Dan!'

Harry's mind was in a whirl, as he fought to make some sense out of what he was hearing. Sober as he had been for weeks now, his brain, unfuddled by alcohol, had recovered

253

all its considerable acuteness, and now a glimmering of understanding began to come to him. He descended the steps to stand face to face with the other man.

'Are you saying that one of the chaps who was with me in George Street that day, has been to your shop and questioned you about things?'

Albert Thomas gusted a foul breath into Vivaldi's face. 'Doon't act the soddin' innocent, Vivaldi. You knows very well he 'as.'

The glimmering of understanding was becoming a strong light, but Vivaldi sought further confirmation. 'Which of them was it?'

Thomas scowled doubtfully. He was starting to consider that perhaps this man in front of him was genuinely ignorant of what had happened.

'It was the Fancy Dan, that bugger who wears a bloody cloak and a big white hat.'

'Adrian West,' the young man murmured wonderingly. He was now remembering the apparently casual questions the actor had asked him about Thomas, such as what the man did for a living, and where he lived. 'But why should he want to go and see Albert Thomas?'

'What's that? What's that you're saying?' the little man demanded angrily, and Harry realised that he had unwittingly muttered aloud.

He shook his head. 'Nothing.'

Now he was feeling cool and calm, and his brain was functioning with an acute cunning. Self-preservation was the name of this game, and he, Harry Vivaldi, was a masterly player.

'I'm glad you've come, Mr Thomas.' He regarded the pinched, grey-grimed face before him with a frank, open expression. 'I was very ill the last time I saw you, and I'm sorry that I wasn't able to help you then.'

Thomas frowned suspiciously, but made no reply, and Vivaldi went on smoothly.

'I'm as concerned as you are about Bella, Mr Thomas. Because the last time I spoke with her, she assured me that she was returning to live with you.'

He assumed an expression of sadness.

254

'You see, it was you that she really loved, Mr Thomas. I was just a plaything for her.'

Contrasting emotions played across the little man's features: anger, hatred, doubt, even traces of satisfaction.

'Oh I'll not try and fool you, Mr Thomas. You're far too shrewd to be fooled, I know that. I'll tell you the truth, man to man . . .'

Harry paused momentarily, evaluating the impression he was making, and what he saw encouraged him to continue in the same vein.

'I'm not going to hide the fact from you that Bella and me lived as man and wife.'

Fury reddened Thomas' bloodshot eyes, and for a brief instant Harry quailed inwardly, but then his resolve returned, and he continued.

'But I swear to you on my dear mother's grave, Mr Thomas, that when I first met Bella, she told me that she was a widow woman. It wasn't until a few weeks before she left me that I found out about you.'

He sighed heavily and shook his head. 'It was a terrible shock to me to find out that she'd been lying to me all that time. And that even while she was living with me she'd still been going to see you. That all the times when I thought she was visiting her sister in Birmingham, it was you she was visiting. She hadn't even got a sister in this country, had she? Just before she left she laughed at me for being such a trusting fool, and told me that her sister lived in Australia. Bella made a real fool of me, Mr Thomas.'

Harry managed to squeeze a couple of tears from his eyes. 'You might want to kill me for living with Bella, Mr Thomas,' he jerked out brokenly. 'But I truly loved her, and she made a fool of me. It was you she wanted all along. And the last thing she said to me on the day that she left, was that she was going back to a real man. And that compared to you, I was only a milksop boy. It was you she wanted, not me.'

He bowed his head and lifted his hand to shield his eyes. Thomas stared hard at Harry, and his face mirrored his inner confusion. His vanity had been stroked by what he had heard, and now he could not help but seek to massage his ego further.

'You say that she told you that she was a widow 'ooman?'

'Yes, that's what she swore to me.'

'And that afore she left she said that she really loved me?'

'Yes!' Vivaldi nodded with bowed head.

'And she was coming back to me, because she wanted to be with a real man?'

'Yes, that's what she said, and she laughed at me as she said it. It broke my heart, Mr Thomas. I don't mind telling you, that when I watched her walk out of the house that morning, I broke down and wept.'

Now Thomas frowned in puzzlement. 'Then wheer did she goo to? Because her certain sure never come back to me.'

'That's what I'm wondering, Mr Thomas,' Vivaldi asserted fervently. 'Because until I saw you I believed that she'd gone back to you.'

He judged it was the moment to offer the little man something else to chew on.

'I'm beginning to suspect that apart from you and me she'd got another chap, Mr Thomas. I'm beginning to think that it was him she went to, and that she only told me she was going back to you to put me off the scent, if I was to go after her.'

The little man's stained false teeth bared in a savage snarl.

'My Bella warn't like that, mate. She warn't a slut! She warn't a liar neither!'

Vivaldi now played a master-stroke. Striking an attitude of a man betrayed and cuckolded by a scheming woman, he stormed angrily, 'Well she lied enough to me, didn't she? She lied about being a widow woman. She lied about visiting her sister. She lied about going back to her lawful wedded husband. She lied about loving me! She lied and lied and lied. That woman's come close to destroying me with her lies. She's broke my heart with her lies. She's ruined my life with her lies.'

Thomas was unimpressed with this bluster.

'Whatever her's done to you, is your own fault, mate,' he

256

grunted in disgust. Then he hissed contemptuously, 'And from what I'se seen of you, it was right what she called you. Youm nothing but a milksop boy, you am. Crying like a babby because a woman chucked you over. Youm nothing but a gutless arsehole. No wonder my Bella chucked you over. No wonder her found another bloke to goo off with.'

He hawked loudly and spat a gob a phlegm onto Harry Vivaldi's highly polished toecap, then turned on his heels and stalked away.

Vivaldi looked down at his toecap with angry revulsion. Then he stared after the little man going away from him, somewhat taken aback at Thomas' abrupt departure. Then he grinned exultantly with the realisation. 'The bugger's swallowed it. He's taken it hook, line and sinker. He believes that Bella left me for another man.'

He felt like cheering and waving his arms in triumph, but kept a tight hold of himself. Then, as the first flush of exulation ebbed away, he frowned.

'But I'm not really out of the woods yet though, am I? What was Adrian up to, I wonder? Why did he go and see Thomas, and say nothing to me about it? What's his game?

'I think I'm going to have to be very wary around that sod. I know he fancies Emma. I wonder if he's trying to take her from me, and he's looking for tools to do the job with?'

Deep in thought, Vivaldi slowly mounted the steps and went to stand in the ticket office, while from the auditorium there came an outburst of loud applause.

Chapter Twenty-Eight

The smells of wet mortar and lime, of damp, foul earth, of human wastes and human sweat wafted to fill Cleopatra Dolton's nostrils as she stood on the rim of the long deep trench watching the navvies plying picks and shovels, while bricklayers and their labourers constructed new manholes for the sewerage system.

The workmen sneaked surreptitious glances at the shapely, elegant woman and exchanged winks and grimaces and muttered comments.

'Nosey fucking cow!'

'What's her want here?'

'Probably fancies you, Tommy!'

'Ahrrr, chance 'ud be a fine thing.'

'Shurrup and get on with it. Her's paying your fuckin' wages.'

'Her's lookin for an excuse not to pay 'um, you means! Miserable tight cow that her is.'

Cleopatra was well aware of the hostile reaction her silent regard provoked. These sweating men, in shirtsleeves and waistcoats, red kerchiefs knotted around their brawny necks, corduroy trousers yorked at the knees, great boots clumped with clay reminded her of her father. And when she remembered what he had done to the powerless child she had been, she drew a perverse and somewhat spiteful satisfaction from exercising her own present power over these, his prototypes.

Behind her was a smart gig with a glossy coated horse between the shafts, and Ozzie Clark was sitting on the driver's seat having a conversation with a man standing by his side. It was the standing man to whom Cleopatra called.

'Mr Newbold, can I have a word?'

Like the workmen, Newbold wore iron-shod boots thick with clay, but unlike them he was respectably dressed in dark suit, high-winged collar and tie, and a curly-brimmed bowler hat.

When he joined her Cleopatra indicated one of the navvies.

'That man is drunk, Mr Newbold. I don't want him working on any project that I'm paying for. Send him away from here.'

Newbold's sun-reddened features frowned unhappily. He peered at the man in question for some seconds, then told the woman, 'That's Teddy Adams, Mrs Dolton. He likes a drink, I admit, but he's a good worker for all that.'

She stared dourly. 'I'm paying you for sober workmen, Mr Newbold. If that man injures himself, then I'll be blamed for letting drunken men put themselves at risk.'

Newbold grinned uneasily. 'But Teddy has always got the weekend's drink still in him on a Monday morning, Mrs Dolton, but it don't stop him working.'

'It stops him working on my contracts, Mr Newbold.' Cleopatra's dark eyes glinted with anger, but she spoke quietly and coolly. 'Now, it's very simple to understand, Mr Newbold. I want that man sent away, and I don't want to see him here again. If you're not prepared to do as I say, then you can collect the rest of your men and take yourself off as well. Do you understand me?'

For a brief moment the man seemed ready to continue the argument, then his eyes slid away from her unyielding regard, and he swallowed hard and muttered, 'Alright Mrs Dolton.' He turned from her and walked away along the trench rim shouting, 'Teddy, I wants a word with you.'

As the other workmen listened to the exchange between Newbold and Teddy Adams and realised what was happening, many furious scowls were directed towards the elegant woman, but she met the glowering looks with a challenging stare as if daring any of them to speak out, and none accepted that challenge. Times were very hard, jobs were very scarce, and these men had no other work to go to.

Cleopatra waited until she saw the offending navvy shambling away from the trench, and then turned away herself and went to get into the smart gig.

'That was a bit harsh, warn't it?' Ozzie said quietly as she settled herself beside him. 'That chap has got a missus and kids to keep.'

She reacted angrily. 'I know that, Mr Clarke. I've seen him kicking and punching her in the street enough times while her kids were screaming with fright. You're forgetting, aren't you, that I used to be a neighbour of Teddy Adams and his family. It's precious little keeping of them that he does.'

'It'll be even less they'll get from him now that you've given him the sack,' Clarke rejoined. 'And it's not our business if he gives his wife a good hiding, is it? If that was the case we'd have to sack half the men on this site.'

She shook her head. 'I didn't give him the sack because he beats his wife and neglects and ill treats his kids, Mr Clarke.' She informed him coldly. 'I gave him the sack because a drunken man on a job is a danger to himself and to his workmates, and Adams is drunk on the job more often than he's sober. And you know as well as I do that under the new Work Acts it's us that will be held responsible if any accident happens because of his drunkeness. They'll say that it's our fault for allowing a drunken man on site.'

Reluctantly Clarke was forced to concede. 'Well, yes. You're right in what you say about that, Mrs Dolton. But I can't help feeling sorry for his missus and kids.'

A momentary disquietude afflicted Cleopatra as she mentally pictured the haggard, battered-looking face of Adams' wife. But then she thought of her own three sons, and her heart hardened as she inwardly reaffirmed, It's to them I owe my responsibility. I'll do whatever I think is needful to make sure that my own children will never know want.

'Where do we go to next?' Clarke enquired, and made an effort to put what had just happened out of his mind. He accepted that life was hard and unjust, and in order to survive he must concentrate on fighting his own battles, not the battles of other men.

The woman looked at the small watch which she wore on a tiny decorative chain pinned to the side of her bodice. Then she glanced at the blue sunlit sky, and the prospect of making the rounds of her various shops suddenly lost any attraction for her. She felt an overpowering need for change and novelty. Then she remembered the invitation from Adrian West that had been delivered to her house the previous day, and smiled.

'Let's not bother with the shops straight away, Mr Clarke. I've a fancy to go and see how Mr West makes his moving pictures.'

Ozzie was happy to agree. When this woman whom he loved displayed a lightness of heart, then his own mood invariably lightened in concord. Cleopatra Dolton was usually sombre in mood and manner. The hardships, degradations and sufferings of her life had left mental and physical scars upon her, and had deadened her capacity for light-hearted enjoyment, so now, when she displayed a rare readiness to seek for some pleasure, he was more than ready to encourage her in that search.

'So it's the Royal yard, it it?' he queried, but she shook her head.

'No, his invitation said that he would be shooting some scenes outdoors. On the Sudan.'

This was a stretch of hilly wasteland to the west of the top slopes of Mount Pleasant.

They made the short journey in companionable silence, and soon arrived at their destination. Despite it being the middle of a working morning there was a sizeable crowd gathered to watch the novel spectacle of a moving picture being made. Ozzie brought the gig to a halt, in the rear of the crowd of spectators, who were being confined to the side of the slope by a rope barrier, and several men acting as stewards.

Cleopatra studied the scene before her with an avid interest. At the bottom of a steep bare slope there were a large number of men dressed as British soldiers of the Boer War, complete with high-coned, pith helmets, khaki uniforms, highly polished leather accoutrements and rifles with fixed bayonets, the steel blades glinting lethally in the

261

bright sunlight. At the top of the slope were other men, dressed as Boers, with long beards, broad-brimmed hats, assorted civilian clothing and bandoliers slung from their shoulders, long-barrelled rifles in their hands. A series of trenches and low breastworks had been constructed, and the Boers were lounging at their ease among them.

Other men and women, variously costumed, were clustered around the tripod-mounted camera which had been set up halfway down the slope, its lens pointed towards the British soldiers.

Cleopatra stared at the cluster around the camera, and recognised Adrian West's flamboyant figure, now wearing hacking jacket, riding breeches, and a large flat cap worn back to front, then drew in her breath with a shock of surprise as she recognised the man in an officer's uniform standing talking to West.

'Johnny Purvis! What are you dressed like that for?'

She narrowed her eyes against the glare of the sunlight and stared hard at the tall strong figure of the man she had last spoken with on the day that he had been sentenced to four years imprisonment for the manslaughter of her husband.

Ozzie noted the focus of her interest, and himself squinted his eyes to stare. His lips twitched involuntarily as he also recognised the man in the officer's uniform, but his reaction was ambiguous. Although he had not been close to John Purvis, he had known and liked him. And now his eyes flickered in quick succession between Purvis and the woman by his side. Despite himself, he felt a stirring of jealousy as he noted the absorbed expression upon the woman's sensual features as she stared raptly at Purvis.

Cleopatra was lost in memories. Although nothing had taken place between them, other than brief exchanges of conversation and that final fatal meeting, there existed between herself and Purvis a tension of sexual and mental attraction, each conscious that should the patterns of their lives have been different, then they might well have been lovers, even man and wife. Now she found herself wishing desperately that she might come close to Purvis, see him clearly, and talk to him, and explore his

262

feelings about what had happened both on that fateful day and since. She wanted to find out if and how he had changed in those long intervening years. She felt that she owed him a tremendous debt, and felt the need to repay that debt in any way that she could. Her lips parted slightly, and she experienced an almost painful constriction in her chest and throat as her longing to go to the man rapidly intensified.

Around the camera a heated discussion was taking place between Adrian West and John Purvis.

West wanted to shoot a scene where the British soldiers, led by Purvis, were attacking up the slope with fixed bayonets. Halfway up Purvis was to fall, apparently mortally wounded, and his men, dismayed by his fall, were to begin to retreat.

Up to this point Purvis was in full accord with the other man. But, after Purvis had fallen, Adrian West then wanted Emma, fetchingly attired in a plumed bush hat, and military style tunic and breeches, to appear suddenly on horseback, ride up the slope, and casting her hat aside to reveal her long flowing hair, to dismount and throw herself on the fallen Purvis with loud lamentations. She was to bandage him up, all the time being subjected to volleys of fire from the Boers, and so save his life. Then she was to take Purvis' sword and pistol and rally the retreating troops and lead them upwards to storm the Boer fortifications. At the very moment of victory with the Boers throwing up their arms in craven surrender, a final treacherous shot from a dying Boer to whom she had given water, was to lay Emma low. The wounded Purvis was to stagger up to where she lay, and kneel beside her for a final harrowing death scene, as Emma slowly expired.

'It will be a sensation!' West declared emphatically. 'There won't by a dry eye left in the house.'

'But that's bloody nonsense, Adrian,' Purvis was objecting. 'Anybody who knows anything about the war will just laugh at it.'

'Why will they?' West demanded to know.

'Because it's just too far-fetched to believe in.'

'Why is it?' Emma interjected indignantly. 'There're a lot of women who are every bit as brave as men. I'd be ready to do it if I was in a battle.'

'I'm not disputing that.' Purvis grinned as he looked at the young woman's indignant expression. 'But to be honest with you, Emma, you would never get the opportunity. Nor any other woman. We don't have any Amazon regiments in the British Army, my dear.'

'Don't you bloody well patronise me, John Purvis!' Emma told him fiercely. 'You'd best remember that it's me who's the leading lady in this picture, not you.'

He couldn't help but laugh, and shake his head. 'Believe me, Emma, I've never once thought that I was the leading lady in this picture.'

'Then why are you against this scene, Johnny?' Adrian asked.

'Because it's got no relationship with reality,' Purvis explained.

'But we're not selling reality, Johnny. We're selling dreams!'

West spoke with forceful, yet quiet sincerity. 'What I'm doing here is to give any little factory girl sitting in the audience an escape from her own dull, drab life. She'll see Emma doing what she or no other woman will ever have any chance of doing in reality. But in their dreams there are hundreds and thousands of them who have such adventures night after night after night. I'm letting them see their dreams brought to life on that screen before their eyes. That's what we're in the business of doing, Johnny. Bringing their dreams to life!'

There was no trace of mockery in Purvis' reflective smile as he looked at the other man. After a short peroid of silence, he nodded.

'Alright, Adrian. We'll do it your way.'

'Good!' West clapped his hands loudly. 'Right then, ladies and gentlemen, let's all get into our places, shall we?'

There was a flurry of movement from all the people around him, which spread out to engulf the soldiers and Boers, as West rushed around shouting orders and instructions.

Cleopatra's lustrous dark eyes glowed with pleasure as she turned to Ozzie.

'Isn't it exciting! I wonder where they found all those soldiers from? Are they real soldiers, do you think? And look at those other men. They look very fierce, don't they?'

Ozzie examined both parties. There looked to be about a hundred soldiers, and perhaps two thirds that number of Boers. He recognised several faces, and told Cleopatra, 'Some of those chaps are in the Territorials. I can see quite a few that I know. There's artillerymen as well as riflemen there.'

'Ready! Stand by for my command . . . action!' West bellowed, and Purvis began to lead his troops up the slope. With colours flying, firing smoke-jetting black cartridges and cheering, the soldiers surged upwards in a long stalwart line, and the watching crowds cheered wildy.

'That's it, lads!'

'Give it to 'um, boys!'

'Kill them bloody Boers!'

'Come on you bulldogs!'

At short erratic intervals, the action would abruptly cease for scenes to be shot again, or while the camera was moved and re-focused, and shots were taken from different angles of both the Boers and the British.

The first time Purvis fell wounded the spectators groaned with dismay, and hissed and booed at the Boers. The sixth time he fell, the spectators reacted facetiously.

'You must have more holes in you than a bleedin' colander by now, mate!'

'You'd best start learning how to duck!'

'Gawd Strewth! Youm up and down more times than a bloody skittle!'

The first appearance of Emma flogging her ancient horse into an unwilling trot up the steep slope, was greeted with cheers and plaudits. The sixth time that the poor old horse laboured up the steep slope, brought a different reaction.

'You wants to get off him and walk, my wench. You'd make better time on it.'

'Oh my, oh my, here's the lady bi-bi-bi-bi-bicyclist again,' one wag carolled turnfully.

'You watch that the Animal Cruelty doon't see you, girlie!'

'It's you oughter be carrying that poor old bugger, not him acarrying you.'

But a few of the simpler-minded spectators remained unaffected by the general levity, and were completely enthralled with what was taking place, so much so, that when the dying Boer treacherously shot the sword-waving Emma in the back, one elderly man charged onto the scene and attacked the dying Boer with his walking stick.

His exploit was greeted with wild cheering from the spectators, and when other Boers came to their comrade's aid, and manhandled the elderly man back behind the rope barrier, some of the onlookers took exception to it. For a few moments the fictional battle scenes were in distinct danger of becoming real, as the hot-heads among them came to the elderly man's rescue.

For Cleopatra, as the hours passed the weary years seemed to slip from her shoulders, and she clapped, and cheered, and hissed and booed, and laughed uproariously as one incident succeeded another. By her side Ozzie watched her in wonderment, and a lump rose to his throat as he saw what this embittered woman might have been like if life had not so cruelly abused her.

The sun was losing its power and the sky beginning to haze over when West finally called a halt to the filming. The crowd of spectators spilled across the rope barrier and mingled with the film makers, and there was a noisy hubbub of talk and laughter as the day's events were excitedly discussed. The costumed extras changed back into their normal clothing, and as the men stripped to their underwear the women blushed and giggled and sneaked sly glances at what was revealed.

Henry Snipe drove the great pantechnicon onto the top of the slope and superintended the loading into it of the camera, and cans of film and the costumes and props. Emma and John were talking with West, and Cleopatra hesitated for a moment or two then climbed down from the gig and started towards them.

'Where are you off to?' Ozzie asked her.

'I'm just going to thank Mr West for his invitation,' she called back over her shoulder.

The imps of jealously danced in Ozzie's brain. 'Oh no. It aren't West youm gooing to see, is it my wench? It's Johnny Purvis.'

Both Emma and Purvis were still wearing their costumes, and as Cleopatra Dolton moved towards them her memories went back to the very first time that she had encountered Johnny Purvis. She had literally bumped into him in the town centre on the day that he had returned from the South African War. With his plumed bush hat and gleaming accoutrements and jangling spurs, he had been a very romantic figure against the backdrop of the prosaic surroundings.

Now seeing him at closer range, she marvelled at how little the intervening years had changed his outward appearance. His close-cropped hair had streaks of grey, his face was a little more lined, but his body was still lean and hard, and he still carried himself erect and proud. The old sexual tension entered her as she studied him avidly, and she was forced to draw a series of deep breaths to slow the sudden quickening of her heartbeat.

'Mrs Dolton, how nice to see you. Have you enjoyed it?'

It was Adrian West who first noticed her approach, and he came to her with outstretched hand, smiling.

'Yes, thank you, Mr West, I thoroughly enjoyed watching you all.'

Her gaze flicked to Purvis, and she saw the shock in his face, which almost instantly was replaced by a neutral expression.

'Let me introduce you to my leading lady and leading man, Mrs Dolton.'

'There's no need for introduction, Mr West. We are already known to each other.'

She exchanged handshakes and greetings with them both.

Purvis smiled pleasantly as he shook her hand, but Emma's manner was cool and offhand. The young woman enjoyed having the undivided attention of these men, and

267

resented the fact that this sensually beautiful older woman was now drawing that attention away from her.

There was a distinct tension immediately apparent, which engendered a momentary silent constraint after the greeting had been exchanged. Then Cleopatra smiled at Purvis, and asked him, 'Did this bring back memories of the war to you, Mr Purvis? I'm sure it must have done.'

He returned her smile. 'Yes, it did, Mrs Dolton.'

'But unlike the war all the dead and wounded get up and go home for their tea,' she remarked quietly.

He nodded. 'It makes the battles easier to fight.'

'You deserve easy battles, Mr Purvis,' she told him quietly, and they stared intently into each other's eyes. It was as if the others with them had disappeared, and the man and woman were enclosed in an intimacy that excluded the outside world.

'Talking of tea, I'm in sore need of some refreshment.' West intruded into that excluding intimacy. 'Will you all be my guests? We can go to White's Restuarant. They do a capital cream tea there.'

Cleopatra reluctantly broke contact with Purvis' gaze, and turned back to the other man.

'That's very kind of you, Mr West, but I'm sorry, I can't accept. My general manager is waiting for me, and we have some matters to attend to.'

She indicated the gig where Ozzie sat staring at her with an air of sullenness that was palpable even at this distance. West did not want to lose this chance of getting to know this sensual woman better, and he tried to coax her to accept his invitation, but she smilingly declined.

'Goodbye Mr West. Goodbye Mrs Vivaldi.'

Emma answered brusquely, resentful of how this older woman had had both men staring at her as if she were a bowl of cream and they were thirsty cats.

Cleopatra's eyes lingered on Purvis. 'I'm so happy that we've at long last met again, Mr Purvis,' she told him, in her low voice, and her gaze was soft and warm. 'I do hope that we shall meet again very shortly, and perhaps have time for a longer conversation.'

The man experienced a frisson of sexual desire, as all

the old attractions that this woman had held for him flooded back.

'I'm sure that we will, Mrs Dolton.'

'Good,' she murmured. 'You know my address, don't you?'

He nodded in confirmation, and with a final smile to the others Cleopatra turned and walked away.

West watched the sway of her richly curved hips and he remarked appreciatively, 'That is a damned attractive woman. I wonder if the camera would like her?'

Emma's face flushed with pique, but she made no answer. In her mind however she silently warned, You'd best not try tomcatting around with me, Adrian West, or you'll soon catch a bloody cold. Two can play at that game, mister.

She smiled brilliantly at John. 'Well Johnny, shall you and I take tea at Cotswold House?'

The man stared ruefully down at his uniform. 'I need to go home and change, Emma. I've promised young Terry Perkins that I'll give him a shooting lesson as soon as I'm finished here.'

The young woman's black eyes sparked petulantly, but she kept the smile on her face, and shrugging, took Adrian West by the arm.

'Oh well then, I'll just have to make do with Adrian's company, won't I?'

Ozzie remained silent as he guided the gig back down the long gentle incline of Mount Pleasant. Cleopatra stole a sideways glance at his sullen expression, and smiled inwardly. She knew how jealous he was of her, and impatient with that, she sometimes maliciously tormented him by paying attention to other men. But that had not been her motivation today. No thoughts of Ozzie had been in her mind when she went over to meet Johnny once again.

Now she settled back on the narrow, uncomfortable seat, and curiously examined her feelings about Johnny. The sexual and mental attraction that he had held for her was still there, perhaps even stronger than it was before. She knew that he had been in love with Miriam Josceleyne, but

269

surely that drab little church mouse had not been able to retain her hold over him for all the long years he had been in prison, and the further years since his release?

Cleopatra was wordly wise enough to know that she still affected him powerfully. She had recognised the expression in his eyes when he had stared so avidly at her.

'Well then, why should we not come together?' she asked herself challengingly.

'Think of the scandal it would cause,' her wary, defensive alter ego warned. 'What would people say if you should have an affair with the man who killed your husband?'

'I wasn't thinking solely of an affair,' she explained. 'But perhaps of marriage, if we were really suited to each other.'

'That makes no difference. You would still be marrying the man who killed your husband. That would be an even greater scandal than merely having a brief affair with him,' alter ego stated firmly.

'I've lived like a nun since Arthur's death,' Cleopatra argued. 'And when I was married I knew no joy in my bed. Only my husband raping and degrading me. But I'm still a woman, and I need a man to love me. I need to know some tenderness and joy in my bed. Why should I have to spend the rest of my life trying to satisfy those needs with my imagination. Surely I've a right to seek for some joy and loving in the remainder of my life. I'll soon be too old to attract any man to my bed.'

'You can have any other man that you might fancy,' alter ego riposted. 'Ozzie here it panting for you. If you just want to scratch the itch between your legs, then take him into your bed.'

'But it's not him I want,' she protested. 'Or just any other man either. I want Johnny Purvis.'

'But think of your children,' alter ego urged. 'How will the scandal and the gossip affect them if you should take Purvis to your bed?'

'My children have lived with gossip and scandal for years. But thanks to the fact that I've got money, I don't need to worry about gossip and scandal, do I? Other people may backbite and tittle-tattle about me as much as they please. It doesn't matter a damn. I'm rich enough to ignore them, because my money will always ensure that to my face they'll be politeness itself.'

'They'll still be blaggarding you behind your back!' alter ego rejoined doggedly.

But although Cleopatra's alter ego might continue to argue further, its will to fight was inexorably ebbing away, and it was already accepting its inevitable defeat.

'So what will you do?' it asked wearily.

'I shall do exactly as I choose!' Cleopatra declared emphatically, and sent alter ego scuttling away in rout.

John Purvis was also engaged in an inner debate as he strode down the Mount Pleasant towards his home.

That's woman's still got the power to excite me . . . But I love Miriam. Then again, perhaps I'm not really still in love with Miriam. Perhaps it's just the memory of her that I'm in love with . . . Cleopatra Dolton is beautiful though, isn't she? Any man would be proud to have her as his woman. She's certainly interested in me, I could tell – there was a definite invitation there. But should I take it up? God only knows, I'm tired of living like a monk. It would be wonderful to make love to a beautiful woman again. We'd make a great partnership, Cleopatra and me. I admire her strength, and her courage, and the way that she faces what the world says about her. She's really a most extraordinary woman, isn't she? And she could be mine, I think, if I was to make the effort to go after her. But there's still Miriam, isn't there. She's still here in my heart . . . If I could meet her again, and talk with her, then I'd be better able to know my own mind. What shall I do? What shall I do?

West's thoughts were also busy as he drove his motorcar down towards the town centre, with Emma sitting beside him.

Since that first occasion, he had only been able to make love with Emma three times. Now that Harry had stopped drinking, opportunities to share Emma's bed had become a very rare occurrence. Of course there were times when they were alone together, but Emma was not a submissive, docile mistress. And when driven by lust he had tried to take advantage of those times when they were alone, she had fought him off with the savagery of a wildcat. For the first time in his life Adrian West was learning what it was like to have a mistress who dominated the relationship, and called the tune to which he had to dance.

His old mistress, Beatrice, had also banned him from her bed. She had suspected that he was having an affair with Emma, and although she could not prove it, her suspicions had driven her to declare that their relationship was over and done with.

He frowned to himself as he thought about Beatrice. She was also causing him considerable problems in other directions. In order to stay here in Redditch and continue with his film making, he had cancelled his theatre's summer touring engagements. Some of the older members of his troupe were quite happy with this. They preferred to stay in one place and avoid the hassle of constant travelling, changes of lodgings, and living out of a trunk. But Beatrice thrived on the touring life, and believed that her big chance to find fame and fortune in her profession was to be found in the cities. Being stuck here in this small, midlands industrial town was not to her liking at all. In her frustration she had taken to creating discord and discontent among the younger, more ambitious, members of the troupe.

West was now facing a constant torrent of moans and groans from these younger members, as they complained with justification of the staleness of repeating the same plays week after week to virtually the same audiences.

He had tried to introduce new plays into the repertoire, but the troupe refused to learn fresh parts, because, led by Beatrice, they said that all their spare time was now being spent in working on his films – for which they were not getting paid any extra fees.

The staleness of the current repertoire was also creating a sharp decline in the attendance numbers at the performances. Even on a Saturday night the seats were three-quarters empty, and he was actually losing money on the Royalty Theatre.

The actor manager was now being forced to reconsider his options and his future plans. All of his available capital had been ploughed into his moving picture venture. Emma's investment in the new company had been considerable, but up until now no new investors had appeared on the scene. There were potential investors, of course, but expressions of interest and promises of consideration were not hard cash. West was facing the unpalatable fact that hard cash was the commodity he was very soon going to be in desperate need of.

His confident expectations of large, quick and easy pickings in the moving picture industry were also somewhat dampened. It was only now that he was beginning to fully realise just how much competition there existed, and how fierce and cut-throat that competition was. Literally hundreds of new films were being produced every month in Britain, France, Italy, Germany as well as the United States, and it was very much a buyer's market. His initial idea that he could churn out a few successful films quickly, to help finance his planned epic productions, had proven to be erroneous. He was learning the hard way that expertise and speed of production had to be acquired by experience and long practise. His rival production companies were making two and sometimes three films a week, nearly all short one reelers lasting for from five to ten minutes running time. By having begun to produce films earlier than he, they had by now built up a considerable stock of films which they could rotate among the various distribution companies, and earn small, but many, rental and sale fees. So far he had not completed a single film.

He sighed heavily, and Emma glanced at him curiously. 'What's the matter, Adrian? You seem unhappy?'

He immediately assumed a jovial air that he was far from feeling.

'Nothing's the matter, my sweet. Now, about tomorrow. If we make an early start we'll be able to finish shooting the final indoor scenes and the picture will be completed.'

'I'm dying to see it all finished,' she smiled eagerly.

273

'Well, it has to be cut and edited before that can happen,' he told her. 'But the house in George Street should be ready in a couple of days, that's if that damned husband of yours has kept his nose to the grindstone. Once we've got our own developing room, and cutting and projection room, then it will be all plain sailing.'

She grinned like a cheeky street gamine, and there was a sly gleam in her black eyes as she asked, 'And we'll start to make our fortunes then, will we Adrian?'

He smiled and took one hand off the steering wheel to pat her thigh, and assure her, 'We shall indeed, my sweet girl. We shall be ready to make our fortunes.' And inwardly he prayed with heartfelt feeling, I hope!

Chapter Twenty-Nine

The ground floor of the house in George Street had been divided by wooden partitions into small developing and drying cubicles, and the bedroom and loft space turned into a projection and store room respectively. A carpenter had been employed to do the work, and Harry had acted as his labourer. Despite his aversion to physical labour, Vivaldi had made no objections when Adrian had suggested this menial task. The young man was anxious to make sure that the flagstones in one corner of the ground floor remained undisturbed.

On the final day of the work, as the two men were fitting and hanging the cubicle doors, their conversation turned to the carpenter's part-time occupation as coffin maker to one of the local undertakers.

'How did you start to do that job?' Vivaldi wanted to know, and grimaced. 'It's a bit morbid, isn't it?'

The man chuckled. 'Not as morbid as what me brother-in-law does. He's the bloody gravedigger down the cemetery theer.' He shook his head. 'I couldn't abear doing that bloody job. Some o' the sights he sees 'ud make me shudder, I'll tell you.'

He went on with ghoulish relish to relate certain horrific discoveries his brother-in-law had made while reopening occupied graves for fresh interments.

Harry listened with avid interest.

'How long does it take then, for a body to become a skeleton?'

His companion shrugged. 'That 'ud depend on a lot of things. The type o' ground, the amount o' drainage, what sort o' condition the body was in when it was put down.

According to me brother-in-law the fat 'uns usually rots away the quickest.'

Vivaldi nodded thoughtfully. 'So after a year or two the worms would have eaten pretty well everything then?'

'They 'udden't if a lead lined coffin was used, 'ud they?' the other man cackled with laughter. 'That's what I'm gooing to have when I pops my clogs. I arn't gooing to give any free meals to no soddin' worms.'

Vivaldi remained silent for a while, and then, as they finished hanging a door, he remarked casually, 'Do you know, from what you've told me about the terrible smells and maggots and suchlike, I can't help but think that it would be healthier for the grave diggers if the bodies were covered in lime. That would burn all the flesh away and leave no stink, wouldn't it?'

'Ahrr, if it was quicklime I should think it 'ud. But me brother-in-law was telling me that one day he opened a grave,' he paused, and stared searchingly at Vivaldi. 'Now I doon't want you to goo blabbing about this, Mr Vivaldi, because it was told to me in strict confidence.'

'I'll say nothing,' the young man assured fervently.

Satisfied, the carpenter continued in hushed tones. 'Well, there was a bad outbreak o' the cholera in this town, years and years ago. And a lot o' the dead 'uns was buried down in the Old Abbey Meadows, in the spot they calls the Monks Graveyard because folks was too feared to let the poor buggers be put in the churchyard. Now folks was so fritted o' catching the cholera that they couldn't get nobody to lay out the dead 'uns proper, so there was bound to be some on 'um who was buried with their wedding rings and suchlike still on 'um, warn't there.

'Well, a few years back a chap, whose name I wun't mention because he still lives in this town, he come to me brother-in-law, and told him that he believed that his grandmother, who'd died o' the cholera, had been buried wearing some rings and jewellery that was worth a good bit o' money. This chap knew the location of the grave in the Monks Graveyard, and he wanted me brother-in-law to goo with him one night and dig her up, so's that he could get the jewellery off her bones.

'O' course, me brother-in-law said he 'udden't do it, because he said it was against the law. But this chap kept on and on at him, 'til in the death he said he'd help. So, off they goes one dark night and does the business. Now me brother-in-law says that most on the cholera corpses was buried wrapped in pitch blankets. But some on 'um had been chucked into quicklime, and this chap told me brother-in-law that he knew for a fact that his old grandmother was one o' them chucked into quicklime. So me brother-in-law warn't feared o' catching anything when he dug the old 'ooman up, because her 'ud most likely be nothing but dust and teeth. Everything else 'ud have bin ate away.'

Harry was forced to lean very close to hear as the carpenter whispered dramatically, 'Does you know, Mr Vivaldi, when they dug the old 'ooman up, her was almost perfect. The bloody worms hadn't touched her, and the lime hadn't ate her. It had kept her intact. Me brother-in-law said that anybody who'd known her when her was living 'ud have known her even after her'd bin buried all them years, because the lime had preserved her almost perfect. He said that he near-on shit hisself when he uncovered her and saw her face alooking up at him. He warn't expecting it, you see. He was expecting bones, not a human face.'

Disquiet struck through the young man, and involuntarily his eyes went to the corner of the room.

'Why hadn't the lime eaten her away?' he demanded.

'Because it couldn't have been quicklime that them who buried her had used,' the carpenter informed with an air of satisfaction. 'It was bloody mild lime. The bloody fools had used the wrong stuff, hadn't they?'

'But surely they could have told the difference?' Harry protested.

'Not necessarily,' his companion explained. 'You see, with quicklime powder you 'as to add water to get it to start burning, doon't you? When they buries a hanged man in quicklime, they knows that the rain and wet is agooing to seep down through the ground and start the quicklime burning. But if it's mild lime, it arn't agooing to burn, is it?

277

Because all the stuff that causes the burning has already bin took out from it. Mild lime is just like chalk really.'

'So how do you know what sort you're getting, if you want to buy a bag of limepowder?'

'Well it's easy to know, aren't it?' the carpenter looked at the younger man with a smug superiority, tinged with contempt for this display of ignorance.

'If youm buying it in sacks then there's different coloured lines on the sacks, aren't there? Quicklime's got a red line on it, and slaked lime's got a blue 'un. And mild lime used to have a yellow line. Unless they'se all bin changed in the last few years.'

He paused suddenly, and stared curiously at Harry.

'Am you feeling alright? You'se gone all queer looking!'

Vivaldi managed a sickly grin. 'It's just the thought of that old woman's body that your brother-in-law dug up. It's made me feel all queasy. I think I'll just step outside and get a breath of fresh air.'

The carpenter grinned contemptuously after Harry's retreating figure, and muttered, 'Fuckin' pansy!'

Outside in the cramped fetid yard Harry was desperately dredging in his memories.

'What colour line was on those sacks I took from Brown's yard? What colour line was it?' He closed his eyes, struggling to visualise. And then memory returned, and his heart sank.

'They had yellow lines on them, didn't they. Yellow lines.'

He paced up and down, his fists clenching and unclenching in his agitation.

'She's not been burned away then. Bella's still laying there all in one piece. God help me, she's still down there in one piece!'

Then doubt invaded his mind.

'Hold on a minute. How long did he say it had been that the old woman had been buried? Years and years ago. The body could never have survived that long, not even in a lead coffin. He's just telling lies.'

Vivaldi began to feel better.

'That's it. He's just shooting a line.'

He scoffed in self-derision. 'Christ Almighty, Harry Vivaldi! You're growing greener as you get older, aren't you? Swallowing such a tall story as that one is.'

He felt so relieved that he returned whistling into the room, casuing the carpenter to remark, 'Youm chirpy, arn't you. I reckon I could do with a breath o' that fresh air meself, if it's perks you up so much.'

Harry grinned at him, but made no answer, and they resumed their work.

But late that evening, when Harry was sitting in the drawing room of Cotswold House in company with his wife and Adrian, the carpenter's story of the preserved corpse returned to his mind, and no matter how many times he dismissed it from his thoughts, it persisted in returning. That night he dreamed once more about the dead Bella, and came awake drenched in the clammy sweat of fear.

Chapter Thirty

Emma always allowed her two maidservants to have the same day off from their work. She did this partly from kindness, so that the girls would have each other's company, and partly for her own convenience. Emma greatly enjoyed being able to sit in the kitchen and share a bottle of gin with her old friend and confidante, Mrs Elwood, without the likelihood of the curious young girls overhearing what was said.

By mid-morning the bottle of gin was already half empty, and the women's eyes were bright with the effects of the strong spirit.

'I heard the bugger shouting out in his sleep again last night.' Emma was referring to Harry.

'I thought he'd stopped doing that since he come off the drink.' The other woman raised her eyebrows interrogatively. 'Does you reckon he's started tippling again?'

Emma shook her head. 'No. He was sitting in the drawing room with me and Adrian till bedtime. And I know he's got no bottles hid away in his room, because I went and checked yesterday, and this morning.'

Mrs Elwood's fat cheeks quivered with salacious laughter. 'Perhaps he's suffering from the night starvation, my duck? Perhaps it's because you wun't let him have a bit that's making him cry out?'

The young woman's black eyes hardened, and her expression was cruel. 'Then he'll just have to keep on suffering, won't he? He's had all the bits he's ever going to have from me. He can keep off the drink just as long as he chooses, but he arn't going to come into my bed again.'

'Why? Am you getting all you can handle from Fancy

Dan?' This was how the cook always referred to West, for whom she had conceived a suspicious dislike.

'He's not got anything from me either for a couple of weeks,' Emma affirmed. 'To tell you the truth, I can't think now what it was I saw in him.' She frowned and stretched her arms wide, and yawned hugely. 'I'm fed up with men, Mrs E. They're all the same – they just want's what's between my legs.'

'It aren't all they wants is it, girl?' Mrs Elwood told her bluntly. 'And it aren't all they gets neither, is it?'

'What's you mean?' Emma challenged defensively.

'You knows well what I means.' The other woman became aggressive. 'Youm a bloody fool to yourself, you am, Emmy Farr. That bloody wastrel husband o' yourn has took hundreds o' pounds from you. And now this bloody Fancy Dan is adoing the same.'

'That's none o' your business,' Emma's gutter devil exploded, and from her mouth there poured a stream of expletives as she reverted to her roots.

The fat cook closed her eyes and sat stolidly until the stream of verbal abuse faltered and ceased. Then she opened her eyes and declared emphatically, 'It is my business, my duck. Because I cares for you, and I doon't like seeing you took for a bloody fool by bloody rotten men.'

The younger woman tossed her head defiantly, but despite her temper was driven to ask, 'Is that what they'm saying then? Your nosey cronies? That I'm being took for a fool?'

'They'm saying nothing!' Mrs Elwood declared ringingly. 'But they'd have plenty to say if they knew all about what I knows, 'udden't they?'

'And what is it that you reckons you knows?' Emma challenged witheringly. 'Because reckoning something arn't knowing it, is it?'

The fat woman was not discomfited by her young friend's tone. She took a gulp of her gin, emptying the glass, and then carefully refilled it from the bottle, and took a further sip. She smacked her lips in noisy satisfaction.

281

'Well then, tell me,' Emma demanded impatiently. 'What is it that you reckons you know?'

Inwardly, she knew that she was going to be forced to face some unpalatable truths. Her friend's mysterious contacts appeared to possess the uncanny facility of being able to penetrate any secrets that she, Emma, thought she held. There were times when Emma visualised Mrs Elwood as a fat old spider sitting in the centre of a huge invisible web, along the threads of which passed information from a thousand different sources.

'Well? Come on! Let's hear it!'

The older woman grinned slyly, and said teasingly, 'I doon't know 'as how I'm agoing to tell you now. Not arter the way you'se bin blaggardin' me.'

Emma could not help but grin herself, at the sardonic humour of this confrontation. And giggling, she urged, 'Come on, you tormenting old cow! What's you found out now?'

The fat red face smiled fondly. The cook was deeply fond of her young mistress, and in many ways regarded her as the daughter which she had never had. Then the smile vanished and she became very serious. She folded her arms before her massive chest and leaned across the table, speaking in wheezy, low-pitched tones.

'Well, just lately I'se bin hearing a lot o' things from a lot of different folks. I arn't said anything to you afore, my duck, because I had to wait to piece it all together afore I could make any sense out on a lot of it.'

She paused to take another sip from her glass, and although Emma was itching with impatience to hear, she knew that she must let the older woman continue in her own way at her own pace.

'The Fancy Dan is fast running out o' money. The takings at that blood-tub of his am right at rock bottom, and he aren't paid them players their full wages for two weeks or more. In fact they'm still waiting for their last week's money. Some on 'um am talking about leaving him. That ginger-haired bit wi' the froggie name is the one who's prodding the rest on to goo. Her used to be his fancy bit until he met you, you know. But it aren't the fact that he went off with you that's bothering her that much. It's the bloody wages he owes her. And theer's a few o' the locals that he's owing bills to as well. Not big 'uns, and not many. But he's keeping 'um waiting for settlement.'

Emma pursed her full lips, and nodded silently. What she was hearing was the confirmation of a developing suspicion in her own mind concerning Adrian's finances.

'Theer's summat else a bit strange agoing on as well, my duck. Theer's bin a bloke asking questions around the town about Bella Thomas.'

'Oh, I know that,' Emma interrupted. 'I saw him myself, didn't I? That little man who said he was Bella Thomas' husband.'

The cook shook her head so vehemently that her hanging jowls swung jerkily from side to side. 'No! It aren't him that I'm on about, girl. This other bloke had the stamp of a copper, so they tells me. He was a big bugger, wi' waxed whiskers and dressed like a plainclothes man. You know how they all looks the same, them sneaky bastards.'

'What does he want with her?' Emma wondered aloud.

'It aren't just him as wants to know about her, in my opinion.' Mrs Elwood leaned back in her wooden-armed chair, causing the joints to creak alarmingly beneath her shifting weight. Satisfaction gleamed in her watery pinkish eyes as she delivered her bombshell.

'This bloke who's bin enquiring after Bella was seen with Fancy Dan in White's tea rooms. They spent a long time in the upstairs room. And when Fancy Dan left he was carrying a big brown envelope, that the other bloke must have given him.'

'I know all about that,' the younger woman declared, disappointment sharpening her voice. 'I thought you had something good to tell me. Not something that I already knows about.'

Mrs Elwood scowled, made irritable by the fact that her bombshell had turned out to be only a damp squib.

'What does you mean, you already knows?' she growled.

'Adrian told me weeks since that he was going to have enquiries made about Bella by private detectives. And he went to see Albert Thomas as well.'

283

'Oh I see,' Mrs Elwood nodded reflectively. 'Then what was in that envelope?'

It was Emma's turn to frown thoughtfully, and she answered the question with another question.

'When was it that this bloke gave Adrian the envelope?'

'A few days since,' the cook told her. 'Why? Aren't he told you about it?'

Emma shook her head. 'No, he aren't said a word. Only that when he went to see Albert Thomas the bloke showed him the door. He's never mentioned this envelope.'

'There, I told you didn't I.' The fat woman's face glowed with triumphant vindication. 'Fancy Dan is a sneaky bastard, right enough. I'se told you all along that the bugger needs watching. He's taking you for a bloody fool, my duck. If he was really to be trusted, then he'd have told you about what was in that bloody envelope, 'udden't he?'

The young woman's expression became pensive, and she remained silent for some time. Then she remarked casually, 'Adrian keeps all his private papers in that big trunk of his, doesn't he?'

The cook nodded. 'But it's always locked, aren't it. It's got a padlock the size of a housebrick on it.'

A broad grin spread across Emma's face, and she rummaged in the pocket of her gown and produced a large, shiny metal key. She held it up before the cook's face and giggled.

'I reckon this might just fit that padlock, Mrs E.'

The fat woman cackled with amusement as her mistress explained.

'Adrian left his bunch o' keys laying about one night, and I took a print of some of them in a bar of soap. I thought that I'd get a couple of copies made.' Her black eyes danced with mischievous glee. 'Just in case he might lose his old keys, you understand. I didn't want him to be inconvenienced.'

'Youm a caution, you am, Emmy Farr!' The fat woman's face shone bright red, and she shrieked with laughter, waving her hands in the air. 'Youm a caution, you am. Youm a bloody caution!'

When her laughter had finally spluttered to an end, she

asked eagerly, 'Does you want me to come up and help you look through Fancy Dan's trunk, my dear?'

'Alright,' Emma agreed. 'Those two arseholes have gone to Brummagem to try and fix up a distribution deal with some bloke that Adrian knows. So there's no danger of them catching us. They'll not be back till tonight. To be honest, I wouldn't care if they never come back. I'm that fed up with both of 'em.'

Mrs Elwood stared knowingly at her friend, and asked with assumed casualness, 'How have you been getting on wi' Johnny Purvis lately?'

Emma's black eyes flashed fire, and she scowled at the other woman's bland face.

'What's that to do with you?'

Mrs Elwood hid a grin and shrugged her meaty shoulders. 'Nothing, I suppose. I was only asking.'

The glossy chestnut hair threatened to become unpinned from its high-piled dressing as the young woman's head nodded furiously.

'Oh yes! Oh yes! You was only asking, alright. You was only asking!'

'That's all I was doing,' the cook declared, with assumed aggrieved innocence. 'Just asking.'

'Well that's what you can keep on doing, just asking. But you'll get no bloody answer.'

Emma drained her own glass and refilled it, and drank the contents down rapidly. Then her mood metamorphosed with its customary perverseness, and she grinned cheekily.

'If you must know, I'm getting on with Johnny like a bloody house on fire.'

'Ahrr, I thought so,' the cook nodded wisely. 'And that's why youm all of a sudden so fed up with Fancy Dan, aren't it? Now that Johnny is back on the scene, youm beginning to have thoughts about him again, aren't you?'

The young woman's grin widened. 'I might be, Mrs E. I might be.'

She refilled her glass yet again. 'Come on, we'll take the bottle upstairs with us. Let's see what Fancy Dan has got hid away in his trunk.'

When Emma had removed the padlock and opened the
lid of the massive trunk Mrs Elwood reminded her, 'Now
doon't go at it like a bull at a gate. Everything 'ull have to
goo back in the proper order, or he'll know that we'se bin
nosing, wun't he?'

The trunk contained clothing and personal possessions
and oddments, as well as papers. At first the two women
laughed and joked as in certain of the large envelopes they
discovered pictures and photographs of naked men and
women in various sexual poses, and Mrs Elwood puffed
between fits of laughter, 'I 'ope you and Fancy Dan didn't
get up to this, my duck. It looks too bloody painful to me.'

Then their mood altered as they saw some of the other
contents of the envelopes. These were photographs of
men, women, children and animals indulging in explicit
sexual acts.

When Mrs Elwood discovered these she frowned with
disgust, muttering, 'Well just fancy him keeping these, the
dirty bastard!'

And handed them across to Emma, who also
experienced shock and acute distaste at the perversions
that the photographs depicted, and she began to wonder
about Adrian's sexual predilections, and to regret that she
had made love with a man who apparently enjoyed such
obscenely perverted pictures.

There were many collections of letters, some written by
women with whom West had obviously had affairs. There
were also letters demanding the payment of debts, some of
which bore very recent dates, all of which added to
Emma's disquiet. Then she found the envelope containing
the reports of the private detective agency that West had
employed to trace Bella Thomas.

Emma split the sheaf of papers with Mrs Elwood, and
both women remained silent as they read. When they had
finished their initial batches they swopped the sheafs and
continued to read on in silence. All laughter had died now,
and when every report had been read they sat staring at
each other with troubled faces.

It was the older woman who broke the strained silence.
'Am you thinking what I'm thinking, my duck?'

286

Emma seemed relucant to speak, and the cook went on, 'These blokes am making out that Bella Thomas has been murdered, or has done away with herself.'

Emma nodded.

The fat woman pursed her lips and expelled a long drawnout breath.

'And from how I'se understood what they'm saying, it could be that your husband knows summat more about Bella Thomas' disappearing than he says.'

Emma was palefaced and tense, as she nodded, and whispered, 'That's how it read to me as well, Mrs E.' She hesitated a moment or two, then blurted out, 'But why hasn't Adrian told me what's in these bloody reports? Why's he kept quiet about them? Is he playing some sort of game, do you think?'

'If he is playing a game, then it's a bloody deep 'un, and no mistake,' the older woman grunted. 'What am you gooing to do about this, my duck?'

Emma shook her head. 'I don't know, Mrs E. I'll have to think about it. Now you keep your mouth shut about what we've found here, while I thinks it all over.'

'I will, my duck, I will.'

The young woman gestured. 'I'd like to be by meself for a bit, Mrs E. I needs to be quiet.'

The fat woman waddled from the room, concern in her face as she turned for a last look at Emma's hunched, tense figure.

287

Chapter Thirty-One

The ratchets clicked metallically as Johnny Purvis wound up the clockwork mechanism of the phonograph, and carefully placed the needle into the grooves of the cylindrical record.

> We from childhood played together,
> My dear comrade Jack and I,
> We would fight each other's battles,
> To each others aid we'd fly . . .

Terry Perkins grinned with delight and kept his ear close to the elongated bell-mouthed horn from where the tinny-sounding voice was issuing.

> And in boyish scrapes and troubles,
> You would find us everywhere.
> Where one went the other followed,
> Naught could part us for we were . . .

'Comrades, comrades, ever since we were boys . . .' Purvis' deep, tuneful voice joined in the chorus, and he waved his arms in time to the music. After a second the grinning boy raised his own thin piping treble in unison.

> Sharing each other's sorrows,
> Sharing each other's joys.
> Comrades when manhood was dawning,
> Faithful what'er may betide,
> When danger threatened,
> My darling old comrade,
> Was there by my side,
> Was therrrre by my side . . .

288

The song continued on to tell the story of the two comrades joining the same regiment and going abroad to fight England's wars.

The final verse was a particular favourite of Johnny's and he sang the words with gusto, acting out the physical combat, using a broom handle as an imaginary rifle and bayonet, while Terry stared admiringly and clapped and cheered.

In the night the foe came over,
And we went for them like hell,
It was rifle butt and bayonet,
And we drove them back pellmell,
There was one chap got me cornered,
I was helpless, wounded sore,
It was Jack that sprang between us,
And my pal was mine no more.

Purvis wiped imaginary tears from his eyes, then grinned at the boy and beckoned him to join in the last chorus.

We were comrades, comrades,
Ever since we were boys,
Sharing each other's sorrows,
Sharing each other's joys . . .

The shrill ringing of the new electric door bell punctuated the final lines of the chorus, and Terry's sharp ears heard the sound before Purvis.

'Theer's somebody at the back door.' The boy ran through the stone-flagged, vaulted passageways to the front of the house.

Purvis, still humming the tune, removed the wax cylinder and began to sort through the racked collection to choose another recording to play.

'It's an 'ooman wants to see you, Mr Purvis.' The boy's expression was puzzled. 'What does an 'ooman want to see you for, Mr Purvis?'

The man could not help but grin amusedly at the boy's manner. 'Didn't you ask her what she wanted then, Terry?'

The tow-head nodded. 'Her 'udden't tell me though. Her just said that her wanted to spake to you personal.'

Purvis nodded. 'Alright. Where is she now?'

'Still at the door I should think.'

'Didn't you ask the lady to step inside?'

The boy shook his head.

Purvis shook his own head, and grinned wryly. 'My Christ, Terry! Will you ever make a butler, I ask myself.'

'A butler, Mr Purvis?' The boy scratched his head in puzzlement. 'What does you mean? Am I gooing to be a butler?'

Again the man shook his head, and chuckled, 'I don't really believe so, Terry.'

As he left the room the boy dogged his heels, and he turned and shooed him back.

'No. You stay here, Terry. Didn't the lady say that she wanted to speak to me personally?'

The spurred heels of his riding boots jingled as he marched through the house, wondering who the woman might be, and what she might want from him.

'I expect it's someone collecting for charity,' he assumed.

But when he opened the front door and saw who was standing in the porchway, he felt a physical shock.

Miriam Josceleyne, pale faced and nervous, swallowed hard and said in a tremulous voice, 'Hello Johnny.'

For a few moments the man could only stand staring at her, and then he recovered his wits, and asked her, 'Will you step inside, Miriam?'

She hesitated, and his heart filled as in his mind the long years rolled back, and he remembered how he had first met and fallen in love with this timid, frail little woman.

'Please,' he stood back from the door and beckoned her in with a motion of his hand, and after a further brief hesitation, she bowed her head and stepped inside.

His eyes studied her avidly. She was wearing a plain white blouse, and grey skirt belted at her slender waist. On her light brown hair was a straw boater with a bowed ribbon around its crown. Her face was thin, and there was a light patterning of lines radiating outwards from her tired green eyes. To him she still looked youthful, and

290

fragilely pretty, and he told her truthfully, 'Do you know, Miriam, you have hardly changed at all.'

A smile of self-deprecation briefly quirked her pale lips, 'I've grown older, Johnny.'

'Come and sit down.' He pushed open the door of the room he used as his study. As she seated herself upon one of the great leather armchairs he asked eagerly, 'Will you take some refreshment, Miriam? Some coffee or tea, or something to eat?'

She shook her head. 'No, I thank you.'

He sat down closely to her and leaned forward with his hands on his breeched knees. His light blue eyes were filled with a genuine pleasure as he told her, 'It is so good to see you again, Miriam.'

She felt a surge of joy, and embarrassed by the strength of her own feelings she stared down at her small gloved hands, entwined upon her lap, fingers twisting and squeezing nervously.

There came the hurried clattering of feet from the stone-flagged passage and Terry Perkins' rosy cheeks appeared in the doorway. His gaze went from the man to the woman and back again, and his curiosity was shining from his eyes.

'Yes, Terry, what is it?' Johnny Purvis was not best pleased at this interruption, knowing as he did what had prompted it.

'I just wanted to know if you wanted me to put another record on the phonograph, Mr Purvis,' the boy asked with assumed innocence, and all the time his gaze was hungrily devouring this woman visitor.

Purvis smiled with a hint of impatience. 'No thank you, Terry. You can get off home now.'

The boy's expression was dismayed. 'Have I got to, Mr Purvis? Only I thought you wanted me to groom the horses later on.'

The man chuckled. 'Alright Terry. You go and groom them now then.'

'Alright, Mr Purvis.' The boy grinned cheekily. ' 'Ud you like me to do anything here for you, afore I starts the grooming?'

'No!' Purvis frowned sternly, and realising that he was treading on thin ice, Terry Perkins scampered off, singing in high-pitched treble, 'Comrades, comrades, ever since we were boys, Sharing each other's sorrow's, Sharing each other's joys.'

The interruption had given Miriam Josceleyne just enough time to master her tense nervousness, and she began to feel more relaxed.

'I think that you've got a devoted follower there, Johnny,' she observed, as the boy's singing echoed through the ancient house.

'He's a good lad,' Purvis told her. 'He's coming into full-time service with me when he leaves school.'

Both the man and the woman wanted desperately to talk of the past, but neither could pluck up the courage to do so.

'I hear that you've become a leader of the Suffragette Movement.'

'Well, I'm not really one of the leaders, but I am active in the Cause.'

For a time they talked of the Suffrage Movement, the man asking questions, the woman answering. Miriam's gaze kept meeting his, then falling away, not in any sly or furtive manner, but rather as if her timidity were overcoming her.

It was Johnny who finally summoned the resolution to tell her, 'Emma told me what she had done with my letter, and with your letters also. And how she had allowed you to go on believing the lies about my relationship with Cleopatra Dolton.'

The woman's thin pale face coloured hotly, but relief flooded through her because she could now speak of what was uppermost in her mind. 'She told me also, Johnny.'

'She wronged us both very badly,' Johnny observed with some bitterness. Although he had been able to forgive Emma, there were still many moments when his anger burned for what she had done to him.

'Have you been able to forgive her for what she did, Miriam?'

The green eyes glimmered with unshed tears. 'Forgive

292

her, yes. But there are times when I could hate her for what she did.'

'Me likewise.' He grinned ruefully. 'I can only draw some bleak comfort from the thought that it was fated to happen, that it was part of our destiny.'

'I've been able to take comfort in some sense from what Emma told me,' Miriam said quietly. 'At least we now know that neither of us had cheated or betrayed the other's trust, that the rift between us was caused by someone else's deceit, and malice.'

John Purvis cleared his throat nervously, and then asked, 'What is there to stop us from healing that rift, Miriam, now that we both know the truth of the matter?'

He reached out to take her hand in his, but she gestured for him to not do so, shaking her head as tears began to fall down her cheeks.

'It's too late, Johnny. It's too late.'

'Why is it too late?' His face showed both pain and puzzlement. 'I still love you, Miriam, and I believe that you still love me. Why would you have come here else? Why is it too late? We have years ahead of us, years that we could share.'

Momentary doubt caused him to hesitate, then he questioned her, 'Have you lost all feeling for me, Miriam? Do you no longer love me?'

She bowed her head, her hands tight clenched before her.

'Is that it?' His own pain was causing him to press her ruthlessly for answer. 'If you can look me in the eyes and tell me truthfully that you no longer have any feelings left for me, then I'll accept it. Can you tell me that?'

Her tearful face lifted to him, and she shook her head and murmured brokenly, 'No, I can't tell you so, Johnny. I do still have feelings for you. I do still have love for you. But it's too late for us. Too late!'

'Tell me why it's too late,' he demanded forcefully. 'I have the right to know why you should say that.'

She wiped her eyes with a wisp of handkerchief, and drawing a deep breath told him quietly, 'I am ill now, Johnny. I have consumption.'

293

Concern and dismay juddered through him, and now he clasped her hands within his own.

'How advanced is it, Miriam?' he questioned gently.

She was able to look him fully in the face, and to hold his gaze with her own.

'It seems to be in recession. But the doctors tell me that the odds are greatly against me ever being fully cured.'

'The fact that you have consumption makes no difference to how I feel about you,' he told her. 'We can still be married.'

'No. I could never marry you, Johnny. We could never live in intimacy as man and wife. I would infect you.'

His eyes grew stubborn. 'I'm not afraid of that possibility.'

'No!' she was adamant. 'I can never marry you.'

'Well if you won't marry me, then be my lover again,' he pressed.

'I couldn't, because I love you too much, Johnny. Every time that we kissed I would be in mortal terror that you were becoming infected.'

He moved swiftly, and before she could draw back, his arms had lifted and crushed her to him, and his mouth had covered her own. The taste and the feel and the heat of him instantly roused her long suppressed, desperate need. Instinctively her body moulded against his, and her fingers clutched his hard muscular body. But in the same instant revulsion for her own momentary surrender to her hungry lusts filled her mind, and she fought to break free of his arms and lips.

'No!' she screamed out as she freed her mouth. 'No! Please Johnny, no!'

He stared down into her tormented face, and remorse and shame filled him.

'I'm sorry, Miriam. I'm sorry. I couldn't help myself.'

She was sobbing bitterly now, her harsh gasping breaths shuddering through her, and gently he cradled her against his chest, stroking her heaving shoulders and whispering, 'Don't cry, honey, please don't cry. I'll never do that to you again. Please don't cry.'

Gradually his soothing took effect and she calmed

down. Her harsh sobbing trailed away into a soft whimpering.

'I'm sorry, Johnny,' she told him brokenly. 'But when you kissed me I had terrible visions of the foulness in me entering you also. I couldn't bear for that to happen, Johnny. I love you, and I couldn't bear to be the means of your destruction.'

His features twisted in sad torment, and tears glistened in his eyes. He was forced to swallow hard to dispel the choking lump in his throat, and it was some time before he could control his shaking voice sufficiently to tell her, 'I still want to marry you, Miriam.'

She started to protest, but he hushed her to silence, and went on, 'No, hear me out, I beg you to hear me out.'

She stared up at him and nodded submissively.

'If you will marry me, then I'll make no physical demands upon you, honey. We'll not share a bed. But we will share our lives in every other way.' He forced a smile. 'There are many married couples who live so, Miriam. Love is not merely the sharing of physical passion. It's the union of minds and hearts as well.'

She shook her head. 'No. Johnny. I couldn't ask you to live like that. You're a man with all a man's natural needs and desires. It wouldn't be fair for you to live in such a manner.'

He grimaced wryly. 'Why not? I've been living like a monk for several years now. I would merely be continuing on the same way, but I'd have you with me to share my life, and so the lack of physical loving would be no hardship to me.'

His protestations could not overcome her doubts however, and she remained adamant in her refusal. But all tensions had dissolved between them now, and they were able to talk without constraint as they walked from the house and out onto the sunlit greensward.

Despite her stubborn refusal to marry him, Johnny was now happier and more content that he had been since their parting. He thought secretly that eventually he would wear down her resistance to marriage. Although he made no further mention of it at this time, he was resolved that he would continue his endeavours to gain that end.

Miriam herself was both happy and sad at the same time, her joy at being with this man overshadowed by the knowledge that they could never share any physical relationship. She felt guilty for coming here. Guilty for not being able to satisfy his bodily hungers. Guilty because of the joy she experienced at hearing him declare his love for her. Guilty because she could not bear the thought of him falling in love with some other woman. But rising above that guilt, was the sweet joy of being together with John once more after so many long, sad, empty years.

The hours passed as they talked and talked, and the suncast shadows of the tree were lengthening across the greensward when at last they reluctantly parted. John stood and watched her slender figure disappear into the long green tunnel of the driveway, and a great surge of happiness filled him.

We will be husband and wife some day, my darling, he told Miriam in his mind. And that day will come sooner than you think.

Miriam began to weep softly as she entered the cool green tunnel, and both joy and sadness battled for mastery within her. It was joy that won that battle. She and John were to meet again tomorrow, and she knew with an absolute certainty that they would meet again, and again, and again.

'Dear God, grant me a miracle,' she prayed fervently. 'Grant me health! Please God, grant me health!'

Chapter Thirty-Two

During the time that had elapsed since Emma had discovered the reports hidden in Adrian West's trunk, the young woman had thought deeply about the possible implications of what she had read in those papers. She had made no mention of the matter to either of the two men involved, but now found that she was looking at both of them with different eyes. Deep down Emma had always in some degree despised men in general, and some men in particular, regarding them as weak-willed creatures dominated by their own bodily appetites, less intelligent and shrewd than herself. Now, however, she was revising those opinions.

In the evenings spent sitting in the drawing room, she would covertly study her husband's handsome features and wonder if he had in fact murdered his old mistress? If he did possess such savage ruthlessness? If he was so cool nerved as to have been able to pay court to and marry her, Emma, while all the time he was intending to kill Bella?

During shared mealtimes she would secretly study the flamboyant Adrian West, and wonder what devious schemes he was formulating in his mind, marvelling at his good humour, and his effrontery in living lavishly, despite his pressing debts, and mounting business worries. She was also beginning to discern that beneath the effete, flamboyant, affable façade, there was hidden a tough and ruthless man. A cold and a cunning man. A daring and dangerous man.

Time and time again she found herself on the verge of challenging either one of them concerning what she had read. But time and time again her innate shrewdness kept her silent. If they were playing some sort of waiting game, then it behoved her to gain more information about whatever that game might be, before committing herself to any action. And so, imperceptibly, there developed between the three of them a watchful wariness, although on the surface they each tried to assume an air of normality in their relationship.

But the cooling of the once friendly relationship that had existed between Harry and Adrian was inexorably becoming more noticeable. On several occasions they indulged in bouts of bickering which threatened to escalate into open acrimony.

Harry was beginning to grumble privately to Emma about the continuing presence of this now unwelcome paying guest, and had several times stated to her his desire for the other man to leave Cotswold House.

Emma herself was beginning to find Adrian's presence irksome. The brief sexual infatuation she had had for him had now completely burned itself out, and she would have preferred it if he had left the house. But knowing what information he was holding, she was not willing to see him go yet. And also she was still eager to act in his films; she had invested a considerable sum of money in the new company, for which she had yet to see any return, another fact which enabled her better to tolerate his continuing residence at Cotswold House.

Emma's feeling concerning the possibility that Harry might well turn out to be a murderer were somewhat ambiguous. The fact that he may have killed a woman did not necessarily cause her fear or revulsion. She had been brought up amid violence, and knew how easily a drunken quarrel could explode and a moment's uncontrollable fury bring tragedy and death. And for her part she was uncaring of what might become of her husband. In fact, she would have welcomed her freedom from him should he die. But the thought of the scandal that it would create should he in fact be found out to have killed Bella filled her with misgivings. Although she despised and fought with her father, she still had some remnants of affection for him. And she loved her mother deeply. She was also very fond of her numerous younger brothers and sisters.

Emma knew that such a scandal as her marrying a murderer would cause her mother shame and heartbreak, and would make her family the butt of mockery and revilement. Although based on a differing bedrock from the pride of the rich and powerful, the pride of the poor and powerless was still a prized treasure to be fiercely protected from insult. Emma's marriage to old Hector Josceleyne had been a source of pride to her family. For no matter what his motivation for marrying her, the old man had been the head of a wealthy and respected family. The poor of the town had admired and respected the young woman for her acumen in snaring such a man. But if her second husband was discovered to be a killer, who had disposed of his mistress in order to marry Emma, then she would become an object of derision and contempt. All those who had previously applauded her would turn and revile her, and include in that abuse all of her family.

So when Harry urged her to send Adrian from Cotswold House, Emma ignored him, and mindful of the use that West might make of the detective's reports, continued to smile on the actor.

The fact that she no longer wanted him as a lover, however, she had not made entirely plain to West. She knew that to jilt him openly might well trigger off unpleasant repercussions. And so she made excuses to avoid making love with him, and tried to keep him sweet by promises of future delights to come when her unhappy marriage situation had resolved itself. The resolution, as she led West to believe, was a matter of getting her husband to agree to a divorce.

West was disgruntled by being deprived of his sexual pleasures, but for the time being was prepared to accept that deprivation, in the expectation of the situation being resolved in the near future.

Unknown to Emma, the reason for West keeping from her the information passed on to him by the private detective agency, was quite simply the fact that the more he had studied the reports, and the more thought he had given to the matter, he was less and less inclined to accept the supposition of Bella Thomas' death. The actor found it almost impossible to visualise that Harry, a man whom he judged to be a physical coward, and a moral weakling, would ever have had the capacity to kill anyone.

Instead he thought it more likely that if in fact she was dead then she had done away with herself in some convenient river or pool, and that her body had been trapped and held hidden by weeds until it had disintegrated and disappeared for ever. But the most likely explanation for Bella Thomas' disappearance was quite simply that she had hidden her tracks too well for the detectives to be able to trace her. And that she was probably living with some other paramour.

Despite that belief however, there were moments during his periodic bickerings with Harry that West could not resist making veiled allusions to certain information he possessed concerning Bella Thomas. And although these allusions would have no apparent outward effect on the other man, West thought that he could discern flashes of doubt and uncertainty in Vivaldi's dark eyes when those allusions were made. In turn this would leave West himself doubtful and uncertain, leave him wondering if despite his own reactions to them, there might yet be some kernel of truth contained within the reports.

The allusions were having an effect on Harry Vivaldi. They were causing him to worry if in fact the actor had discovered something about Bella's death. He knew that West had been having enquiries made by private detectives, and he was beginning to worry about what, if anything, they might have discovered. Harry was also beginning to consider the unpalatable possibility that he himself might have unknowingly given to the actor some inkling of what had happened to Bella. He knew that in his nightmares about the dead woman he shouted out, and now he began to wonder if those shouts might have been bellowed aloud, and the actor might have heard what he was shouting.

Yet despite all these fearful worries, Harry was discovering within himself attributes which he had only previously devoutly wished for. He was discovering a capacity to control his panic and his fears, and to utilise those emotions to mobilise all his scant resources of physical courage. To use them to nerve himself to face possible danger, and to plan and calculate with a considerable degree of cold resolve. Now he was possessed of a growing confidence that should disaster threaten to overwhelm him, he would be able to meet that threat head on, and to find some way of dealing with it.

And so, the days and weeks passed and the summer slowly passed, and within the confines of Cotswold House Emma, Adrian and Harry ate together, and drank together, smiled and talked pleasantly together, and circled each other watching and waiting like feral birds of prey.

Chapter Thirty-Three

The sulphurous fumes produced by the gas works permeated the air as Laura and Miriam walked towards the high block of the retort house and the massive rounded gas holders.

At the gatehouse a man wearing a battered uniform peaked cap challenged the pair.

'Yes ladies, what can I do for you?'

'We're looking for Mrs Jakes,' Miriam told him.

'Mrs Jakes?' He frowned doubtfully. 'I doon't know the 'ooman, ma'm. Theer aren't no women works here, you know.'

'She doesn't work here,' Laura put in. 'But we've been informed that she comes here with her child to let it breath the air.'

His frown cleared. 'Oh I see. Well theer's a lot on 'um brings their kids down here. But I doon't know many o' their names.'

'Are there any ladies here now with their children?' Miriam asked.

He nodded. 'Theer's a few went through a while since.'

'Well then, may we also pass through and go and look for them?' Laura's voice was curt – she possessed less patience than her friend. 'Only we've not much time to spare.'

The gatekeeper appeared to lose interest in them, and nodded, 'Ahrr, goo on through then.'

Miriam stared doubtfully at the complex of filthy, coal-dusted structures and buildings, the myriad steam jetting, hissing lines of pipes and vast gas holders. 'Where will the women be?'

He gestured towards the tall walls of the retort house. 'Up along by theer somewheres, ma'am. I doon't know exact. But take care wheer you walks. Theers a lot o' muck and water lying around.'

'Thank you.' Miriam nodded, and led the way up the steep entranceway into the noisy, busy complex. Flat capped, dirty-faced men in greasy soiled clothing hurried about on their tasks and errands, and a long train of coal-filled railway waggons drawn by a raucously puffing engine rumbled and clattered over steel rails.

As the two friends neared the retort house Laura pointed.

'There's Mabel Jakes. Over there with those other women.'

There were four shabbily gowned, shawled women with several children clinging to their skirts, and two with swaddled infants in their arms, huddled in a group close to an outlet pipe which jutted from the grimy wall of the retort house, periodically emitting jets of swirling steamy waste gases.

As they joined the group one of the children, a small boy, was coughing and whooping noisily, his face blue-tinged, saliva and mucus pouring from his nose and mouth. As one of the women bent anxiously to him, a stream of urine ran down his sticklike legs as he involuntarily voided his bladder. Another of the woman exclaimed irritably, 'Just look at the little bugger. He's bin and gone and pissed hisself agen. And I aren't got anything else for him to wear.'

Another of the children, a tiny girl, began to cough, breath whooping noisely in her throat as she fought to inspire.

Miriam shook her head in near despair at the ignorance which caused these woman, and countless others, to so fervently believe in the efficacy of gas works fumes as a sovereign cure for whooping cough and other respiratory diseases. Ever since she could remember Miriam had seen pathetic little processions of sick children being led and carried by their anxious, careworn relatives, towards the gas works. In rain, snow or sunshine, heat or cold, balmy

breeze or freezing wind, they would huddle against the
walls of the retort house breathing in the foul waste fumes
for hours.

She sighed sadly at the sight of the present misery of the
small boy and girl, and she wanted to urge the women to
take their children back to their homes. But she knew
from experience the futility of such urgings, and so kept
her counsels to herself.

Mabel Jakes was a young woman in her mid twenties,
but looked a score of years older. Her body was gaunt and
bent, her cheeks sunken into her toothless mouth, and on
one side of her withered throat a hugely swollen ball of
flesh, the skin red and shiny tight, forced her head into an
unnatural posture upon her narrow shoulders.

'Hello Miss Miriam, Miss Laura,' she greeted, and her
eyes were fearful.

'I've got some good news for you, Mrs Jakes.' Miriam
smiled reassuringly. 'There's no need for you to be
anxious.'

'Oh yes.' The ball of flesh prevented the woman from
nodding fully; her head could only move fractionally. Any
extension of movement caused her extreme discomfort.

'Yes.' Miriam's manner became somewhat strained,
because of her uncertainty as to how the woman would
react when she went on to tell her what she had to say.

'Doctor Peirce has had a reply from Birmingham. I'm
very pleased to be able to tell you that Doctor Holmes has
agreed to examine you, and if the examination is
satisfactory, then he will operate immediately. He will see
you in Doctor Peirce's surgery at ten o'clock on next
Tuesday morning. You'll be in very good hands, my dear.
Doctor Holmes is considered to be the most expert
surgeon in the country for this type of operation.'

Dismay filled the woman's eyes, and she made no
answer.

Miriam stared at her with concern. 'Are you alright, Mrs
Jakes?'

The woman's head twitched slightly forwards in
acknowledgement.

'Then what is troubling you?'

304

Still the woman did not answer, and Miriam gently pressed her. 'Come now. You must tell me. What is the matter, my dear?'

'I can't have any operation, Miss Miriam,' Mabel blurted out.

'But why ever not?' It was Laura who questioned. 'The doctor will only operate if he considers it absolutely safe to do so, Mrs Jakes.'

'No!' the woman's head twitched jerkily in negation. 'No! I can't have it!'

'But there's nothing for you to be afraid of,' Laura argued. 'As I've already told you, Doctor Holmes will not operate unless he considers it absolutely safe to do so.'

'No! I can't have it. I can't have no operation,' Mabel repeated doggedly.

'Why?' Laura Hughes persisted.

'I'se got no money to pay for it.'

'But you know very well that the local suffragette branch is going to pay. It will not cost you a single penny. I've already told you that many times, since we first discussed this operation,' Miriam reminded her.

'Who'se to look arter the kids while I'm in 'ospital?' Mabel wailed.

'We will make arrangements for them to be cared for while you're away, Mrs Jakes,' Miriam assured her.

The young woman continued to protest, 'Who'll see to me 'usband?'

'Surely he can see to himself for a time?' Laura Hughes challenged impatiently. 'He's a grown man, isn't he, not a helpless infant.'

'No! I can't have it.' Mabel Jakes' head jerked agitatedly.

'But you must have it.' Laura Hughes' patience seemed near to snapping. 'How can you be so stupid? Don't you realise that if that lump on your throat continues to grow at its present pace, then there will shortly come the time when it will literally stop you breathing? It will choke you to death!'

The young woman's eyes screwed tight, and she wailed in fear and misery.

'Theer, look what you'se bin and gone and done now?'

one of the other women angrily rounded on Laura Hughes. 'You'se fritted the poor soul half to death! Who the bloody hell does you think you am, coming down here blaggardin' this poor wench?'

Laura was unabashed by this attack. 'I'm trying to save her life,' she stated forcefully. 'If that swelling is not operated on, then it will most surely kill her.'

Mabel Jakes' wailing increased in volume, and she wrung her hands together in terror. Her distress and loud cries frightened the children, and they began to cry and wail themselves, and all the while the two afflicted children coughed and whooped uncontrollably.

'Gerroff from here, 'ull you,' the angry woman pushed Laura Hughes hard on her chest, sending her staggering backwards. 'If you doon't bugger off, I'll bloody well swing for you, you interfering cow.'

Dismayed by this turn of events Miriam attempted to intervene. 'Please, calm yourself,' she moved to try and comfort the wailing woman. 'Please, Mrs Jakes, don't distress yourself so. There's no need for it.'

'Just fuck off, 'ull you,' the angry woman shrieked wildly. 'You'se done harm enough for one day. Fuckin' suffragettes, coming poking your bloody noses in wheer they arn't wanted. Just fuck off.'

Realising that the situation had deteriorated beyond redemption Miriam reluctantly took Laura's arm and led her away from the cacophony. Neither woman spoke until they had reached the base of the Prospect Hill and were beginning the ascent to the town centre. Then Miriam murmured remorsefully, 'I wish now that I'd never mentioned the possibility of an operation to Mabel in the first place. But I never dreamed that it would cause her such distress.'

Laura frowned. 'She was eager for the operation when you told her that it might be possible for her to have it. It isn't your fault that she's a stupid, hysterical woman, Miriam.'

She shook her head dismissively. 'There are some people whom it's well nigh impossible to help. They're just too stupid and ignorant to know what is good for them. I can't help but consider that Mabel is one of that number.'

'Oh no, Laura. You're too harsh on the poor creature,' Miriam protested. 'Her ignorance is not her fault. She has never had any chance to gain knowledge, has she?'

'That's as maybe.' The younger woman was not prepared to abandon her stance. 'But she's wasted our time and effort, and also the doctor's time and effort, hasn't she?'

'It's not her fault that she's so afraid of an operation,' Miriam argued doggedly. 'She can't help her fears.'

'No, and neither can we help her fears.' Laura's thin features were sternly obdurate. She came to an abrupt standstill, and taking Miriam's arm brought her also to a standstill.

'Listen to me, Miriam,' she spoke with a burning intensity. 'When you decided that as the local branch of our movement we would no longer go into the streets with flags and banners to preach our message, but instead further our aims and influence by trying to give practical help to women in need of it, I was in full agreement with you. I thought it to be a good idea. But now I have to tell you that I think we are travelling the wrong road. It's the middle of August now, isn't it? In all these weeks that we've been trying this new idea we've achieved almost nothing to further our cause in this town – in fact, quite the opposite. Some of our supporters have fallen away, because they say that they didn't join the movement to become imitation Sisters of Mercy, but to win the right to vote.

'And what little good we've managed to achieve in giving practical help has been far outweighed by the number of times we've been fooled into giving help to worthless cheats and wasters. Do you realise that people are beginning to laugh and sneer at us behind their hands because they say that we are trying to act as Lady Bountifuls, and are mainly wasting our efforts even in that capacity? They are saying that we do more harm than we do good.' She hesitated, and then finished despondently, 'And after today's debacle I have to accept that there is considerable justification for them saying that.'

307

Miriam was stung by the harshness of her friend's criticisms, and turning away she continued on up the steep hill, her expression troubled and sad. Laura sighed regretfully, and followed behind, not attempting to shorten the distance of several paces that now separated them.

On the brow of the hill where it merged into the flat plateau of the Church Green, Miriam slowed to a halt and turned to wait for her friend. When Laura Hughes reached her she asked, 'What should we do then, Laura?'

'We should be concentrating on getting you well. Instead of rushing around trying to sort out the problems of these wretched women, you should be resting, and allowing your body to heal.'

The concern in the younger woman's grey eyes belied the scolding tone of her voice.

'But I'm getting well,' Miriam asserted. 'I am much stronger, and I don't cough half as much. Johnny tells me that I'm improved beyond measure.'

'John looks at you through love-hazed eyes,' Laura smiled wryly. 'And he always tells you what you wish to hear.'

It touched her heart to see her beloved friend and John Purvis together. The man was a frequent visitor to their house, and they to his.

The young woman both envied and pitied her friend's love affair. She knew how desperately Miriam wanted to get well. She knew the bitter frustration of the older woman, and how much she wanted to give herself both physically and mentally to her lover. Laura could only admire the self-discipline and restraint exercised by Miriam in refusing to surrender to her own hungers, because she knew that by doing so she would almost certainly infect the man she loved with her own terrible affliction. But despite Miriam's protestations of returning health Laura feared that her friend's illness was slowly but inexorably worsening. The unhealthy flush of the consumptive was now constant in her pale cheeks. There were some nights when Laura lay awake listening to the older woman's racking bouts of coughing; some mornings when she went into Miriam's bedroom she could feel the dampness of the bedclothes created by heavy night sweats.

'Well, Laura? I'm still waiting for an answer to my question? That's if you can tear yourself away from your daydreams.'

Miriam was smiling, and Laura realised that she had been lost in her own thoughts.

'I'm sorry Miriam, I was thinking about something.'

'So I could see. Now, what shall we do if we're going to abandon our efforts to be Lady Bountiful?'

'Well,' Laura's broad brow creased in consideration of the question. 'We could begin by calling on the supporters that have fallen away from us locally, and telling them that we're now going to concentrate solely on the struggle for the vote. We could tell them that we've abandoned being Lady Bountiful.'

Miriam Josceleyne frowned slightly, but nodded. 'Go on.'

'Then we can begin organising for the demonstration in Birmingham. We need to take as many sisters as we can from here. And that will take money. Then there are the uniforms for Mary Leigh. We promised to have them ready for the Prime Minister's visit, and they're not even halfway finished. We have to recruit more sempstresses.'

Laura's enthusiasm visibly kindled as she went on, and her grey eyes sparkled excitedly. 'Wouldn't it be wonderful, Miriam, if we could take every sister who wished to go from here up to Birmingham. If we can raise sufficient money we could do it, you know. We could pay their fares and wages they'll lose, and pay to have their children looked after for that day.'

The older woman's own enthusiasm was roused as her friend continued talking. And when Laura fell silent, she agreed.

'You're right, Laura. There's still about four weeks before Asquith comes to Birmingham. We've time enough to do it, you know.'

'I know.' Laura smiled quizzically. 'But we'll have to concentrate solely upon that. And not allow ourselves to be distracted by other matters.'

309

'Johnny can help us,' the older woman stated, then blushed, because she had once again betrayed how constantly the man was in the forefront of her thoughts.

Laura laughed fondly. 'I wasn't referring to John, Miriam. I was meaning that we mustn't allow ourselves to be distracted by trying to do any more good works, not until we're fully organised for Birmingham, anyway.' She paused, and then asked, 'Do you agree?'

'I do.' Miriam nodded, and then the two friends linked arms and went happily on their way.

Chapter Thirty-Four

The weather swung unseasonably, and for more than a week clouds had blotted out the sun. Every morning crowds of colourfully costumed extras, dressed in the uniforms and clothing of the English Civil War gathered upon the slopes of the Sudan, and then waited in rain and drizzle, the long plumes of the hats of the cavaliers drooping as the water drenched their feathers, the buff coats of the Roundhead troopers darkening as they became saturated.

Adrian West became increasingly angry with the weather as the days passed, and increasingly worried about his fast diminishing finances as he continually paid the extras to do nothing but wait for the clouds to rift and the sun to shine through.

To add to his misfortunes, following an altercation with certain local magistrates, councillors and prominent religious bodies because of a risqué play he had presented in an effort to boost audience attendances, his license to perform in the town had been suspended. He had been forced to have the wooden theatre dismantled, and its components stacked in forlorn piles at the side of the rented shed in the Royal yard. Inevitably his troupe of players had dissolved and dispersed following a heated dispute about the wages they claimed he owed them.

Now, at three o'clock in the afternoon, he gazed despairingly up at the lowering skies and again prepared to pay the extras for yet another wasted day.

Sheltering beneath the raised hood of the white Mercedes motorcar Emma, wearing the ornate courtdress of a high-born Stuart lady, her glossy chestnut hair hanging down in long ringlets, a cloak covering her naked shoulders and lowcut bodice, was also feeling disconsolate, and more than a little worried about her own considerable investment in this present moving picture. It was to be an epic about Royalists and Roundheads, with herself as the leading lady. But from the very first moment that work on it had begun the film had been beset with difficulty and delay. But still the money flowed outwards, and her bank manager had requested several urgent meetings with her.

After each of those meetings there had followed acrimonious arguments with Adrian, as she questioned why he must spend so recklessly on costumes, the hiring of nearly a hundred saddle horses and several hundreds of extras, the building and rebuilding of lavish indoor and outdoor sets. Always he met her accusing questions with the same answers. He was creating the greatest moving picture in history. It would bring them both immortal fame, and make them rich beyond the dreams of avarice. He was revolutionising the art of the moving picture, and carrying it into the future. When it was finished, and the wealth began to roll into their pockets, then she would go down on her knees and thank him for the vision and foresight.

At first these answers had overawed her. His utter conviction had stilled her doubts, and there were times that she had felt mean and unworthy to share in his dreams so fervent and palpably sincere were his protestations. But lately these answers had begun to lose their power to move her. Instead she was witnessing the daily drain on her own finite financial resources with an ever increasing uneasiness and foreboding.

With an open ledger on his knees, Adrian sat on a tall stool and the extras formed a long line and began to pass before him. Each man called out his name and had it ticked off in the ledger as he passed. Sitting on another tall stool by West's side, the dour-featured Henry Snipe counted out coins from the large moneybag between his feet and placed them into the outstretched palms of the passing men.

When the last extra had been payed, the lean whiplike

312

figure of Walter Read came to West and pointed to the mass of horses corralled by rope fences at the bottom of the slope. Their flanks were wet and steaming from the weeping drizzle.

'They'm gooing to need a good rub down tonight, Mr West, or we'll have 'um sickening else.' The horsebreaker grinned, displaying yellow horselike teeth. 'I'll have to hire a few more hands to help out. They'm too many for me and me lads to manage.'

West grimaced, and objected, 'Surely a little bit of dampness won't hurt them, Mr Read?'

The man stared at him knowingly. 'Well Mr West, if you wants to risk it, then youm the boss. But if any o' these beasts sickens because o' the wet, then their owners 'ull be claiming full value for damages from you.'

After a few moments consideration West reluctantly conceded the point, and he nodded curtly. 'Alright Mr Read, take on the help. But try and manage with as few as you can. Money doesn't grow on trees you know.'

'Doon't it now,' Read replied sarcastically. 'Well theer's summat I didn't know afore. It just goes to show, doon't it? If a man keeps his ears open he can learn summat new every day of his life, carn't he?'

He held out his hand towards the scowling Snipe. 'You'd best give me four sovereigns, Mr Snipe. I'll make account tomorrow, and if it's cost more or less we can settle up then.'

Read walked away jingling the coins in his hand and whistling happily, and West miserably watched him go.

Snipe scowled sourly at his employer. 'Doon't let 'um see you looking like that, or they'll know how bad things are.'

Instantly the strained expression disappeared from West's florid features, to be replaced by the customary look of jovial insouciance, and he asked laughingly, 'Is that better?'

The dour man nodded, and picking up the money bag, he rattled the pitifully few coins remaining in its capacious folds.

'You're going to need to fill this a bit sharpish, if you intends shooting tomorrow.'

For a moment the jovial mask slipped, and West snarled

313

viciously, 'I know that, you old fool. Just leave such matters to me, and do what I pay you to do.'

'Pay me to do?' the little man returned snarl for snarl. 'You aren't paid me for two weeks now!'

'You don't need paying, you thieving old bastard,' West riposted. 'You steal twice your wages from me every bloody week.'

Snipes was unabashed. He grinned ferociously. 'If I didn't do that I'd never get a bleedin' penny out of you, would I?'

'Give me that bag, and get the camera and other stuff stowed away,' West grunted. 'I've got more important things to be doing than standing here talking to you.'

Carrying the almost empty bag and the big ledger West stalked towards the Mercedes.

Emma greeted him shrewishly, 'More good money wasted today then.'

Controlling the urge to bite her head off, the actor smiled sweetly. 'It's just one of those things, my darling. I can't control the weather, unfortunately.'

He cranked the engine into spluttering roaring life and got into the car.

'I'll take you home, and then I've a business appointment to go to.'

'Who with?' the young woman questioned suspiciously.

'A potential investor.'

'Who's that?'

This time West made no reply, but concentrated all his attention on guiding the lurching motorcar over the slippery, muddied turf and out into the narrow rutted lane which led up to Mount Pleasant.

Emma snapped impatiently. 'Well?'

'Well what, my darling?' He beamed at her.

'Who is it that you're going to see?'

'I've already told you, a potential investor,' he evaded maddeningly. Before she could return to the attack he went on to strike first.

'Are you going to tell your husband tonight that you want a divorce so that you and I can be married?'

It was Emma's turn to make no reply. Her full lips

thinned into a hard set line, and she glared sullenly ahead.

He glanced sideways at her sullen profile, and frowned. 'Are you going to tell him?' he repeated, with a sharp edge to his voice.

Still she stayed silent.

The man hissed with exasperation. 'I'll not stand for being messed about in this way, Emma. I'll tell him myself.'

She remained glaring sullenly straight ahead, and West lost his temper. 'Will you bloody well answer me?' he shouted.

She tossed her head petulantly, causing the long glossy ringlets to tumble about her cloaked shoulders.

'I'm not sure that I want a divorce Harry. And I'm not sure that I want to marry you.'

'Oh, that's the game is it? You just used me for a bit of fun. And now that you've had your fun you think that you might be able to drop me, do you? Well, you're making a terrible mistake if you think that, my girl.'

His manner became threatening. 'Don't think that you and that damned worthless husband of yours can make a fool out of me. Because I know something that can get your bloody husband's neck stretched. That would bring you down into the muck as well, wouldn't it?'

This provoked a reaction, but not of the sort that he might have expected. She turned to face him, and her black eyes danced with malice, but held no trace of fear.

'You know something do you? Well use it then! I don't care what happens to Harry Vivaldi. And as for bringing me down into the muck, let me tell you something. I was born in the muck. I was reared in the muck. And in the eyes of this town I'm muck myself. So you can't bring me down into the muck, because I've never crawled out from it. I'm already there.'

Taken aback by this totally unexpected reaction, he could only stare bemusedly. Recognising the success of her counter-attack she jeered, 'You'd best watch the road instead of gawping at me. Or you'll have the bloody car arse over tip.'

To give emphasis to her warning the offside wheel struck a pothole and the car bounced and skidded, and

315

West swore as he wrestled with the steering wheel to regain control.

The shock engendered by this near-accident drove out his anger, and he experienced a sickening sense of dismay. 'Jesus Christ, I've messed up here! Stupid bastard that I am!' he castigated himself bitterly. 'Why couldn't I have kept my big mouth shut? Why couldn't I have controlled my temper?'

His mind raced as he sought for some way of mitigating the effects of his rash words. At his side Emma was also thinking hard. A fast accelerating contempt for West was throbbing through her, but so was the unwelcome recognition that unless she trod warily this present situation could rapidly worsen and bring all that she dreaded down upon her head.

Neither of them spoke during the remainder of the journey, and West eventually brought the Mercedes to a juddering halt outside the Cotswold House. For a while neither of them made any attempt to move, and they remained seated side by side, staring straight ahead. Then Emma gathered her full skirts and would have got out of the car, but the man laid his hand on her arm to stop her.

'Please Emma, hear me out?' he begged huskily.

She stayed stiff and silent, but remained in her seat, eyes still facing to the front.

'I'm truly sorry for losing my temper just now.' West was playing the role of a grievously wronged man, whose noble spirit had been sorely wounded. 'It was not the act of a gentleman. My only excuse is that my love for you drives me near to madness at times. What I said was madness also. I could never ever do anything to cause you distress, or to harm you in any way. I am totally ashamed of myself.

'I will of course leave your house immediately. But I hope that our business arrangements may be left unchanged for our mutual benefit.'

As Emma listened to his halting tones, she jeered inwardly, Youm a real trouper, arn't you, West. I wonder what fuckin' play youm taking these lines from? Well two can play at this game, West. And I reckon I'll prove a better gamester than you in the death.

When he had finished speaking, and was gazing at her with sorrowful, soulful eyes, she bowed her head, and toyed with her fingers for some moments. Then she murmured hesitantly, 'I don't wish you to leave my house, Adrian. I do want to marry you, and I do want a divorce from my husband. But you must give me time. It's a big step for me to take, you know. I do need time to steel myself to bear all the scandal and disgrace that my divorce will cause. It could kill my mother to hear what I've done. She's not strong Adrian. Please be patient with me. And please say that you'll stay in my house.'

Relief surged through him, and that sensation was so strong it blotted out his native scepticism.

'Anything, my darling! Anything that you want! Of course I'll stay. And of course I'll be patient. Please just tell me that you forgive me for ever doubting you.'

Tears fell from her black eyes and she murmured broken assent, taking his hand and squeezing it gratefully. Then gathering her skirts she left the car and hurried indoors.

West puffed out a long sigh of relief, and congratulated himself. 'Well Addy old boy, you managed to bring the cavalry to the rescue in the nick of time.'

Fresh confidence exploded, banishing all doubts. 'I've saved that situation, and now I'll save my picture.' He jumped out and cranked his engine into life, then remounted his seat and roared away.

Up in her bedroom Emma stood watching the man from behind the net curtain of the window. Her gutter-devil was roused and wrathful, and her black eyes glittered cruelly.

'You'll drag me down into the muck, will you, Adrian West? Well, it'll take a better man than you to beat me.' Her lips twisted in scornful contempt. 'You think you really got something over me doon't you, with those detective reports that youm keeping so secret? Well they aren't worth the paper they'm written on.'

In her mind a cold resolve was hardening.

I'll get free of both of the bastards someday,' she promised herself. But I'll make use of them in the meantime. I need West to make me a star of the moving pictures, and I need my bloody husband to keep West out of my bed. But just soon as I've got what I want, then it'll be the soldier's farewell for both of the sods.

She threw herself down on her bed and lay with her arms stretched wide, and her thoughts turned as they so often did, to the detective's reports concerning the disappearance of Bella.

I wonder what did happen to her? I wonder if she really is dead? I should have thought that if she'd done away with herself then somebody or other would have found the body by now.

But what if somebody has hid the body away? The unbidden thought was followed by the inevitable question: Was it Harry who hid her away?

She tried to dimiss that notion. No! He'd never have the guts to do somebody in.

But the memories of gossip retailed to her by Mrs Elwood returned in full force to her mind.

But Harry used to knock Bella Thomas about didn't he? She used to be walking about with black eyes and busted lips. And women don't always get them from falling downstairs all the time, do they? He could have killed her in a flash o' temper, couldn't he? He could have hit her a bit too hard one night when he was in drink.

And how about his bloody nightmares? And the way he kept on running off to George Street as soon as he used to wake up. He don't do that anymore, but I still hear him shouting out in his sleep as if all the devils of hell were after him.

Again she tried to dismiss these disturbing thoughts. No! It can't be. Harry would never have the guts to kill her, and then carry it all off like he's done, as if nothing had happened.

But the dismissed thoughts quickly returned: It wouldn't have taken any guts to kill her, if it was done by accident, would it? If he'd hit her, and she'd fallen and broke her neck, or something similar. But then he'd have to get rid of the body, wouldn't he. And she was a big woman to handle. He wouldn't be able to just chuck her over his shoulder and carry her.

Suddenly Emma drew a sharp breath, as abruptly she realised, He needn't have carried her anywhere, need he? He could have hid her in George Street, hid her in the bloody house. Is that why he used to goo charging down there after he had a nightmare? Has he got her buried under the floor in that house. Or hid in the roof somewhere.

Although all her rationality clamoured to reject this conviction, still it persisted. Rather than repulsing her it instead gradually created a perverse excitement, and even a trace of grudging admiration for the man's nerve in covering up what he had done.

Emma's lack of revulsion was not an indication of any inherent wickedness in her character, and her callousness about Bella Thomas' possible fate was not unexplainable. In the slum she had been born and raised in life was bitterly hard, and very cheap, and death an intimately familiar companion. From infancy she had witnessed death come in many different forms, and she believed that murder wore many different faces, and could at times even be a justifiable act. She knew also that it could be an act of omission as readily as it could be an act of commission.

In her opinion all those countless people who died prematurely worn-out in mind and body by ceaseless grinding toil had been surely murdered by the employers who so ruthlessly exploited them. All the women of the slums who died screaming in childbirth because they could not afford to have proper medical treatment were victims of the murderous neglect of their rulers. The infants and tiny children of the slums who died in such abundance from endemic deseases were the victims of that same murderous neglect. And all the tens of thousands of her fellow countrymen and women who died in bitter poverty after a lifetime of polluted water, rotten food, adulterated beverage, poisonous cesspits, wretched housing, had been murdered by those set to rule over them, just as surely as if those same rulers had taken hammers in hands and battered their brains out.

If any clergyman had taxed Emma with being a wicked

319

sinner because she felt no revulsion for what she thought Harry might have done, she would have spat in that clergyman's face and called him a hypocrite, and have challenged that same clergyman to live the life she had led, and then see if he would prate so confidently of wicked sinners?

Made restless and unsettled by her thoughts Emma rose from the bed and quickly changed into outdoor clothes.

In the hallway she called to Mrs Elwood, 'I'm going out for a walk, Mrs E.'

The fat cook came waddling, wiping floured hands on her voluminous white apron. 'Gooing anywheer special, my duck?'

The young woman shook her head. 'I'm only popping down to see me Mam, and then I might goo and have a look at that new set in the Royal yard.'

'Alright, my duck. I'll see you later.' The fat woman smiled fondly, and watched the slender elegant, parasol-carrying figure of her mistress until she disappeared from view along the Church Green.

Chapter Thirty-Five

Cleopatra Dolton opened the door herself to greet her visitors, and invited the two men to follow her into her office.

Once there she wasted no time in meaningless small talk. 'I've studied your proposals with great care, Mr West, and if we can clarify certain matters, then I'm prepared to invest some money in your moving picture.'

The actor beamed with pleasure, but the other man, Ozzie Clarke, frowned and shook his head.

Cleopatra's dark eyes noted her manager's reaction. 'What's the matter, Mr Clarke? Don't you think it to be a sound investment?'

Again he shook his head, and told her bluntly, 'No, I don't.'

West cursed inwardly, but outwardly retaining his pleasant expression, he enquired with a show of good humour, 'But why not, Mr Clarke?'

'Because it's all too airy-fairy,' Clarke grunted sourly.

A gleam of annoyance came into Cleopatra's eyes, but knowing that Ozzie was only acting protectively towards her, she kept her voice equable.

'You'll have to explain what you mean by airy-fairy, Mr Clarke. I don't think either Mr West or myself fully understand your meaning.'

'The meaning's plain enough to my reckoning, Mrs Dolton.' Clarke did not bother to hide his own annoyance, and spoke sharply. 'This moving picture business is all pie in the sky. There's nothing solid there, nothing that you can take hold of. Money should be invested in bricks and mortar, in land or livestock, in something that has got a

321

sure return. But this picture business is all fancies and pipe-dreams. And all you end up with after spending hundreds o' pounds is some cans of celluloid.'

'But it's what's on that celluloid that's important, Mr Clarke,' West was stung to protest. 'It can't be measured in pounds, shillings and pence. It is an art that we're discussing here, not simply commerce.'

Clarke's face reddened with irritation. 'Can you eat art? Can you wear it? Does it shelter you from rain and cold? Can you sleep on it?'

'Tcchhaa!' the actor clucked his tongue in disgust. 'You're nothing but a philistine, Mr Clarke!'

'I'm a what?' Clarke demanded angrily. 'What was that you called me?' His meaty fists clenched and he seemed ready to spring at the other man.

Cleopatra, hiding a smile, hastened to intervene, and scolded with assumed sharpness, 'That's enough, gentlemen! I didn't ask you to call here to fight about this. And I'll thank you both to remember that you are guests in my house.'

Clarke subsided into disgruntled silence, while West smiled charmingly.

'I do apologise most sincerely to you, Mrs Dolton, and to you also, Mr Clarke. I assure you that I had no intention of causing you any offence.'

Cleopatra took up the written contract proposals and began to go through them clause by clause with the two men. At length she seemed satisfied, and laying the papers aside told West, 'There's just one thing more that I'd like to satisfy my mind on, Mr West. I trust that you will feel able to answer fully?'

'But of course, Mrs Dolton,' West was all bluff frankness. 'Ask me anything you wish. Anything at all.'

The woman returned his smile. 'I'd like to know who the other investors are, Mr West, and the sums that each one of them has invested. And I wish to see their contracts.'

And I'd like to see some evidence of security from this flash bleeder, Clarke added in his mind. He mistrusted the other man profoundly, and feared that once West had laid his hands on Cleopatra's investment money then he

322

would simply disappear with it.

The actor did not seem in the least disconcerted by the woman's request. 'But of course you shall know whom the other investors are, Mrs Dolton.' He beamed. 'Mr John Purvis, Mrs Emma Vivaldi and myself are the sole investors at present. Mrs Vivaldi and myself are joint partners in the New Age Moving Picture Company; we each put in five hundred guineas. Mr Purvis agreed yesterday evening to purchase two hundred and fifty shares at a cost of one guinea per share. I am proposing that you purchase the same amount for the same price. Should the picture I am working on at present prove as successful as I anticipate, then I shall further propose that we four shall become equal partners in the next venture I have in mind.'

'And what venture is that?' Cleopatra was intrigued.

'The Battle of Waterloo, Mrs Dolton. To be recreated on the actual battleground, with a cast of thousands. It will be the greatest, most spectacular moving picture ever made.'

West's eyes took in a fanatical gleam and his voice throbbed with fervour. 'Just imagine it, Mrs Dolton. People will be able to see Napoleon, the Duke of Wellington, old Marshall Blucher, and all the armies. The audience will be at the Duchess of Richmond's ball, they'll march away with the soldiers, and weep with the women left behind. They'll be with the Iron Duke in his moment of victory, and see Napoleon weeping in the hour of his defeat. They'll see the British redcoats sweeping the field in triumph and the Old Guard dying to the last man. It will be spectacular, Mrs Dolton. Spectacular and awe inspiring!'

Cleopatra's vivid imagination was fired by the man's own fervour, and she murmured with shining eyes, 'It will be awesome, Mr West. It surely will be.'

It was the more phlegmatic Clarke who brought them both back down to earth. 'I reckon you should get this present picture finished first, shouldn't you? Afore you starts to fight any battles o' Waterloo. And from what I hears you'm having more troubles than enough getting this 'un finished as it is, never mind starting any new pictures.'

Elated by his own splendid visions, West was dismissive of his present difficulties. 'They're merely hiccups, Mr Clarke,' he said airily. 'Passing clouds which will very soon be blown away completely, leaving only clear blue skies.'

The mention of John Purvis being a fellow investor had given Cleopatra certain ideas. And now she was eager to be rid of the two men.

'Very well, Mr West, I'm persuaded to sign our contract,' she told the actor. 'I shall have my solicitors draw up the necessary documents, and as soon as that is done, then we'll complete.'

She waved aside her exclamations of pleasure, and his profuse thanks and assurances.

'If you will excuse me, gentlemen, I have many domestic matter to attend to. I'll leave you to see yourselves out.'

As soon as the outer door closed behind them she hurried upstairs shouting for the housekeeper, 'Mrs Danks, will you run my bath for me please, and then lay out my dark blue dress? I have to go out.'

Chapter Thirty-Six

Emma's entrance into the hot, stifling air of the narrow rancid alley known as Silver Street was greeted with excited cries by the ragged urchins. There were words of welcome from the assortment of haggard women sitting on chairs and stools and the doorsteps along the fetid length of the alley to gain a respite from the stuffy, over-heated interiors of their wretched tenements.

'Here's your Emmy coming.'

'Doon't her look grand.'

Halfway down the long alleyway Emma's mother, Amy Farr, was sitting with a knot of neighbours, and she called to her oncoming daughter, 'Has you passed your Dad, our Emmy? He's only just this minute gone out.'

The young woman grinned and quipped, 'No, he must have ducked into the Red Lion when he saw me coming.'

'What's all this about you being in the moving pictures, Emma?' a neighbour asked. 'Our Albert said he's seen you up at the Sudan all dressed up like a soldier at fust, and then like a bloody queen.'

'Yes Mrs Green, I'm making moving pictures in partnership with Adrian West.'

'Is he the chap what's got the theayter?' the neighbour winked lewdly. 'I 'udden't mind giving him a bit o' whatfor!'

'I'll let him know, Mrs Green. Perhaps he'll come and call on you,' Emma joked, and the woman cackled with laughter and shrieked.

'Well tell him to be sure and call when me husband aren't in.'

'That wun't be any good, Hetty. The bloody kids 'ull still

325

be theer, wun't they?' a second woman chortled.

'That wun't matter.' Hetty Green again cackled with laughter. 'I can bloody soon send them out to play, so we shan't be disturbed.'

All the women joined in the general laughter, and Emma shared their salacious mirth.

Despite her comparative wealth, and her enjoyment of her own creature comforts, there were times when Emma found herself missing the rough and ready camaraderie that she had known in the Silver Street, and wished in a way that she could could have been content to remain there. Because she certainly had found no friendship, companionship or even acceptance among the upper social classes of the town that her marriage had brought her on a material level with. Emma was a child of the slums, and the respectable classes of the town would never forget that fact. In her turn, Emma's rebellious, high-spirited nature impelled her openly to mock the respectable classes' mores and codes of social behaviour. Emma had escaped from Silver Street, only to find that she was exchanging one type of social prison for another. Since she could accept neither she had become in a sense an outsider who no longer really belonged in any of the myriad social groupings of the town.

One woman went into her hovel to bring out a stool for Emma to sit on, and the young woman willingly sat down and joined in the exchanges of gossip and anecdote and laughter.

Periodically her eyes lingered on her mother's hugely pregnant belly, and she experienced burning resentment against her father, Winston Farr, for his callous disregard for her mother's physical wellbeing. For as long as Emma could remember her mother had been either pregnant or recovering from childbirth, the only blessing being that during the past few years nearly all of the babies were either still-born or died soon after birth, and so did not add to the almost impossible burden of feeding and clothing the numerous children the couple already had. Without Emma's continual financial help the family would have virtually starved. Winston Farr neglected to practise

326

his trade of chimney-sweep, and instead spent most of his time, and almost all of the family income, in one or other of the numerous public houses in the town. Now, in concert with that resentment against her father, came the realisation that for all her moments of nostalgia for the friendship and company of Silver Street she could never have borne to become like one of these women: poverty stricken drudges, perenially pregnant, used by their menfolk at best with some degree of comradeship, and at worst as mistreated beasts of burden.

After a couple of hours Emma slipped some money into her mother's hand, and made her farewells.

She stood for some moments on the pavement beneath the arched entrance to Silver Street, and toyed with the idea of going the scant distance into George Street.

I'd like to have a close look inside Harry's old house. I'd like to see if there's any sign of anyone being buried under the floor, she thought.

She knew, however, that Henry Snipe would almost certainly be there working at developing the film shot earlier that week on the indoor sets. So reluctantly she concluded that her examination of the house's interior would have to wait until a more suitable time and opportunity presented itself.

She strolled towards the Market Place and the Royal yard.

Now she was in the big shed examining the newly completed indoor set. It was the interior of a lavish banqueting hall, and no expense had been spared on the richly embroidered tapestries and drapes, the great table laden with silverware and fine plate, and the genuine marble statues and busts and paintings lining the walls. There was even a musicians' gallery erected against the end wall.

She frowned as she mentally computed the cost entailed. 'The mad bugger will bankrupt me if I don't watch it.'

The great double doors at the front of the shed swung ajar and West came hurrying in. When he saw her he called exultantly, 'Emma, I've done it! I've done it!'

He came rushing to her and clasped her hands in his.

327

His florid face alive with joy.

'Everything is going to be alright, darling!' He was almost babbling with excitement. 'I've got the money. I've got enough to finish the picture. Everything's going to be alright! We're going to be rich, sweetheart. We're going to make our fortunes!'

She stared at him bemusedly, and he laughed down into her face and told her, 'John Purvis, and Cleopatra Dolton have both agreed to invest. We're made now, darling. We're made! All our troubles are over!'

She hardly dared to believe what she was hearing, and the doubt was in her face.

'It's true, Emma. It's true what I'm telling you!' he crowed delightedly. 'They've both agreed to sign contracts. They've both agreed to invest. Everything is alright now, darling. We'll be rich!'

Now she did believe him, and experienced a wave of relief that her own money might now be safe.

'When did they agree?' she sought to know.

'Johnny Purvis agreed last night, and Cleopatra Dolton this afternoon. I've been at the solicitors with her general manager for the past couple of hours getting the details of the contract straightened out. She'll be signing tomorrow, and so will Johnny Purvis. Isn't it wonderful, my love!'

He laughed elatedly, and she could not help but laugh herself as his mood enveloped her. Adrian drew her to him and kissed her passionately, his arms straining her slender body hard against his own, and because he had brought good news she responded willingly enough.

Just outside the great double doors footsteps slowed and a man's figure appeared in the doorway, but the couple were unaware of his advent. For long long moments Harry Vivaldi stood watching their passionate embrace. Watching West's hand greedily searching the shapely body of his wife. Watching her fingers caressing the man's shoulders and neck and hair. And in Harry Vivaldi's being there pulsed a rage to kill.

She's put the horns on me! The fuckin' whore has put the horns on me! I'll fuckin' well kill her! And him as well! I'll kill them both! he thought.

Impulsion to throw himself at the pair and rend their flesh with his bare hands roared through his brian. But another force compelled him to immobility.

Box clever, Harry! his inner voice warned. Think before you act, Harry! Box clever! Box clever, Harry!

And the man heeded that voice, and obeyed its commands and he moved to conceal himself behind the shelter of the door, and watched with murderous eyes until the couple broke apart and talking together in excited voices began to move towards where he was hidden. Then he turned and hurried away, and was gone from view when they came out of the shed.

Chapter Thirty-Seven

A circuit of various obstacles had been set up around the greensward and John Purvis was schooling his new horse to jump the hurdled fences, the barrels, the heaps of brushwood. When Cleopatra Dolton reached the end of the tunnel-like driveway, she halted in its shadows and stood watching the horse and rider.

Purvis was hatless, and coatless, wearing only an open necked shirt, breeches and riding boots. Although she was not a horsewoman herself, Cleopatra could recognise the consummate skill of the man's riding as he took his mount over jump after jump, and she found herself admiring this further facet of Purvis' character.

After clearing the final obstacle, a brushwood fence some five feet in height, Purvis took the horse across the greensward at a gallop, tufts of turf flying out from beneath the thudding hooves. He passed within yards of the driveway entrance, and Cleopatra saw his head turn towards her, and then he slowed his mount and circled around, easing down to a trot to come back to where she was standing.

'Good afternoon, Mrs Dolton,' he saluted her with raised riding crop, and regarded her with appreciation in his light blue eyes. Her dark blue gown was of silk, and she wore a small veiled bonnet on her soft dark hair, and carried a small parasol. 'This is a pleasant surprise.'

He dismounted, and stroked and patted his horse's neck and muzzle, telling it, 'Good boy, good boy.'

The beast whinnied and pushed its muzzle against the man's caressing hand. Smiling fondly he said to the woman, 'He wants his sugar lumps. But he'll have to wait until he goes back to his stable. I've forgotten to bring them with me.'

He looked at her in silent questioning, and she smiled and told him easily, 'You're doubtless wondering why I'm here, well it's a case of Mahomet and the Mountain. You haven't come to my house, so I've come to yours.'

He chuckled appreciatively, then glanced up at the hot sun and invited her, 'Will you take some tea with me, Mrs Dolton. Or perhaps some chilled wine?'

She nodded and they walked side by side across the lush grass, the man leading the horse.

At the house he indicated the open front door. 'If you go inside and take the second door to your left, Mrs Dolton, you'll find my sitting room. Please make yourself comfortable and I'll join you there just as soon as I've put this one into the paddock.'

The room was sparsely and simply furnished, with no fripperies or ornaments to clutter its space. Its high, vaulted ceiling and thick stone walls created an atmosphere of peaceful seclusion.

Cleopatra went to stand gazing out of the window, her eyes sweeping across the wide vale with its fecund pastures and woodlands, and did not turn as Purvis entered the room and came to stand by her side.

'It's a fine view you have here, Mr Purvis,' she congratulated him, and he nodded.

'It's the view that I always dreamed that one day I would overlook from this very house.'

She turned towards him now, her dark eyes curious. 'Do you mean while you were in prison you thought about this view?'

'Oh yes, of course I did. But even as a young boy I dreamed of owning this house, and having this view spread before me.'

His light blue eyes drank in the opulent landscape and he uttered fervently, 'I love this part of England, Mrs Dolton. I really love it. For me it's the most beautiful place on earth.'

'But you must have seen many other beautiful places, Mr Purvis. You've travelled the world, have you not?'

331

'Yes, I've travelled widely.' He grinned ruefully at her. 'But as the old saying has it, there's no place like home, is there?'

His manner became brisk. 'Now, will you take a glass of chilled wine?'

She willingly accepted, and he fetched in a dark bottle beaded with moisture and they sat and drank together. Cleopatra told him of the contract she was to sign with Adrian West.

Afterwards they talked of the event that had bound them forever in a strange intimacy, the death of her husband, Arthur Dolton.

'Do you ever feel bitter towards me for what I did to your husband?' Purvis asked curiously. 'I know that you were not happy with him, but I robbed your children of their father, after all.'

'You acted only in self-defence. It was his fault, not yours. And he was a brute of a father to my sons.'

Cleopatra shook her head, and her dark eyes glowed. 'I'll not be a hyprocrite by professing to have any regrets for his death, Mr Purvis. I was glad that he died. I hated him while he lived, and I still hate his memory. My only regret concerning his death was the trouble and disgrace that it brought upon your head.'

It was the man's turn to shake his head. 'You need have none concerning me, Mrs Dolton. I'm a fatalist, and I believe that our lives are mapped out for us from the day of our birth.'

They went on to talk of many things, and there grew between them a warmth and an easiness and an ever deepening pleasure in each other's company. By the time they had finished the first bottle of wine, they were on first name terms, and by the time that the second bottle of wine was nearly empty a strong mutual liking had developed. The sexual tension between them had metamorphosed into an unspoken recognition that each found the other sexually desirable. But that fact created no sense of strain between them, and only added a pleasing frisson to their conversation.

Both were basically lonely people, but it was a loneliness

332

that was to some extent self-imposed. Because both of them preferred solitude to company that did not suit them. Johnny found to his own surprise that he could talk frankly of his love for Miriam, his instincts telling him that this woman sat facing him could be trusted with his confidences. In return Cleopatra told him of her relationship with Ozzie Clarke, and of how in her softer moments she regretted that she could not return Clarke's love for her.

'Will you marry Miriam Josceleyne, Johnny?' the woman wanted to know, and could not help but feel sharp pangs of jealousy.

'I would marry her tomorrow,' he admitted, and shrugged his broad shoulders. 'But she refuses. She is ill, you see, and afraid that she might infect me also.'

'What's wrong with her?' Hope was burgeoning in Cleopatra's mind.

'She has consumption,' he told her sadly. 'But really I believe it's only a very mild condition. I would be prepared to take the risk.'

Cleopatra nodded understandingly, but made no other comment. Yet in her mind the sensation of hope expanded. She knew now that she wanted this man for herself. But she knew also that if she were to try and take him from Miriam Josceleyne at this time then she would only encounter his rejection. Cleopatra was a very shrewd and a very patient woman. Consumption was a killer. Sometimes it took years to destroy its victims, but destroy them it inevitably did.

I can wait, she told herself now. And when Miriam Josceleyne dies, then I'll be here to comfort Johnny.

Her dark, lucent eyes gleamed and she rose from the chair, leaning to kiss him lightly on the cheek, smiling at his exclamation of surprise.

'We are friends now, Johnny,' she told him. 'And friends may kiss each other's cheeks when they say goodnight.'

'Must you, go so soon?' he queried. 'I'm enjoying our conversation so much that I'm very reluctant to see you go.'

'I'm enjoying it also, Johnny,' she replied truthfully. 'But

I really do have to go now. But from now on I hope that we shall be having many, many other conversations. I feel that I've found a true friend in you, Johnny, and I hope that you may feel that way about me. Because I am your true friend. And that is quite apart from the debt of gratitude that I owe you.'

After she had gone, Johnny returned to the living room and opened a third bottle of wine. He sat sipping his drink, gazing out across the verdant countryside, and thinking about the woman who had just left him.

As the hours passed and the shadows lengthened and dusk fell upon the land he found that his sense of loneliness had intensified and he wished that Cleopatra Dolton was still here with him, and he hungered to hear the sound of her low husky voice. Then was assailed with an uneasy guilt that he had wished for Cleopatra's company, rather than the company of his beloved Miriam.

That sense of guilt persisted in lurking in the back of his mind, and when he went to bed he made an effort to drive all thoughts of Cleopatra from him. But with sleep there came dreams, and those dreams were of Cleopatra's dark, glowing eyes.

Chapter Thirty-Eight

As if to atone for its previous misbehaviour, the weather during late July and August was ideal for West's film making. Day after day the sun shone from cloudless skies, and in a very short space of time he was able to complete his picture. As soon as he and Snipe had finished cutting and editing the work West telegraphed an invitation to an old business acquaintance, Walter Harriman.

Harriman was an American, presently residing in London, who owned a large film distribution company, and also several theatres both in England and the United States. A tall, lean, lantern-jawed, steel-rimmed spectacled Yankee from the state of Maine, quietly spoken, austere in dress and manner and almost puritanical in his mode of life, Harriman nevertheless shared Adrian West's passion for moving pictures, and was equally convinced that they were the entertainment media of the future.

He arrived in Redditch late in the afternoon of Thursday the twelfth of August, and was met at the railway station by West in his Mercedes motorcar.

Harriman looked down his long nose at the opulent vehicle and sniffed disapprovingly. West chuckled easily. 'Now Walter, I'm sure that your disapproval of my machine won't prevent you from riding in it. There are a great number of steep hills in this town, and you'll very soon get tired of trudging up and down them.'

The American stared dourly. 'Extravagance has ruined a deal of better businessmen than yourself, Adrian,' he spoke in clipped nasal tones.

West's smile did not falter, and he announced jovially, 'I've taken a suite of rooms for you at the best hotel in the

335

town, Walter. But you don't have to worry about the expense. As I told you in my telegraph I'm paying for everything.'

The American frowned and asked curtly, 'Will you still be paying for my return fares to London even if I don't like what I've come to see?'

West burst out laughing. 'Of course I will, you Yankee miser! But you're going to love what you've come to see. I'm fully confident of that.'

'Then I suggest that we put that to the test immediately,' Harriman challenged. 'Because my time is very valuable, Adrian, and I've none of it to waste.'

By now the porter had appeared wheeling Harriman's luggage trunk on a small trolley, and West tossed the man some coins. 'See that that's delivered to the Royal Hotel, will you.'

The porter grinned and saluted. 'I will, Mr West.'

Walter Harriman's frown deepened at this further display of needless extravagance, but he made no spoken comment. Instead he mounted the seat beside West, and sat with folded arms, his Homburg hat crammed low on his long head as the motorcar roared away from the station forecourt.

The vehicle's arrival in George Street brought the usual grouping of interested spectators to gawp and exclaim with admiration, and West grandiosely tossed coins to a couple of shabby men.

'Keep an eye on my motorcar for me, will you lads?'

Then he led his guest through the covered entryway and into the tenement. Upstairs in the bedroom, which had been converted into a small viewing room, Snipe was waiting with a loaded projector, and a surly scowl.

The new arrivals settled themselves down in comfortable armchairs, the room was darkened, and Snipe worked the projector. Harriman sat in frowning silence as the black, white and grey images flickered across the small screen, but behind the steel-rimmed lenses of his spectacles his cold eyes began to gleam with appreciation as Emma Vivaldi displayed her talents.

When the final reel had chattered to its end, and the

thick black coverings were removed from the window to allow the daylight back into the room, West turned eagerly to his guest.

'Well Walter, what do you say?'

The American's thin lips set in a hard line, and still he frowned.

'Well, tell me something,' West badgered impatiently. 'At least give me some reaction.'

Harriman fingered his lantern jaw, and his lips pursed judiciously. Then, after a long pause, he nodded slowly.

'It's a good product, Adrian.'

'Then you'll take them?' West asked eagerly.

Harriman ignored the question, and instead himself questioned, 'The leading lady? What's her name?'

West grinned knowingly, and in his turn evaded the question. 'You liked her, did you, you old dog! You can see a star in the making in her, can you? I told you that she was superb, didn't I?'

For the first time since his arrival in the town, the American's sour frown lightened, and he smiled bleakly.

'I think that you've found a British Vitagraph Girl, Adrian. Only you've gone one better than Vitagraph. Put that young woman and Florence Turner side by side on the screen, and Turner wouldn't get a looksee.'

'Then you'll take both films,' West stated confidently. 'I won't be greedy on the price, Walter.' He grinned slyly. 'Not at this stage of the game anyway.'

The bleak smile had disappeared from Harriman's features, and he once again was wearing his customary dour frown. 'I haven't said that I'll take them, have I, Adrian?'

West knew his man of old, and now the confident smile left his face, and he asked guardedly, 'What do you want from me, Walter?'

The American steepled his fingers beneath the point of his lantern jaw, and answered softly, 'I want a couple of dozen one-reelers featuring the young woman. They need to be of all varieties, drama, burlesque, high comedy. I'll need a dozen singing and dancing reels as well, that we can use with the cinematophone and auxetophone.'

'But I don't know if she can sing and dance!' West protested, and the bleak smile briefly touched the American's thin lips.

'Any fool-woman can fake a few dancesteps, Adrian. And if she can't sing, then find someone who can, and let her mime to their words.'

West tried to hide his disappointment, but could not resist complaining, 'I thought that these two films would create enough excitement about her.'

Harriman shook his head decisively. 'No Adrian, good as they are, they won't be enough to make a star of her. She needs to be presented in shorts first, and these two longer pictures kept back until her face and name is known to our audiences. The we can whip up a whole lot of publicity about the longer films.'

Once more the guarded look appeared in Adrian West's eyes. 'You do realise that she's under an exclusive contract to me, don't you, Walter?' he lied blatantly.

A slyness entered his companion's voice. 'Oh yes, I realise that, Adrian. But if I'm to put my distribution network and my theatres at her service, and to make a real big star out of her, then I'm going to be wanting a piece of her for myself. So I think that we'll have to discuss that exclusive contract, won't we?'

Seeing the doubt in the other man's expression, Harriman chuckled mirthlessly. 'You mustn't be too greedy, you know, Adrian, and try to keep her all to yourself. With my help she can become a real golden goose for both of us.'

He spread his hands expansively. 'Let's be completely straight with each other, Adrian. The only reason that you got me up here is because you haven't got the necessary resources yourself to make a big star out of her. I've got those resources. So you need me more than I need you. And we've done business before, haven't we? So you know that you can trust me.' Again the bleak smile touched his thin lips. 'After all Adrian, it's better the devil you know, isn't it?'

West knew that he would have to bow to the inevitable, and he comforted himself with the knowledge that half of

338

the golden goose was better than no goose at all. And he also knew that with this man behind her, Emma could become a very large golden goose indeed. There would be a more than ample share for both he and Harriman if all went well.

He grinned, and held out his hand. 'I agree.'

'I knew you would, Adrian.' The American shook hands, and then became briskly businesslike. 'I'll have the new contract drawn up as soon as I get back to London. Now let's have another looksee at those pictures, shall we?'

Once more the room was darkened and the flickering images cavorted upon the small screen. West was glad that his companion's interest was completely absorbed by the films. He needed to think carefully about his next moves, and as he thought problems arose to bedevil him. Those problems centred on two main themes, one of them being the existing contracts he had already made with Emma, Cleopatra Dolton and John Purvis.

Now that Walter Harriman agreed to join him in launching Emma upon her moving picture career, he no longer needed in the long term the financial backing of Cleopatra Dolton or John Purvis. But in the short term he would still need money from them to finance the making of the short pictures that Harriman was demanding from him. The American would not advance any money for this. He was only interested in marketing a finished product. West knew from past experience that the American would drive a hard bargain, and that he would most certainly refuse to accept any other partners such as Dolton or Purvis.

I'll have to find some way of dropping them both, West knew. But I'm still going to have to get more money from them to make these shorts. I'm too strapped for cash to do it, and from what Emma tells me, her investments have been going badly these days so she's got next to nothing in readies.

West was not overly concerned about Emma's reaction to any proposals he might make concerning the change of partners. She was utterly besotted with the idea of becoming a moving picture star, and he was confident that she would go along with anything that would further her ambitions in that direction.

His major problem, as he saw it, was Harry Vivaldi. The man was continuing to lead an abstemious life, and was always affable and willing to do any menial tasks that he, Adrian, might delegate to him. Outwardly Vivaldi seemingly accepted with equanimity his continued banishment from his wife's bed, and to West's chagrin the relationship between the marital pair was apparently warm and very amiable. So much so that at times West suspected that Emma might secretly be considering resuming conjugal relations, that was if she had not already done so on occasion. This unpalatable suspicion was provoked by the fact that she had not permitted him to make love to her for some considerable period now, always evading his advances with promises of future delights to come when her marital situation should be resolved. Yet, to West's angry bafflement, she was still refusing either to seek a divorce from Harry, or to press her husband to leave her house.

West wanted Emma solely for himself. He wanted her for his wife. He wanted her lustfully, and he wanted her lovingly. He wanted to dominate her both mentally and physically. And he wanted to control her career and her earnings from the career. Because of the frustration he was experiencing in all these aims West was beginning to think irrationally about the situation, and in his mind Harry was becoming the intolerable obstacle to his achievement of his desires. Once Harry was out of the way, out of Emma's life, then West was convinced that all his plans would be able to be brought to a swift consummation.

Now, sitting here before the flickering screen in the small darkened room, the image of Harry rose loomingly in West's mind, blotting out the images on the screen. With Harriman's advent, Harry's removal now became of paramount importance in West's mind. The man had got to go. He must be got rid of once and for always. And he must be got rid of very soon.

All of the inherent ruthlessness in Adrian West's

340

character now came rampaging to the forefront of his resolve. I'm going to get rid of you, you bastard, he silently told the metal picture of Harry Vivaldi. One way or another you are going to go!

Chapter Thirty-Nine

As early as the middle of August the authorities in Birmingham began preparing for the coming 17th of September visit to their bustling city of the Prime Minister of the Liberal government, Mr Herbert Asquith, accompanied by Cabinet Ministers and many of the Honourable Members of Parliament. Even before the opening days of September tremendous efforts were being made to whip up enthusiasm for the meeting in Bingley Hall of the rulers and the ruled. This meeting was promised to be of great import, because it was widely broadcast that Mr Asquith intended to throw down his challenge to the House of Lords that their power to veto should be abolished, and that the will of the House of Commons should reign supreme and so the voice of the ordinary people of England should prevail over the voice of hereditary privilege.

Such an admirable and desirable proposal did indeed attract a great deal of interest and support from among the ranks of the ordinary people, but the Women's Social and Political Union received it with a more cynical and jaundiced reaction. They pointed out to anyone who was prepared to listen that if freedom for the common people to voice their will, and see that will prevail, was what the Prime Minister truly wanted, why was it that he continued to deny that freedom to a full half of the population of Great Britain? Namely, the female half. And so the Women's Social and Political Union decided that since the Prime Minister had displayed no real intention of rectifying the current state of affairs, they in their turn would do all that lay within their power to disrupt his visit to Birmingham.

342

Accordingly, while the authorities made their plans and arrangements for the Prime Minister's visit, the suffragettes likewise began to organise, and to make their own plans and arrangements. During the weeks leading up to 17th September Miriam and Laura attempted to mobilise local support. Night after night they tramped the streets of the Needle District pushing handbills through letterboxes, talking to small groups and individuals among their sympathisers, enduring insults and threats of violence from their opponents, and once even experiencing actual violence.

After this incident in which the two women had been jostled and manhandled by a gang of half-drunken roughs, Johnny Purvis insisted on accompanying them on their nightly rounds of the streets, and from then on although they still encountered many instances of verbal insult and threat, the sight of Purvis' strong muscular body, and the heavy, club-headed walking stick he carried deterred any potential physical aggressors.

But despite their tireless efforts the actual numbers of women who had definitely promised to travel up to Birmingham on the day of the seventeenth remained small.

Tonight had been a particularly disappointing time in this respect. The trio had gone to the nearby village of Feckenham and had spent weary hours travelling the surrounding lanes to call upon the numerous isolated cottages and farmhouses, but had obtained only one firm promise to join the Birmingham demonstration. It was very late, and darkness had fallen when Johnny drove the horse and gig back up to the house in Mount Pleasant.

'You'll come in for a while, won't you Johnny?' Miriam pleaded.

He smiled at her and nodded. 'Yes, I'll come in. But I'll not stay for long. You need to rest.'

Her face was thin and very pale, and the deep pools of blue-black shadow beneath her eyes were not caused by the effects of moonlight.

There was great concern in his eyes as he regarded her frailty. During the past weeks she had driven herself

343

remorselessly, and Johnny feared that she was grievously overtaxing her strength. Repeatedly he had tried to dissuade her from making such heavy demands upon herself, but she had stubbornly refused to stop, and rather than precipitate an angry clash, he had unwillingly accepted that she would go her own way in this matter.

Inside the kitchen the gaslight hissed to drive back the darkness and while Laura bustled to fill a kettle and place it upon the gas stove, Miriam gratefully sank upon a chair at the table side.

John could not restrain himself. 'Miriam, you're doing too much. You must rest.'

She smiled tiredly at him. 'There'll be plenty of time for resting after the seventeenth.'

'You'll be in no condition to do anything on the seventeenth if you don't stop driving yourself so,' he told her sharply, and sought support from the other woman. 'Is that not so, Laura? You agree with me that Miriam should rest more, don't you?'

The young woman tossed her head impatiently. 'I've long since given up trying to talk any sense into Miriam,' she snapped. 'I'm resigned to waiting for the silly creature to collapse bodily.'

In Miriam's green eyes there burned the glow of fanaticism as she immediately counter-attacked, 'I shall do whatever I consider that I must until the seventeenth is passed and gone. So both of you can leave me alone, and stop this continual nagging. It will make no difference to my intentions, not if you both nag until you're blue in the face. So you may as well keep quiet about it from this very moment.'

Miriam's whole being radiated an inveterate stubbornness, and knowing her as they did, both the man and the younger woman accepted their impotence to deflect her from her chosen course.

Laura grimaced and shrugged her slender shoulders. 'There, you see Johnny, there's nothing you or I or anyone else can do to make her see sense. We're just wasting our breath in the face of such obstinate stupidity.'

She turned and busied herself in preparing a pot of tea,

and the scowl on her features registered her mood. When the tea had been made she slammed the filled pot, cups and saucers, milk and sugar on the table, and announced, 'I'm going to bed. I have the sense to realise that the human body needs to rest even if Miriam hasn't. Goodnight Johnny.'

She flounced away, and Miriam giggled. In that moment she resembled a mischievous girl-child, and because he loved her, Johnny could not help but smile in sympathy with her mood.

'You're a wicked woman to torment and worry poor Laura like you do,' he stated, but the warmth in his eyes and the softness of his tone belied the admonishment of the words.

He leaned over the table towards her and took her thin hand between his strong fingers. 'I know that there's nothing that either Laura or myself can say to you that will make you give up this cause that you're so set upon, my darling. But for my sake, if for nothing else, I wish that you would try to take things a little more easily and slowly. It won't serve any good purpose at all if you set back your health by overtaxing your strength as you're doing.'

Her eyes were tender as she looked into his concerned face, and the love she bore for him shone through them. 'I will take things more easily, Johnny,' she promised with a patent sincerity. 'But not until after the seventeenth. After that date has passed, then I'll do anything that you ask of me. I promise you that from the bottom of my heart.'

'Will you marry me then?' he was driven to urge. 'After the seventeenth, will you marry me straight away?'

All her being clamoured to tell him yes. But even as the words of acceptance rose to her lips she was forced to bite them back, bitterly though it grieved her to do so.

'You're much better in health now, my honey,' he tried to coax her. 'I can see that you're recovering. And even if you don't achieve a full recovery, it still doesn't have to prevent us from being wed. I shan't be in any danger of becoming consumptive.' In his need for her he was driven to lie. 'The doctors have assured me of that. There'll be no danger of my becoming infected. I've asked several

345

doctors about it, and they've all told me the same, that there is no danger to me.'

Tears lurked in her eyes, and she blinked hard to keep them from falling. Unable to hurt him by direct refusal she sought to avoid it.

'We'll still have to wait, Johnny. I want to marry you, you know that. I want to marry you more than I have ever wanted anything in my entire life. But we must wait, until I'm assured that I'm recovered, or nearly so.'

He sighed heavily, and then reluctantly nodded. 'Very well, honey. But I shall keep on badgering you until you do agree to marry me.'

'But I've already agreed to marry you, haven't I? We must just wait a while, that's all.' She smiled and lifting his hands to her lips kissed his fingers one by one.

For another hour they sat with clasped hands, and John told her what he planned for their shared future. She smiled and nodded, and felt her heart swelling with the love that she bore for him. At last, aware of how tired she was, John forced her to promise that she would go to bed and rest immediately he had gone. Having received that promise, and satisfied that she would indeed go to her bed, he left her.

Not wishing to break her word to him, Miriam went upstairs to her room, and laid down fully clothed upon her bed. There in the darkness she let her tears fall freely. Knowing that she would never be able to marry the man she so desperately loved. Because despite all that the doctors could do, and despite all their confidence that they would achieve a betterment of her condition, Miraim knew that the disease she harboured was inexorably killing her. She knew that the relentless progress of her disease was hastening, and that now death was eager to enfold her in its shadowed embrace.

Chapter Forty

Henry Snipe tuned his ukulele and began to play, and Emma hummed along with the plucked jingling notes.

Three times the man played the tune, and then Emma nodded to him. 'I've got it now, Henry.'

He scowled dourly. 'Let's run through it with the words, then.'

Once more his spatulate fingers moved deftly upon the metal strings, and this time Emma sang.

> Down by the riverside I stray,
> As twilight shadows close.
> And the soft music of the spray
> Lulls nature to repose . . .

She sang slowly, and dreamily, and the husky timbre of her voice possessed a quality that evoked memories in some of her listeners of those warm summer evenings now long past when they too had searched for love.

> Beside the stream a maiden dwells,
> My star of eventide,
> Pure as the water lily bells,
> Pure as the water lily bells,
> Pure as the water lily bells,
> Down by the riverside . . .

Walter Harriman and Adrian West sat side by side on a plain wooden bench in front of the young woman, and as the song went on they exchanged glances of mutual satisfaction. On the bench behind them Harry Vivaldi sat smiling pleasantly, but in his brain a murderous fury raged:

Pure as fuckin' lily bells! That's not you, is it you fuckin' whore! You were never pure! You fuckin' prostitute! You rotten stinking whore!

But even while the filthy abuse bellowed within him, his lips remained curved in a smile, and his dark eyes betrayed nothing of his inner turmoil.

At the open doors of the vast shed a small crowd of loungers were clustered, and as Emma's husky voice sang the last lingering notes they burst into spontaneous applause.

She grinned in delight and curtseyed low, then stepped down from the platform and came towards Harriman and West who rose to meet her, both men clapping their hands in congratulation.

'You're going to be a big star, my dear,' the American told her, and behind his glasses his eyes were hungry as he stared at her beautiful face, flushed now with pleasure.

'Now Harry, you're the recording expert, how soon can you get the discs made? Shall we plan on a week at most?'

Harriman did not so much question, as order, and at his side West frowned in resentment at the other man's assumption of authority.

Emma noted that frown, and spitefully twisted the figurative knife by smiling radiantly at the American and telling him admiringly, 'You certainly know how to get things moving, Mr Harriman.'

'Please my dear, call me Walter. You and I are going to be very close associates from now on, and I hope very close friends as well.' Harriman could not help but preen under the admiring regard of this beautiful woman, and boasted, 'I've the name in my business of being the man who gets things done, and done quickly, my dear.'

He turned to Adrian West, whose resentful frown was instantly overlaid by an attentive, eager-to-serve expression.

'Adrian, I want you to begin filming just as soon as the discs are cut. I should think that you can shoot at least one song and dance short a day. So I want the twelve reels

348

from you three weeks from today. That allows you plenty of time in case you hit any snags.'

He turned back to Emma. 'Emma, my dear, I'm going to work you like a slave for these next few weeks. But believe me, it is absolutely necessary to do so. The harder you work, the sooner you'll become a star. And you truly want to be a star, don't you?'

She nodded, and assured him breathlessly, 'Oh I do, Walter. I want that more than anything else in the world!'

He could not resist touching her smooth cheek with his fingers, and with a heavy gallantry told her, 'A woman as beautiful as you are, Emma, deserves nothing else but to become a big star. And I'm the man whose going to make you a star. You can count on that as a sure thing.'

She smiled flirtatiously into his eyes, and told him huskily, 'I do, Walter. I really do.'

Piqued by this intimate exchange between the pair, West asked sarcastically, 'What about all the other shorts that you want me to shoot, Walter? Do you expect delivery of them a week after the twelve song and dance shorts?'

The American's eyes hardened as he detected the sarcasm. He swung to face the other man and told him harshly, 'I expect you to fulfil your part of our agreement, Adrian. If you feel that you can't do that, then perhaps you should tell me so right now, and I'll make other arrangements to have Emma's pictures made.'

All four of them, Harriman, Emma, West and Harry Vivaldi instantly recognised that this was the moment of truth. This was the moment when the controlling dominance of their enterprise was to be established, and Emma's moist red lips opened slightly and she felt excitement surging within her as she watched the two men facing each other in this struggle for mastery.

Harry, hating West as he did, lusted to see him crumble and accept defeat at the hands of the American.

West's heart began to thud heavily. He realised now that Harriman had known that he, West, had been bluffing about possessing an exclusive contract with Emma, and that now the American was calling that bluff. His glance flicked to the faces of the other man and woman. On

349

Harry's face was the overt malicious glee he had expected to find. But Emma's expression was of expectant interest, and her black eyes were dancing with excitement. His gaze came back to Harriman.

The American's face was hard and challenging, and his eyes cold and watchful. 'Well, Adrian? I'm waiting to hear your answer?'

A sickening sense of impotence flooded through West. The other man held all the strongest cards in this particular hand.

But if I give in to this Yankee bastard now, then he'll take control of Emma's career! he realised, and with that realisation there came surging a terrible anger. West was not, and never had been a coward. He was a tough, courageous man who had had to fight for his livelihood all the years of his life. And he was not prepared to let any man dominate him.

He drew a series of long deep breaths to control the painful thudding of his heart, and then answered firmly, 'I'm your partner, Walter. Not your bloody lapdog! You'll get the shorts delivered as and when they're completed.' As he spoke he decided to hold nothing back, and to risk everything. 'Emma is my partner in the two films that we've already shot. I've no further binding contracts with her. If she thinks that some other man will make a better job of directing her pictures then of course she is quite at liberty to say goodbye to me. I shan't try to make any difficulties for her, or to place any obstacles in her way.'

He looked briefly at the young woman, who was staring at him with surprise, and a dawning admiration.

'I'm going to be completely truthful with you, Emma. Walter has the resources to make you a big star, I haven't got those resources. But, I know how to make moving pictures that are better than any other pictures now being produced. In my pictures you will outshine every other star, because I'm the finest director in the world.'

He turned again to face Harriman, whose eyes were betraying a grudging respect.

'So Walter, I'll tell you again. If we are going to be partners, then we are going to be equal partners. I'm no man's lapdog.'

There was a silence which began to lengthen uncomfortably. Emma's gaze went from one to the other of the men in rapid succession. She admired the way in which Adrian had reacted to Harriman's challenge, and though she knew that she needed the American to further her career in moving pictures, she, like West was not prepared to let him dominate their joint business relationship.

Emma's shrewd brain rapidly evaluated the situation, and she suggested very firmly, 'I think that the three of us should form a new company, and we'll all be equal partners in it. There won't be one of us who's the boss. We'll work as a team.'

The American's dour features remained impassive for some seconds, then a smile came to his thin lips, and he chuckled dryly. 'So be it. Emma. So be it.'

The tension dissolved into the nervous laughter of mutual relief, and the two men and the woman exchanged handshakes and brief hugs. Only Harry Vivaldi was excluded. He stood forgotten and alone. Still the pleasant smile remained on his handsome face, and his lips moved in muttered congratulation. But in his heart bitter resolve steeled.

Enjoy yourselves while you can, you bastards, he told them silently. Because very soon it will only be me who'll be laughing!

Chapter Forty-One

On Tuesday the 14th of September, Miriam and Laura travelled to Birmingham by train to meet with the suffragettes who were organising the demonstrations against the Prime Minister.

At New Street Railway Station they encountered their first evidence of the authorities' security measures. Nine feet high wooden barriers had been erected along the platform where the Prime Minister's train was to arrive.

At the station's entrance they were met by Mrs Mary Leigh, who was the principal organiser for the coming demonstration. A pretty little woman in her early thirties, she had recently formed the Women's Social and Political Union Drum and Fife Band, of which she was the drum major. In the month of May the band had created a sensation when they had marched through the streets of London in their military style purple, white and green uniforms, with the mace-twirling Mary at their head.

In the mean streets surrounding the Bingley Hall, Mary showed the visitors the further wooden barricades which the police would man on the day of the seventeenth to seal off those streets and deny any demonstrators access. Across the glass roof of the hall itself great tarpaulins had been stretched, and tall fire escapes placed on each side of the building, with hundreds of yards of firemen's hoses laid across the roof.

When told of this, Miriam smiled amusedly. 'Do they intend to drown us then, Mary?'

'I'm sure that's exactly what they would like to do with all of us.' The little woman laughed. 'However, even if they manage to do that I think that we'll be like Charles the

352

First. I think that we'll be an unconscionably long time dying.'

'But when these barricades are manned by the police how will we be able to get into the hall?' Laura wanted to know. 'They look very strong, don't they? I can't see how we'll be able to pull them down, especially with the police fighting to stop us doing so.'

Miriam also voiced grave doubts, and added, 'Do you think it would have been wiser for you not to have issued that warning to the public to stay away from Bingley Hall because we are going to demonstrate there and disrupt the Prime Minister's speech? Surely all that you've achieved by that is to put the authorities on their guard, and give them time to erect all these defences. They've turned this area into a fortress almost.'

'They can double the number of barricades if they want,' Mary Leigh declared confidently. 'But it won't do them the least bit of good, because we're already inside their walls.'

She laughed at the puzzled expressions on her companions' faces.

'Surely you remember the story of the Trojan Horse? Well, we've got a Trojan Horse of our own.'

Still not fully understanding Miriam and Laura could only nod politely.

'See down there.' Mary Leigh pointed along the length of the mean street with its rows of grimy, red-brick terraced houses. 'There are a lot of rooms to let. These people are poor and need to earn money in any way that they can. It's the same in every street around Bingley Hall.'

A dawning understanding brought smiles to the faces of her listeners, and Mary Leigh nodded. 'Yes, we've rented some rooms, and our sisters will be in those rooms when the police man these barricades. So while we shall still attack from the outside, we shall already have our shock troops inside the defences.'

'I still think it was a mistake to issue that warning though,' Laura remarked.

'It was done for a purpose, Laura,' Mary told her happily. 'We knew that the Prime Minister's visit would only attract a certain amount of interest, for all the fuss that's been made about his challenge to the House of Lords. But the prospect of seeing us fighting with the police will bring thousands of people flocking to see the fun. We shall create enormous publicity for our cause, and there'll be thousands of women everywhere who will join our movement as a result of that publicity.'

Privately both Miriam and Laura did not share in that optimism about fresh recruitment to their course as a result of the demonstration. But neither wished to dampen Mary's enthusiasm, so both voiced murmurs of agreement.

After the inspection of the authorities' defence measures, the three women went to the house of another of the Birmingham activists and spent the remainder of the day putting the final touches to the plans for the Redditch Branch's contribution to the forthcoming demonstration.

They returned to Redditch on the last train of the night, and found Johnny Purvis' tall figure waiting for them on the gloomy station platform, standing beneath the weak halo of the single guttering gaslight.

He lifted his curly-brimmed bowler hat in greeting, and smiled. 'I've come to carry you home. I'm sure you're both tired out from your journeyings. I thought that you'd be earlier. This is the third train I've met.'

'You shouldn't have put yourself to the trouble,' Miriam protested, but a warm glow of happiness suffused her at this further confirmation of her lover's kindness and consideration.

'It's a pleasure, not a trouble, my honey,' he told her softly.

The three of them squeezed tightly together on the gig's seat, and as the powerful horse strained to draw its load slowly up the steep incline of the Unicorn Hill, the women chattered excitedly about their day.

Johnny listened with a fond smile, and during a lull in their accounts told them, 'I shall be going up to Birmingham with you on the seventeenth.'

They stared in surprise, and Laura asked eagerly, 'Do

you mean that you're going to join in our demonstration Johnny? I thought that you weren't really interested in Women's Suffrage.'

He shrugged his broad shoulders. 'To tell you the truth, Laura, I'm not really very interested in any sort of suffrage. I don't believe that obtaining the right to vote will make any difference to the general condition of women in this country.'

'But of course it will!' Miriam retorted spiritedly, and began to lay out all the reasons for that enfranchisement, until Johnny laughingly begged her to stop.

'Please honey, please. No more! I've heard it so many times, that I could recite it in my sleep.' To soothe any possible resentment his words might cause the two women, he went on, 'You know that I support you whatever you both do, because if it makes you happy, then it makes me happy also. But I'm not a political animal. I believe that this country is an oligarchy, and that that oligarchy is mainly drawn from the same families that have ruled over us for centuries. I think that so-called democracy is a farce. The same faces are forever there in the Houses of Parliament. No matter which political party is elected, the same greedy, self-serving, hypocritical pigs are stuffing their fat bellies at the same trough. So whether a vote is cast one way or the other, it makes not a jot of real difference to the governance of this country. The Lord will still be in his castle, and we peasants will still be standing at his gate. I don't like that state of affairs, and I think it is corrupt and rotten, but all I can do is to do my best for myself and my loved ones.'

Both women protested heatedly, but he was adamant. 'There's no use in you trying to convince me otherwise, ladies. That is my belief, and will remain so.'

'Then why are you coming up to Birmingham to demonstrate with us?' Miriam demanded to know.

'I'm not going to demonstrate in the streets with you, my dear,' he informed her with a smile. 'I'm going to listen to Asquith's speech. I've got a ticket for the Bingley Hall meeting.' He chuckled at their expressions, and told them gently, 'But that's only my secondary reason for going. My primary reason is that I want to be there to protect you both.'

'But how can you protect us, when you'll be inside the Hall and we'll be outside?' Laura challenged.

He looked quizzically at her. 'You won't be inside then?'

'Of course not. How can we? Only ticket-holders are allowed inside.'

He pulled an envelope out of his pocket and handed it to her, telling her with a grin, 'I thought that you might like to be inside when Asquith speaks, so that you can put your views to him face to face, as it were.'

Laura tore the envelope open to disclose a thin sheaf of cardboard tickets, and her eyes shone as she saw what they were.

'I've a close friend in Birmingham who had contacts in the Liberal Party, and he managed to get hold of a few tickets for me,' Johnny explained. 'He doesn't like Asquith any more than I do, and when I told him that I knew some very militant suffragettes, he was only too pleased to give me these for your use. I rather think that he's hoping you might take the opportunity to take Asquith to task about a few promises he has made and broken.'

Miriam laughed in delight, and threw her arms around Johnny to hug him.

'Steady now, honey.' He joked, 'What will people say if they see you behaving like a factory girl?'

'Let them say what they like,' she declared, and kissed him on his cheek. 'Thank you, darling. These are the finest presents I could ever have had.'

He grimaced ruefully, 'I hope you'll still be of that opinion after the riot you'll undoubtedly cause.'

'You'll be able to judge that for yourself, won't you,' she beamed at him, 'because you'll be sitting right in the middle of us when the riot starts.'

He chuckled wryly and nodded. 'That's true.' He raised his eyes to the heavens and beseeched rhetorically, 'Oh God, what have I done? What have I done?'

The horse breasted the hill and the gig wheels spun faster as it broke into a fast trot, and the shared laughter of its occupants rang out along the quiet street.

Chapter Forty-Two

During the afternoon of Wednesday 15th September, Miriam and Laura received an unexpected visitor at their home.

Miriam felt embarrassed as she faced Cleopatra Dolton in the small living room, uncomfortably remembering her rudeness towards the woman during the last occasion of their meeting. Her embarrassment made her stiff and constrained in manner, but Laura felt no such constraint, and she told the visitor, 'This is really a great surprise, Mrs Dolton. But a most welcome one. Please, do sit down. Will you take tea?'

Cleopatra shook her head. 'No tea, thank you, Miss Hughes. But I would like a glass of water. This hot weather has made me thirsty.'

Laura hastened away to fetch the water, and Cleopatra seated herself on one of the plain wooden-armed chairs that flanked the fireplace.

It was Cleopatra who broke the strained silence. 'I expect that you're finding this meeting as difficult as I do myself, Miss Josceleyne.'

Her low voice was as sensual as her physical appearance, dressed as she was now in a dark green gown with a tight bodice that showed off her full breasts. Behind the wisp of veil that fell from her broad-brimmed hat, her lucent dark eyes and olive skin enhanced the exotic beauty of her features.

Miriam felt plain and dowdy by comparison. As she had done so many times in the past she found herself marvelling at the fact that after meeting this woman, Johnny should still profess his love for herself.

But the fact that the other woman had confessed to feeling uneasy served to make Miriam feel more relaxed,

357

and she was able to smile tentatively and reply.

'Yes, I am finding it somewhat difficult, Mrs Dolton. You see, I don't really know what to say to you. I was so rude at our last meeting, particulary in view of the way you had helped myself and my friends that day. And since then, the only thing that I've done to make any apology or amends for my behaviour, has been to write that letter to you.'

Cleopatra lifted her hand. 'Please, Miss Josceleyne. There is no need for any explanation, or for you to feel in the least apologetic. That is all long past now, and we should be looking to the future, not dwelling on what has gone by and allowing that to make us feel unhappy in any way.'

Miriam nodded grateful agreement. 'Yes, you're right, Mrs Dolton. We must look to the future now, and forget the past.'

Suddenly she experienced a sense of ease, and the first faint kindling of liking for her visitor.

Laura reappeared with a glass of water, and Cleopatra took it from her with a smile of thanks and drank from it. When her thirst was eased, she smiled at the two women facing her and told them, 'The purpose of my coming here is to offer my help, ladies.'

'Your help?' Laura queried, and the older woman nodded smilingly.

'For more than two weeks now I've been hearing about your plan to join the other suffragettes in Birmingham to demonstrate against the Prime Minister. My maids and my housekeeper have talked of nothing else but that there will be a party of women from Redditch going there.

'Naturally your names were mentioned as the organisers and leaders of that party.'

'Do you wish to join us there, Mrs Dolton?' Laura questioned eagerly. 'You would be more than welcome to, wouldn't she, Miriam?'

Miriam nodded instant confirmation, and murmured, 'Indeed you would, Mrs Dolton.'

The olive-skinned features were regretful. 'No, I can't join you in person. To speak frankly, although I do sympathise whole-heartedly with the suffragette cause, because of my business interests in this district I cannot afford to antagonise those who oppose you.'

She smiled with a hint of irony. 'I'm far too selfish to jeopardise my own financial well-being by becoming known as a supporter of the Woman's Social and Political Union. However, I think that I can be of help to your movement in another way, which must remain anonymous.'

She paused, as if waiting for their permission to continue, and Laura told her, 'Please, do go on, Mrs Dolton.'

Cleopatra did so. 'According to what my maids have been telling me, there are several women in the district who are not able to accompany you to Birmingham, even though they would greatly like to. Some can't afford to lose wages from work, others can't afford the fares. What I'm prepared to offer as my contribution is to pay the lost wages and the fares of those women. On condition that you do not tell anyone of what I have done.'

Her listeners exchanged a long look, and a silent question and answer passed between them.

Then Miriam turned back to Cleopatra and nodded emphatically. 'We would like to accept your offer, Mrs Dolton, and to give you many thanks for it. But I should warn you that there might be as many as fifteen women who'll want to take advantage of it. Will that be too many?'

Cleopatra shook her head. 'No, it's not too many. I am prepared to pay for a greater number if need be.'

She snapped open the large handbag she was holding on her lap, and took from it a leather purse, which she placed on the small table beside her chair.

With a smile lurking on her full, shapely lips she told them, 'I've made an estimate of what the total cost might be, allowing for twenty-five women taking advantage of my offer.'

She tapped the purse with her silken-gloved finger. 'This should cover all those expenses adequately enough.'

'But I doubt that there will be twenty-five women,' Miriam protested. 'I should think the highest number will be perhaps fifteen or sixteen.'

'Then whatever sum if left over you may use in the work you are doing for the poor of this town.' Now Cleopatra's lips parted and her white teeth gleamed in a smile. 'My maids have also told me about how you have been helping some of the most desperate cases of poverty hereabouts.

There's little or nothing remains a secret for long in this town, ladies.'

'Yet you are still prepared to make this contribution to us,' Laura pointed out. 'Even though if news of what you are doing comes to light it might damage your business interests?'

The other woman laughed throatily. 'I shall merely deny it.'

She rose and told them briskly, 'And now I must go. I'll see myself out.'

Before they could even get up from their chairs she was gone from the room and seconds later they heard the front door closing behind her. They sat staring at each other in pleasurable bewilderment.

Outside in the warm sunlight, Cleopatra walked quickly away from the house. Her lips were still curved in a smile and her thoughts were pleasing. She knew that neither of the women had sensed her real reason for calling on them this day, and that they had fully accepted that her motive was only to offer her aid to their cause.

Although she bore no malice towards Miriam Josceleyne for having won Johnny's love, nevertheless she wanted the man for herself, and was determined that she would some day have him.

She had been very desirous of meeting Miriam Josceleyne face to face for the simple reason of wishing to see in what state of health the woman appeared to be. What she had seen today had confirmed her hopes that someday soon Johnny would be free of Miriam Josceleyn's entanglement. The woman was dying! Cleopatra had had a vast experience, and could read the signs of sickness and mortality. This afternoon she had detected in Miriam Josceleyne's thin, wasted features the portents of approaching death. She exhaled a sigh of deep satisfaction.

Soon you'll be free again, Johnny, she spoke to him in her mind. And then you'll turn to me. I know that you'll do that, because I shall make sure that I'm there when your lover dies and leaves you all alone in the world once more. But you won't be alone, Johnny, because I shall be with you. You'll belong to me then, and I'll never leave you. We'll spend the rest of our lives together . . .

Chapter Forty-Three

Birmingham, 17th September, 1909

From the Queen's Hotel to Bingley Hall the streets were thronged with crowds, and sweating policemen fought to clear the way for the procession of vehicles that carried the Prime Minister of the Liberal government and his entourage. Those who had tickets to enter the hall also had to fight their way through the crowds, and to pass through a series of barriers and between lines of stewards and policemen who continually roared at them.

'Show your tickets! Show your tickets!'

Johnny, with Miriam literally hanging on to his coat-tails, led the small group of women through the narrow gangway at the final barrier and on into the hall itself.

Inside the hall it was overheated and stuffy, and the smell of packed human flesh saturated the thick air. A band of trumpeters were blaring out the tune of 'Rule Britannia', and hundreds of sweaty, red-faced men bellowed the chorus, stamping out the rhythm with their feet to create a thunderous noise.

Rule Britania, Britannia rules the waves,
Britons never never never shall be slaves.
Rule Britannia, Britannia rules the waves,
Britons never never never shall be slaves.

As Purvis battled his way through the densely packed crowd the women behind him attracted hard suspicious stares from the numerous stewards and policemen. But no one moved to challenge their progress, and eventually

361

they were able to find a place to stand near the centre of the great auditorium.

Miriam's thin face was flushed and her eyes sparkled with excitement. Although she was the smallest and frailest of her party, the other women clustered close around her as if to seek her protection, and stared nervously at the men surrounding them.

Johnny smiled down at her, but his eyes were concerned as he saw her smother a fit of coughing, and when that fit had passed and her shoulders had ceased to heave, he questioned anxiously, 'Are you all right, Miriam?'

'I'm fine, thank you,' she assured him, and on impulse reached out and squeezed his muscular forearm.

'Isn't it wonderful, Johnny? We've penetrated to the very heart of the enemy position. I wonder how Laura is getting on?'

'I expect that she's getting on very well,' he answered drily, 'She's another fireater, like you.'

Laura had elected to stay outside and join with one of the groups of suffragettes that were to attack the barricades.

'Isn't it wonderful, ladies!' Miriam exclaimed happily to the other women. 'We'll be able to attack the Prime Minister beautifully from here, won't we?'

The three other women with her could only manage sickly grins of assent. Now that they were actually here in the lion's den, their fighting spirit had all but evaporated.

The trumpets had ceased to blare now, and the roared chorusses had quietened to a hubbub of talk and laughter. Then on the platform in front of the crowd, a body of frock-coated dignitaries appeared, to be followed by the distinguished, grey-haired figure of the Prime Minister himself, the Right Honourable Herbert Asquith, Leader of the Liberal Party.

A roar of cheering greeted his entrance, and he bowed in acknowledgement.

'Boo!' Miriam shouted, and giggled like a mischievous schoolgirl. Johnny frowned warningly as he saw the angry looks directed at her by the men around them, and shushed her to silence.

362

As the Prime Minister prepared to speak, the crowd hushed, and the shufflings of booted feet, and hoarse coughing stilled.

'For years the people of this country have been beguiled with unfulfilled promises . . .' he declared in ringing tones, and immediately a heckler at the front of the crowd shouted, 'How about the unfulfilled promises that you've made to the women of this country, Mr Asquith? What have you to say about them?'

It was a male voice that had shouted, and Miriam stared with wide eyes at Johny Purvis and exclaimed in shocked surprise, 'It's a man! And he's speaking up for us!'

The next instant a scuffle erupted as the heckler was set upon by men close to him and driven to the floor by volleys of kicks and punches. Then he was dragged upright and hustled through the jeering crowd by stewards. The unfortunate man passed close to Miriam's party, and the women blanched with fear as they saw the blood streaming down the man's features.

The Prime Minister continued speaking, but time and again other men shouted interruptions concerning the vote for women, and each interruption was dealt with as the first one had been, and the interrupter battered unmercifully and ejected from the hall with bleeding wounds and bruised body.

Miriam was simultaneously delighted by these demonstrations of support from the men, and appalled by the brutality with which those men were treated. She ached to raise her own voice in challenge to the Prime Minister, but forced herself to remain silent and to obey the instructions she had received from the organisers of the demonstration. These were to wait until they acted from outside the hall, before beginning her own disruption inside it.

Outside in the streets a full scale battle was developing. Led by a women with a hatchet in her hand, the suffragettes repeatedly surged forwards against the barricades, succeeding in overthrowing the first barrier time and time again, although opposed by a thousand police.

'Votes for Women! Votes for Women! Votes for Women!'

Their screamed war-cry was cheered by thousands of sympathisers in the crowds, and many of those sympathisers joined forces with the suffragettes and charged the barricades shoulder to shoulder with them. Snatch squads of policemen darted out from behind their defence lines to seize and arrest individual suffragettes, but each time they grasped a woman, her friends fought to prevent the snatch squad returning behind the barriers with their prisoner and succeeded in freeing her.

Laura was in the very thickest of the fight, and had lost her hat and had her sash torn from her chest. But wild with excitement, she was laughing as she returned again and again to the charges against the barricades.

The tumultous uproar, from the streets and the screams of 'Votes for Women', penetrated the interior of Bingley Hall, and the Prime Minister's supporters muttered angrily and mouthed cursed and threats against the suffragettes.

Another heckler challenged the Prime Minister, and was instantly swamped by the stewards, and Miriam could not restrain herself, and shouted at the attackers, 'Shame! Shame on you! You're nothing but cowardly bullies!' as the bleeding, half-conscious heckler was dragged past her.

Then there was a sudden crash of smashing glass as a missile came hurtling through one of the ventilators, and women's voices screamed.

'Down with the government! Votes for Women! Votes for Women! Down with the government!'

As the dusk had fallen the suffragettes had emerged from their Trojan Horses. From the windows of the rented rooms directly facing Bingley Hall volleys of missiles rattled against the room and walls of the hall. The police reacted swiftly, bursting in the doors of the houses and storming up the stairs to grab the women and drag them down into the streets. From one house the ear-splitting banshee howl of a electric horn ululated, and when police tried to burst in the front door they found it barricaded from the inside, as were the windows likewise. Infuriated Liberal Party stewards came running from Bingley Hall to smash their way into the house by brute force and roughly handle the women who were blaring the horn.

Inside the hall Miriam shouted with all her power, 'Down with the Liberal government! Votes for Women!'

'Gerroff out on it!' A man pushed her roughly, and other men began to jostle her companions, who squealed in fright and cowered back.

Miriam was not deterred by this opposition. She struggled to fight her way through, all the time shouting, 'Votes for Women! Votes for Women!'

John was torn by conflicting emotions. He wanted to leap forward and protect her, but at the same time he was mindful of her impassioned pleas to him earlier, that he stand back and let her fight her own fight.

Then he saw a clenched fist land high on Miriam's head, sending her flying backwards, and white hot fury exploded in him. He surged forwards and with a single short chopping blow to the jaw dropped the man who had hit Miriam, then was himself attacked from all sides. He fought with grim savagery against overwhelming odds, breaking noses, cutting and bruising flesh, but was slowly brought down and battered senseless by sheer weight of numbers. Rough hands grabbed and lifted his inert body and he was carried out of the hall, while Miriam and her companions were manhandled after him.

Then on the roof of a house on the other side of the hall, thirty feet above the ground, the small agile figure of Mary Leigh suddenly appeared, together with a tall, fair-haired girl named Charlotte Marsh. Working by the light of a tall electric lamp standard they began to pry the slates off the roof, using an axe to do so, and to hurl those slates onto the roof of Bingley Hall, and down into the street below. Cheered on by their comrades still seething around the barriers, the two girls sent a barrage of slates whirling and smashing, driving back the police who had erected a ladder against the house wall and were trying to mount it.

A firehose was dragged forwards, but the brass-helmeted fireman refused to direct it, and after a heated altercation Liberal Party stewards and policemen turned the water on and aimed the jet of water at the two women on the roof. The slates became slick and slippery with running water, but the women removed their shoes and stockings so that their bare feet could retain purchase, and they continued to hurl slates at their attackers. Finding that the water jet was not going to force the women down, the men grabbed bricks and stones and began a counter-barrage. Their throwing was more powerful, and their aim more sure than the women and in scant minutes the tall girl's face was streaming with blood from a gash inflicted on her forehead, and Mary Leigh had been hit several times. The unequal contest could not continue long, and the women were hit repeatedly, but they kept up the fight until the Prime Minister came hurrying out from the hall and entered his car. As it drove away a slate smashed against its rear, and then it was out of range and the Prime Minister was gone.

Now the two women surrendered, and the police mounted the ladder and brought them both down from the roof. They were frogmarched through the streets in their bare feet and drenched garments and thrown into the police station cells to join other suffragettes and their supporters who had been arrested earlier.

In the streets outside crowds still surged, but the fighting had stopped, and the general mood of the crowd although still excited, was more good natured than aggressive, and both of the principal opposing sides were claiming the victory: the authorites because the Prime Minister had been able to make and finish his speech, the suffragettes because they had created such a riotous uproar that they were assured of it becoming news all around the world.

Inside the police cell, Miriam tried to comfort the three women who had been arrested with her in Bingley Hall. This was the first time that any of them had ever been in trouble with the law, and Miriam could remember her own fears on the occasion of her first arrest.

'You'll not be mistreated,' she assured them. 'Later tonight we shall undoubtedly be allowed bail, and you'll be able to go home.'

366

'My father will kill me, when he finds out that I've been in a police cell,' one young woman asserted tearfully, 'He'll never forgive me for bringing such disgrace on the family name.'

Miriam smiled grimly. 'It's no disgrace to fight for what you believe in, my dear. And we are fighting in a just cause.'

As a hardened veteran of police cells, arrests and jail, she was not in the least concerned for herself. But her major worry at this moment was about what happened to Johnny. Her last sight of him had been his inert body being loaded onto a handcart and pushed away from Bingley Hall by two policemen.

From the adjoining cells the sounds of women's voices singing the 'Marsellaise' rang out, and Miriam felt very proud that her comrades could still proclaim their undaunted defiance in this way.

Heavy boots stamped on the stone flags of the corridor outside the cell door, and keys rattled. Then the door was flung open and several policemen appeared.

'Come on girls,' a grizzled old sergeant instructed. 'You're wanted.'

They followed him into the charge room, where on a tall stool behind a high lectern-like desk a grim featured inspector was waiting to charge them.

Miriam moved to the front of the group and announced firmly, 'Inspector, I wish to make it clear that I am responsible for these three ladies being here. They were acting under my impress.'

The inspector regarded her closely.

'What's your name?' he growled.

'Miriam Josceleyne.' She faced him unafraid.

He ran his finger down a list of names noted on a sheet of paper that was lying on the open ledger before him. His lips moving soundlessly as he read.

Then he nodded, and stared hard at her. 'Yes, Miss Josceleyne. We were expecting you. Now stand back and wait your turn.'

For a moment or two Miriam remained stationary, and the man warned her, 'If you don't do as I say, Miss Josceleyne, then I shall order my men to shift you.'

Knowing the futility of further defiance, she did as she was bid and moved back into line with her companions.

One by one the other women were called to stand in front of the desk and to give their particulars, which were carefully entered into the large ledger. They were then told that they would be charged under the Public Order Acts, and each given bail in her own recognisance.

As each woman was dealt with she was hustled out of the charge room, until only Miriam remained together with the sergeant and the inspector.

'I've already got your particulars, Miss Josceleyne. You're very well known to us by repute. You're quite notorious, in fact,' the inspector informed her, and a mocking smile curved his lips beneath his clipped moustache. 'But you'd best give me them again while I check that our information is correct.'

She was anxious to ask about Johnny, and knowing that if she provoked the policeman by being recalcitrant then she would have no chance of finding out what she wanted to know, she obeyed his instructions.

When all his questions had been answered the Inspector told her, 'I'm keeping you in my custody, Miss Josceleyne, because it's my belief that you are a confirmed troublemaker, and I don't want to risk further riot on the streets tonight.'

'Is it because you know that we are winning that makes you afraid to give me bail, Inspector,' she gibed. 'Are you so afraid of the truth that you need to keep me locked up? Are you afraid of we suffragettes?'

He grinned savagely at her, and his eyes were contemptuous. 'No, Miss Josceleyne. I'm not afraid of you, or a thousand like you, because I think that you suffragettes are nothing more than a lot of silly women who are only playing games to entertain yourselves. In keeping you in custody I'm merely obeying my orders. You and the rest of the ringleaders of tonight's riot are going to be taught a hard lesson, and not before time, in my opinion. You're going to be taught to respect the law. The authorities have decided to show the world just how weak you lot really are. They're going to teach you a lesson you won't forget in a hurry. After we've done with you, you'll all be only too happy to act like good little women, and stay in your kitchens where you belong. You're going to learn to leave mens' business to men, and to stay at home to play your stupid games.'

'That remains to be seen, doesn't it, Inspector. I for one do not intend to give up the struggle, no matter what the authorities might do to me. It's not a game to me, you see. It's a cause, and a just and a noble one.' Her defiant words were not uttered with any hint of braggadocio, but merely stated with a firm matter of factness. This caused the man to stare speculatively at her, as if he were considering whether or not his scathing opinions of suffragettes might be wrong.

She then asked quietly, 'Please Inspector, can you tell me how John Purvis is? He was arrested with me, and he was injured.'

The inspector stared questioningly at the grizzled old sergeant, who shrugged in answer and shook his head.

'I can't tell you, Miss Josceleyne. We've no information concerning the man at present.'

Miriam's anxiety caused her to protest spiritedly, 'But surely that information can be obtained very easily, Inspector.'

'I'm not here to argue with you, Miss Josceleyne,' the inspector retorted irritably, and jerked his head in signal to the sergeant.

'Put her back in the cells, Sergeant.'

'I won't go!' Miriam declared heatedly. 'I won't go anywhere until you tell me what I want to know.'

The inspector hissed with impatience, and slamming the big ledger shut, got off the stool and went out of the room.

Miriam felt near to tears with vexation and worry, and she turned to the sergeant and appealed to him, 'Please Sergeant, can't you tell me anything about John Purvis? He is a very dear friend of mine, and I am very worried about him. He looked to be badly injured when they took him away.'

'He most probably looked a sight worse than he was,

369

missy.' The sergeant spoke with a gruff kindness. 'Now you come on with me, and if you behave yourself, then I'll try and find out what you want to know.'

Before she could thank him she was racked by a terrible fit of coughing, which left her with streaming eyes, and a sharp pain in her chest. For a moment she felt near to collapse, and she clung gratefully to the policeman's arm for support.

'Here missy, are you poorly?' he questioned her with real concern. 'Does you want me to fetch the doctor to have a look at you?'

Wheezing for breath she shook her head. 'No, I'm perfectly well, thank you. It's only a cold.'

Leaning on his arm she was led back to the cells, and sank down onto the wooden pallet that served as a bed as the door was slammed and locked behind her.

Once more hacking, retching coughs tore from her throat and agonising pain lanced through her head and chest. She tasted the metallic saltiness of blood in her mouth, and when she looked at her handkerchief she saw an ominous red stain spreading across its white expanse.

Despite the awful nausea and the bodily weakness she was feeling, the image of the inspector's contemptuous eyes rose to the forefront of her thoughts. That image aroused all her stubborn courage.

'I'll not give him the chance to point the finger and gloat at my weakness. I'll not allow him the proof of his words.'

She tore a square of cloth from her white cotton petticoat to use as a handkerchief, and hid the blood-stained handkerchief in her bodice. Then, spent and sick, she lay back upon the hard wooden boards and thought worriedly about Johnny.

'Please God make him all right!' she begged over and over again. 'Please God let him be all right.'

Chapter Forty-Four

It was not until the early evening of the following day that John Purvis arrived back in Redditch. He left the railway station and walked up the Unicorn Hill, aware of the curious stares directed at him by his fellow travellers and those he encountered on the road. This curiosity was invoked by his torn and dirtied clothing, the numerous bruises and cuts on his head and face, and his splinted and bandaged left arm, which he was wearing in a sling. At the central crossroads he turned southwards and walked along Evesham Street. Then the sound of his name being called brought him to a halt and he turned to find Emma hurrying towards him.

She presented a very fetching picture in her white blouse and dark skirt, with a ribbon-bedecked straw boater perched saucily on her high-piled chestnut hair.

'What's happened to you? You look as if you've been put through a mangle,' she asked with concern.

He smiled. 'I feel as though I've been put through a mangle, Emma. I'm afraid that I bit off more than I could chew this time.'

'Were you up in Brummagem yesterday then?' she questioned eagerly, and here eyes danced with excitement. 'From what they tells me it was a rare old punch-up, wasn't it.'

'It certainly was,' he confirmed. 'I've just come back from there.'

'Was Miriam with you?' the young woman wanted to know, and he nodded.

'Yes. She's been remanded in custody.' He grimaced unhappily. 'We were both arrested yesterday, and put in front of the magistrates this morning. I got let off with a fine, but Miriam was sentenced to prison for refusing to be bound over to keep the peace. She just wouldn't listen to me; she was determined to defy the authorities.'

'The silly cow,' Emma stated with heartfelt feeling. 'How could she behave so stupid! My old Dad always says that when you're up in front of the beaks, then the best thing that you can do is to eat humble pie, and touch your forelock. You only make things worse for yourself if you give them any sauce.'

The man nodded ruefully. 'Your Dad is telling the truth, Emma. But you know how stubborn Miriam can be at times.'

'Was she the only one sent down?' Emma asked.

He shook his head. 'No. I think there were about nine or ten given jail sentences. Some got two months hard labour. Miriam was lucky in one way, she only got a month in the Second Division.'

'How about her friend, Laura? What did she get?'

'The police never arrested her. She's stayed up in Birmingham to see if she can manage to persuade Miriam to give in and accept being bound over to keep the peace. Apparently the magistrates will sometimes agree to let that happen in cases like this, even after sentence has been passed, if the prisoner grovels enough. But she's only wasting her time, Miriam will never give in.' Again he grimaced ruefully. 'But Laura is just as stubborn as Miriam, and nothing I could say would persuade her to come back here with me.'

'Where are you going now?' the young woman asked.

'Home,' he told her. 'I need to bathe and change my clothes, and have a couple of stiff drinks.'

'I'll walk up with you.' Emma grinned like a cheeky urchin. 'I'll even come in and have a couple of drinks with you, if you'll invite me.'

'Well, of course you're always welcome, Emma,' John seemed a trifle doubtful. 'But what will your husband say if he finds out that you've been drinking alone with me in my house?'

She tossed her head dismissively. 'I don't give a bugger what he might say, or anybody else for that matter. I'm my own woman, Johnny. Besides, it's his fault that I'm walking the streets at this hour.'

Purvis could not help but smile. He had always liked and admired this young woman's courage and spirit, and found her gamine-like ways engagingly charming.

'Why is it his fault?' he asked.

'Because him and Adrian West are sitting in the bloody house glaring at each other like a pair of bull terriers waiting to fight. You could cut the bloody air with a knife, it's so thick. I couldn't stand sitting there between them, I was beginning to feel like a bone that they both wants to crunch up.'

'What's causing them to behave like that?' Although he voiced the question, Johnny already knew the answer, and thought, You're driving them both half mad with jealousy, I expect, my girl.

She stared flirtatiously up at him from beneath her thick dark lashes. 'They both reckon that they're madly in love with me, don't they? The silly buggers!'

Johnny made no reply, only the hint of a smile quirked the corners of his mouth, and a sly gleam entered her eyes.

'Of course, I don't give a toss for either of them. I just wish that they'd both bugger off and get out of my life. There's another man that's caught my fancy.'

There was an implicit invitation in her voice. Johnny recognised it, and answered guardedly, 'Well Emma, you must have cared for your husband at one time. You married him freely after all.'

'He was just a passing fancy,' she said airily. 'After being wed to old Hector any young bloke would have looked tasty to me. It was just my bad luck that he was here at the time.' She paused, and her eyes glinted. Then she said deliberately, 'He was here, and you weren't, Johnny. Or it would have been a very different story, I can tell you. Harry wouldn't have got as far as my front door, never mind into my bed if you'd have been here in Redditch when old Hector died.'

She drew a long breath, forcing her breasts to jut out beneath the silken blouse. Johnny Purvis could not deny that her beauty was a strong temptation. It was, however, a

373

temptation that he was easily able to resist. Quite apart from the fact that he loved Miriam, and had no intention or even real desire to be unfaithful to her, his present bruised, battered and sore physical condition definitely prohibited any sexual dalliance.

His expression was very serious as he quietly told the young woman, 'I'm in love with Miriam, Emma. And I intend to marry her just as soon as she'll have me.'

Although her black eyes glinted in pique, Emma still smiled, and replied light-heartedly, 'Well Johnny, you're a man who knows his own mind best.' She ran her hands down her shapely body, and winked broadly, 'But you really don't know what you're turning down. I could prove to be the best thing that has ever happened to you, you know.'

He smiled wryly. 'Maybe so, Emma. But I'm not likely to find that out, am I?'

He touched his fingers to the rim of his curly-brimmed bowler hat in a parting salute. 'I really have to get home now, Emma.'

'I'll still walk the way with you, Johnny,' she informed him cheerily. 'And I'll still like to have those drinks. There's no reason why we can't remain good friends, is there?'

He shook his head and chuckled. 'No, there's no reason against that, Emma. I think that you and I will always be good friends. And you're very welcome to come in and have a couple of drinks.'

She fell into step beside him. 'Now, I want to hear all about what happened up in Brummagem.' She questioned eagerly, 'How many of the buggers set about you?'

Chapter Forty-Five

Tendrils of smoke curled about Adrian West's head as he drew deeply on his cheroot and exhaled lingeringly. Sitting opposite him in another deep armchair, Harry Vivaldi was also smoking a cheroot, and long tendrils of smoke likewise wreathed around his dark curly hair.

Although they were silent, that silence was charged with a tangible hostility, and the atmosphere in the room was tense. Their eyes periodically met, held for a few moments in challenging regard, then slid away. Each man was playing a waiting game, hoping to force the other to speak first.

It was West who eventually did so. 'If you had any pride or self-respect, then you'd leave Emma,' he suddenly blurted out angrily. 'You know that she doesn't want you, and yet you cling on like a leech.'

Harry's hatred for the other man seethed within him, but he smiled mockingly, and replied in a jeering tone, 'You sound like a spoilt little brat whose Ma won't give him a sugar plum, West.'

West's florid complexion darkened ominously as the lust to jump up and smash the other man's sneering features to a pulp surged through him. Vivaldi experienced a tremor of fear as he recognised how close West was to a violent explosion. But then his own hatred overlaid that fear, and he went on jeeringly.

'Emma's my lawful wedded wife. And that's how she's going to stay. You and that Yankee bastard are going to be making a lot of money out of her, and I intend to have my share. So you might as well learn to like that fact, because you're definitely going to have to lump it. Emma and me are going to stay wedded, for just as long as I want her for my wife.'

'She'll not put up with that,' West asserted heatedly. 'She'll leave you, and very soon as well.'

Vivaldi shook his handsome head in negation. 'Oh no, West. Emma will never leave me. You know that for a fact, don't you? Because you've been trying to talk her into doing just that for a long time now, haven't you? But she won't do it.'

A flash of jealous rage showed briefly as he gritted out, 'I know that she's been to bed with you, West. You didn't think that you could fuck my wife without me knowing that you had, did you? I know what happened between you two. And I know that it hasn't happened again for quite a time now. She's tired of you, West. You were only a passing fancy for her. I know Emma better than you could ever know her. I know what she's like, and the way her mind works.'

Now he grinned in sneering triumph, 'She'll never leave me, because deep down she knows that we're two of a kind, her and me. We suit each other, West. We'll stay together for the rest of our lives, Emma and me. That's if I choose for us to stay together.'

The other man' rage was almost beyond his control. But he knew that there was a lot of truth in Vivaldi's sneering words, and he feared to test the strength of his own relationship with Emma by physically attacking her husband. So he made up immediate reply, and exerted all his willpower to hold his anger in check, and to think calmly and cunningly.

After some considerable time he suggested, 'Look Vivaldi, if it's the money that Emma will earn that is keeping you with her, then I'll give you all the money that she earns. If you divorce her, then I'll sign a binding contract with you, to pay you the equivalent of Emma's earnings for the next five years if needs be.'

Vivaldi snorted with contempt as he heard this, and shook his head in rejection. 'Five years' earnings! You must take me for a bloody fool. Emma could be making a fortune for the rest of her life. Never mind five years!'

'Let's make it ten years then,' West offered desperately. 'Ten years is really the longest period that can be logically expected for Emma's career in the moving pictures. I'll sign a contract for ten years with you.'

Again Vivaldi shook his head contemptuously. 'There'll be no contracts signed between you and me, West. Not for five years, not for ten years, not for any length of years.'

West decided to play what he regarded as his trump card. 'All right then, Vivaldi. I didn't want to do this. But you leave me no choice. Just wait here for me, I'll only be a minute.'

He rushed upstairs and took the envelope containing the private detectives' reports from his trunk; returning downstairs he thrust the envelope into the other man's hands.

'Read these, Vivaldi. And read them very very carefully,' he challenged. He remained standing, staring down at Vivaldi's bowed head, as the man extracted the sheaf of papers and began to read through them.

As he realised what the reports contained, the blood suddenly drained from Harry's face, and his hands began to tremble as fear flooded through him. He swallowed hard in a fruitless attempt to loosen the panic-engendered constriction in his throat and chest. But out of the depths of that panic and fear his sense of self-preservation rose to his aid.

He finished reading the damning reports, and grey-faced stared up at the other man.

'This is all rubbish.' Harry attempted to brazen it out. 'I don't know why you're even bothering to show this stuff to me. It's all bloody rubbish!'

Believing that he now held the mastery of the situation, West smiled gloatingly as he took the sheaf of papers from the other man's nerveless hands and stuffed them back into the envelope.

'I wonder if the police will think that it's all rubbish?' he baited. 'I think that I'll drop these in to them now, and see what their reaction will be.'

'Do what you want,' Vivaldi snarled, and his lips curled

back from his teeth and he looked like some savage beast caught in a trap.

West gusted out a harsh breath, and nodded. 'All right, I'll go to the police station right now, and I'll give these reports to them.'

He turned away and moved towards the door. Harry realised that his own bluff was going to be called, and his panic became momentarily uncontrollable. 'No!' he cried out, and jumped to his feet. 'No! Wait! Please wait!'

West halted and grinned in awareness of victory. Slowly he turned back to face Harry, and moved to stand close to him. In a low voice he asked, 'Are you going to do what I want?'

Vivaldi's face was sheened with a clammy sweat, and his skin was pallid. He nodded silently.

West's grin broadened, but in this moment of victory he felt no impulse towards mercy. Rather he wanted to break the other man's spirit into little pieces, to force him to plead and grovel for mercy.

'You're going to leave this house this very night, Vivaldi,' he instructed harshly. 'You're going to leave Emma with me, and you're going to stay away from us for ever. Do you understand?'

Vivaldi nodded slowly, and West brandished the envelope under his nose.

'If I ever so much as even hear of you again, then these will be put into the hands of the police.'

'But where can I go?' Vivaldi wanted to know. 'I've no money.'

'Here.' West pulled some coins from his pocket and dropped them onto the floor in front of Vivaldi. 'There's your train fare.'

He took some more coins from the same pocket and with a grin of utter contempt tossed them down onto the floor also, and some bounced and rolled across the thick carpeting. 'And there's some money for food and lodgings, until you find a way of earning more. Now pick it up and go, Vivaldi. That's all that you'll ever get from me. Because if I ever see or hear of you again, then I'll take these reports to the police.'

For some moments Vivaldi stood motionless, his face a mask of utter despair, and West pointed down at the coins lying scattered around their feet.

'Pick them up, and get out, you piece of worthless shit!'

Vivaldi went down on his hands and knees, and moved around scrabbling at the coins with hooked fingers, West stood gloating above him.

Breathing hoarsely, his dark eyes wild and staring, Vivaldi rose to his feet and pushed the coins into his trouser pocket. He went to move past the other man, who stopped him and pointed to the fireplace.

'You've missed one, Vivaldi. There's a sixpence there. Next to the fender. Pick that up as well.'

As Vivaldi bent in obedience, West roared with laughter, and turned away to place the envelope upon the armchair. At the sound of that mocking, jeering, triumphant laughter something seemed to click in Harry's brain, and a red mist suddenly veiled his eyes. His fingers touched the fallen sixpence, then moved onwards and wrapped themselves around the handle of the heavy steel poker that was lying within the fender. He straightened, turned and his arm rose high and came down with all his strength.

The heavy steel rod bit into the back of West's skull with the sound of an axe cleaving soggy wood; the man's knees crumpled beneath him, and he slowly sank down and fell forwards upon his face. For a few seconds his body twitched violently and his feet drummed against the carpet, then he emitted a long sighing moan, and sagged into stillness. Trickles of blood welled out of his ears and ran from his mouth and nose and began to pool and spread out from beneath his head.

Vivaldi stood staring down at the motionless figure, and he marvelled at his own lack of fear, and at the way in which his brain was thinking coolly and planning his next moves. His full lips curved into a smile of satisfaction.

'Who's the piece of worthless shit now, West?' he muttered.

Mrs Elwood had gone to her own home some hours past, and Emma had given the maids the evening off so that they could go to visit their families. But Emma herself

379

might be returning at any time, so he must move quickly.

He bent and swiftly went through the dead man's pockets, taking out a wallet, which he opened to find several high denomination banknotes. He stripped the rings and personal jewellery from the dead man. Removing his own engraved, initialled gold signet ring, he fitted it on the dead man's corresponding finger, and also placed his own inscribed pocket watch into the dead man's fob pocket. Then he went into the storeroom at the rear of the house and brought back with him a can of paraffin oil, which he poured over the dead man, saturating the face and head, and splashed the remainder around the room and hallway.

Hurrying upstairs he put on West's voluminous driving coat, goggles and cap and crammed the rest of the man's clothing and personal belongings into the travelling trunk and reticules and loaded them onto the motorcar parked outside the front gate. He blessed the dusk and the rain which had started to fall, keeping strollers and loiterers off the streets so that there was no one passing or sitting in the recreation garden, and ensuring that if any of the neighbours looked out of their windows, they would not be able to see clearly enough through the murk to penetrate his disguise.

Then he returned to the drawing room, and striking a match, set the oil-soaked body and furniture ablaze, taking care that the sheaf of reports were destroyed by the flames, before hurrying from the house, leaving the front door locked behind him. Outside he stared briefly at the thick drawn curtains of the drawing room window, noting with satisfaction that the flames within the room could not yet be seen through them.

He cranked the car's engine into life, mounted the driving seat, and motored sedately away. On the brow of the Prospect Hill a man standing in the doorway of the Crown Inn shouted and waved to him.

'Good evening, Mr West.'

Vivaldi waved back in friendly acknowledgement and went coasting down the steep hill.

Inside the Cotswold House the flames swiftly spread

380

and took a firm hold, and the outer curtains of the windows caught fire and the glass darkened then cracked and splintered from the intense heat.

A passerby, head bent against the murky rain, came past the house and halted, staring with shock at the blazing curtains. Then he began to bellow, 'Fire! Fire! The house is on fire!'

The man ran to the front door, and as he mounted the steps of the portico a sudden explosion of combusting gases from within the hallway sent the coloured glass of the door bursting outwards, and he ducked and retreated hurriedly back into the roadway.

'Fire! Fire! Somebody come and help me!' The man stood waving his arms and shouting wildly, and then from the neighbouring houses curious faces peered from windows to see what the noise was all about.

'There's a fire! The house is on fire! Fire! Fire!'

Then suddenly the deserted street filled with shouting, gesticulating figures, and one of the neighbours who had come out of his own house ran back inside and cranked the telephone handle and shouted wildly to the answering operator to inform the fire brigade.

In the fire station situated behind the council offices at the far end of Evesham Street, the duty fireman answered the shrilly ringing telephone, and listened intently to the operator's gabbled report.

In his turn the fireman ran to toll the big alarm bell which hung above the arched entrance of the station, and within a few minutes men came running towards the station from all directions.

Teams of horses were fetched from the nearby stables of the Co-Operative Society and hitched to the resplendent brass-glinting, steamer pump engine and the ladder fly. Brass-helmeted firemen, fully clothed in blue serge tunics and knee-length boots, their axes slung at their thick leather belts, mounted the steamer and the fly. With bells furiously jangling, the appliances erupted from the station and careered furiously towards Church Green, the galloping hooves of the horses striking sparks from the roadway, the tall-funnelled steamer pouring out clouds of smoke and glowing cinders. The onlookers cheered excitedly and hurried after the charging brigade.

By now a crowd had gathered to see the burning house, and the police were having difficulty in holding back the ever increasing numbers. As the fire engines galloped up the crowd eddied and swirled to give them passage, then surged forwards once more against the line of policemem.

Hoses were uncoiled, water-supplies tapped and the steam pump brought into play to exert pressure and send the jets of water arching high from the brass nozzles that the teams of firefighters fought to hold steady and direct upon the flames now leaping from the broken windows.

Gradually the fire was brought under control and finally conquered, and firemen entered the smoking, steaming interior of the house to search for victims.

Returning light-heartedly from Johnny's house, Emma smelled a whiff of smoke carried by the faint breeze as soon as she came to Church Green, and when she passed the front of St Stephen's Church she could see the crowd and hear their excited voices. She quickened her pace, and suddenly realised that it was Cotswold House that was on fire.

'Oh my God!' she gasped in shocked horror, and began to run towards the crowd. Reaching it she forced her way through the dense mass, ignoring the outbursts of protest and abuse that her battering progress created, until she was brought to an abrupt halt by a policeman's outstretched arms.

'Let me through!' she demanded, and the burly constable told her, 'Just stay theer 'ull you. Nobody's to be let get any nearer.'

'But it's my house!' she shouted wildly. 'Let me through! It's my house!'

The altercation attracted the attention of those around her, and suddenly her two maids were at her side, crying out their relief that she was here, and not lying dead in the almost gutted interior of Cotswold House. Moments later the massively fat bulk of Mrs Elwood came buffeting through the clustering onlookers, and the cook wrapped her young mistress in her meaty arms and cried out over and over again, 'Thank God youm all right, my duck! Thank God youm all right!'

The news that Emma was the owner of the house spread rapidly, and the fire brigade officers, Captain Perrins and Lieutenant Huntley, in company with police Superintendent Davis hurried to speak with her.

They led her within the police cordon and questioned her closely as to who had been inside the house that evening.

'My husband and Mr West were both there when I left,' she told them.

'Are you sure that there was no one else?' the policeman pressed, and she shook her head.

'No. No one.'

The men's faces were very grave and they exchanged looks. Then the police Superintendent again asked, 'You are sure that the two men were there when you left the house, Mrs Vivaldi?'

'Yes, of course I'm sure,' she answered, and now an uneasy sense of apprehension troubled her. 'They were both sitting in the drawing room.'

'That will be the room there at the front of the house, will it, Mrs Vivaldi?' Captain Perrins sought confirmation.

'Yes,' Emma told him, then questioned anxiously, 'Are they all right?'

The fireman's smoke-grimed features were sombre, and he warned, 'You must prepare yourself for some bad news, I'm afraid, Mrs Vivaldi.'

Mrs Elwood took Emma's arm and pressed it to her side, murmuring comfortingly, 'I'm here with you, my duck. I'm here.'

Despite the fact that she cared little or nothing for either her husband or Adrian West, Emma still felt a sense of dread sweep over her, and her heart started to pound furiously.

'Tell me,' she demanded. 'Tell me what's happened to them.'

It was the police superintendent who answered her demands. 'I'm sorry to have to inform you that a body has been found in the drawing room of the house, Mrs

Vivaldi. As of yet we've not been able to identify who it is. The firemen are continuing to search through the remainder of the building for any other people who may have been trapped inside.'

'One body?' Emma stared in puzzlement. 'Only one body?'

'Yes, Mrs Vivaldi,' the man repeated gently. 'One body only as of now.'

Emma felt dazed and badly shaken, and the policeman asked Mrs Elwood, 'Is there anywhere that this lady can go and lie down? It's been a terrible shock to her.'

'She'll come to my house,' the fat cook declared firmly, and swung to beckon to the two wan-faced maids. 'Come on you pair, you'll all on you stay wi' me tonight.' Then she informed the policeman, 'Me name's Mrs Elwood, and I lives down at Creswells Cottage in Easemore Lane theer. You'll find Mrs Vivaldi theer when you'se got summat more to tell her.'

'Very well,' the superintendent accepted, and assured Emma Vivaldi, 'You have my deepest sympathy, Mrs Vivaldi. I'll come and talk with you when I know more myself.'

Like a mother hen with her chickens the vast bulk of Mrs Elwood moved away, shepherding the three young women protectively. The crowd parted to give them a clear passage, and murmurs of sympathy and compassion followed their progress.

Chapter Forty-Six

By noon of the following day the news of the fire had spread throughout the length and breadth of the Needle District, and many curious onlookers came to view the damaged house. The finding of a single charred corpse and the disappearance of the second man from the scene caused tongues to wag suspiciously, and wild rumours to be floated.

The man who had seen the Mercedes motorcar pass the Crown Inn came forward and told the police that he had exchanged greetings with Adrian West some minutes before the discovery of the fire. This information, coupled with the discovery of Harry Vivaldi's inscribed signet ring and pocket watch upon the charred corpse, served to confirm in the minds of the police that it was indeed Vivaldi who had been killed. The preliminary examination by the police surgeon of the charred remains brought forth the further discovery that the dead man's skull had been shattered by a savage blow. The police now decided to treat the case as a possible murder enquiry.

It was Superintendent Davis and Inspector Wagstaff who brought the ring and watch to Mrs Elwood's home for Emma to identify. Paradoxically, although Emma had wanted to be free of Harry, now that she was presented with this apparent proof of his death, she wept for the manner of that death.

The two policemen stolidly regarded her until she had recovered and dried her eyes. Then Davis asked, 'What was the relationship between your husband and Adrian West, Mrs Vivaldi?'

A warning note sounded in Emma's mind as she heard

the question, and she queried cautiously, 'Why do you ask me that?'

'Just answer the question please, Mrs Vivaldi.' Davis's manner was grim, and his eyes were hard and suspicious.

Emma shrugged. 'They were not friendly. But why are you asking me such a question?' A sudden dawning of understanding caused her eyes to widen, and she asked incredulously, 'You don't think that Adrian killed Harry, do you?'

The policeman hesitated, then answered, 'It's not our business to deal in speculation, Mrs Vivaldi. We are merely trying to ascertain the truth of what happened in Cotswold House last night.'

Emma frowned, and her thoughts raced.

The policeman went on to ask further questions concerning her own relationships with both men, and about the business and financial dealings between them. He also wanted a detailed account of her whereabouts and movements during the previous day and evening.

She was shrewd enough to sense that she herself was under suspicion as being somehow involved in what had happened the previous night. But she answered fully and forthrightly, and in the end the policemen seemed to be satisfied with what she had told them, and took their leave of her.

As she saw them to the door she asked Superintendent Davis, 'Please tell me the truth. Do you really think that Adrian West killed my husband?'

For the first time since his arrival the man's eyes held a gleam of sympathy as he stared into her strained features. He shrugged, and told her in a low voice, 'I can't tell you anything officially, Mrs Vivaldi. But unofficially, and just between you and me, it appears that there is a strong possibility that West is the man we'll need to look for if we're to find out how your husband met his death.'

In thoughtful silence Emma returned to the small living room and seated herself by the fireplace.

Mrs Elwood had been shopping in the town when the policemen had called, and when she returned Emma told her what had occurred. The fat woman nodded, and in her turn regaled Emma with the wild rumours that were sweeping the town, rumours in which the dead man had been murdered because of West's desire for Emma.

The young woman grinned ruefully. 'I reckon I was born for trouble, Mrs E.'

The other woman nodded with certainty. 'As the sparks fly upwards, my wench. As the bloody sparks fly upwards.'

Emma rose to her feet. 'I think that I'd better go and see me Mam, and put her mind at rest. She's bound to be worrying about me.'

'I'se already popped in to see her, my duck,' Mrs Elwood told her, 'so she knows that youm all right.'

'What about me Dad? Was he there when you called in?' Emma asked anxiously.

'Ahr, he was, and sober for a bloody change, as well.' The fat woman smiled grimly. 'He said for me to tell you that you'se brought disgrace on his name, but that he'd still stand by you.'

Emma chuckled and remarked ironically, 'Oh, yes, the old bugger 'ull stand by me for just as long as I've got money in me purse to give him.'

By now the shock that these events had engendered in her was rapidly wearing off, and her indomitable spirit was reasserting itself.

'It's a good job that we'd nearly finished shooting all the shorts, aren't it, Mrs E. Otherwise I'd be right up the creek without a paddle now that bloody Adrian West has done a bunk.'

She looked about the room for her boater hat. 'I'm going up to the post office to send a telegraph to the Yank. I'll have to let him know what's happened here.'

'Does you think that's wise?' Mrs Elwood looked doubtful. 'I mean to say, what if he drops you because of what's happened? I mean, it looks as if it could turn out to be a real scandal, doon't it. And you knows what folks am like, my duck. They'll try and plaster you with any muck that's gooing, wun't they?'

'Let 'um!' Emma tossed her head defiantly. 'I doon't give a damn what they might say. Folks round here has always talked about me, aren't they, and bad-mouthed me. So what's the difference this time?'

'But the Yank might not think like you does, my duck,' the older woman argued, and her eyes were worried. 'I doon't want to see you lose your chance of being a moving picture queen. Perhaps if you doon't tell him what's happened here, then he'll not come to know of it until it's all bin forgot.'

'And pigs might fly, Mrs E,' the younger woman retorted in scathing dismissal of that notion. Then she grinned cheekily, and winked. 'The Yanks's a man, aren't he. And he's the same as all the other men I've known, never mind his sour looks and miserable ways. He'll do exactly what I wants him to do, Mrs E. You just wait and see if he wun't.'

Emma pinned her hat onto her luxuriant mass of hair and moved to the outer door where she turned and giggled. 'Do you know, I've suddenly got a mind to goo and see what America looks like, Mrs E. I reckon it might suit me very well. Especially now that I'm going to be a moving picture queen . . .'

Despite her misgivings the fat woman could not help but chuckle and wryly shake her head.

'Youm a caution, you am, Emmy Farr. A proper caution!'

Chapter Forty-Seven

Miriam and the other suffragette prisoners were finally transferred from the police station cells to Winston Green gaol on Wednesday the 22nd of September. As the two Black Marias passed through the tunnelled entrance of the castellated gatehouse and the great iron-studded gates closed behind them with a resounding crash, Miriam heard the young suffragette confined in the neighbouring cubicle start to weep noisily. She tapped the wooden partition and told the girl, 'Don't cry, my dear. It's really not so bad as you fear.'

Female wardresses in black uniform gowns and small black toque bonnets were waiting for the prisoners, and they hustled them into the forbidding greystone block where the reception cells were situated. One by one each suffragette was put through the reception process. Their names and particulars were entered in huge ledgers, their clothing and personal belongings taken from them. They were made to get into iron bathtubs which contained six inches of tepid, scum-topped water, and wash their bodies and heads; then they were issued with their prison garb: old brown serge gowns patterned with yellow arrowheads, long white canvas aprons, dirty looking whitish-grey cotton vests, long drawers and stockings, and lastly small flat white canvas caps with long ribbons to tie beneath their chins. Although the clothing had been put through the prison laundry before reissue, the knowledge that countless other prisoners had worn it before caused the more fastidious of the new arrivals to feel itchy and unclean.

Some of the suffragettes had never been imprisoned

before, and they looked very pale and frightened as the wardresses barked orders, and keys rattled in locks, and doors slammed loudly. But for Miriam and the other veterans it was all very familiar territory, and they exchanged whispers and made plans as they waited to be marched to their individual cells within the women's wing of the prison.

Miriam was called out of the reception cells and issued with her bedding, consisting of three rough, threadbare grey blankets, two coarse grey sheets, and a shabby wafer-thin quilt that smelled of stale sweat. She was also given a tin pot, a tin bowl-like platter and a metal spoon, a strip of rough towelling, and a square of hard yellow soap. Then a pleasant-faced young wardress led her into the women's wing. A high, vaulted hall with three tiers of cells facing each other across the open central space of the gloomy building. From landing to landing nets of strong wire netting had been secured to catch suicidal prisoners who might hurl themselves over the railings in an attempt to dash themselves to their deaths on the stone slabs below.

The two women's footsteps echoed past the long rows of blank cell doors set into the white-washed walls, each door locked and barred, with no sound coming from behind it.

When they reached Miriam's designated cell the young wardress smiled at her in a friendly way and stood in the doorway while Miriam laid down the bedding on the wooden pallet and headrest that was to serve as her bed.

'Your number's D 18.' The Wardress handed her a large round badge made of yellow cloth, with the black numerals and single letter printed upon it. 'Your cell task is sheet-sewing, so when you gets your needle amd thread you can sew your badge on.'

'Very well, ma'm,' Miriam answered, and the wardress nodded.

'You've been inside a few times now, haven't you? I read about you and the others in the papers.'

Miriam nodded and agreed ruefully, 'Yes, I've served several sentences, ma'm.'

'Is it worth it? Doing all this time?' the young wardress questioned curiously.

390

Again Miriam nodded. 'Oh yes, ma'm. It's worth it.'

'Do you really reckon that you'll win the vote for women?'

'Definitely we'll win,' Miriam asserted confidently. 'But it may take some considerable time to achieve our victory.'

The rosy face stared wonderingly. 'But you're a lady, aren't you? How can you stand being shut up in here along with all the dregs and scum of the streets? Don't it turn your stomach sometimes?'

Miriam considered for a moment or two, then said thoughtfully, 'There are times when being in prison does turn my stomach. And yes, there are some women in here that I can only agree are the scum of the streets. But most of the prisoners are just poor unfortunates that life has treated very unjustly. They're more to be pitied than condemned.'

'There's some truth in that, I suppose,' the wardress conceded, then went on, 'But how can a gentrywoman like you bear to keep on coming back inside, when you know how rough and hard the life in here is?'

Again Miriam carefully considered her words, and then said slowly, 'Well, for me the suffragette movement is like an army that is fighting a war. I think of myself as a soldier of that army, and these prison sentences are like the battles and campaigns that a soldier must endure in a war.'

The young wardress nodded understandingly. 'I suppose, then, that that makes me and the other wardresses a part of the enemy army, does it?' There was no hostility in her tone.

Miriam smiled wryly and nodded. 'I suppose it does really. But I don't think that it's necessary for us to hate our enemies, is it? I find that I can respect, and even like, a good many of them.'

The other woman beamed good naturedly. 'That's a good answer, that is. And to tell you the honest truth, I'm all in favour of what you lot are after. I think that us women should have the vote. But I haven't got the guts to go out and fight like you lot are doing. And anyway, I've got to make a living. I can't afford to risk losing this job, and maybe ending up in here on the wrong side of the cell door.'

'Of course you can't,' Miriam agreed sincerely.

A bell jangled in the distance, and the young wardress grimaced. 'I'll have to go now. You know how to lay out your bedding, don't you? It's the same in here as in the other nicks. There's your brick and cleaning rags for your brightwork. I should get cracking straight away and make everything shipshape. There'll be an inspection of you new intakes shortly. So make sure everything's in parade order, soldier!' She smiled and saluted, then disappeared behind the closing door.

The keys rattled in the lock and the bolt slammed home. The sharp echo of her footsteps died away, and Miriam was left in lonely silence. She sat down on the wooden stool which was part of the sparse furnishings of her cell, and made an evaluation of her physical condition. To her own surprise she found that she was feeling quite fit and strong, and that the dull ever-present ache in her chest was hardly noticeable.

Mentally she felt clear-headed, and very determined. She reviewed the plan that she and the most militant of her fellow prisoners had formulated while they were in the reception block. That plan was to continue their protest even while in gaol by any means at their disposal: mainly refusal to obey orders, destruction of prison property, and finally, a hunger strike. This last method was a recently introduced weapon into the armoury of the suffragette movement, and during the past months thirty-seven suffragettes had gone on hunger strike while in prison, and had been released early because they had done so.

Miriam drew a long deep breath, then got up, lifted the stool in her hands and carefully smashed the small glass panes of the cell window. Using a shard of the broken glass she slashed the sheets and blankets to ribbons, and then sat down on the stool once more, and with hands folded on her lap, patiently waited.

Time passed and Miriam lost all track of it as she lapsed into reverie. Then the sounds of footsteps and the jangling of keys roused her. Her door was unlocked and swung open, and a woman's voice shouted, 'Stand to attention, Number Eighteen.'

There were two wardresses, and the prison matron. She

was short, dumpy bodied, middle-aged woman, uniformed like her underlings in a black gown and small toque bonnet, but wearing the star of her rank upon her sleeves.

'Stand up for the matron, Eighteen,' the taller of the two wardresses shouted, and glared fiercely.

Miriam ignored her, and remained seated with her hands folded upon her lap.

The matron gestured for the tall wardress to stand aside, and came into the cell herself. Her eyes passed over the slashed bedding and the broken panes of glass, and her lips tightened. Then she turned her attention to Miriam, staring closely at her.

'Are you sure that you want to do this, Eighteen?' she asked quietly, with no trace of hectoring or aggression.

Miriam met the searching gaze levelly, and nodded. 'Yes, Matron. With all respect to you, I am quite sure. I would like to make it clear that this protest is not directed against yourself or your staff, but against the authorities who are refusing to give women their basic right to vote.'

'All right Eighteen, all right,' the matron told her wearily. 'There's no need to go on. I've heard all this before.'

Miriam subsided into silence, and the matron left the cell, taking the wardresses with her. The door was slammed shut and locked, and the footsteps marched away.

Miriam gusted out a sigh of relief. Despite her courage, she had been very nervous when the moment for confrontation had arrived, and she was happy that it had all passed off so easily. But now she knew that the gauntlet of challenge she had hurled down would be quickly taken up, and she nerved herself for whatever ordeals might lie ahead.

Within a very few minutes serried footsteps again approached her cell and the door came crashing open. Four wardresses entered and without a word grabbed her and frogmarched her along the landing and down the spiral iron staircases, then across the ground floor and down a further flight of stone steps to the basement punishment cells. Cold, dark cells containing nothing but the bare walls, where the daylight penetrated only faintly.

She was pushed into one of the cells and a wooden plank bed was brought in.

'Strip off your dress, stockings and shoes,' a wardress ordered curtly.

Knowing that any physical attempt at resistance would be futile, Miriam obeyed. Barefoot, wearing only vest and long drawers, her hands were handcuffed behind her back, and then she was left alone in the cold darkness.

She remained standing, shivering as the chill clammy air penetrated her thin vest and drawers, and in an attempt to keep warm began to pace up and down the cell. Three paces forward, turn, three paces back, turn, three paces forwards, turn, three paces back, turn. For a while her determination wavered and she feared that her courage was ebbing away. Then she deliberately filled her mind with thoughts of Johnny Purvis, concentrating hard on building mental images of him, and this served to distract her fears and help to steel her resolve to fight on.

It was fully dark when the wardresses returned to her cell. The gaslight, set into the wall beside the door and shielded by thick glass, was lit from the outside, and the door opened. A tin tray holding a bowl of gruel and potatoes, a piece of hard dry bread, a mug of cold water, and a spoon was placed on the wooden bed. Then one of the wardresses unlocked and removed the handcuffs, only to replace them on Miriam's thin wrists, but this time with her hands in front of her, palms facing each other so that she could use her hands and fingers to hold the spoon and utensils and left the food to her mouth.

Miriam drank thirstily from the water mug. Then shook her head when a wardress offered her the spoon.

'No ma'm, I am refusing all food.'

'More fool you!' the most senior wardress grunted, and jerked her head at the others. The tray of food was taken away, and the gaslight turned out. The door slammed shut, keys rattled in the lock, and Miriam was once more left to the darkness, the cold clammy air, and the intensely depressing feeling of abandoned loneliness.

Chapter Forty-Eight

Within days following the fire at Cotswold House police
'Wanted' posters were being issued for the whereabouts of
Adrian West, and it became general knowledge in the
Needle District that the missing man was suspected of
murdering Harry Vivaldi.

The initial sympathy for Emma as a tragic young widow
was quick to evaporate as malicious gossip spread stories
concerning her relationship with Adrian West. Soon she
was being hooted in the streets and openly taunted with
having driven West to kill her husband.

Some people, such as Mrs Elwood, the two maids,
Johnny Purvis and others close to Emma still supported
her and remained firm in their friendship, and their
disbelief in her having been the cause of the murder.
Emma herself faced her accusers with a defiant courage,
and when openly reviled her gutter-devil would rouse
itself and she would give as good as she got and more in
the matter of abuse and taunts. But inwardly she was
racked with doubts, and was wondering if in fact it had
been her fault that the tragedy had occurred. Also she
feared that when the coroner's inquest took place, the
resultant publicity would cause Walter Harriman to
withdraw from their business partnership, and thus put an
end to her dreams of becoming a moving pictures star.

Harriman did not reply immediately to Emma's
telegraph informing him of what had happened. Instead
he telephoned a freelance reporter that he knew who lived
in Birmingham, and employed the man to find out as
much as he could about the tragedy, and what people's
reaction to it was. Some days later he received a very

detailed report, and it was only then that he travelled to Redditch.

The first thing he did upon his arrival in the town was to go in search of Henry Snipe. The subsequent interview was highly satisfactory to both men, and when it was completed Snipe had been engaged by Harriman as head cameraman and process editor of the Harriman Moving Pictures Corporation.

'Now get every single inch of Mrs Vivaldi's shorts printed and ready to roll just as soon as you can,' was Harriman's parting instruction, and Snipe, happy that he had now found another master, grumblingly set to work.

Harriman's next calls were on Johnny Purvis and Cleopatra Dolton. He found it easier to purchase Purvis' shares in West's moving picture company, than Cleopatra's. The beautiful woman proved to be a shrewd businesswoman, and she drove a very hard bargain. But Harriman paid the inflated price with as much good grace as he could muster. By the time he went to Cresswells Cottage to call on Emma he was the owner of all the moving picture company's shares, except for those owned by Emma herself, and the missing man's estate.

The young woman looked very beautiful dressed in widow's black, and the American was forced to remind himself that his primary objective was business and making of a great deal of money, rather than the attraction that Emma exerted over him.

He seated himself in the cramped living room of the cottage and wasted no time.

'I'm not going to be a hypocrite, Emma, and tell you that my heart is bleeding for your grief,' he stated bluntly, 'because I know that you didn't really give a damn for your husband, or for Adrian West.'

His bluntness gave Emma a moment of shock, but then she admitted frankly, 'No, I didn't. But what's going to happen now, Walter? There's a lot of gossip being spread, and none of it is in my favour. People are saying that it was my fault that my husband was killed. They're saying that it was me who put Adrian up to doing it. There's going to be an inquest very soon, and when that happens and the newspapers catch hold of the story there'll be a scandal, and I'll be in the middle of it. So, is there anything you can do to keep the story out of the papers?'

He shook his head. 'No, my dear. There's nothing that I can do, or want to do to keep the story out of the papers. Quite the contrary, in fact, I intend to get in touch with a couple of newspaper guys that I know, and get this story plastered all over every front page of every newspaper in England and the United States, and the rest of the world if I can manage it.'

Her mouth opened in shock, and his thin lips smiled bleakly.

'The publicity that this case can create for you is a dream come true, Emma. It'll bring people flocking into my theatres to see your moving pictures. Given the right sort of build-up you can become the modern Jezebel, Delilah and Salome rolled into one. You'll be the original scarlet woman, Emma. Every man's secret desire, and every woman's secret envy. This can make you the biggest star in the world.'

Emma shook her head in bewilderment. 'But I thought that you would hate this publicity,' she told him. 'I thought that a man like you, who lives such a strait-laced life, wouldn't want anything to do with me. I thought that any scandal at all about me would have you tearing up the contracts.'

He shook his head, and said solemnly, 'I never let my personal preferences interfere with business, Emma. What happened between those two guys is a godsend for your career in the moving pictures. It's a dream come true, and that's no exaggeration. All we have to do is to take full advantage of it. And you can leave that to me. All you have to do is what I say, and I'll make you the biggest moving picture star in the world.'

He paused and behind the glass lenses his eyes were cold and calculating. Then, satisfied with what he read in her expression, he went on.

'But you must do exactly as I say, Emma, and be guided by me in all things. You must wear what I tell you. You must behave as I tell you. You must even say what I tell

397

you to say. And above all, you must trust me completely. If you can agree to all this, then I can guarantee that I'll give you everything and more that you've ever dreamed of having.'

Again he paused, and his eyes measured the effects of his words, and he frowned slightly as he detected a gleam in her black eyes of what could be taken for mocking contempt. But then that gleam disappeared, and the black eyes sparkled with pleasure, and greed, and she told him eagerly, 'I can agree, Walter.'

He nodded, and breathed out a satisfied sigh. Then he instructed her, 'Right then, get your things packed, we're going to London to buy you a new wardrobe, and to meet some people who'll be helpful to your career.'

'But what about my maids, and Mrs Elwood?' she protested. 'I don't want to go off to London all by myself and be among strangers.'

'I can find you another maid.' He frowned at this evidence of wilfullness, as she shook her head stubbornly.

'I don't want another maid. I want the two I've got already. And I want Mrs Elwood to come with me as well. She knows how to look after me properly.'

'But Mrs Elwood's a married woman. She won't want to leave her husband,' he argued.

'She dying to leave the old sod,' Emma stated positively, then put her hands on her shapely hips and stated firmly, 'Before we do anything else, I reckon that we'd best get things clear between us, Walter. Now I'm prepared to be guided by you, and to do anything that you tell me to as far as my career goes. But we're partners, Walter. Not master and slave! I'm going to take my maids and Mrs Elwood with me, and that's that!'

'But that's a needless extravagance. Two maids and a travelling companion!' he grumbled.

She giggled at his sour expression. 'It's no use you counting pennies anymore, Walter. You should start thinking in pounds. If I'm going to be a star, then I've got to behave like one right from the beginning, haven't I? So stop worrying about what I'm going to cost, and start thinking about how much I'm going to be earning.'

Reluctantly he accepted defeat. 'Very well then, Emma. Now will you please begin the preparations to leave here? I want to be in London as soon as possible.'

Emma laughed with delighted excitement, and going to the bottom of the staircase called upstairs, 'That's it, Mrs E. Becca, Molly, get your things ready, we're off to London!'

Delighted exclamations and giggling sounded from above, and Emma beamed at Harriman, mischief dancing in her sparkling black eyes.

'I'll just go and see me Mam and Dad, Walter, and tell 'um to get their bags packed as well. Them and the kids 'ull enjoy a holiday in London . . .'

Her laughter pealed out at the sight of his shocked features, and then she was gone, leaving only the fragrance of her perfume behind her . . .

Chapter Forty-Nine

The three visiting magistrates were alike in their sombre frock-coats, eyeglasses, and forbidding scowls as they listened to the charges brought against the prisoner of destroying the property of His Majesty's Prison Commissioners, and the evidence of the matron and wardresses concerning those charges.

Miriam, fully dressed and with her hands handcuffed in front of her, stood facing them, her gaze fixed on a point on the wall above their heads. Her mind was detached and her thoughts far away from this bleak room.

'Do you have anything to say in your own defence?' the senior magistrate questioned, and his fingers stroked his long full beard.

Miriam heard his question, but ignored it. It seemed to her that these proceedings did not concern her at all.

'Did you hear me, young woman?' the man demanded, his voice rising angrily.

She glanced briefly at him, and shook her head. 'No. I've nothing to say. What the matron and wardresses have told you is the truth.'

Then she once again gazed at the wall above the man's head.

The magistrates conferred briefly in whispers, and exchanged nods of agreement. Then the senior told Miriam, 'You have committed a very serious offence, young woman, and it is our decision that your punishment shoud be set accordingly to show the gravity with which we view your conduct. You have been sent here for breaking the law of the land, and yet you persist in disobeying that law even here. You are accordingly sentenced to nine days' close confinement with bread and water for diet, and to pay twenty-five shillings damage.' He nodded to the matron. 'You may remove the prisoner, Matron.'

'Very good, sir.' The matron jerked her head at the other wardresses, and they led Miriam from the room and back down to the punishment cells. Once there she was again ordered to strip to vest and long drawers and her hands were then handcuffed behind her back.

Once during the course of the long drearily-passing day she was taken out of her cell and made to walk for an hour up and down the corridor which ran the length of the punishment block. Afterwards her handcuffs were briefly removed so that she could wash her hands and face, and make use of the watercloset that was set in an alcove at the end of the corridor.

Then she was re-handcuffed and returned to her cell. Three times during the course of the day the wardresses brought her two slices of hard dry bread and a mug of water. Each time she drank the water and refused to touch the bread. The wardresses accepted her refusal in silence, their faces remaining blankly indifferent.

Hunger was painfully gnawing at her, and she was beginning to feel weak and light-headed, but she lay on the bare planks of her wooden bed and tried to detach herself mentally from her body.

She was sleeping fitfully when at midnight the gaslight was turned on and the matron and a wardress entered her cell.

'Stand up for the matron,' the wardress barked, and Miriam obeyed and stood swaying, her senses dazed and still half asleep. The matron herself unlocked and removed Miriam's handcuffs, and then without another word both women left the cell and the gaslight was once again extinguished.

Thankfully Miriam rubbed her sore wrists, and experienced a real sense of pleasure now that she was able to lie down more comfortably and pillow her head on her arms.

For the next two days the routine continued, but the handcuffs were no longer used. Once a day she exercised in the corridor for an hour, then was allowed to use the watercloset, and to wash her hands and face. Three times a

day the wardresses brought the two slices of hard dry
bread and the mug of water into her cell, and Miriam
drank the water and refused to touch the bread. None of
the wardresses attempted to reason or even to speak with
her, and only barked short sharp orders.

Now her gnawing hunger pains had abated and she felt
only a sick emptiness. Her bodily weakness was slowly
becoming more noticeable, and the curious feeling of
light-headedness had metamorphosed into a dazed sense
of detachment from her physical body and a general
disorientation in regard to her surroundings.

At noon on the third day a wardress came to her cell and
told her, 'Here's your uniform. Get dressed and come with
me. The matron wants to speak to you.'

Miriam obeyed without question, and followed the
wardress up the flight of stone steps and across the vaulted
hallway into the room used as a doctor's surgery. She
blinked in surprise as she entered the room and saw that
two frock-coated doctors, the matron and half a dozen
wardresses were ranged around the walls. On the floor in
the centre of the room a battered old leather armchair
chair had been placed with a sheet spread underneath it.

The two doctors stepped to confront Miriam, and the
elder of them, a white haired, kindly looking man with pince-
nez and a goatee beard told her to sit down in the chair.

Feeling giddy and weak Miriam was grateful for that
command, and she sank onto the leather seat, revelling in
its supple comfort. The elderly doctor produced a blue
official form which he held out for her to see.

'These are my orders from my superior officers,
Number Eighteen. You must listen very carefully to what I
am going to tell you. It has been decided that no
suffragettes are to be given early release from their
imprisonment even on medical grounds. I know that
during the past few months a number of your movement
have used that method of the hunger strike to compel the
authorities to release them. That is no longer permitted.
All suffragettes will now serve the full length of their
sentence, and will not be allowed to continue in any
hunger strike. Therefore, if you persist in refusing your

food I am instructed to compel you to take it.'

Miriam stared at him disbelievingly, then asked, 'If I continue to refuse to eat, how will you make me do so?'

'I shall use whatever methods I deem necessary.' His manner softened, and he urged her, 'Be sensible, young woman. Your friends have all agreed to take food, so why should you persist in refusal?'

She shook her head. 'I don't believe you. My friends would never surrender, and would resist to the death any attempt to coerce them.'

His voice hardened. 'I am asking you once more. Will you agree to take food?'

For a brief instant apprehension whelmed over Miriam, and she was sorely tempted to accede. But then her courage returned in a rush, and grimly she shook her head. 'No Doctor, I will not take food.'

'Very well, young woman. You leave me no choice in this matter.'

He stepped back from the chair and signalled to the matron, who in turn snapped out, 'Secure the prisoner.'

Before Miriam could react the group of wardresses sprang to the chair, her arms and legs were gripped and pinioned, her head was forced backwards, and the chair itself tilted back at an angle. The doctors came forwards and the younger man grabbed Miriam's mouth and jaw in his strong fingers and forced her mouth open, while the other man measured liquid from a bottle into a large table spoon and poured it into her pouched mouth. Miriam tasted brandy and milk and she gagged and swallowed. The process was repeated several times, and then the other doctor sprinkled eau de cologne upon Miriam's face and neck and she was pulled to her feet and taken back to her cell by wardresses.

Immediately they had locked her inside its dark confines Miriam pushed her fingers deep down her throat in an effort to induce retching, but although her stomach heaved and she gagged repeatedly only a taste of bile came into her mouth.

A clammy sweat started from all the pores of her body, and she felt near to fainting. She lay upon her wooden bed

403

and tears fell from her eyes, and in that moment of bitter chagrin she could have wished for death to take her and put an end to her sufferings and degradations.

Paradoxically, despite her torment of mind she slept that night far more soundly than she had done since her imprisonment, and when she was roused by the wardress early next morning she felt refreshed and strengthened, and more than ready to continue the lonely battle.

Her breakfast of two dry slices of bread and a mug of water was brought to her cell, and she drank the water and pushed the bread away.

This time one of the wardresses advised her in a kindly tone, 'Listen to me, ducky, you should eat this bread, because they'm intending to start the full force-feeding if you don't. They'se already give some of your mates the treatment yesterday, and it was really horrible for them, I can tell you. If you've got any sense at all you'll eat a piece of this bread now.'

The well-meant warning had the opposite effect upon Miriam than that the wardress had intended. The news that her comrades were still carrying on the fight filled her with exultation, and she became more determined than ever that she would not surrender.

'Thank you for your kindness in telling me,' she told the woman with heartfelt sincerity. 'I know that you mean me well. But I'm afraid it's impossible to persuade me to do anything other than continue refusing food.'

'All right,' The woman shook her head regretfully. 'I just hope that you know what you're doing, ducky.'

It was midday when they came for her and this time she was only marched a short distance to the end of the corridor and taken into a cell there. Miriam stared with horror at the padded walls and floor, and one of the wardresses jeered.

'Yes, that's right, it's a cell of the loonies. It's the right place for all you bloody suffragettes to be in.

'Be quiet, Benton, leave her alone,' another of the wardresses snapped curtly, and the first one lapsed into sullen silence.

More wardresses and the matron entered the cell, to be

followed by the two doctors. A wooden plank bed was brought in also, and then the elderly doctor asked Miriam, 'Are you prepared to take food, Eighteen?'

Pale-faced with apprehension, Miriam summoned all her courage and shook her head in refusal.

The doctor nodded to the matron, who in turn ordered, 'Secure her.'

Many hands grabbed Miriam and bore her down onto the bed, and held her motionless. Although she was unable to move she could see the doctors from the corner of her eye, and terror mounted in her when she saw the younger man produce a funnel with a long thin rubber tube dangling from it. A wardress handed him a large tin jug, and then the older doctor took the free end of the rubber tube and bending over Miriam he thrust it up her left nostril and began to feed it down into her throat. She cried out and gagged violently as terrible pain exploded in her nose, throat and chest, and an agonising pressure built up against her eardrums until she feared that they would burst. The chest pains spread lower down her torso as the doctor continued to push the tube deeper into her body. Miriam heaved and struggled but could make no impression against the pinioning hands of her captors. The younger doctor held the funnel high and started to pour the mixture of beaten eggs and milk down it.

Through a dark haze of pain Miriam heard the older doctor complaining in a querulous voice, 'It's going down very slowly, MacCarthy. I haven't got all day to spend here, you know.'

Then his fingers pinched hard on her nostrils and throat, and the pain became even more acute.

When the contents of the jug had been absorbed Miriam was lifted into a sitting position and a basin of warm water was brought into the cell and held beneath her chin. The elderly doctor pulled out the tube and plunged the end of it into the water.

Miriam moaned and sagged near to fainting, and agonising pain throbbed in her chest, throat, nose and ears. The basin was removed, and Miriam was dragged bodily upright to enable the doctor to test her heart and

405

make further examinations.

Satisfied he told the matron, 'Take her back to her cell.'

Miriam was so sick and faint that the wardresses had to half carry her along the corridor, and the faces of some of them were concerned and sympathetic as they helped her. She heard one whisper to another, 'It aren't right to treat the poor cow like this. It's wicked, so it is.'

'Shut up, Smith,' the matron warned. 'Any more talk like that and you'll be looking for another position, my girl.'

In the cell the matron produced a pair of handcuffs and used them to secure Miriam's hands behind her back.

'This is to make sure that you don't put your fingers down your throat to fetch your food up again, Eighteen,' she explained matter of factly, and went on, 'What's just happened will go on happening twice a day, until you give up this stupid hunger strike, Eighteen. So just think on.'

Miriam fell back upon the hard wooden plank bed and felt that she was drowning in a sea of pain, and her mind filled with doubt that she would be able to sustain this unequal battle.

She shook her head. 'No, I won't give in. I won't give in.'

The repetition of the words seemed to infuse her with re-newed determination, and helped to keep the doubts at bay.

The empty hours wore on and the day resumed its normal pattern. She was taken out of her cell and made to exercise by walking up and down the corridor. Two slices of dry bread and a mug of water were brought to her, and she drank the water and refused the bread. Then, as the dusk of the coming night cast her cell into darkness, they came for her again.

'Stand up, Eighteen. It's time for you to go for your supper.'

Miriam slowly struggled upright, her heart thudding, her breath quickening, her body trembling with dread and fear of the approaching ordeal. But when the moment to undergo that ordeal came, she met it with the mystic fervour of some medieval religious martyr, and in the midst of her agonies her mind cried out in triumphant exultation.

'I'm keeping the Faith! I'm keeping the Faith! I'm keeping the Faith!'

406

Chapter Fifty

The news of the forced feeding of the suffragettes caused a storm of outrage, and the Labour MP J Keir Hardy attacked the Home Secretary, Herbert Gladstone, for ordering this mode of action against the defenceless women. But amid gales of laughter and anti-suffragette gibes in the House of Commons, the Home Secretary refuted all allegations that the treatment was cruel and barbarous. He even let it be known that His Gracious Majesty, King Edward the Seventh, had written from Marienbad the previous month to express his approval of the fact that more stringent measures were to be taken by the authorities against hunger-striking suffragettes. If the sovereign in his benevolent wisdom was in favour of such measures, then surely those measures must be perfectly acceptable and legitimate.

From a sympathetic wardress in the Winson Green gaol the suffragette movement received almost daily bulletins on the progress of the hunger strikers, Mary Leigh, Charlotte Marsh, Jane Edwards, Miriam Josceleyne and the others. But despite the public outrage, and the opposition of many Members of Parliament and other prominent people, the forced feedings continued.

Johnny and Laura took rooms near Winson Green, and tried daily to obtain some access to Miriam. But all their efforts were fruitless, and they seethed in impotent anger and dismay as the unequal battle behind the great stone walls of the prison continued to rage. Through the offices of the sympathetic wardress messages were smuggled into the suffragette prisoners from their friends and supporters outside, and Johnny took advantage of this to

407

send repeated messages to Miriam, begging her to abandon the hunger strike. But all his entreaties met with stubborn refusal, with the added admonition that he was to let matters take their course, and not try to interfere in any way, on pain of losing her love forever.

For a few days he managed to restrain himself, and take no action. Then his anxiety for Miriam became too much to be borne, and he told Laura, 'I'm going to fetch Doctor Peirce and Doctor Dickinson up to see the governor. He must be told about Miriam's health.'

'You mustn't do that!' Laura was adamant. 'Miriam will never forgive you if you interfere in such a way.'

He scowled at the young woman. 'Would you sooner let her kill herself then?'

'Of course not!' Laura protested indignantly. 'I'm just as concerned about Miriam's health as you are, John. But she has expressly forbidden us to attempt to interfere in any way with what she is doing. And I love her enough to respect her wishes.'

'And I love her too much to respect her wishes on this occasion!' he shouted furiously. 'I won't let her kill herself by carrying on with this madness.'

'She'll never forgive you if you interfere!' Laura declared.

'I can live with that, so long as she is all right,' he stated, and the young woman stared into his hard eyes, and accepted defeat. She admitted to herself as she did so that deep down she was both relieved and happy to find him so adamant.

In the event it proved unnecessary to bring the Redditch doctors to the gaol. Miriam haemorrhaged during the course of her next force feeding, and was rushed into the prison infirmary. Upon being informed of her condition, the Home Secretary signed the order for her release, and Johnny and Laura were waiting for her as she was carried out of the prison in a horse-drawn ambulance.

Overriding all her half-hearted objections, Johnny brought Miriam back to his own home, where he had rooms prepared for her and Laura. He had engaged trained nurses to care for her on a twenty-four hour basis, and Doctor Peirce was also there to make a careful examination of her condition. When that examination was completed the doctor called Johnny and Laura into the living room downstairs and held a long conversation with them.

Later, when Miriam was settled comfortably in her bed next to the window, through which she could see the sweep of wooded hillside and the fecund green valley of the River Arrow, Johnny came to tell her, 'You're home now, honey. And this is where you'll stay until you're well again. Then we'll get married, and we'll travel wherever you want to go. I'm never going to let you leave me again.'

She smiled up at him, her green eyes huge in her pallid, wasted face, and she nodded contentedly.

'So be it, Johnny.'

He seated himself by her side and took her thin hand between his own strong hands, and stayed with her as she smilingly drifted into sleep.

As he sat tenderly cradling her hand, gazing at her pallid face so peacefully happy in dreams, tears brimmed and fell to trickle down his cheeks. Doctor Peirce had told him that death was already reaching out to claim Miriam, and that the end was very near. It could only be a matter of weeks, perhaps days, and then she would be taken from him.

'I love you, honey!' he whispered brokenly, and now his cheeks were wet with tears. 'I love you . . .'

Final Chapter

The April winds danced over the tombstones and gravemounds of the cemetery. The boisterous gusts rattled the budding twigs and branches of the tall elm trees, and caused the thick green foliage of the ancient yews to sway and rustle and shimmer in the bright sunlight. Johnny Purvis smiled as a small red squirrel came bouncing as lightly as thistledown onto the fresh white marble of the gravestone, and perched upright on its hindlegs, its bright eyes regarding him curiously.

'We have a visitor, Miriam,' he murmured, and rose from his crouching position at the foot of the grave.

'I have to go now, honey. But I'll come and see you again tomorrow.'

His eyes lingered sadly on the vase crammed with fresh flowers, and he read for perhaps the thousandth time the gold inscribed lettering on the upright stone.

'Miriam. The beloved wife of John Purvis. Laid to rest 15th October, 1909.'

The wedding ceremony had taken place in her sickroom only days before her death, and now six months later the poignant memory still brought tears hotly stinging his eyes. He sighed heavily, and immersed in his memories, slowly walked away.

At the entrance to the cemetery an elegantly dressed woman was waiting, and when he neared her she called softly. 'Johnny?'

He looked up in surprise, and smiled. 'Hello Cleopatra. What brings you here?'

'I often walk this way,' she told him. 'I find it very peaceful here.'

410

He smiled wryly. 'It's certainly that.'

She fell into step beside him. 'Do you mind if I walk with you, Johnny. I'm feeling a bit lonely.'

'I'll be glad of your company. I'm feeling lonely myself,' he told her.

For a while they chatted easily, exchanging gossip about mutual acquaintances. Inevitably the talk turned to Emma, and the sensational success her moving pictures were enjoying both here and in America, where she had now gone to make a triumphal tour of personal appearances, taking with her an entourage that included her two maids, Mrs Elwood, her mother and father and her numerous brothers and sisters.

Johnny laughed fondly. 'She's a caution, isn't she?'

'Oh yes she is indeed,' Cleopatra agreed ironically. 'Young Emmy Farr has always been a proper caution!'

For a while they discussed the mysterious disappearance of Adrian West. Although his white Mercedes motorcar had been found abandoned in a wood near to Manchester, no trace of the man himself had ever been discovered. It was as though he had vanished into thin air.

Cleopatra asked about Laura, and Johnny told her that in her most recent letter to him she had said that she was going to stay with the suffragette movement in London, and continue the fight for women's enfranchisment from there.

'Of course, she still has the house in Mount Pleasant that Miriam left to her. So she'll never be without a home of her own to come back to.' He smiled reflectively. 'I could never really understand why she and Miriam were so fanatical for women to have a vote,' he admitted.

Cleopatra shrugged her shapely shoulders. 'Nor me either.'

They continued to talk companionably and Johnny Purvis found that his low spirits were raised, and a sense of happiness infused him.

At last Cleopatra slowed to a reluctant halt. 'I have to leave you now, Johnny.' She smiled warmly at him, her eyes soft and loving as they lingered on his face. 'The boys are coming home for a holiday, and I need to be there to meet them when they arrive.'

'Of course you do.' Now that the moment of parting had come, he was loath to let her go.

'They'd all love to meet you again, you know,' she told him truthfully. 'They often mention you. I think they admire you as their ideal of what a soldier should be like.'

'I'd like to meet them,' he told her.

'Then come to my house tomorrow afternoon,' she invited him. 'We can all have tea together.'

'I'd like that very much,' he accepted eagerly.

She held out her hand and he took it within his own.

'Until tomorrow then, Johnny.' She smiled, 'Come as early as you like.'

'I will.'

Their hands parted reluctantly, and she stood watching his tall, soldierly figure until it had gone from her sight, then she made her way towards her own home.

Many men watched her pass and there were those among them who wished that they were by her side. But they knew that the beautiful widow always walked alone. Cleopatra, however, knew that from this point on in her life, she would no longer walk alone.

A smile wreathed her lips, and her heart sang within her as she walked onwards towards the future that she would share with Johnny Purvis . . .